T0049335

A NEW LAND

A NEW LAND

BOOK ONE OF TWIN MOONS SAGA

C. RAY SMITH, JR.
WITH MATT ROBERTSON

authorHOUSE®

AuthorHouse™
1663 Liberty Drive
Bloomington, IN 47403
www.authorhouse.com
Phone: 1-800-839-8640

© 2011 by C. Ray Smith, Jr.. All rights reserved.

No part of this book may be reproduced, stored in a retrieval system, or transmitted by any means without the written permission of the author.

First published by AuthorHouse   11/07/2011

ISBN: 978-1-4670-4087-7 (sc)
ISBN: 978-1-4670-4088-4 (ebk)

Library of Congress Control Number: 2011917112

Printed in the United States of America

Any people depicted in stock imagery provided by Thinkstock are models, and such images are being used for illustrative purposes only.
Certain stock imagery © Thinkstock.

This book is printed on acid-free paper.

Because of the dynamic nature of the Internet, any web addresses or links contained in this book may have changed since publication and may no longer be valid. The views expressed in this work are solely those of the author and do not necessarily reflect the views of the publisher, and the publisher hereby disclaims any responsibility for them.

Contents

Thanks for encouraging and editing assisting of:
Rachel McCleary
Jake Martin
Nicole Woolsey
Nikki Watkins

Chapter One

Shadow of Death
....

> "Yea, though I walk through the valley of the shadow of
> death, I will fear no evil . . ." Psalms 23: 4

Leaning over the rail of a pitching ship, puking one's guts out is probably not the best time for reflection. This was not how he thought it was supposed to be! It just could not be happening to him.

"Please Lord, let me wake up from this nightmare!" the boy exclaimed to himself.

The five foot, four inch, preteen's name is Ray, and he is the second—although oldest living son of Kelric, Marquis of Retúpmoc. His wavy, dark brown hair was unusually disheveled, and somewhat dirty. The length was not enough to tie in back, but was too long to be considered short either. It was growing out for the winter, but still an in-between length.

Ray's kingdom, Candlewynd, was a small one, and had been at war with a neighboring kingdom, Chimera, off and on for most of the past twenty years. Chimera was a landlocked kingdom that wanted Candlewynd's coast land. Also religion was greatly different—Candlewynd was strongly committed to the Holy Church, which was at odds with the Muslim faith of the Chimerans. In our world this would be similar to the Moors and the Spaniards in Spain before and during the Reconquista.

In a world where most of the land was divided into small kingdoms, warfare was a constant companion to the people. Ray's small coastal kingdom, which consisted of the capital city of Candlewynd and several small towns was, like many others, ruled by a king and nobles. Many of Candlewynd's nobility were Mentans, and had ruled with the aide of mental abilities, called psionics, much different from what our world would consider normal. Spell casting was not totally uncommon, and was considered a noble skill. Not just arcane spells, but many of the clergy had their spells granted by God. Not exactly the world we live in today, but that was another time, another place, another world. They knew of unhuman peoples, and creatures, but they were supposedly not near these lands.

Life for a twelve-year-old is confusing enough under normal situations. For his friends and him, or at least his companions, normalcy was far removed. The lives of the children he had worked with since becoming a page at eight years of age were changing. Some of the friends and he were promoted to junior squires, with the privileges and responsibilities. Others with whom they had worked were preparing to be sent for other types of training. After the elementary training in reading, writing, mathematics, preparatory mind focusing, and other learning, they were to move into our professional fields of training—for Ray, that of a warrior.

All the nobles' children went to the castle for this initial training beginning at age six. One, of course, did not develop mental powers that early, but since almost all of the nobility in the realm had some psionic powers, early understanding was needed. Usually the psionic powers began with the other physical changes—around twelve. Background skills and theory began early, as did focusing to channel power and to rebuild one's reserves. Every now and then a commoner was found with some psionic skills and they would be brought in for training also. It seemed strange to Ray, but some of these commoners' children reminded him of other children at school.

The nobles of this and other lands were called Mentans, at least those who possessed mental powers. Not all the nobles had these skills, but the more powerful families possessed them, to differing degrees. Some of those studied—psionics abilities and worked to develop these talents. Others were just born with some abilities and it was luck or happenstance. The pure Mentans attempted to keep their blood lines pure, but this was not an easy task, as war took a heavy toll on the noble and commoner alike.

At age eight they began more specialized training where their skills would take them, whether arcane arts, priestly callings, martial, or other skills. Other children—commoners with special talents—began training at eight to twelve, when testing was done by the Healers to determine if they had the "*spark*."

Let's face it, some of the smaller children were more suited to the arcane arts and did not need the same type of training that he needed as a fighter, nor did those especially bent for religious studies. Ray believed the strange ones were those that were being taught how to deal with locks and traps. All these children could have been trained at the castle, but the king wanted them to be the best trained that was possible—especially with more than just the specter of war looming around them. Not all of the children were being scheduled to go these training centers, only the ones who tested the highest. Even though one was of noble birth, it wasn't guaranteed; just those whom had won approval through many testings and strict discipline. Some of the squires, many of common birth, were being allowed the opportunity to go to the fighting. Ray didn't think it was fair, and he wanted to go with his father to the front, not to do more training. The teenagers that were training for mages might need to go for more schooling to learn their trade with spells, but as a fighter, he believed he could train in real battles.

In Ray's world, at sixteen a boy became a senior squire, was considered of legal age, usually returned home from the training schools. He began serving in the king's army; and a marriage was arranged, if it had not already been done. Some of those arranged marriages did not occur for several years, depending on where the bride was in her training, still others could occur very soon. Those who had stayed and trained at the castle also began a more active service in the army. The training was quasi military, so the older students had some authority over the younger. Usually the senior squires were over the junior squires, not so much with the seniors being just a year older—usually they were three years older. The senior squires were usually quite tough on the younger squires and being disciplined by one of them could be awfully painful. But they had to have a good reason to discipline a squire, they could not do for just general principles—if they did that, they got in severe trouble and disciplinary actions were much worse than they gave the younger squire. A senior squire still received corporal punishment.

Those who went away to learn the arcane arts or priestly duties usually did not return until they were between eighteen and twenty-one. Their training was a bit longer, and as Ray understood it, more complex. Somewhere about that time, twenty years old, a senior squire would become a full-fledged warrior, and if noble, knight, and both would assume a great deal more responsibility—marriage was expected, if duty was not already discharged.

"But thank God that is still a long way off for me!" the boy had thought.

Their school was hard work, but that gave them the chance to know other children of the nobility and they would be well trained when their time came to serve the king and/or whatever other adventures came their way. Besides, where else was a better place to meet other nobility that might one day be their life partners, and learn other things of court? Dancing and other social amenities were also taught. The students mixed with the students those who would be differently trained most of the time, not just those who would wield swords.

In Ray's world the Biblical passage "Spare the rod and spoil the child" was taken literally. Misbehavior was punished painfully to "beat the devil out of the child." It was believed if you knew you would be punished for misdeeds, you only got what you deserved. It seemed that the twelve and thirteen year olds were the ones most commonly requiring discipline. Younger children wanted to do good, but since these children were trying to grow, they also needed more instructions.

———————

My thoughts took me back to August. It was at the yearly send off party where my life really started to unravel. Those of us going off for additional training were to have the Grand Send Off. This was also a party for those whose castle training was finished and would be taking a more active role in the affairs of the kingdom—or in the war. The king was to speak, the food was well prepared, and that aroma was great. There was dancing, singing, some crying, and celebrations as we were preparing to begin a new leg of our journey to adulthood—as there was each year when children were sent off to their special training centers. I would be gone for most of four years—with only time off for Christmas to come home, and maybe briefly at the time of a Great Send Off. Children from the city who were younger, those who were older who had not been sent away to learn, the families of those leaving, and most of the nobility of the land that were in the kingdom were attending the festival. We danced, ate, and in general were having a wonderful time—as the events always were.

I spoke to and danced with the beautiful, younger girl that I had kissed in the hallway at the castle school. I had heard from the older boys how much fun that could be. It turned out to be one of the most painful events in my life.

She had dropped her handkerchief and I picked it up and returned it to her and stole a little kiss; it was kind of interesting, but not like the older guys made it sound. I did not even know her name, as she was at least two year younger than me, and she did not seem to mind. I thought it was kind of fun, until I went to sword practice.

We were assembled and about to begin practice when the Master of Arms sent for me to meet him in the stable. This was not normally a good thing, but I could not think of anything I had done that would result in my being reminded of my manners, and many times it was the senior squire that was responsible for discipline. I had not been disrespectful to any instructors, nor had I missed any assignments, and did not remember leaving out any equipment I was responsible for out.

When I walked into the stable and saw the old Master of Arms holding a hickory rod, I knew I was in big trouble. I was to receive a dozen stripes for kissing the girl in the hall. As I was still a page, a leather strap was normally used, or for twelve-year old squires, my age six stripes from a cane were normal, ten licks was a severe punishment—but a dozen with a cane!

I wanted to protest, but was informed I could have a score if I did not quickly assume the position over a saddle. I felt like I had welts on the welts when he finished. It was the worst disciplinary action I had ever received. I was certainly glad that we were not working on horseback. When I got home, I complained to Mother, who had already heard about the caning from my eight-year old little brat—I mean brother. She not only didn't give me sympathy, she said that if my father was home, I might be getting another good strapping *or* caning from him, and that it might still happen when he did return from the war. I was sore from that whipping for a long time.

I found out a couple of days later the girl I had kissed was the king's granddaughter, and through friends, that her evening lessons were similarly unpleasant . . .

The party was going well, everyone was dressed in their finest livery, and the prince sent word that I might dance with his daughter—dance only, no kissing.

The kissing—that was a month ago. Our farewell party was going well; my father and other of our relatives that were normally on the front line of the combat area had been given leave to attend this special event. It had been a long time since I had seen him, and since the death of my oldest brother two years ago, I had become very special to him—but that may have been partially due to the results of my testings.

I was still my father's child, but I was given more respect from him now that I was to be a squire and go on for additional training, just as my brother had done before me. I was just starting to become mentally aware, gaining my psionic powers and knew that I was developing those, as well as hone my fighting skills.

Father was more than a little upset about the kissing incident, but believed that I had already been punished enough. But said if he heard of future indiscretion, I might not be able to sit on a horse for several days. He suggested that if I wanted to kiss a girl it would be much healthier and less painful to kiss someone other than a princess!

Father had been there beside me when I was given my red sash and spurs as a junior squire. He had taken me around and formally introduced me to many of the officers that served under and with him in the war. I had met them before, but this was a formal military introduction, as I was now able to take part in war. Even though I was not going to be allowed to go—I was off to school for more training. Many of the noblemen knew of the testing results from the Healers and told me they hoped I would quickly reach my initial potential and be able to aid the king's troops in battle. My head was starting to swell both from this and the small amount of watered wine that we were allowed.

My father brought reality back into the scene by reminding me it would be at least four years, until I would be allowed to join them in battle, as a senior squire.

"I hope the war is over long before then. I would like you to have a chance to grow into full manhood without the strain of war. If your brother had been able to continue a little longer, he might have survived," he said.

"Father, I know Kelvin died in the war, but I want the chance to serve God and king. I also would like the chance to avenge his death." My voice cracked as I said it, embarrassing me. It was the first time I noticed it.

"Ray, you know your brother was larger built than you are, at least for your age. He had an earlier growth spurt, but remember he was larger than everyone else his age. But you have a stronger mind and your psionic talents will need to time to mature also. If Kelvin had not been in such a hurry to join me at the front, his mental skills might have been able to save him, and others.

"I don't want to hear any more talk of your finishing quickly to join the fray. If it is still going, then you can wait until your strength is to be a real asset. Besides, if you remain at the academy a bit longer, you might be able to assist your little brother there. Shall I write your instructors, and direct them that any talk of an early exit from you should be seared out of your system?"

I didn't have to ask how this searing was to take place, and my mother came up with my brother and her brother, John, who was one of father's staff officers. Father quickly changed the subject. Mother still would cry when she thought about Kelvin.

"I believe this is the best party we've had in years," she said. "The music seems a little better, and the appetizers seem to suit my tastes. Then again, it could just be because of the special importance it holds this year."

It seemed to me that more senior squires were preparing for deployment to the front than normal, and even more without noble livery. Since livery is not worn in our training, I was not really aware how many of the older students were not of noble birth. I remembered some, from the yearly parties before. The only thing I needed to know about them when they were older pages (and later, squires) was that they were older, and I had to follow their orders, at least until I was commissioned.

The dancing was fun—and several of the female members of our group were also going to the fighting academy—so I felt compelled to dance with them. Female fighters were not unheard of, but it was not as usual. The girls normally inclined to the spell casting arts, including the clergy. My mother had been trained as a Healer, although she had done little to practice her skill after she began to have a family, almost none since my birth.

The great feast was about to begin, with all the other preliminaries out of the way. Roasted beef's, venison's, pork's aroma wafted through the air, and was available in ample portions, as was a wide assortment of fowl. Vegetables, breads, and drink were also served in bountiful portions and a grand time was being enjoyed by all. Then the dessert trays were brought and I just knew someone would really explode from all that we were eating.

Then it was more dancing and mingling. Many of the younger children had been taken off to bed, and I was fighting hard to keep my eyes open to enjoy as much of this as I could, especially when Princess Charissa told me that she wanted to dance with me again.

———————

The princess was in a powder blue, floor length gown, with some beautiful sparkling stones along the top, and down the front of the dress. She also had a lovely ruby necklace around her neck, and a small golden tiara—with small rubies on it—sat on her wheat blonde hair. Her hair was braided back in a long single plait, which reached near the middle of her back. The blue in her dress brought out a lovely color in her deep blue eyes. She looked every bit the princess that she was.

———————

Now since I was two years older than her, she was, well too young for me. But she was a princess—so I was willing to dance with the child. Besides, she was kind of cute, and she looked older than ten. So we danced several dances. Then I realized that there was not anyone else her age still at the party.

"Did you get in trouble when we kissed—when I kissed you last month?" I asked her.

"Oh my—yes I was punished ever so severely!" she exclaimed. "My grandfather was extremely displeased that I would allow a boy to kiss me, and not at least slap his face. But I heard you were punished quite harshly—is it true?"

I told her, "I have had better afternoons than that one turned out. The Master at Arms had my attention much longer than I wanted him to. And I was sore for a couple of days."

Then she looked me in the eyes, and scared me so badly that I was concerned that I might soil my clothes. "Next time you kiss me, maybe it should not be so public," and shook her head, to toss her blonde hair in the back.

"I . . . I . . . I," was about all that would come out, and my voice betrayed me with a funny sound again. It was a good thing there was low lighting by this time—otherwise, it would have been noticeable that I was shaken up by her comment.

Then another older student came over and asked for the next dance. I hope I did not agree too quickly and move overly rapidly away to get some punch to drink. Then I stepped out for some fresh air. In the warm autumn night air, the smell of her perfume was still in my nose. That was a lot to take in, not to mention a bit more danger than I wanted to consider.

Let's see, a dozen stripes with a cane for a quick spur of the moment kiss. What would happen if it were planned . . . ?

That was where the thinking ended as our world came crashing in.

The King's herald then got everyone's attention and King Harold made the announcement that strong forces were moving toward us from three directions, and they had overrun many of our outward positions. The party was ended, senior officers would meet immediately, and all other military personnel were to make preparations for immediate redeployment to the battle. They were to get their gear and return, ready to leave within the hour.

Father found me, and told me to get his gear—which was already packed—load it on the pack horse, saddle Thunder, his charger, and bring them back to the castle and wait for him on the front field.

"Father, may I saddle my horse to ride with you part of the way?" I knew better than to ask to accompany him to the battle.

"You must be the man of the house, while I'm away. This may postpone your departure for further training. Stay home until you are sent, take care of your mother, Megan (my very annoying fifteen-year old sister), and assist Cord. You know Cord is not nearly as big as you are."

I was not sure how this might postpone my going off—the war had been going on all my life. I thought it might just go on forever.

Things were apparently not going well. A large number of wounded began to come into the city. Mother was asked, to begin helping at the hospital. She spent a lot of time working on her skills as a Healer at home, with a lot of big old books. It was something I had never seen her do before.

Things were not going well. Even at school the instructors were sharp with us, and several children learned painfully that it was not a time for misbehavior. Even the older squires were having problems with the instructors, and that meant additional problems for the younger squires and pages. Many, if not most, of the senior squires were even called up to duty at the front.

Also, it seemed to many of us that we were spending more time with archery since the party than normal. And we were doing it from higher positions toward lower targets; we even went and shot from the city walls one day. I asked Mother about this. This felt extremely "wrong," "bad," something . . .

"Well, dear, I don't teach those subjects. I would think your instructors just think you have not been practicing that enough—thus the extra practice. You could always ask the instructors, but from what you've told me about everyone's mood—I wouldn't if I were you," Mother told me.

I did not believe questioning a senior squire at this time would be too smart; they seemed to be looking for an excuse to remind a younger student of their manners. I knew I did not want another of "those" trips to the stables for that.

For months it had been getting worse. Wounded were coming in quicker from the battles, which meant the battles were getting nearer. Rumors said that many of the outlying estates had been overrun. One cold morning, late in November, we heard that there had been a destructive raid in the capital.

A group of the enemy had come into city and cast *fireballs* into a warehouse, and into some barracks. The fire and smoke could still be seen from the warehouse district, as other buildings caught fire from the first.

If the enemy had successfully entered the city, we must be in dire straits. All types of wild rumors were going on how they got in (and worse) out of the city. What types of magic had been used—beside; the arcane that brought the *fireball* into being? There was concern that psionics had moved the raiders from town and that there might be a Teleportation Pad set in some unknown location in town.

During this time, between the party and the raid of our beloved city, some of the children who had been sent off to study returned home, by ship. Then most of the older of these returnees went to assist in the war. But nothing seemed to help. The losses kept mounting up, and then another strike in the city—this time against the palace itself. The palace was not the only target, just the most disheartening. Other military targets were included in the raid.

The next morning, while the fires where still being fought, we went to our classes to learn our chosen professions. I was to report to work on mind focusing. Mother had been assisting me—to give me extra training, in the evening. Shortly after we began, one of the instructors in the arcane arts came into our class.

With a sad and a weary expression, he said, "You are to return home, and pack for a long sea journey. Get your weapons of war, armor, and other items you will need. Information has already been sent by servants to your parents or with whom you are staying to begin preparation. The city is to be evacuated!"

We sat there in shock, like he had cast a spell on us. We were hardly even breathing.

Then my older cousin Luke, Uncle John's son, came into the room. Luke was one of those that had returned from the training schools after the party. He was a Healer, and not only was he able to cast spells of curative nature, he learned the psionic devotion of *cell adjustment*, which was also curative. He was already fourteen (and about to be fifteen), and we had attended his going away ceremony and party just two years ago. Luke looked a lot like both my mother and uncle, dark green eyes, and light brown hair. He was normally very conscious of his personal appearance, but today he was a bit unkempt. He was mud splattered, carrying a riding quirt, and had a slight trace of blood on his emerald green robe.

He looked about the room, then slammed the quirt across a table and shouted, "Move—or you will desperately wish that you had!"

That got us up and moving. I started going toward the door, and Luke motioned for me to stand to the side. We had been close growing up, although he was much fonder of my big brother—I think a kind of hero worship. Kelvin was much larger built, being a fighter, while Luke was much slimmer, and Luke and I both looked up to him.

"The next time an instructor tells you to move, dear cousin, you had better not just sit there. Should you continue to do it—there may be some consequences!"

"Why are you pulling rank on me like this—you're not a warrior, and I'm not one your apprentices?" I responded. "This is extremely unusual for you to be giving me orders in the classroom."

"I can do so if I want to—having been in battle, but I didn't mean it like that, I just meant with the way things are; you could really catch a good one. And if the instructor has other things he is busy with, I don't want to be the one that has to carry it out. We're too close for that, but I'd have to follow orders, and I'm not that much older than you."

"We need to find Cord and get you both home to pack. Looks like you two are stuck with Caroline and me," he told me giving me a quick hug then pushing me out the door. Caroline was his younger sister, and she was nine.

"Are you going to tell me what is going on, or do I have ask the correct question to get any information?" I queried as we started down the stairs to find Cord. "I know you were up in the battle areas practicing your healing arts—which I hear are pretty good, for your age."

"I don't think either of us want the discipline that would cause for discussing that here," he said in a somewhat lower voice. "I'll tell you, Mother, Megan, and Aunt Martha what I can, when we get the two little kids and get back to your estate."

We found Cord and Caroline, and quickly made our way across town, in the carriage that Luke had brought from the estate. He had brought a dispatch from father, and knew we were to evacuate. Father had ordered him to stay and assist us in the evacuation and in caring for the family. Father knew Luke's mother and sister needed someone to help them cope with the disaster.

Uncle John's family had lived with us in the city estate since their hereditary home had to be evacuated, about six years ago. So Luke was almost like a brother, even though we were quite different.

I still could not explain to myself why he was allowed to go up to the battles and I was not. He is only a couple years older than I am. His healing spells must have really been needed—that is the only thing I could come up with. Megan didn't think it was fair at all, since she was a year older than Luke.

———————

Luke told them how badly things were going in war, and that they would not be able to stem the tide. Both of their fathers were alive when he left. The plan—as he understood it—was to hold out long enough for us to evacuate the city. Then they would ask for terms of surrender. After that they would attempt to rejoin us. He wanted to return to the battle, but he been given a direct order to stay. He told us also that arrangements for leaving by sea had been going on for a lengthy time.

Preparations for a sudden departure were quickly finalized, some supplies were kept permanently in the two large ships—for this emergency. These ships, the *Golden Quiver* and the *Silver Goose* were recently purchased to escape as the war worsened. They had magical enchantments which would give the ships favorable winds. The devices on board the two ships would cast *Sailor's Wind*, which would increase the speed of the ships about two to two and half miles per hour, or a little more than two knots per hour. The ships were double decked about 250 feet in length and about 50 feet across. Each of these vessels would be carrying a little more than 850 people including crew, livestock, supplies and a small amount of personal belongings of the occupants. Besides the two large merchant ships, other vessels were there. The fishing fleet was staying close to home. About fifteen small ships which could carry no more than ten people and one other merchant vessel had been acquired to assist in moving the important guilds of the city. The smaller vessel was much faster, but did not have the magical enchantment to aid its movement. It also only carried about 150 passengers, besides its crew. Also in port were two ships of war with crews of about 250 men, which had been hired to serve as escort vessels for the ships being readied for the escape. The populace hoped they would not have to leave. The city prayed that those who went back to the battle lines would be able to stem the tide of the war—but it was not the case.

The two large merchant ships, and the rest of the convoy departed the next afternoon, with the tide. Very little livestock went with them; just enough to start up new herds and flocks, and the best of the people from the city, common (this would include artisans) and nobility. The poorest and the slaves remained, as they would not be treated harshly by the advancing armies—at least that was what the children were told. The two young boys wanted to go to Marquis Kelric and aid him. Ray felt that as a squire he knew something of battle. They were not to be permitted, and argued the issue long enough almost to be disciplined by the Master of Arms.

The trip by ship to King Harold's cousin's kingdom of Kloridus was to take several weeks, and by the second night, most on board had been seasick. Winter may have been officially a couple of weeks away, but it felt incredibly cold on the ships. The weather made sailing difficult—so the squires were to perform most of the lookout duties and other types of watches. It was not certain how much they were needed for this or if it just gave them something to do.

"Please Lord, let me wake up from this nightmare!"

It was starting to snow, and the wind coming off the sea was biting cold. How could I still be throwing up? I hadn't eaten anything in twenty-four hours. But even the cold, fresh air was not helping my upset stomach. The pitching deck just kept me wishing I was dead.

Several of the larger fishing boats decided to go with the evacuation, along with some of the wealthy merchants that had the small merchant ship, which was moving additional people. The ships were attempting to keep together, and certain lights were to be placed on the ships at set locations, to help other ships from losing their placement as our little fleet moved out in the angry sea. The fishing boats were starting to have some troubles, it seemed to me. They kept moving along with the rest of the fleet.

Ray decided this was not what he expected of an ocean cruise. His noble family did not have a suite, and he was not even staying with them. Worse still, his family was not even on the king's ship, the *Golden Quiver*. Luke and he were both housed in the common quarters with many other former classmates. Because Luke was a couple of years older, he had extra responsibilities, although he was not in charge, and treated just like any other junior squire age boy. There were some squires that returned from training and some senior squires who were not deployed, plus other older spell casting students—similar to the senior squires with them in the fleet.

Ray's mother, younger brother, aunt, and younger cousin were all in the same area of the ship with just a canvas curtain to separate them from other families. There was not much distinction between nobility and the commoners. Almost no one had an individual room. The captains had one, because it was required for information and charts, the king had one—but he and the royal family were on the other ship, and some of the more powerful mages and priests were in semi-private rooms. Other spell casters just had a small chest in which to store their spell books. The few adult warriors had their fighting gear: armor, weapons, etc. in a chest at their hammock. Things were more than a bit cramped, and that many people crammed into close quarters would soon begin to cause unpleasant odors. At least some of the spell casters were able to alleviate part of those problems.

The fourth morning of their journey the seas had calmed to a slow roll, much to all the passengers' stomach's relief. It was still cold, but they were able to assume some duties without a great fear of being washed overboard.

A commotion was created by a signal from other ships in the tiny fleet. People gathered and looked to the south for the cause.

As Ray continued to stare in a southerly direction across the vast expanse of ocean water, the nature of the new threat soon became apparent. A number of warships had come into view on the edge of the horizon. Ray thought there were perhaps two or three ships roughly the same size as the two frigates escorting the Candlewyndian fleet. In addition, there were at least four to five smaller ships accompanying the enemy frigates. At this distance, Ray could not make out many details about the ships but he could see that each ship was painted black, each had long, black oars and each was rigged with dark black sails. They presented a very ominous appearance indeed and Ray was sure that was why they were painted in that way, to inspire fear in the hearts of their prey.

Now a frigate in Ray's world was not the same as might be seen on earth. There were no cannons, as gunpowder was unknown to them. They did have catapults, usually refereed to as cats, and large crossbow type weapons called ballistas. These ships were normally 150 to 175 feet in length, about 30 feet in width, and had a fighting crew of around 200 men plus additional officers. Also these sailing ships had oars, which could be used to increase a ship's speed—especially if they were attempting to ram another ship, as war ships were equipped with a ram, which could be raised or lowered.

Looking around him, Ray could tell that the enemy ships were achieving their desired effect on his shipmates. The atmosphere on board the ship was tense as crew, soldiers and passengers went about preparing themselves for the coming trial. Those women who were not adventurers were herded below decks along with the smaller children and such aged persons as had come along. Meanwhile, the maritime soldiers positioned themselves at their assigned stations to await the coming attack. On nearly every face was a look ranging in varying degrees from concern to outright fear. Everyone knew the two large ships carrying the bulk of Candlewynd's refugees could not maneuver well enough to spar with faster warships; even with the magical aide. The various fishing boats and other assorted smaller craft that had followed along with them would also be easy prey. Their only real defense was the two Kloridites frigates that had escorted them. But how could two frigates hope to prevail over a squadron of warships?

Though Ray tried as hard as he might to suppress his fear, something of it must have shown on his face because one of the crewmen fell in beside him and clapped him on the shoulder. Ray recognized him as one of the men who had earlier laughed at his bouts of seasickness. There was no mirth in the man's gaze now, however, as he looked down at Ray with something akin to pity in his eyes.

"Ye can go below, if ye like, lad," said the seaman, shifting his cutlass to rest on his shoulder. "No one'll think any less of ye in the mornin', of that I can assure ye."

I knew the man was expressing some measure of kindness in telling me that I could sneak below with the women and children, but I had no intention of doing so.

"I am a squire, sir, and I will do my duty," I said training to sound brave and proud.

The crewman smiled at Ray and said, "Aye, lad, so ye will." He then moved on down the line to take up his station near the aft catapult.

Bleakly, I stared out across the expanse of ocean separating me and the black ships of the enemy. I thought of home, the manor, and other property that had been left behind when my family was forced to flee. I longed to curl up once more in my own bed. My thoughts turned to mother, Cord, and

Megan—I knew that it was my responsibility to do whatever I could to keep them safe. Father is depending on me to protect our family. I thought about father and wondered where he was and how the battle for the city was going. I offered a short prayer to God, praying father was well, and then briefly murmured another silent prayer that God would keep him safe. Then I thought about Kelvin, who had died so young in the fight against Chimera, but was still four years older than I am. I remembered fondly the time we had spent together. Even though I, along with the rest of his family, had mourned for Kelvin, I had never really admitted to anyone how much I missed my older brother.

It was a brief interlude of thought, that all of these things and more had come to me. I thought about all of the unhappy things that had occurred in the preceding months and, although I was still afraid, I began to get angry. It seemed as if this small black fleet threatening us had become the embodiment of everything wicked and cruel in my world. It may be that they would all die that day, but I was determined that I would not die a coward's death, skewered like a boar in some hole within the depths of the ship. I'll swing my long sword until I could swing it no more and I'll take as many of the enemy with me as I can.

Ray's reverie was broken as he caught a flash of light in the corner of his eye. The flash appeared to have come from the quarterdeck of the king's ship, the *Golden Quiver*. As he turned in that direction, several other flashes of light followed in rapid succession. Ray was startled at first, but he soon realized that the captains were gathering to confer with the King on the quarterdeck and the flashes of light were caused by dimension doors opened for the captains by their ships' mages. Captains Ramirez and Duran of the Kloridites frigates were joined by Captain Drake from the *Silver Goose*, the ship Ray was on, one of the large Candlewyndian passenger ship. As one, they doffed their hats and made their bows to King Harold. Also, present on the crowded quarterdeck were Captain James of the flagship along with his executive officer and most of his staff officers. Finally, to one side, seemingly unaware of the military personnel around him, stood Gerron, the King's wizard. The enigmatic wizard was staring in the direction of the enemy warships and his concentration was so intense that Ray thought nothing could possibly distract him.

Just at that moment, someone slapped a hand on Ray's shoulder, startling him so badly that he nearly jumped out of his skin.

"You are just a bit on edge, aren't you, cousin?" asked Luke with a laugh. "I guess we all are." Luke stepped up beside Ray along with Ray's friend Timothy, who had a very distinct appearance with his closely shorn blonde hair and a small birthmark above his left eye, that appeared to resemble a small bird.

"Wouldn't you just love to know what they're saying?" asked Timothy, pointing toward the quarter deck. All of them looked in that direction. "Too bad none of us have *clairaudience*."

The boys and others from the *Silver Goose*, and the other vessels of the tiny fleet looked on wishing they knew what decision that determined their fate were being made aboard the *Golden Quiver*.

"What have you learned, wizard?" the King was saying. "Who are they and what are they about?"

Gerron did not answer immediately. Instead, the hooded wizard turned and regarded each face in turn, as if gauging in his own mind their ability to accept and comprehend the information he was about to impart. He turned back to King Harold and began to speak.

"The fleet is not Chimeran, but they are in league with Chimera," Gerron began.

"I could have told you that," scoffed Captain Ramirez, interrupting the wizard, "they don't have a fleet. They are pirates from the Isles of Samara and their black ships are quite distinctive. We have dealt with them in the past. Usually, there are never more than one or two ships together, however, due to the fact that they do not enjoy spreading their booty too thinly. The leader of the Samaran pirates, such as they have, is Lord Malpheus. He captains a ship-of-the-line called the *Panther*, though thankfully it is not one of the ships we see here. Chimera has apparently paid him enough gold to muster the pirates against us. This is a small fleet, however. If they are truly united in this effort, there could be as many as fifteen to twenty ships arrayed against us. But I have never seen . . ."

Captain Ramirez trailed off into silence when he noticed the wizard favoring him with a withering stare. Plainly, Gerron did not appreciate being interrupted.

The hooded wizard continued to glare at Captain Ramirez for a few seconds and then began to speak once more.

"As the Captain indicated, the ships belong to pirates from the Isles of Samara," said Gerron. "They are in league with Chimera and, apparently, they have been promised a portion of the plundered riches of Candlewynd should they encounter and sink our ships. The Chimerans want several of us, including the King, his family and myself, killed on sight. They want none left breathing who can lay claim to Chimera by divine right of sovereignty. The rest of our people can be killed, captured and sold into slavery, or whatever else suits the fancy of these pirates, particularly insofar as our women are concerned."

This produced frowns and growls all around, and a snort from the King.

"These ships we see before us do not represent their entire fleet. There are other squadrons, including the ship of this Malpheus fellow, patrolling farther down the coast. Now that our vessels have been spotted, will probably send one or two of their ships off to signal the others while the rest remain behind to prevent us from continuing south toward our destination. The corsairs know that if we reach Kloridus, we will be safe and they will never see their blood money."

"Your Majesty, the wizard is right!" said one of the junior officers, peering through a looking glass at the enemy fleet. "One of their frigates is sailing off in a southerly direction and another, smaller ship is sailing sou' by sou'west! Five ships remain, one frigate and four sloops. They are holding their positions steady."

"They seek to block us from sailing any farther south," muttered Captain Duran.

"They won't attack us yet," added Captain James. "They'll wait until their fleet is at its full strength."

"We did not plan for this eventuality," said Captain Ramirez. "If we had known the Samaran pirates were in league with Chimera, our entire navy would have sailed. This is a threat to Kloridus as well as Candlewynd. As it is, with only two frigates, we may be in a position to give battle to the squadron currently arrayed against us but there is little we can do against a fleet of any magnitude. Especially if the *Panther* prowls these seas against us. Upon my soul, neither of our frigates are any match for a ship-of-the line, the rest of their fleet aside. The *Panther* is armed to the teeth and carries more than 600 bloodthirsty warriors."

"Indeed," said Gerron. "Even assuming we can battle our way through the remaining ships in our path, we will soon be set upon by their entire fleet."

"Then what, in God's name, are we to do?!" King Harold barked. "Sit here and wait for them to gather and fall upon us? Or should we sail back to Candlewynd and face the Chimeran legions who have probably overrun the entire country by this time?"

"We certainly cannot hope to outrun them," Captain Drake was saying. "Both this ship and my own might with the magical aide we have aboard. The other merchant will be easy prey for warships. These ragtag fishing boats and other wrecks following along with us won't stand a chance either."

"Again, I ask, gentlemen," growled the King, struggling to control his temper. "What are we to do?"

Gerron sighed.

"As you have already observed, our options are limited, Majesty," said the wizard. "They will expect us either to give battle in an effort to continue sailing south and win our way through to Kloridus, to sail back the way we came into the waiting arms of the Chimerans, or to beach our vessels, go to ground here and somehow attempt to escape overland. If we hope to survive, we must do the unexpected."

"And what might that be?" asked King Harold, in a tone of exaggerated patience.

Instead of answering the King immediately, Gerron directed his attention to Captain Ramirez, who was the senior of the two Kloridite naval officers.

"Captain, do your frigates have the strength to confront the ships currently arrayed against us?"

Captain Ramirez looked thoughtful.

"We face one frigate and four sloops of varying sizes," the Captain said. "It would be no easy fight, but it is possible that we can defeat them. They probably do not expect an attack, with the advantage of surprise and a large measure of good fortune, we might defeat them."

"And even if we defeat them, what will that accomplish?" asked Captain Duran. "Our losses will be heavy and we would still have somewhere upwards of fifteen ships, including the *Panther*, gathering and prowling the seas between here and Kloridus."

Ignoring Captain Duran, Gerron directed his gaze once more at King Harold.

"Again, Majesty, I think we must do what they will least expect," said Gerron. "I propose that Captains Ramirez and Duran, if they are willing, give battle to the Samaran squadron. Meanwhile, we will sail with all possible haste westward toward the open sea where, if we sail far enough, we can hope to elude our pursuers long enough for the Kloridite navy to muster and sail forth to answer this threat. I will send word of our kingdoms' mutual plight to their wizards through otherworldly messengers."

Captain James looked doubtful.

"Yes," said Captain Ramirez thoughtfully, looking at Captain Duran. "It just might be possible. Assuming we can defeat the current enemy, we should be able to easily elude the bulk of the pirate fleet since we will no longer be slowed down by our escort duties. Not to mention the fact that they will be more interested in finding their prey than bothering with us. Meanwhile, if this wizard can persuade our King to muster the entire navy, we can link up with our own fleet."

Captain Duran nodded.

"And perhaps we can put an end to Malpheus and the Samarans once and for all," he said with a grim smile.

"It would do my heart good to see the *Panther* sent to Davy Jones' locker with all hands and Malpheus as well," said Captain Ramirez, returning his colleague's smile.

"Then let's be about it, gentlemen," said King Harold. "Captains Ramirez and Duran, we pray that God's hand be with you in the coming battle. Captains James and Drake, send the signals out immediately. Let us make preparations to sail on a westward track toward the open sea. We will sail on the turn."

Captain Drake and the other captains were returned to their ships and orders were given in preparations to the quickly created plan aboard the flagship.

At Timothy's urging, the three boys walked past the mizzenmast and quarterdeck to arrive at the stern. There, they joined other squires, maritime soldiers and seamen at their posts. They waited while the signals were all sent and the helmsmen set new courses out to sea. Before long, they felt the huge, lumbering ship slowly changing directions from the southerly course they had been taking which led directly to Kloridus and safety, to a more westerly course leading them directly out to the dangers of open sea. As ordered by the King, they were sailing with all possible speed on the turn of the glass.

As the civilian ships began to make their way out to sea, the enemy squadron also began to move into action. One of the sloops hove to and sailed off in a southerly direction. The remaining black ships formed a loose horizontal line formation with the frigate in the center and moved forward, apparently with the intention of following the Candlewyndian refugees and marking their progress.

Meanwhile, the two Kloridite frigates suddenly sailed past and headed straight toward the four enemy ships. Captain Ramirez's flagship, the *Sea Lion*, was in the lead with Duran's *Golden Eagle* sailing directly behind the flagship. Ray thought this was an odd formation and voiced that opinion to Luke and Timothy.

"It's a maneuver the Ancients called *diekplus*," said a voice coming from behind Ray.

Ray spun around and saw the seaman who had spoken to him earlier. The man gave Ray a toothy smile and stepped up between him and Luke to watch the coming battle for as long as they could see what was happening.

"What is *diekplus*?" asked Timothy.

"Ramirez is a smart commander. He knows that his ships are faster and more maneuverable than those of his opponents and he thinks that he can use that to offset their advantage in numbers," explained the sailor. "Watch."

The two Kloridite frigates continued to sail straight at the enemy, picking up speed as they went. Splashes to either side of the *Sea Lion* gave proof to the fact that the black ships were firing their aft catapults, thus far ineffectively, at the approaching frigates. Suddenly, when they had covered about half the distance between them and the enemy, Ramirez's flagship veered off to the left and swerved to approach the line of black ships from an angle while the *Golden Eagle* maintained its course. At that precise moment both ships surged forward with an incredible burst of speed. With full sails and their oars plunging in and out of the ocean with one accord, Ray was sure he had never imagined that ships could move so fast.

The *Sea Lion* then lowered its ram and sailed straight at one of the sloops in the enemy line. From the deck of their ship the boys could see that the commander of the black ship was taken by surprise and would be unable to maneuver his ship out of the way in time. Men began jumping from the sides of the smaller black ship in an effort to get away. Others began to fire flame arrows at the *Sea Lion* in a panic, most of them falling short or missing their target altogether. Then came a loud crashing sound of splintering wood as the frigate's ram took the sloop amidships in its gunwales. Even at their ever increasing distance from the fight, Ray and the others could hear the shrieks of dying men as they were thrown into the sea. Incredibly, the larger frigate plunged completely through the black sloop, which was torn asunder and immediately began to sink.

Meanwhile, the *Golden Eagle* careened head-on into the enemy line, passing straight through the line with oars held aloft and, in the process, sheering off the oars of the enemy frigate.

"*Diekplus*," said the seaman. "One ship is down, another crippled. This fight is as good as over."

Both frigates swung around and began to hunt for new targets.

What resembled an intricate dance with each ship tacking for better position. The captains of the three remaining enemy sloops knew that they could not hope to ram a frigate and maintain their own ships intact. Therefore, their goal was merely to avoid being rammed themselves while attempting to sail in a pattern which would enable them to join forces with their own disabled frigate and to keep the Kloridite frigates busy until their frigate can become functional again. It was probably as good a plan as any with one of their ships down and their flagship disabled.

However, the two Kloridite captains were too good. After another turn of the glass, another black sloop had been sent to the bottom of the sea and a second sloop had fled in a southerly direction. Although the fight was so far away now that Ray could barely see what was happening, he could tell that the two Kloridite frigates had sailed on each side of the disabled black frigate and attached multiple grappling hooks. Maritime soldiers were swarming from both ships onto the deck of the enemy frigate and a melee had broken out.

Although the pirates fought bravely, Ray knew that they were hopelessly outnumbered and Captain Ramirez would easily capture the frigate.

Meanwhile, with the frigates almost out of sight, Ray was startled when he looked off to the southeast and saw that the lone remaining black sloop was sailing straight at them, possibly tacking toward some of the fishing boats. When the sloop came within range, the aft catapults on both merchant vessels began firing at the sloop, with very little success.

Suddenly, as the black ship was sailing past and bearing down on a fishing boat laden with people and supplies, Luke saw and pointed to the king's ship. There Gerron along with the two enchanters, were casting spells at the sloop. Transfixed by their incantations and by the grace of their hand movements, Ray stared at the three mages.

The three wizards finished their spells at almost the same time, and a ball of light shot from the hands of each mage, flying toward the enemy ship. Turning, the boys watched as a small explosion rocked the quarterdeck of the sloop. A second, slightly larger ball of fire exploded in the ship's rigging and sails. Finally, a massive explosion of fire took the sloop amidships and engulfed the middle of the vessel in fire. Ray could hear the screams of the dying pirates as they jumped off the burning ship, perhaps preferring a cold, watery death to the searing flames of the Hell to which they would soon awake. Worse, a horrible odor of smoke, brimstone and burning flesh came wafting across the sea.

———————

"God's wounds!" Luke whistled. "Did you see that?"

"How could anyone miss it?" I asked sardonically. "Even if you didn't see it, you can still smell it."

"How true," muttered Timothy. "I think it is my turn to be sick."

"You lads have weak stomachs," taunted Luke. "Perhaps you both should still be playing with wooden swords."

"Those pirates are the scourge of the seas and they mean to kill every one of us," said Richard, Ray and Timothy's Senior Squire. "But, as God is my witness, no man deserves to die like that."

This statement sobered all three of the boys, even the usually irrepressible Luke.

"I'm going to my bunk," I told them.

"Probably a good idea, lads," agreed Richard. "All three of you should get some sleep while ya can, especially you two to younger ones."

With that, Ray went below and flopped down in the hammock that he had strung to sleep in. He was tired but still a little sick and, truth be told, he was a little frightened to know that they were sailing out into the deep ocean. He lay there staring at the top hammock for what seemed an interminable length of time before finally dropped off into an uneasy sleep. After a while, he thought he was somewhere else looking at a scene—detached, like a play.

They had been hidden most of the day in a small cave, just big enough for the ten of them and their horses. Now, they were just waiting for the sun to go down so they could ride under the safety of the night sky. They would continue riding for the southern border and safety. Their leader knew that the Chimerans would be hunting for them, but thus far they had eluded their pursuers and he believed that they would likely reach their destination within the next couple of days.

After another couple of turns, they decided it was safe to be on their way. So far, they had kept to little known forest paths and now they were heading into the southern hills. The border was so close. Soon they would not only be safe, but they would rejoin their loved ones who had fled by ship to Kloridus. When Kloridus and other nations were shown evidence of Chimera's consort with the Orcs and other unholy creatures, alliances would be formed and they would rally a host to retake Candlewynd and destroy the Chimerans. What a beautiful day that would be! The stars were shining brightly in the sky above and the night air was chill. Vapor steamed from the horses' nostrils with each breath as they galloped along the path.

The small party had ridden perhaps half a turn of the hourglass when they heard the sound that each man had been dreading. From back along the path behind them, some distance away, erupted the ferocious baying of hounds on the hunt. By the Heavenly Gate, but they were so close! Sensing their peril, the warhorses stepped up their pace without being urged. Two abreast, the chargers pounded down the path until they were lathered and panting. Impossibly, however, the baying sounded ever closer and closer behind them.

At last, it became obvious that they would not be able to outrun or elude their pursuers. Some forty paces after a turn in the path, the warriors dismounted, knowing the path would be too narrow for horse combat. They gathered, drew their weapons and prepared to give battle. If the dogs were accompanied by only a small party, some of them might yet make it to Kloridus alive.

"Remember what we are fighting for, lads," said the leader. "The free nations must know that this was more than just another land grab. Chimera and its demi-human allies will not be satisfied with Candlewynd alone. When they have raped, pillaged and defiled our homeland, they will look southward again."

Their hopes soon faded, however, when their opponents turned the corner of the path and came hurtling toward them.

"Good Lord in Heaven," breathed the leader. "They've brought hell hounds."

Indeed, running at them were half a dozen enormous black dogs, lathered as if after a long run but showing no lack of energy for their efforts. The dogs were snorting as they ran and with each snort, a belch of fire spewed from their nostrils. Upon sighting their quarry, the hounds began to howl gleefully and their eyes shown with a fiendish, unearthly glow. Behind the hounds, followed a company of Orcs bearing a hammer and sickle emblem upon their shields. The Orcs rode upon huge Wargs and brandished long spears. The Orcs were chanting something in their savage tongue.

The Candlewyndian warriors barely had time to notice this because the hounds were soon upon them. The first two warriors in the line were engulfed in flames as the hounds stopped to belch out their fiery breath, three apiece on each man. After this, they leapt forward into the line. The warriors fought bravely and two of the hounds were down with a third missing a leg, when the hounds breathed their unholy fire again, incinerating a third warrior.

With a fourth man hamstrung and down, only six soldiers were standing when the Orcs hit the line. After that, the fight was soon over. Within moments, only the leader was alive, bleeding from a dozen wounds, three of them mortal, and cornered with his back to the stone wall. Nearly a score of Orcs surrounded him in a semicircle. His blade dripping with the black blood of Orcs and hell hounds, the leader beckoned them forward.

"Come to your deaths, you dogs," he panted.

He had not long to wait. A huge Orc chieftain stepped out of the pack and skewered him with a wicked looking spear coated with some black poison. As the leader sank to the ground, the Orc chieftain barked something unintelligible to the rest of his company and they were riding off in the direction they had come.

The leader, barely holding on to life, could feel the black poison coursing through his veins and he knew he would soon be dead notwithstanding his other wounds.

"Ray . . ." whispered the leader. "Ray . . . you must be the Protector now. Watch over your mother, brother and sisters. Ray, Ray . . ."

Chapter Two

Trouble at Sea
....

"He who spares the rod hates his son, but he who loves
him is careful to discipline him."—Proverbs 13:24

"RAY!! Wake up!"

He awoke with an almost unbearable sense of loss. He
didn't have long to dwell on this, however. As he opened his
eyes, he was looking up into the face of his friend Timothy,
who was shaking him.

"At last, you're awake!" exclaimed Timothy. "Come on,
you're supposed to be at your post, standing watch along with
the other squires in our group. You don't want Lieutenant
Lyons or Richard to catch you late, do you?"

Spurred into action more by the possibility of this last
threat, Ray jumped out of his bunk and the two scurried out
onto the deck to take up their posts.

Those that were squire age and over were to spend a great
part of the day learning their way about the ship, climbing in
the rigging, and duty stations in case of an attack. Ray heard
from Luke that those with spell casting skills are to be placed
where they may work their magic with less chance of being
interrupted. A ship's officer, Lieutenant Lyons, was to be in

charge of his group. Other officers would be working with other students.

Lieutenant Lyons was an officer on board the ship. When the voyage had commenced, the squires were divided up into groups according to age and experience. The groups were then expected to stand watch in shifts and to learn everything they could about naval combat, including climbing the rigging, arming and aiming the catapults, swinging the boom and lowering the ram, fire prevention and assorted other tasks. This was to be done in their spare time between watch shifts and weapons training. Richard's group, which included Ray and certain other of his peers, was one of the groups led by senior squires of whom the Lieutenant had been placed in charge.

Ray and the other junior squires suspected that Lieutenant Lyons chafed under his responsibility for their group of squires because he always seemed to have a scowl on his face whenever he spoke to any of them. The man could be quite intimidating when he wanted to be. He was a large, barrel-chested man with a huge, bushy black beard and long black hair which combined to form a mane which would make his surname name seem all the more appropriate. The Lieutenant really did look, and roar when he was angry, something like a lion. He generally wore his hair oiled back and tied from behind with a small leather strap. He also had bushy black eyebrows topping large dark eyes which always seemed to blaze with anger. In spite of his burly stature, the Lieutenant was deceptively nimble as well, often dishing out punishment, such as a cuff on the ear, before his charges even knew it was coming. His baritone voice, which was loud and usually stern, could be heard from one end of the ship to the other when Lieutenant Lyons was in a lather. It seemed to Ray that this was most of the time.

As he and Timothy tried to slip into their posts, Ray hoped that their tardiness had gone unnoticed. Unfortunately, this hope proved fruitless. Both boys jumped as they heard the sound they had been dreading.

"Avast, you lazy dogs, what are you about?!" bellowed Lieutenant Lyons from behind them. "You are nearly half a turn late in taking your posts. I've seen ships attacked and sunk in less time than that!"

"Children! They expect me to turn *children* into maritime soldiers," Lieutenant Lyons roared. "Children—be sure to heed what I say! I have little patience with youthful misdeeds, and they will be treated quite severely. I have been informed that many of you are of noble birth. You are aware of the consequences of misbehavior or poor work. Further that punishment will be given the same for any young ladies just as for the young gentlemen, and I will not spare the rod should the occasion require it," he stated, as he looked sternly at us. He looked extremely intently at the three girls who were training as warriors with us.

Ray guessed he thought the girls had been somewhat pampered at the castle. As far as Ray could tell they were held to the same expectations as they boys did, and were punished when those in charge felt it was warranted. The fact that they matured quicker than the boys had, made them a great challenge with sword exercises, and they were better with a bow than almost all of the lads. Ray blushed as he recalled that even Charissa had been punished when they had been caught kissing.

Mistaking the source of Ray's discomfiture, the Lieutenant continued, "Good! At least *you* have the grace and good sense to be embarrassed for your laziness. Don't be the first to learn personally of shipboard discipline, you will regret that for a long time! Richard, I'm willing to let the young pup that was late off with extra marching duty this time. **IF** there is a next time you will ***warmly*** remind any tardy child of their shortcomings! However, you may discipline him as you see fit as you're the senior in charge of the boy. After yesterday's events, I'm inclined to be too lenient today!"

With that said, Lieutenant Lyons stalked off and began yelling at some unfortunate crew member on the other side of the ship. They all breathed a bit easier after the lieutenant left. Richard assigned Ray two hours of marching duty in leather armor, shield, and sword for being tardy—which Ray believed was much better than a caning from the senior.

———————

We then began a lesson in the terms of the ship, especially the rigging. We had to know where we were to be deployed, if an attack was launched against the ships, how to quickly climb the ropes to the crow's nest, and a bunch of other things that were completely alien to us.

Timothy came up while we were catching our breath from a quick climb to the crow's nest and back down.

"I am beginning to think this voyage is going to be harder than lots of training at the castle—my arms are starting to really hurt. I heard the lieutenant talking to one of the midshipmen, betting that our legs would really be sore in the morning."

"Timothy, I believe he may have understated the bet—I'm sore now," I told him. "My hands are little sore, probably because of the cold, but it is a good thing we spent so much time with a sword and shield. Can you imagine what our hands would be like it we weren't use to using them for weapons?" my voice cracked again—it couldn't make up its mind how it was going to be.

The lieutenant snapped back to the training, and twenty-five very tired, mostly twelve year olds, were extremely glad when he eventually sent us to have a small noon meal. After that we would start to learn the drum signals for actions that were required of us. This lasted about two hours, and most of us were thoroughly confused at the end of the time. We were extremely glad to be going to work on mental exercises. What we did not realize was how difficult it was to focus when you're that tired.

"You children must learn to focus through fatigue," rasped our instructor, an aging gentleman wearing a robe of the same color gray as his long hair and beard. "In war, one does not have the luxury of being fresh when attempting to refocus one's mental energy. You must learn to quickly focus your energies while being harried by enemies and fatigue."

That night was a welcome relief from the day's hard struggles. Luke said the spell casters had a similar type of day. They had been in other parts of the ship training on the ropes, learning to judge distances on a ship. Not that any of the students were going to drop a *fireball* on the deck of the ship, none were that skilled in spell casting, but a *sleep* at the wrong spot could be fatal to those in the area affected.

Luke proceeded to tell them all a story about a novice who had cast *sleep* on the bozun's mate's cat as a joke only to be shocked when the cat keeled over and fell overboard. Luke thought this was exceedingly funny, although Ray felt it was rather cruel.

"You should have seen the novice's face!" exclaimed Luke. "You would have thought he had been caught inside the King's treasury with two bags full of gold slung over his back! And later, the bozun's mate came on deck and asked around after his cat. The novice went deathly white! It's all I could do to keep from laughing!"

"Cousin, I'm afraid you have a very warped sense of humor," I quipped, "especially for a healer, who has seen war. Now, if you don't mind, I'm going to bed. And I suggest you do the same. I'm sure tomorrow will be just as long as today was."

We did not talk any more of the day's events—sleep quickly overcame us. And I, for one, was extremely thankful to God that: I did not have duty this night, my stomach had gotten use to pitching of the ship or at least for the calmer weather, and I didn't have any nightmares.

The morning came too early to me.

"It's still dark outside, not even a hint of the sun showing itself," Seth, who was another of the boys in my group, said echoing my thoughts. Seth, a second year squire, was already thirteen, and had returned from training after the party.

I heard several groans from the others about the pain in their legs and arms from all the climbing yesterday. I wonder if the lieutenant had any takers on his bet about the soreness, because he was completely correct.

Before first meal we were up and down the rigging four or five times, twice with a bow and arrows to fire from the rigging, and then for a race that the two slowest of our twenty-five would be given extra duty—to help motivate them to be faster. I was glad I was one of the quicker ones. Timothy and Seth were not quite so lucky.

This type of routine went on for a week, or more. It was very physically demanding, and seemed that the adults' tempers were very short, not only in the physical training, but also in our other studies. Many of the young squires were put across a chair or table and caned. Even the older squires were not exempt from disciplinary actions, nor were those in magical studies, nor were there gender exceptions. If you did it wrong too often or too much, you felt the instructor's wrath with a hickory or birch rod. I was glad to have missed those extra training sessions.

Even with these brutal training techniques, there were very few injuries; only a few more than would have occurred in the fencing or jousting arenas at home. This gave the Healers a chance to practice their craft with real patience. Curing spells, ointments, and mental healing were all practiced by the Healers.

We finally got a day off—besides the Sabbath. We had a Monday off—two days in a row without the training. Some of us still had duties or watches, but no up and down ropes, sword drills, etc. What made it even better was that the sun was out—it was still cold, but the bright sun lifted our spirits and the rest allowed our young bodies to recuperate.

Luke came up while I was talking to Timothy and our senior squire—he was not as hard to get along as many of the older boys. At nineteen, Richard had been in the war. He had returned to the city with a slight injury, and been given escort duty to assist the more severely injured, and get his wound cared for.

Then it struck me. "Richard, there doesn't seem too many adults or even senior squires on the ship. Are there a larger number on the King's ship?"

Richard made kind of a face, sucked in a little extra of the cold air, "We're not supposed to bring that subject up."

I was a little concerned with his tone, but still went on, "Sir, you did not bring it up—I did. Are you allowed to answer, or is this a subject I'm not even allowed to ask about? I don't want to get you upset with me."

By now both Luke and Timothy began to look about the ship, most of those who were training on the ship were junior squire age, not many senior squires or adults.

Richard then motioned for us to sit, looked around and started, "You three have to promise not to talk about it to anyone else. If I get in trouble because of this, I'll do something that I would really hate to have to do. I'll take a rod to the three of you, and your discipline will be more severe than what I get. Do you understand?!"

We all three shook our heads, replied, "Yes, sir" and listened intently to what the senior squire was to say.

Richard began, "I'm the only senior with you two—correct. Most of the groups have two senior squires, I think two groups have three senior squires on both ships combined. The bulk of the fighting force on the two ships are made up of the two hundred squires, in eight, twenty-five man groups. Of that number most of you are twelve and thirteen, and not all are male. I'm not sure what the break down of spell casters are, but we are a very young group. Most of the adults are on the two support war ships. I know that there are more seniors and adults on the merchant ships, but many of them are wounded and are recuperating. Each of the fishing or other vessels also has at least one warrior on them—I think."

The boys let that sink in for a while. It was a good thing their society allowed squires to be so involved. But that still meant only about sixteen to twenty senior squires, about the same, maybe a few more, in young knights, a few instructors, and the king's staff for all the warriors in their kingdom—if you didn't count the two escort ships. They weren't sure how many of them were soldiers. The sailors could also fight, but they were not really trained for warfare. The other vessels had some warriors and squires on them, but how many? How many would survive the journey, or what about those who were badly injured? They are were off on their estimates, but they were still indeed a young group on this adventure; as it turned out, one of the smaller ships had a high percentage of senior squires on it.

———————

"God's wounds, this is a dire situation!" exclaimed Luke.

Richard continued, "Luke, I know you are not one of my squires, but the promise of what will happen if this discussion gets out still applies."

I thought Luke was going to try to argue the point, but later he told me he was concerned Richard might show him right then that he outranked him, was enough older, and could wear him out. I guess my cousin is smarter than I thought.

Instead Luke added to the information, "There are only seven healers on this ship, counting the instructor. I don't believe there are more than four training on the other ship. That number doesn't count any of the parents who are taking care of children below, like Aunt Martha, or if the ship has a Healer on staff. The Priests are helping taking care of curing on the other ship. And from what I can tell the mages are split on both ships, but I have not paid attention to their numbers."

Timothy's eyes were almost glazed over "I guess that is why they are working us so hard? We are the army!" His voice cracked for the first time that I had noticed.

Richard reached over and rubbed Timothy's head and told us, "Yes, and why discipline has been pretty severe.

"I know you're still sore from last night's reminding of keeping alert on watch?" Richard asked Timothy.

"Yes sir. You were quite harsh with me. I didn't think I deserved one that bad."

"Would you like to go take it up with Lieutenant Lyons? If you believe I was unfair in my discipline you know you can do that," Richard said—more than a little annoyed at being somewhat challenged.

"No—no sir, I don't want to get any officers involved. Please don't take me to him. I apologize for my comments, I did not mean to be critical," Timothy pleaded almost tearfully, with his voice cracking also.

Getting an officer involved would probably get someone in trouble; Richard if he was incorrect in disciplining Timothy, or Timothy again for questioning his superior. Luckily for Timothy, Richard was easier to get along with than many of the senior squires, who might have been more offended by his statements, and used them for an excuse to punish him.

We took time to visit with our family again that day. We usually only saw them on Sunday, as the rest of the week we were training. It was good to see Cord, and even Megan wasn't too hard to get along with—she had been kept really busy as a Healer also.

Luke and I discussed what Richard had told us later that evening, very careful not to be overheard. We did not want to betray his trust, not only for fear of what Richard would do to us, but because it might make it more difficult to work with him in the future, and I was in his unit. We both decided we would have to work harder in the future.

As a result of the conversation with Richard, Ray decided to really try much harder, as he saw the importance of training. He became very difficult for the other students in his unit to compete with due to his increased intensity. As a result, the oldest student and a girl, about fifteen, became his new sparring partner. Sherry would sometimes attempt to distract Ray by flirting and keeping the youngster off balance. She was one of the better junior squires on board with a sword, definitely the best girl, and beyond doubt, she was the best archer among them. She would be devastating if she developed the strength to draw a strength bow. She definitely had the best eye.

Sherry was also very comely and fair of skin, with exotic, almond-shaped green eyes and, chestnut brown tresses, which she often wore in a ponytail when they sparred. She was lean and athletic but hauntingly soft as well. Ray discovered this on the brief occasions when they would come together in the middle of a sparring match. Sherry also had delightful swells in the area of her chest that Ray had never really noticed on a girl before. Charissa certainly had nothing of the kind.

"Luke, Sherry and I spent a lot of time working against each other while training. But there is another student, Adam, that seems to consider her his girl, and does not like the extra attention I was giving to her and her to me. He was assigned to another group, but he still thought I was attempting to steal his girlfriend. Think I should say something to her about it?" I asked my older cousin.

To my chagrin, Luke began to laugh.

"I should have known better than to confide in you, the way you've been behaving lately!" I growled, kicking my cousin in the shin.

"Yow, that hurt!" exclaimed Luke, still laughing.

"What exactly is so very funny, cousin?" I asked through clenched teeth.

"Not to give offense, cousin," Luke said, grinning, "but you are only twelve summers. She is fifteen. She more likely considers you a very cute child, albeit good with a sword, rather than someone she would consider as a potential love.

She flirts with you because she wants to win and she knows it distracts you. Don't look so outraged!"

"All right, but what about Adam?" I asked, glowering at Luke. "If she really has no interest in me, why is Adam so upset at me?"

"Who knows?" quipped Luke. "Maybe he just is a very jealous lover, or perhaps he's just not very intelligent, have you considered that? Or . . ." Luke got a speculative look on his face.

"Or what?" I wanted to know!

"Perhaps she is simply trying to make him jealous," suggested Luke. "Sometimes girls do that when they don't think you are showing them enough attention. She may be showing attention to you when she knows Adam is watching just to make him angry. You'd better be careful, Ray. Adam is much bigger than you are and her actions may even goad him into fighting you. Some girls even enjoy being fought over."

This idea had not occurred to me.

"You don't really suppose Adam would want to fight me, do you?" I asked, appalled.

"Oh, surely not," said Luke in a comforting tone. "He is, after all, much larger than you and he must know that you would both get severe punishment for fighting.

"No, with most marriages arranged I'm not sure what his complaint is. Besides you're just twelve," he stated, emphasizing my age.

After a very hard workout session in which Sherry and I fought as a team against two of the oldest students in our group, and won, she gave me a slight kiss on the cheek. It was almost like an older sister might give a little brother, but it shocked me. The last time I kissed a girl it proved to be very painful.

That evening after we ate Adam found me, and informed me of what he planned to do with me. He challenged me to meet him in the hold of the ship where it was more private and we could have a nice long discussion about my relations with his shield mate. At twelve I am very good with a sword, but I'm not a match for a fifteen-year-old in a fist fight.

Fighting of this type is against the rules, and if we were caught, Richard or Lieutenant Lyons would tear me up, plus I would probably get killed in the fight. I attempted to explain this all to him, and was getting more than just a little scared. Also, by now we were getting some attention from other boys in the compartment.

His threats were becoming much more personal, and one of his friends suggested they should "haul me down and beat the snot out of me." Then it was decided that I was too much of a coward to go down to the hold and defend myself.

A boy can only take so much before he has to defend himself. I asked if there was another way this could be settled, and was answered with a laughing no.

We started to go down to the hold, and I was scared to death. Not so much about getting beat up—that was going to happen, he was just too much bigger and older than I was. I was concerned that I would not even be able to get any punches to land, and that I might appear to be too much of a baby. Or even worse—cry.

There was a loud bellow from the door that got everyone's attention and before I knew what was happening, Richard had grabbed me, seemingly by the scruff of the neck, and pulled me back. There was also a ship's officer there and a knight wearing chain armor, a winged helmet and a flowing, forest green cloak bearing an emblem with an eagle on it. I knew the emblem, and assumed he was the knight in charge of Adam's group of squires, Sir Stephen.

"You *children* will return to your quarters, *now*," barked the knight. "I know each one of your faces and I can assure you that you *will* have enough extra training this week to help you remember the rules for the rest of your *miserable* lives. I will teach you the penalty for interrupting my evening meditations with this foolishness!"

Everyone was sent back to their sleeping berths, except Adam and me. Adam went with his knight, who quoted the scriptures as they left, "'he who spares the rod hates his son, but he who loves him is careful to discipline him.' You will learn the meaning of those words."

I had to face Richard. I was almost in tears from fear of the fight I thought I was going to have. Richard's voice was extremely stern, and he appeared to be very upset.

"Your cousin came and got me," Richard began through clenched teeth. "I'm extremely disappointed in you for being willing to have a brawl, like a common street urchin!"

I felt his criticism was a bit unfair—I had not wanted the fight. In fact I did not want anything to do with it. I started to tell him, but I decided that anything I said would probably just get me into more trouble. Richard did not appear to want to listen to anything.

Richard sighed and sat down on a crate, frowning at me.

"Why are you so mad at me?" I asked. "I know I made a mistake and that I'll be punished for it. I will accept my punishment, however severe you decide it should be."

"You've embarrassed me, Ray!" Richard replied. "The knight who was here earlier, his name is Sir Stephen, younger son of the Count of Windborne. He is an Eagle Knight, a member of the elite scout and combat unit who ride into battle and for reconnaissance purposes, with very fast—almost racing steeds. They are feared by the enemy and greatly respected by the army for their bravery. I hope to gain admission to that unit after my advanced training is complete. Now, Sir Stephen probably thinks I'm not fit for his father's unit or for command anywhere else. If I can't even manage a group of twenty-five young squires, how can I manage their type of missions? Why did you have to get in a fight with a squire from Sir Stephen's group, of all things?! My record with him was spotless before this!"

Now I felt worse than I could recall ever feeling before.

"Richard, I know who the count is, and I'm sorry," I said with a lump in my throat. "I guess I just wasn't thinking."

"You've got that right," Richard replied. "Now go on up to bed."

I started to say something else, but Richard interrupted me.

"You get to bed, and in the morning after first meal we will have a lengthy, one-sided conversation about your manners, or maybe I should say the neglect of them," Richard said. "If you say anything to me before then—you will regret it."

I quickly went to bed, but it was hard to sleep knowing that I was really in trouble when the morning came.

"Thanks, Luke, for getting help. He was going to beat me up—bad," I squeaked to Luke before turning over to go to sleep.

"What did Richard say?"

"He did not say much tonight, but tomorrow I'm a little concerned about being able to sit. I don't want to talk any more tonight—I'm kind of shook up after that encounter," I told my cousin.

"Good night then—I guess we should be thankful that you can still talk, and your eyes aren't swollen shut also."

He is soooooo encouraging!

Ray closed his eyes and tried to rest but sleep just wouldn't come to him. For a while, he lay awake worrying about his "appointment" the following morning with Richard and Lieutenant Lyons. Then he started thinking about the fight he almost had.

Tossing and turning, Ray wondered why he had gone down to hold of the ship. He knew that part of his motivation had stemmed from the reasons he gave Luke before going down. He needed to be respected if he ever hoped to follow in his father's footsteps as a commander of men. His father had always told him that. Also, Adam had embarrassed him in front of other squires, that was true.

God's wounds, but he missed Kelvin so much. He also missed his father. It already seemed as if they had been sailing for months and months. Ray wondered how the war was progressing. His mind went back to the dream he had the previous week and he wondered if he would ever see his father again. Did they even have a home to which they could return? Even if they did, it would never be the way it was when Kelvin would come home from squire training for the yule or summer season and play sticks and stones with Ray and Megan in the grass under the warm sun. Those happy times were gone forever. Who knew what tomorrow would bring? Not just the immediate date with Lieutenant Lyons in the morning, but the future itself.

Quietly, with his head buried under his pillow, Ray began to cry. Eventually, he drifted off into an uneasy sleep.

I saw Adam during first meal the next morning—he was moving extremely sorely. His look at me was none to kind.

It appears that Sir Stephen and he had already discussed his manners. That did not give me any comfort.

I knocked on the door to Lieutenant Lyons's room, where I was to meet with Richard. I was shaking.

"Come in," came the Lieutenant's voice.

As I open the door to the small room Lieutenant Lyons, Richard, and Sir Stephen were all there.

"Reporting, as ordered, sir!"

They got up from sitting on a bed and the single chair, and Richard ordered, "Down to the ward room!" He also picked up an ominous birch rod leaning against the wall in a corner of the room.

As I started down the hall Richard came up behind me, and placed the rod over my shoulder and quietly said, "Just in case you hadn't figured it out—better be on your best manners this morning. Adam got a bad beating last night, and you are not in for an easy time either, don't make it worse. You should know better than to lie—Sir Stephen will be *truth reading* you."

I wasn't sure if Richard was trying to scare me worse or help me—I don't think I could have been much more afraid even in mortal danger. I knew I would not die from this—I might wish I could, but I wouldn't.

The ward room was already empty when we came into the room. My three superiors sat at a table facing me, with the rod across the table.

Sir Stephen began the questioning, "Would you like to tell your side of the events that were taking place last night—or should we beat you first, then ask the questions, to make sure we have your attention? And by the way, do you know the penalty for a seaman fighting aboard ship?"

I was really shaking now. I never been questioned like this, even when I had been in trouble other times at the castle. I was not sure if this was because I was now a squire, or because of the circumstance. My voice began to quiver as I spoke, "Sir, I have heard the penalty for seaman fighting is a flogging—two dozen lashes at the grating. But Sir, the squire is not certain where the knight wishes me to begin, sir." My voice was quivering.

"Boy, you start crying and your senior squire will give you a good reason to cry," the Lieutenant said firmly, and yet in a very low tone. "Why was Squire Adam wanting to use you for pugilistic practice?"

"Sir, the squire doesn't understand what that means, sir," I said, afraid that my lack of knowledge would have me in more trouble.

"Fighting, punching practice then," the Lieutenant said.

I took a deep breath, to calm myself, and try to get control of my fear, then started, "I have been working extremely hard the last several days, trying much harder, and none of the squires my age have been able to challenge me in the drills . . ."

"What has that to do with Adam?" Lieutenant Lyons interrupted.

"Begging the Lieutenant's pardon, I was getting to that. As a result of my extra efforts, I was paired up with the oldest member of our group, Sherry, to get a better challenge and to challenge her. Adam seemed to be upset with my working with her. When we won a team competition yesterday, she gave me a sisterly kiss on the cheek for my effort. I believe Adam took exception to that," I stated.

"So you kissed his fiancé," the Lieutenant stated.

Sir Stephen moved from his *truth reading* and stated, "It seems Sherry needs to be here also, as she seems to be part of the problem or at least may have part of the answer. Also, why did you increase your personal intensity on the training so much more than the other students?"

I glanced over at Richard, a bit startled by the knights's remarks and question.

"I asked the question, son; you need to address me, not your senior squire!" Sir Stephen exclaimed.

I quickly recovered, concerned that they might discover our conversation with Richard about the number of adults with us. "Begging your pardon sir, I was concerned I had gotten one of my unit in trouble by accident. I was not trying to get Sherry involved, sir. Nor did I know she was his fiancée."

The knight got up from the table, went to the door, and said "You sit for a moment, I will be back in just a moment, and we will continue then."

As he turned to leave the room he spotted a page going up to get some fresh air, and called for her to go get Sherry, who was in mathematic or writing class at this time.

"That will save me a walk and we may continue with you," Sir Stephen said returning to his chair. "Back to attention for questions, boy!"

As I quickly got back up and at attention, I wondered why this knight seemed to be in charge instead of Lieutenant Lyons or my senior squire? Sir Stephen began a new line of questions. "What motivated you to try so much harder than the others in your unit that you had to be paired with a student three years your senior?"

Now it was going from bad to worse, if I got Richard in trouble for telling us about the fighting force situation, he would be in trouble, and then he would probably discipline Timothy, Luke and me for that—as he promised.

I nodded to Richard and began, "The senior squire and I were talking one evening about the importance of our training, and I decided that I needed to try much harder to take advantage of the training we were getting. And since we have not heard from our troops in the city, I may have to accept that I am the new Marquis of Retúpmoc."

Lieutenant Lyons and Sir Stephen began at the same time, stating they believed there was more to it than that. I did not believe the lieutenant could *truth read*, but just saw more in what I said than I meant for them to. They exchanged a few words in private between them.

Sir Stephen then asked Richard, "Would you care to add to this? I don't believe your squire is telling everything, and by his continual looking to you in this line of questioning, I believe you may elaborate more than the boy."

I had been very careful not to lie, so I was not sure what the adults were getting that shifted the questions to Richard.

At that time there came a knock at the door. When told to enter, Sherry came in, and said that she was reporting as ordered. Sir Stephen told her to wait outside for a moment and they would bid her to come in then.

"Richard, I believe you were about to shed more light on this line of questioning," the knight stated.

The adults continued to question Richard and me more about the increased focus on training and our conversation. Finally Richard explained in detail about our conversation on that cold Monday night on the deck of the ship, and that he had sworn me to secrecy about it, that was why I had been evasive about it, attempting to keep my word.

"Richard, we will continue this discussion in much greater detail tomorrow. You may find yourself across the table, but today let's concentrate on the business with which we began. Ray, have Sherry come back in, and you wait outside," Lieutenant Lyons said.

When I went to the door to get Sherry, she gave me a rather disapproving look. I mouthed that I was sorry. She already knew about the incident last night, and probably what Adam had received for his part.

They questioned her for about fifteen minutes then I heard four resounding strikes of the birch and yelps of someone being disciplined. Sherry emerged from the door with tears in her eyes and told me, in a quiet voice, "They want ya back inside, and we will talk later, after lunch in the *hold*."

I was not comforted by her statement nor the look she gave me. I also was not sure that going down to the hold after this morning was going to be something I wanted to do, but she knew I would follow her instructions—I really had no choice, she was enough my senior to require me to follow reasonable orders.

I stood at attention while the three of them discussed matters for a minute or so. Then I was instructed to lean over the table and the knight began, "You apparently are in this trouble, but not by your own doing. You're to be punished for accepting the challenge for the fight in the hold. But since the fight did not take place and your efforts to improve your skills are more at the cause of the problem than youthful misconduct, we will be lenient on you for the present. You are only to receive three stripes this time."

I could not believe I was getting off so light. I'd never been disciplined with only three swats with a cane while I had been training, usually six was more typical for a young junior squire. As an older page I might get ten with a leather strap. It been many years since my father had only given me four or five swats with a leather strap when I was in trouble at home.

Richard was instructed to give three well-laid swats, and they still hurt badly, but I had been afraid I would get at least ten, and after the question about seamen fighting, I thought I might get something like that.

After I was allowed to stand up and rub my aching backside I was dismissed. On the way out, the knight reminded me, "Eight tomorrow morning, you are to meet back in here and we will finish our discussion with you and Richard about the other topic."

My heart sunk, as Richard and I left to go to our classes I tried to talk to Richard. "I didn't try to get you in trouble about our private conversation. Really, please don't be upset with me about that," I pleaded.

"We'll discuss it after our meeting in the morning. I'm sorry I had to bust you this morning, but I'm glad it was a light one. You took it pretty well for your age. I laid them on really hard, like I was ordered."

"Are you going to whip us for the officers finding out about our conversation," I asked?

"Didn't I tell you we would deal with that tomorrow? Are you wanting another whipping right now?" he exclaimed, obviously not pleased with my continued questioning.

"No sir," I said and hurried off to the remainder of my mental combat class.

After class I talked briefly to Timothy, and told him I got caned, but did not mention to him that it was a light one. I also let him know we might be in trouble with Richard, but not to mention it to him.

We had close quarter sword drills with sticks for swords immediately afterwards, and prior to lunch. The wind was cold, but the sun was shining through quite nicely. I was a bit concerned about working with Sherry. This was the first time she would have been mad at me while working with weapons.

As we approached each other to begin, she gave me a slight nod, a smile, and said a bit louder than needed, "Boy—I am going to kick your little butt!"

She called me some name that I did not understand, but I don't think it was nice—pre-pub something another, and sent me sprawling with an elbow to the chin. I got back up to continue the drill, when she spun around after I blocked her sword thrust and caught me with her other elbow in the stomach. This was not going well. I had not practiced the close quarter drill much, and Sherry apparently had done so many times.

By now some of the other students had started watching. I became a little more cautious, but attempted to attack also. This time she caught me with the hilt of her wooden sword and split my lip wide open. As she came over to put what would have been the killing blow, she whispered "Just about all of the students near my age know that I got caned, because of ya. So ya better be ready for a rough session!"

Richard came over to see how badly I was injured. "You two trying to repeat this morning's exercise in the ward room? Are you all right?"

The blow had brought tears to my eyes, but I quickly told him, "I want to continue. Her extra training—because she is older, she just got started better than I did. I can go."

After that the lesson became one of constant pain. My chin and lip were really starting to hurt, but I became more careful. I landed several good blows, as did Sherry. Her spin moves with the short weapons kept me off balance. I was used to the long sword, not this twelve inch blade.

We got the chance to take a break, and Luke came up to tend to the lip which was still bleeding. Sherry walked off without talking to me. I that hurt worse than the bruises she had given me. Luke took care of the battering I had taken by using his mental skill of *cell adjustment*.

After he stopped, I asked him, "I wish you coulda gone ahead and taken care of the whelps I got this morning?"

"I'm not allowed to relief anyone of that type of pain, and you know it. If I do, then I get what I cured. And the word is "welt" not "whelps," that's a like a puppy. But those were much less than I expected," Luke explained.

"Well don't tell anyone that I got off light, it might create additional problems. Oh, I almost forgot, they found out about the conversation we had with Richard. Don't say anything to him, just get ready. Can't use your skills on yourself, if he whips us, can you?"

"God's wounds—NO! I'll talk to you later," he said leaving.

Sherry walked up behind me, without me knowing and whispered, "I warned ya to get ready. Quit holding back or ya'll get hurt! We are still meeting in the hold after lunch!"

As I turned to talk to her, she told me, "Don't turn around or say anything, pretend I didn't say anything."

Now I was confused.

We began again, this time I was more ready. She was still older and more experienced in this than I was, but I started doing better. She still kicked my butt, just like she said.

She did not say anything else to me, and I saw her sitting with Adam. I'd probably seen that before, just didn't notice. I was quite sore when I got to sit and eat with Timothy—sore, in more than one way.

"Sherry really worked you over. You'd think you got her in trouble, instead of the brute trying to kick your rear. Maybe she is just mad at you because he got in so much trouble? What do you think?" Timothy asked.

"She did get in trouble, and if she stays mad at me, Luke may become my personal Healer."

We finished eating and I got up to go. Sherry was still sitting when I left, but since she was older, I figured I'd better wait on her. I was a little nervous.

I made my way down to the hold, and sat gingerly on a sack of some grain to wait. I didn't have to wait long. She came down the stairs, thankfully alone. I was worried that Adam might come to complete last night's plan. Her hair was still damp from the sweat and ocean spray of our earlier workout.

I stood up and looked down out the deck, "I'm sorry I got you in trouble—I, I didn't mean to—honest. Please forgive me."

"I got in trouble for a kiss, I kissed ya like a little brother and all this happens," she said.

I was thinking that this kissing stuff was not what I expected. Maybe I should become a paladin—a holy fighter. Then I wouldn't have to worry about this stuff.

Then she grabbed me and kissed me full on the mouth—wow! I could hardly breathe. That was nothing like when I kissed Charissa, I couldn't explain it—it was so unexpected!

"That is a kiss," she told me. "Do ya understand the difference?"

"I told them you gave me a sisterly kiss. It was because we worked so well together on the competition," and my voice made that funny sound again. I hated it.

"Adam got a dozen lashes with the rod, and was warned it would be two dozen if it happened again," she told me coldly. "I didn't tell him how badly I was beaten, but I suspect ya heard the birch from outside the door. Ya are not to let anyone know the number of stripes I received. Ya just tell anyone that asked that ya were not inside when I got whipped. Do ya understand me?"

"Yes, but I still don't understand why . . ."

"Ya don't have to understand anything!" she cut me off. "Ya have to follow instructions, and ya better give me the respect that my being three years your senior deserves when ya are given instructions—do ya understand?!"

"Yes ma'am, I understand, and will obey," I told her.

"There is no doubt ya will obey, or I can make life quite unpleasant with the difference in our age. If I was noble born, I would have probably already been married. As neither Adam nor I are neither noble the marriage was arranged and we will be wed early next year, after his sixteenth birthday. I'm not really upset with ya, but to keep Adam from more trouble and hurting ya I will play the part. And ya will play it also until I give ya the word that ya are forgiven" she told me.

I wanted to tell her most nobles weren't married that early, but decided it would better to just listen.

"I've enjoyed working with ya, Ray, and I think of ya as my little brother that I never had. But just like if ya were my kid brother, ya better follow directions or pay the price," she told me and then finally smiled.

"I'm just so glad that you're not really mad at me. I didn't know you were promised either. I'll play my role then," I sobbed. I was so relieved that she was not really angry with me.

"Should I apologize to Adam—to make it better for you?" I asked. "I'll do it if you want me to. Even if he is not noble and I am!"

"No, not yet. After it appears ya have been forgiven ya might do that just to avoid a thrashing after we land. When we get back to training this afternoon, we are to be working in leather armor, and wooden long swords—while we are waiting, ya will polish the brass on my armor," she told me.

"Sherry, that is a servant's job. I'm noble and shouldn't have to do that."

"Ya will do it because I said so, it's punishment, that I can demand," she told me. "And ya will show me respect!"

"Yes ma'am!" and I saluted her.

"Be careful, little brother!"

We went back on deck separately, and then to get our armor. Timothy was already in his leather armor when I got back up to our area.

"Where you been?" he asked innocently enough.

"Getting reminded that I'm twelve, and better give respect to my elders, but only verbally. No rod this time," I added quickly.

We came on deck and heard the order of pairs for training. Sherry and I got to go first, since we were the top two with the weapons. Richard gave a quick demonstration of what he wanted and expected of us, as Lieutenant Lyons looked on.

We saluted and got ready to begin when Sherry said something to Richard. He held up his hand to wait and came over to me. "She said to remind you that she is still kicking your rear today. I believe she is a little upset with you about this morning. You could be in trouble for a while."

"Yes sir, I am in trouble with her. Any chance I could have a new partner until she gets over this?" I asked as my voice cracked again.

"Boy, you will have to cope with her and your voice. Good luck—you may need it," he told me. Then stepped back and signaled to begin.

After making me look like bad for a couple of moments, I began to do much better. She still worked me over pretty good, but after—I guess—getting over being anxious I started keeping up with her. We had a pretty tough session, and then were allowed to take a break. She motioned me over, then turned, opened her arms up, and had me remove her armor. Then she had me sit at feet her feet and clean the armor. I was getting upset at this insult. When we got up, she had me put her armor on her, like I was a servant. Now I was really mad.

"Sherry, don't make me do that again!" I told her through clenched teeth.

She tossed her head, gave a slight laugh, and put on the helmet to begin another session. "Get ready, little boy," she told me.

I was so mad that I was starting to get tears in my eyes. I couldn't believe she was humiliating me this way. This time I went quickly on the offensive, I faked with the sword and caught her with a shield butt. This staggered her, and I quickly followed with a slash with the wooden sword, that caught her on the side of her helmet. She crumpled and went motionlessly to the deck—and lay there.

I just stood there watching her, then I heard Richard yell, "HEALER!"

That brought me out of my—I guess—trance or something. I ran to her and pulled her helmet off, and held her, and started to cry. I didn't care that the kids saw me crying, I was so worried about Sherry.

Megan was on duty, and had been hovering nearby, expecting to be needed. She just figured I would be the one needing the curing powers that she had. My sister had also heard about me getting Sherry in trouble—she had recently turned sixteen, and was about a couple of month or so older than Sherry. She ran over, and did a quick look over check then went almost immediately into a healing trance for *cell adjustment*.

Shortly thereafter I was flung into the air, with my shield still on my left arm, and the wooden sword tied around my right wrist. Adam was charging me, and had a clear path as the other younger students gave way. Lieutenant Lyons and Richard were seeing after Sherry and did not see Adam approach. I scrambled to my feet and defensive practice took over. As he ran at me to attack me with his metal practice sword—not a wooden one, I ducked under and slammed by wooden sword in his mid-section with all my might. As he doubled over from the blow, caught him across the back of his helmet and he went down and stayed there.

I was breathing very hard when Sir Stephen ran up from where their group had been working out on another part of the ship. As he bent over to check on Adam, he ordered his senior squire to escort me below deck and stand guard with me in the ward room.

My world was, spinning and I was not sure what people were saying to me. The senior squire took me below and was saying something to me, but it did not make sense. His words just sounded all jumbled up. Lieutenant Lyons came into the room and as I stood to attention the room swirled, like a whirlpool, and then went all black.

I woke up in sick bay an hour later, with my mother sitting beside me, in a healing trance. My eyes fluttered, and as I tried to move, she held me back down and told me I needed my rest.

"What about Sherry? Is she okay," I asked quickly?

"Everybody is doing fine, just some bumps and bruises that will mend," she told me comfortingly.

"Am I a big trouble," I asked?

"No more questions—sleep." Then she did something that I had not seen her do before: she cast a spell, and I was asleep.

A *sleep* spell only lasts about half an hour, but when the body is ready for more, I guess it lasts until you're ready to wake up. I woke up, and just lay in the hammock. Shortly afterwards I heard four bells chime and got up.

I went down for first meal, and saw Timothy and Luke. I went over to sit with them and see if I could get some information about Sherry. Just as I sat down, a voice from behind me asked, "Hey, little boy, can I sit with ya? Your little friends look like they're getting ready to leave."

It was Sherry. Luke and Timothy weren't even close to being through eating, and Luke was close enough to her age to tell her so. She then asked them to find another bench where we could talk. I was not sure I wanted to talk to her alone, and I wanted to talk to the two guys. I asked if they could stay, because I needed to ask them some questions afterwards. Maybe they could move down a bit and give us some room first.

"Are ya trying to tell me what to do little brother?" she asked in a nice way, as the two boys moved off.

"No ma'am, we just have a possible problem with our senior squire that we need to discuss also, with your permission," I responded—trying to be quite respectful, as others were watching.

She started, "Ya caught me pretty good yesterday. That was the first time I have ever been knocked out. I guess I really pissed ya off pretty good."

"Sherry, I'm sorry. I didn't mean to hurt you. When you went down, it scared me to death. I thought I might have killed you. I really am sorry!"

"Stowe it ya little snot. Ya still have to be on my bad side for a while, especially after ya embarrassed me like that yesterday afternoon."

"I embarrassed you," I said a little too loudly. "What about what you did to me, treating me like a servant. That was embarrassing, and you knew it when you did it."

"Ya might better be a little quieter, or I might have to report your poor manners to the senior squire. Ya wouldn't want that, would ya?"

"No ma'am," I said humbly. I definitely did not want to get reported to Richard for that.

We continued our conversation for a while and I found out she was okay, and not mad at me, but I had probably made a permanent enemy of Adam. I suggested that I ask for forgiveness for his action of attacking me, considering the circumstances yesterday, to see if it would go easier on him. That would be a good excuse to get on her good side quicker. She said I could try, but it would still be a couple of days before it could appear to be okay between us. She called me her little brother again to let me know we were okay, but we just could not show it yet. I think I was in love—but couldn't show it or say it.

I did not get the chance to talk to Luke and Timothy about the meeting that morning with Lieutenant Lyons, Sir Stephen, and Richard. I just hoped I didn't get Richard into too much trouble, and he decided to beat the daylights out of us.

By seven that morning I was looking for Sir Stephen, to see if I could help keep Adam out of additional trouble. It then occurred to me that I could be in trouble for that too. I located him on deck. He appeared to be deep in thought.

"Begging your pardon Sir, may I have permission to speak with the knight?" I asked.

"We have an appointment already this morning—or did you forget?"

"No, Sir, but I wanted to discuss a different matter, if the knight will allow it."

He appeared to be extremely stern, and did not wish to be bothered by any child for whom he was not responsible. I didn't believe that he liked me very much.

"You may proceed," he finely told me.

"Sir, about yesterday's events involving Adam and myself," I started. "I don't know what has been discussed concerning that, but I was worried that Adam might be in trouble. If he is in trouble, I wanted to request forgiveness for him, considering the reason for the action."

"Son, you might not be so forgiving when Lieutenant Lyons finishes with you on that subject. You may be in for a considerable punishment yourself, because of your actions, which were discussed just yesterday!" he exclaimed.

I was getting a little worried now, but I told Sherry I would still try. "Yes Sir, but my request stands, and I forgive him for his actions, even if I am to be punished for it."

"I'll consider your request, but I don't think you are making a good decision, because of what you may receive for the actions."

I thanked him for his time and willingness to at least listen. As I turned to go, he told me that he knew my father and brother, and that there were some of thier good qualities in me.

The meeting with the adults at eight that morning was much better than Richard or I had hoped. Timothy and Luke were called in also, and we were given extra marching duties for the demerits we received, but we did not get caned. They felt that I was being perceptive and would not be unduly punished for this. We all were ready to leave, feeling pretty good about the situation.

As we were dismissed Sir Stephen had Richard and me remain. "While you are here, we need to discuss yesterday's events. I have very little input into those events, but it should be handled swiftly. Timothy, locate Adam, and have him wait outside."

Richard and the Lieutenant agreed that no punishment was deserved regarding what happened to Sherry. Since I had been warned before about my actions with Adam, there was some discussion about that, and I was sent out while they discussed it.

Richard was then dismissed and Adam and I were ordered back into the room. Sir Stephen then asked Adam, "You were warned as to the severity of the punishment you would receive if you repeated actions that got you caned yesterday. So what punishment do you deserve?"

"Sir, you promised me at least a score of stripes for my actions, up to two dozen stripes with the birch, Sir!"

Sir Stephen then motioned to the table, and said, "Assume the position!"

"Begging the earl's pardon, Sir," I interrupted.

"You may not speak, you are at attention," Sir Stephen cut me off! Then he proceeded to cane Adam. After the fifth stroke he stopped, and told him he could get up. He told him about the discussion that he and I had earlier. Then dismissed him.

It was my turn—I was afraid. I had seen how hard Sir Stephen had given Adam his swats. Adam had tears in his eyes from only five swats, and he was fifteen.

"Is that enough mercy for his actions?" the earl asked.

"Thank you, Sir, for the mercy," I said. Hoping I would not receive too much worse, but expecting to be in big trouble for everything combined.

I was dismissed without a caning, but was warned to be more careful. Also, I was questioned about what I did in the attack. I left surprised and happy only to have demerits to march off, not multiple sets of whelps, I mean welts, from more than one caning.

Our training was going well, except for the weather. Sherry gave me a rough time for a couple of more days, but I did not have to polish any more armor. She just had to make it look like I had to pay for getting her in trouble, then I was back in her good favor. She "adopted" me as her little brother, which helped keep some of the older boys from giving me a hard time, and got me off of Adam's "garbage list." Adam knew I saved him a lot of pain by requesting Sir Stephen to forgive his actions. We weren't friends after that, but he wasn't trying to kill me either. Richard gave me a few extra details for the costing him demerits and marching duties, but they were light, and he did not make Luke and Timothy do anything extra.

The weather remained cold, and sleet pelted us for many days. The winds had not been what we had hoped for most of our journey, and this would add to our travel. The two priests with the skill to do so added to our supplies with the magical skills by *create food and water*. The food wasn't too good, but it was better than going hungry and having to ration the food. The king's ship was doing the same, and we passed food off to the other vessels with us. Some fish were caught and added to the food supply.

Then the weather and the sea really took a turn for the worse.

Chapter Three

Landfall
·············

> "Rescue me from the mire, do not let me sink; deliver me
> from those who hate me, from the deep waters."
> Psalms 69: 14

It was his birthday, Ray turned thirteen. It was strange not to have a party or presents, but this was not his old way of life. He was allowed to have dinner with his family: Mother, Megan, and Cord. Even the meal was plain, but he did get to visit them, and since Christmas was only a few days away, the ship would plan a festive day and a grand Mass was planned. That evening, a foul storm struck the little fleet. It was almost as dark as night all the next day. They were really worried about the smaller ships, and their pace slowed as sails were brought in to keep from tearing them and the shearing masts in the storm. The crew had to work hard to keep the signals lit for the other ships trying to keep up with the larger ships, and of course everyone was trying to stay with the flagship, and the king.

That night the wind and sea increased in fury. A titanic, ominous cloud front loomed in their path. All the students twelve and older were taking turns manning the pumps; this allowed the seaman to do what needed to be done for the ship. Sherry thought it was just to keep the kids busy and tired when they were not able to practice on deck.

The lightning and thunder gave the sea an eerie, small look, as the fleet was pulled closer to the foreboding cloud before them, forever on the horizon. With the sea surging and the wind blowing directly toward it, the ships could do nothing but move toward it. The ships' officers and other military people attempted to calm everyone by telling them it was all right, not to worry. But most of those who saw the mountainous darkness did not believe them. A few of the younger children and others that came up from below had almost all the passengers in panic. Their stomachs revolted on them again with the tossing of the ship. This gave the ship a more unpleasant ododr. Besides far too many bodies crowded together, upset stomachs made the whole ship smell in need of a good lye soap bath.

The ships got closer to the edge of the dark clouds, and the sea became even rougher. Most did not think even the larger ships would be able to survive the storm—and tried not to think of those in the smaller ships, who braved the open sea to stay with their king.

Most of the passengers spent time in prayer for their souls and lives on the ships, which they expected would not survive the storm. To make the situation even worse, ice was starting to form heavily enough on the rigging and masts that they were in even greater danger of breaking.

As the small fleet entered the darkness of the cloud, it became calm, and the ships, all of them emerged on the other side in a brilliant, but cold, winter day. There was no explaining this—it must have been a miracle sent from the Angel of God. A Christmas Eve day present.

Then everyone crowded on deck. The seamen went aloft and started breaking ice off the masts and rigging, while officers sent everyone below, to avoid the falling ice. A couple of groups of squires were kept topside to assist in this task, but Ray's group was sent back below to start cleaning their part of the ship. He would have preferred to stay on deck. Gosh, it stank down there.

Things went very well for the rest of the day. Everyone's spirits were high after the miraculous deliverance from the storm. But as night approached a new panic seized the fleet, as two moons emerged that evening!

———————

"This is all wrong," Timothy whined.

"You think so—Birdy," Sherry taunted. She had begun calling Timothy, "Birdy," when she was irritated. She did it because of his birthmark, and I told her I thought it looked like a bird.

I gave her a sharp look, wanting her to stop because Timothy didn't like it. As I got ready to say something to her about it, she cut me off.

"Did you know my birthday is next week? I'll be sixteen," she stated, and looked at us as what she said sunk in. "Other people have birthdays too. Yes, I will be a senior squire. I do hope my first official duty will not be to remind some twelve, or thirteen year old of *his* manners. Do I make myself clear?"

Timothy and I responded, "Yes ma'am!" Then Timothy went below.

"Why'd you do that? Neither of us have given you any problems, well at least on purpose. And you are being rude to Timothy," I quickly added.

"Little brother, you only recently got to be off the wrong list—are you wanting a return trip there, with me about to have more authority over you? You're a good kid, and a great little partner, but remember the age difference. And stations," she added somewhat sadly.

I believe she may have figured out that I liked her, but I never said anything because she was already promised, and in a few years I would be promised to someone else. I decided a new tactic.

"Okay, sis," the first time I called her that. "I don't want to be the first to get a whipping from you that way. I've taken enough in practice from you. And it wouldn't be any fun if I couldn't swing back."

"Or sit afterwards," she laughed "Too bad, you're still such a little kid, and noble. Otherwise, Adam and I might take you for a personal squire."

"Sometimes I don't think your attempts at humor are very funny," I said, not very pleased with the idea of her giving me a whipping. Most of the younger squires were in trouble enough, without her making a joke about it.

The next morning was Christmas. The ships and the little boats got close together and Christmas Mass was held for the fleet and many decorations were hung on the ships to commemorate the festive occasion. The students waved back and forth to each other from the ships and the smaller boats came along the side to get additional supplies. The students were allowed the day off to be with their families. Ray had asked his mother, on his birthday, if Sherry might join them for the day. Sherry had no family on board—they had not made the voyage. So Sherry joined Ray's family, which also included his aunt Beth and cousins. They had a cold, but wonderfully, great day. Extra food was given for the holiday, and the sea was calm enough to allow the people to enjoy it.

Caroline thought Sherry was fantastic, and that Ray brought his partner for her sole benefit. Caroline, of late, felt like the only female child, as Megan was on duty all the time, stationed with other girls her age, and never around. It seemed having Sherry around made her feel less outnumbered. Sherry gave Caroline a great deal of attention, and spent most Sundays with Ray's family from then on. Ray's mother knew she could learn much more of her son from Sherry than Ray would ever volunteer. Cord thought she was great, because she could beat Ray with a sword, and rumor has it that older brothers have been known as a source of torment toward their younger siblings.

Training resumed the next morning, the day after Christmas, for students on board the two ships. It was not sure how far they were from land and signals between the two royal ships were quick in the morning light. The ships then maneuvered closer together and dropped sails again. Ray's ship put the captain's boat over and the captain and several of the other leaders went over to the king's boat. A party from the king's ship came over and a competition was held between the junior squires that were selected from each of the ships in different contests. Ray and Sherry were chosen to compete in a sword competition. The other crew made some comments about a girl and a young squire being their opponents. Both of the boys were about Sherry's age, and had been sent off to school and returned.

Comments stopped when Princess Charissa came forward and extended her hand to Ray before any of the competition began. He kneeled and politely kissed her hand. She led him to where she was given a chair to sit and watch the competition, and the boy kneeled beside her. She was attired quite nicely—with a dark blue dress and a beautiful fur coat. She was wearing the tiara, that she had worn to the send off party, but no jewelry.

"I hope a kiss on the hand will not get us in trouble, like our first kiss did, my princess," I said in a low tone when I had gotten her attention.

"It was quite polite and courteous, but not what We expected. We do not think any chastisement will happen for the action. How have you been doing?" she asked.

"It would take a long time to tell, and a much less interrupting place, my princess," I replied, not knowing how to react to her. I wasn't used to hearing her use the royal "We" in referring to herself. She hadn't done it at school or the party. But at least my voice wasn't cracking—right then.

We watched the other students compete, with both ships being close in the wins, but I guess a slight advantage was to the king's ship. Sherry and I were the final competition for the morning two-person teams. As I got up to prepare, the princess asked, "Won't you introduce Us to your partner in this event?"

In a grander and louder voice than was really required, "My princess, I am proud to present Sherry a squire, who will become one of His Majesty's senior squires within the week. She has provided me an excellent opponent and partner in our exercises on this voyage. I will hate to lose her at promotion and impending marriage."

Sherry blushed, the first time I remembered her doing so. She kneeled and also kissed the princess's hand. "I'm honored, your highness, that you have allowed me to kiss your royal hand," she said in a very quiet and subdued voice.

We prepared for the competition. Both pairs were in leather armor, a helmet, a shield, and a wooden long sword. Both pairs were introduced, including their family names. Only Sherry was a commoner among the four. "Well—little brother, you better get ready. Both of these boys are very good, and bigger than we are. Give it your best and you'll be fine."

"Come on sis, we'll do fine. Besides, I'm ready to see someone else get their butt kicked by you, instead of you kicking mine for a change," I told her, as my voice cracked again—that was getting really tiresome.

The combat was a lot longer than anyone expected. Most thought the bigger boys would quickly dispatch the girl and much smaller younger boy. It appeared their size would wear the smaller kids down. Sweat was pouring down all four kids, even in the cold weather. Sherry was the first to miss a parry with the shield and was hit on the sword arm. She was required not to use the arm for the remainder of the competition, and switched her sword to her left hand. When Ray saw this, he gave an excellent fake, and gave his opponent a crashing shield butt. It wasn't as effective as it had been against Sherry when he had knocked her out, but effective enough to get credit for a death blow with the following sword thrust. He then quickly came to Sherry's aid and distracted her attacker enough to allow her to make what counted for a killing blow.

The four students then bowed before the princess, and moved off for some water. Sherry and Ray were given a great deal of congratulations by their shipmates. Adam gave Sherry a huge hug and then surprised Ray by lifting him off the ground with a huge bear hug, and then almost threw him to Sherry. Sherry gave him a big hug and a little kiss on the cheek, with Adam looking on.

Sherry had a pretty good bruise on her arm, and Megan was attempting to get her to move inside or at least away from the other students to examine it. Finally she was able to move her from the crowd to stairs down inside the ship where a closer look revealed that she would require healing.

While Megan was healing Sherry, Richard came up and whispered something to Ray, and he quickly left to go where the captain's boat was tied to the ship. Princess Charissa was there waiting to talk to him. She wanted him to come to the other ship and tell her how things were going on this ship. She really had not seen much, being forced to stay below with the other younger children. He convinced her that Sherry should come too, that way it would not look bad. He did not want to face the Master at Arms for any mistakes again. The princess told him she was not going to allow him to kiss her in public—maybe if they could sneak away for a bit she would like to try a real kiss. That thought scared him, but maybe Sherry could teach them how or at least be a lookout.

He went back to get Sherry, who wanted to go back for a change of clothes. But the princess's messenger came up and told them to get in the boat. They would find something for Sherry to change into.

As they were seated on the boat for the trip over, Sherry suggested that if she got embarrassed over at the king's ship, a certain young squire might be in for real pain. Ray laughed and said she would be fine, but she was not laughing.

The princess and Sherry quickly disappeared below deck, and true to her word a lovely dress was found for Sherry to wear. This was the first time Ray could remember seeing Sherry dressed up. There was not time for that on the ship while training. As the two young ladies entered the room, Ray stood, and bowed to them both. Then he gave each of them an arm to escort them into a lunch with the king, several military officers, and the captains of both ships—not quite the private dinner Ray thought they might be able to have.

The two squires were questioned at length about training on the ship, but it was very enjoyable. The ladies were then dismissed and Ray was questioned about his observation on the lack of adults, and how that affected his training. It seemed they were surprised that a barely thirteen-year-old and a girl were able to defeat two of the better Mentan squires on the king's ship, both of whom were already sixteen. He was questioned about a great many things, not as if he were in trouble, but to see what the squires thought of things. It was a truly gratifying afternoon.

It was getting close to dark by the time the two students and the others returned to their ships. Before leaving, Princess Charissa asked her grandfather, the King, if Sherry might be her personal tutor, in front of everyone. She said it would be nice to be around a girl who could fight for a change. Sherry turned bright red again, and gave the boy a very harsh look, that made him swallow hard. Her grandfather told her that he and the council would give it some thought. The princess tried to make Sherry keep the dress, but she said there was no place to wear it on board ship.

As the two teenagers stepped into the boat, one of the king's advisers asked Sherry, in whispers, when the wedding was to be. She informed him that the date had not been set. He informed her that the princess wished to be informed and would like to attend, if Sherry did not mind. Then the captain's boat rowed back to the other ship and the children went back to get ready for bed, after spending half a day and much of the evening on the king's ship and in the presence of royalty. That and watered wine made sleep very pleasant that night.

"Did you really kiss her in the hall of the castle?" Sherry asked as we were finishing first meal the next morning.

I nearly spit out my water with the question. "I don't believe that is something polite you should ask, ma'am."

Timothy chimed in, "Yes he kissed, and then a hickory kissed him a bunch of times across his butt. His next kiss is from you and he gets another whipping. Maybe he should quit kissing the girls—it seems to cause him a lot of pain!

"Or maybe he should leave kissing to those who are better at it." Timothy's voice cracked, but he still chuckled, rather pleased with himself.

"You better hope I don't get the chance to have a go with you in any of the exercises," I said, not finding any humor in his statement.

Then turning to Sherry, I asked "It seems that you got along well with the princess, yesterday. What did you talk about?" I hoped this would change the subject.

"You," Sherry said with a smile, and fluttered her eyelashes at me.

Shipboard life continued, as it had, for another week—lots of hard training, both physically and mentally for most. Those, like Sherry, who did not possess psionic powers worked on other skills warriors might need: reading, writing, map reading and making maps, but this was only to give them something to do. Most school type work was over after their second year as a squire. The groups were redefined based more skills than the random assignments that had placed them originally on board, two days after Christmas. Ray found himself in with a group of much older squires, some of whom could have been promoted to senior squires, but those promotions were on hold until the ships landed and proper testing and ceremonies could take place.

Ray was sitting with some of the other kids his age one evening after drilling. He enjoyed getting to spend some time with those his own age. One of the other boys had to spit. That action started a spitting contest. Now as unpleasant as that might sound, it is not an unusual thing for boys to do; even two of the girl junior squires decided to take part. It just works much better in a barn than indoors, or on a ship. After they had been at the contest for a while, Ray decided to go in and get some of his class work done. The other five kids continued the contest. Ray found out the next morning one of the older senior aged healers came by, and she was appalled by their actions. She marched them down to Richard who disciplined all of them, fortunately for Ray, no one told that he had been involved earlier.

Ray attempted to give Sherry a difficult time, one evening, after turning sixteen, not being a senior squire, and having to wait til landfall to give him the whipping she had threatened him with. That attempt was short lived when she asked him if he really enjoyed cleaning armor that much.

———————

"You've been giving me a hard time about that since—well, a long time. I start getting a little back and you act like that. That's not right, sis," I told her.

"You realize little boy, with the new unit, any number of the boys could and would take care of that task for me on any given night. They could do it while Adam was on watch, so he wouldn't be a suspect—if somehow the adults found out about it. Now it might not be a proper birch or hickory rod, but the training swords would work well—don't you think? And they might not stop with six or ten stripes. Remember this unit is made up mainly of the kids I grew up with—my age. Not your little friends," she stated rather cooly. There had been no humor in her voice.

"Come on sis, why are you being so hard on me the last couple of days? Did I do something that I didn't know I did?"

"I have not been feeling very good yesterday or today, and you're an easy target. So, don't push me or it could be unpleasant," she warned me.

"You've been a real . . ." I caught myself about to make a dangerous mistake, and changed, "grumpy old bear. Besides I'm almost as tall as you now, so you could quit calling me 'little boy.'"

"You're dismissed!" she told me.

"What!" I stood up and looked at her. I was mad—dismissing me like she was a senior squire already wasn't right.

She looked up at me, then turned to one of the other, older boys in our group, "Aaron, please escort—this squire back to his berth. He is to remain there the rest of the evening, and there may need to be a discussion about his manners on the morrow!"

"Yes ma'am," I said as I saluted and turn to go with the surprised looking fifteen or sixteen-year-old squire.

"What did you do to earn that—Sherry thinks pretty highly of you to be such a young snot?" Aaron said as we walked.

"I don't know, and I'm not that young. I'm thirteen, and as tall as she is. Can she give you orders like she just did?" My sentences all kind of ran together.

"No, not really, but if she took you down and made that statement to Richard or Sir Stephen you'd have been in more trouble than either of you'd have wanted. You handle yourself really well, especially for your age. I don't think you're off the hook with her, there may be some demerits," Aaron told me as he left me at my hammock.

I started to go talk to Luke, and then realized she had given a direct order. If I left, I would really be in trouble, and saying that she wasn't being fair would not have changed my disobeying an order. So, I read and studied a little extra.

———————————

Just before lights out Aaron and three other boys about his age started walking back toward Ray's hammock. Aaron was carrying a wooden practice, long sword. He kept popping the end of it onto his left palm. As he and the others walked up to Ray, he handed him a small leather strap, about four inches long, with teeth marks in it.

"Sherry thought we might need to have a little conversation about your attitude. You may want to place that in your mouth to keep from yelling out." Aaron informed him as the four boys surrounded him.

Ray's eyes got a bit large. Four to one and all of them bigger was not a good place to be. The lights would be turned out in a couple of minutes, and Ray felt cold sweat starting to run down his back and his heart was racing. He tried to talk to the boys, but they told him to keep very quiet, or it could get a lot worse. Then the call for lights out came, and the lanterns were extinguished.

"Your adopted sister wanted you know that you're in for a rough couple of days, with any of us you have to work with. You need to keep your mouth shut and just face it with good spirits. If you complain about our treatment of you, then she will report your manners to your senior squire. You want to face us in training or take a chance on dealing with Richard in the ward room?" Aaron calmly, and very quietly asked me. "By the way 'little brother' you're shaking!"

"I'd rather face you tomorrow—one on one than this or the senior squire," I said. "And if four, bigger guys—like knights, came up to you like this you'd be shaking too!"

"Don't get too big for your britches, or I'll give you get a bit of a reminder this evening with his sword. I'm of nobility also—so don't think that will keep you untouched," one of the other boys stated in the dark.

"I've never tried to pull that with Sherry or anyone else. But I'll be glad to give you the chance with that sword tomorrow in drills, unless you think you need your three friends to help in with that also" I stated. Probably wasn't the smartest thing to say under the circumstances.

The unidentifiable boy suggested that when we got to land and they all got their promotions to senior squires, that they get a birch rod and have a birch party with me. I might be a bit less mouthy with five or six swats from each of them. Then he cuffed me across the right ear.

"Knock it off—leave the kid alone."

"Sherry said she'd see you on deck—if you wanted to come up and talk to her," Aaron told me. "It wasn't an order, but your option."

That was a good excuse to leave, before I said something else stupid and made the older guys really mad.

"You're being awfully hard on me, sis; I don't think I deserved that," I complained when I came on deck. "What if I'd tried to fight my way through them when they came in?"

"You wouldn't have come up to talk to me, and I'd have to have had another fencing partner for tomorrow," she said and reached out and tousled my hair.

"Ray, you're not our age, you fight well enough, and you will probably out rank us all one day. For now you have to give us the respect I—we deserve, and you didn't earlier. Someone other than you, like Birdy or another kid your age, and we'd gone to Richard then. You still have that option. I thought the other idea was being lenient with you."

"Yes ma'am, but I'm going to be pretty well beat up on by the end of the day. I believe I can defend myself against any one of your friends, but by the end of the day they will wear me down, because they are bigger—especially when they are trying to dish out pain."

"Yea, but like you told me about it, at another time, at least you'd get to swing back. Besides you've grown enough I can't kick your butt as easily as I could when we first started, and you've improved too. Okay, little brother?"

She gave me a little kiss on the cheek, and a slight hug.

"Sherry, can I ask you something—but you have to promise you won't pull rank on me for it? Please?"

She looked at me, and then said, "Okay—but remember you go too far and it might make it worse tomorrow."

"If you weren't engaged to Adam, I'd like to kiss you! Like in the hold that time, not just you giving me a light kiss on the cheek."

"If I weren't engaged, I might let you. But that is not the case and don't mention it again, or you will be in serious trouble. You can be my little brother, but that's it, kid! I need to talk to your mother."

"Oh God's wounds, Sherry, please don't tell my mother! I didn't mean to be out of line!"

"Ray, if I were upset about this I would not report you to your mother—like for your little brother Cord. I'd be taking you to Sir Stephen, who would probably leave you some long lasting welts and bruises. I wanted to discuss something else with her, if she doesn't mind and has time to see me. By the way, that was sweet. But someone besides Adam might be jealous."

Ray sent word to his mother, early the next morning, that Sherry wanted to talk to her. He was concerned that Sherry was going to tell his mother that he wanted to kiss her. As the training started with book work that day, his brain was quickly filled with other things. Math was giving him some problems, but in the rest of his studies, he was doing well. He believed he was starting to understand navigation and reading the star charts, but had not much practice with that—since they had gone through the cloud, the world seemed to have changed.

The military side of training the next several days was strenuous for other reasons. Ray felt some of the boys were taking unfair shots at him. He would do relatively well early in the practices, but his smaller size and youth would betray him by the end, and he would take a great deal of abuse then, when paired with Sherry or her bully boys. After three days she had them stop. In practice she still gave the outward appearance that everything was fine, she told him she didn't want anyone to notice he was in trouble—this time. The other boys had learned by the end of three days to be aware of his shield butt, and he had learned a few things from them, but he was glad to be off their pain detail. Sherry told him he had done well, but he was still hurting. He hadn't seen Luke to get any help from him with the pain, and had not been injured enough for a healer to be called for.

These tough sessions did have some advantages. The three other girls, about a year younger than Sherry, had noticed him taking the extra abuse and had given him some encouragement. Sherry hadn't been with them during many of those sessions; she was working with a longbow instead. She had spent more time with that the last week before Christmas, and it seemed that she was working even more lately: extra sessions while Ray was in the mental focus and training classes. Ray could not challenge her with a bow, but then it seemed no one else in the unit was close to her skill with the bow. Supposedly there was a commoner's kid on the king's boat that was as good.

The second week in the new world was extremely exciting. Early in the week a whale and her calf were spotted. The ships gave them a great deal of space, but the people enjoyed seeing the magnificent creatures. Only the sailors had ever seen a whale, and those that had did not recognize this type. A couple of days later dolphins were spotted. These animals were great fun to watch. Toward the end of the week sea birds were spotted by one of the fishing boats. Word was sent by signal flags. This caused a great deal of excitement. Most of the students were confused.

"What was so great about birds," they wondered?

When informed that birds have to have LAND to nest it, sunk in, that they might be close to land. The ships steered toward where the birds appeared to be heading that evening.

Rain and a slight squall made the efforts challenging that night, to remain on the course the birds had shown. Rough seas continued for several more days, which meant more book type training for the students, as it was dangerous to train hard on deck, and not enough room below decks.

Ray asked his mother, one Sunday, about what Sherry wanted. His mother said that it was between ladies, and none of his business, and he had better not ask Sherry! He did not understand girls, but according to his cousin, neither did anyone else.

The storm abated three days later, and on the fourth morning the lovely sound of "LAND HO!," was heard from king's ship and several others took up the cry.

Land was sighted, and that caused quite a stir among those on ships. As they approached the land, the ships stayed a couple of miles from the coast, while sailing up the coast looking for a good place to land. Those who had been training were ordered to armor up and get weapons ready—and it wasn't for practice this time.

After sailing for most of a day, a location was discovered that looked very promising. A wide harbor of several miles opened up, with decent hills overlooking both sides, of the crescent shaped harbor. The cliff-hills would allow defensive positions above the sea, and a lookout spot, and it was only about five or six hundred yards apart across the opening to the harbor. A fair sized river emptied into the harbor, and trees lined the river, although most were devoid of leaves, as it was still winter. A few evergreen trees were spotted amongst the empty branches, but most of the trees were hardwoods. The ships did not enter the harbor until morning the next day, and the ships dropped anchor a half mile out from the shore. Long boats were sent out from each ship with a carefully selected crew to explore the immediate coast. Ray was extremely disappointed that he was not selected to go on the expedition, although Sherry was selected because of her skill with the bow. The expedition was made up of senior squires, or those that should be, adult fighters, a mage, a priest and a healer for each boat. Both healers came from the ship Ray was on, and Luke was not selected either, but Megan was. Luke did make a strong case that he had been in a combat area before being sent back, and that knowledge would make him a better candidate. It didn't change the minds of those in charge, and older, female healers were selected. The two long boats landed on the beach and went in opposite directions, to determine if this area was inhabited. They returned shortly after noon, to give their reports. Food was sent to the crews, and only the leaders came aboard the king's ship to report.

After about an hour, two of the fishing boats came over, unloaded their passengers on to the two ships and reloaded those from the long boats. They then set sail to the base of the cliffs that overlooked the harbor, one ship to each cliff. They landed where they were able to go up the hills and see if they were guarded or to see if they could observe anything from them.

Some of the other fishing boats also unloaded their human cargo early that day and spent the rest of the day fishing in the harbor. Most of the students were kept too busy with training to keep much of an eye on the search parties. Working with the real weapons, they trained that day with a different purpose. There were double the lookout and guards that day. With many of normal teachers out, it was a bit different. Still the youngsters work hard, as they believe they might finally get off the ships.

The fleet spent that night in the harbor. Ray could hardly wait to talk to Sherry about what she saw. He was extremely disappointed when she did not come on board that evening. He went to find Adam, to see if he had any news.

"Sir, did you hear from Sherry?" I began, making sure that I was respectful. I figured he would be a senior squire pretty soon, so I better get used to the idea now. I did not want to make any mistakes in military procedures.

"What makes you believe I would tell you, if I did?" Then he gave a short laugh and asked me to sit down. "You don't have to call me sir right now, this can be informal."

"Thanks, I, I wanted to make sure—with your friends around, that a kid my age wasn't appearing not to be respectful" I told him.

"Most of these guys know you and what you are, but it was still correct, until you were given permission otherwise, for somebody year ahead of you and older.

"Sherry did not send any messages to me; I was going to see if you heard anything, you have contacts that I don't have," Adam said.

"No, not really. The people I know are mainly my age. Those that I know because of my family still see me as a new junior squire, not yet gone off to train. So, they don't tell me anything, they just watch and make sure I'm properly trained in all my responsibilities," I said, wishing I knew more.

"I've been informed that you are to be in our wedding—if you are willing and able to," Adam then stated. He looked hard at me, but did not say anything after that.

"Sherry, giving orders again?" I asked.

He shook his head yes.

"Sir, do I want to take part?" I shocked him with the question. "I'll find a reason not to be there, if you don't want me there. We have not always been on the best of terms, and I . . ."

"Boy, if you know what good for you—you'd better be there, if you can! Sherry would never forgive either of us, if you didn't show and could. We're okay, as far as I'm concerned.

I still think you're a little twit, but Sherry thinks highly of you," he added jokingly.

"I'd love to be there. I'm still not used to having her as a big sister, and she is easier to get along with than my real one. They're a little harder to figure out than a brother," I told him.

"No joke," he said under his breath as I left to go back to my berth.

———————

The next day the ships moved in closer to land and unloaded most of their occupants, and a lot of the cargo. Ray's ship and most of the squires on it were to travel farther up river to see if the land was occupied. The last thing they needed was to get embroiled in another war. The king*s ship stayed, began making a wooden palisade, and chopping additional wood that either would be used in making shelter or to take with us for additional supplies if we had to move on. The two long boat groups continued to scout around both sides of the river and harbor for inhabitants, looking more inland.

Ray's ship returned a day and a half later, having seen nothing, and most of the instructors and students were longing to get back to being on land, after their time at sea. It was also difficult going upstream, in the shallow winter waters.

Returning to the base camp site was not exactly what they expected. They were to spend almost no time in their normal training duties, but all in manual labor; building crude shelters and other domesticated structures. The few stallion war horses did not seem to take too well to being used as beasts of burden, and most of the females had colts on the way, so they were not worked too hard.

After about a week of construction work, ceremonies were held promoting some of the junior squires to senior squires, etc. Shortly after the ceremonies, Sherry, with Adam standing there, asked Ray if he wanted what she discussed with him. He worked hard to dissuade her from that, until he did something to deserve being punished. She said she didn't really plan to whip him, just thought she'd give him the chance to ask for mercy again.

Ray did not think it was nearly as humorous as the two senior squires did, but at least he was not in trouble.

Wedding preparation was the next thing on Sherry's agenda. Ray's mother offered to assist in the planing. But his mother's normal plans would not work in a city under construction, as this was. Finally it was planned to use the little tabernacle. Caroline and Cord would be a part of the wedding, and Sherry asked Ray if he would give her away. He was shocked, but agreed to whatever Sherry wanted him to do.

The princess was in attendance, as she had requested, and provided a much more suitable dress than Sherry ever could have found. It was a white gown that would have never done for a princess's wedding dress, but for a commoner—it was a dream dress. Ray's mother found a white veil to add to the dress and occasion.

It was a lovely wedding, with much more nobility taking part than Adam or Sherry ever would have imagined. Ray and his family had done their part to make her feel like a sister, and the priest was overjoyed to get to have a wedding after all the problems of the last several months. They were even able to have a small dance aboard their ship, to honor the wedding couple. Most of the guests in attendance were not of noble birth, and seemed in awe of Sherry's hostess.

After the palisade was built for initial protection, places to live to protect the inhabitants from the winter's cold and wet were to be completed. Almost all moved into the makeshift city. Barns were also constructed for the animals that had been brought. Then a real city was to be planned with stone walls, towers, and strong gates. Real houses were to be built also.

Ray's family, due to their rank could have had one of the first houses, but stayed on board ship with apartments being constructed for them there—like a floating inn. Ray and Cord went back and forth from ship to land each day for training (and in Ray's case, work details).

Being the man of the family now meant much more responsibilities, which for a thirteen-year-old is tough to deal with. Ray was reminded on occasions that he was still not an adult, especially when his younger brother and he had some *strong arguments*. He believed it was rather embarrassing for a squire to have his mother take a hickory to him, and tried to convince her of this. His mother felt the reminders were required to make sure his attitude and actions remained acceptable—and at least, he thought, his little brother got a similar lesson, even if it was with a leather strap instead of a rod. She asked if he would prefer Sherry to administer the discipline to him, since she was a senior squire, or she could always request one of the adult males to perform the parental duty. That wasn't what he had in mind, and definitely did not want one of the knights to take on that responsibility.

The new city was laid out, and the preparations for the new walls were made. Lots of digging was required for the foundation. Squires had many of these work details, as they made up much of the labor force. Some of the commoners were trying to get land ready for farming in the spring, so the wood was cut from those places first. It was used for construction and fuel. One of the first things that had been constructed was a saw mill. The river would be a great source to power the saws. Other saws were manually operated to aid in the construction process, but the saw mill was great benefit.

The king's most powerful but very old mage was capable creating a wall made of stone—magically. Some wished he was an expert in that school of magic, so he could've cast an extra of these *wall of stone* spells per day, even if they were not very thick—about two and half inches. But by placing these over the palisade, they greatly reinforced the existing walls. When the outer wall of the city was being constructed, he made the walls much smaller but thicker. It was much easier than trying to locate and quarry quality stone, but it would take a long time to create a city wall, so a search for a place to quarry stone was to be made.

The search party was to have consisted of a couple of knights, four senior squires, and four junior squires. Sir Stephen was to be in charge of the expedition, even though a higher-ranking noble would be also be going. Sir Stephen requested magical support—just in case it was required. So a mage, priest, and healer were sent with the party. Not much spell support from any of them, but a *sleep* spell could be powerful.

Sherry and Richard were both selected as senior squires to go. Richard because he had seen battle, Sherry because of her skill with a bow. Adam wanted to go because he was her new husband, which was why he was not selected. He might not be able to concentrate on the mission and the welfare of the entire group if his wife was in danger. Sherry requested that Ray might go as her junior squire. Sir Stephen wasn't thrilled with this idea, because of his age, his rank as a noble, and besides, older junior squires were available. In the past he believed those of higher nobility were not good at following orders from a lower social rank. Sherry convinced him Ray would do as he was told—she had trained him well on the voyage over. Sir Stephen and Richard laughed at that, thinking back on what she put the boy through.

"Let me talk to his mother first," Sherry asked, "after that I can assure you of his complete attention."

She spoke to his mother before Ray knew there was a planned mission, or that he might get go. After their conversation, Sherry was asked to stay until the boys came home to the ship that evening. She had not seen much of Ray or his family since the wedding.

The boys were arguing when they entered the room and saw Sherry.

"Sherry!" they both shouted and move close to give her a hug. Both boys were extremely glad to see her.

"Is that the proper way to greet your superiors?" she said laughingly as she hugged us both.

"Since you are in our apartment, yes!" I said. "Oh, it is good to see you. Are you still my sis?"

"That depends on how you act. If you're a good kid, yes—if not, I'll just be a mean old senior squire. I still owe you something—don't I?" she asked teasingly.

"What does she owe you?" Cord asked.

"A good whipping for being so mean to me while we were training partners," she answered my brother.

"Can I watch—he needs a good one?" the little brat responded.

"Hey—don't encourage her, she could be serious," I said remembering her temper and Mother's questions at another time.

"If I agree to take you with me on a little expedition, can you follow orders?" she asked in a quite serious voice. "And not attempt to pull any nobility type rank?"

"I can't believe you would even ask that of me. I've never tried that with you, or anyone else around you, even when you were kicking my . . . well, beating me pretty bad in our training," I said, somewhat offended by her tone and comments. "I thought we were closer than that."

"It should have be 'badly' dear," Mother said, correcting my grammar.

"You've been treated according more to your rank since we landed, than on the ship, where I held a tight rein on you. And don't give me that 'poor me attitude,' do you understand me little boy, or mister?" she said to me.

"Yes ma'am."

Then she told me about the expedition to look for a good quarry. Mother informed me that Sherry had permission from her—in writing—to make sure I toed the line, just in case there was any question of authority. AND she could pass it onto a knight if needed.

I was feeling double teamed and I hadn't done anything. "Why are you both mad at me? I haven't done anything to deserve this. And yes, I want to go with you."

After that we had a nice dinner, before Sherry went back to land.

"Report an hour before first light. Be in your full leather armor, and long swords. Go ahead and bring your bow too," she instructed before leaving the ship.

That night I made sure my sword was sharpened and well polished. Cord oiled my shield and helmet for me, to help me. I didn't even have to ask him—he might be a useful page after all. I got there early the next morning and waited as the others showed up one or two at a time. I was glad to see Richard; I hadn't seen much of him since Christmas.

"I guess this means Sherry got you in. I'm not sure you're up to this, you're going to be youngest by a couple of years. Almost of all of the junior squires are already fifteen," Richard told me, not too encouragingly.

"Not the first time I've been the youngest in a group. I did all right with the unit Sherry and I transferred to after Christmas. I took more abuse than the others 'cause I was younger, and I'll keep up here. Sherry wouldn't allow me any other choice."

"Just remember if we get into a skirmish, follow orders," Richard said.

"Richard, sir, when did I not follow orders? Just because I'm younger doesn't mean I can't hold my own. You've seen that."

"I've also seen some more noble born unwilling to follow orders from those more experienced," Richard said coldly.

"That won't be a problem," Sherry said as she walked up. "I'll keep him in line, and have the authority to do it—don't I?"

"Yes ma'am, but you won't have need to exercise it, ma'am," I said quickly, and extremely glad to see her.

"You can leave him to me," she told Richard, and he walked off shaking his head. "I'm surprised Richard was acting that way. I thought he would believe in you too."

As the time approached to leave, some of my other unit mates came up and gave some good natured kidding, "I thought this was to be a serious expedition. I didn't think we would have to be babysitting." That was okay, I knew those I had worked with would be quick to accept me. Sir Stephen was a different matter.

The knight took Ray aside before leaving and had a long talk with him, and then Sherry came over when she saw the discussion taking place. They sent the boy off some ways and continued their discussion. Finally the knight motioned Ray back over, and said that he would accept the young squire, but the boy was Sherry's responsibility.

"I'd better not be called on to remind you of your manners, because she is unable to deal with you," he told the junior squire. "For either of your sakes!"

Ray told Sherry that she could depend on him for whatever she asked. She said he better, and with all joking aside it was serious business here. He might have to guard her privacy, since she was the only female on the expedition, and a woman needs some privacy at times. She also told him if Adam heard that he didn't behave right, and that she had a problem, when they returned, Adam would finish any problems much more thoroughly than she was able. Sherry told Ray that she told her husband there would not be any need for that. Her little brother would act gentlemanly and respectfully, as his mother had already ordered him.

Ray explained that he did not need to be treated like a small child, he should be treated like the rest of the junior squires that were going. If he deserved to be discipline, then do it, but quit acting like she thought she would need to.

She agreed; he always had been good at following orders, and she was just trying to look after her little brother.

The party started inland, where they had seen some larger hills from the top of the cliffs at the entrance to the harbor. Light fortifications were to be built on the cliffs, to alert those on land for vessels coming from the sea and up the river.

Catapults were being constructed to help defend the harbor from an attack by sea.

The party was moving by foot. The horses were needed too much in the building. A couple of large war dogs were also with them, and served as pack animals of sort.

Ray was to Sherry's immediate right serving as her guard, and she kept her bow out in case of trouble. It was a bit cold for a bow, so every now and then Sherry would wrap it back up and put between her tunic and armor to keep it warm and flexible. The ground was uneven and covered with a light snow and ice. This made walking difficult.

Ray and most of the others were just glad to be doing something besides building a city.

The land was supposed to be good, according to the farmers, who had been clearing land and getting ready for spring planting. It would still be a long time before any of those crops were ready, but fresh food after being on a ship was a pleasant thought.

Fishing had not been very good, but no one expected it to be in the winter. There was hope that the fishing would be able to add a steady food supply to the city, both salt—and fresh-water fish. Some scouting parties had spotted deer further inland, but hunting parties had not been sent out, as the food supplies was adequate for the time being.

The party had been walking several hours, through snow-covered ground and winter dead trees. A few squirrels had been spotted chattering in the trees, but not much else, including animal tracks. With a small grove of evergreen trees spotted ahead the party decided to stop for a short break in them. They would block some of the wind that chilled the youthful group as they walked along.

Sherry spoke to Sir Stephen and another knight, Sir Robert, then motioned for Ray to come with her. They walked backed away from the others and where had Sherry spotted a small cave.

———————

"Get your tinder box out and light your lantern for me," Sherry said as she set her shield down. She took off the sword belt, but took the sword from the sheath before setting it down.

"You're not going in there?" I asked as I knelt to light the lantern. "There might be a wild animal or something."

"I need to," she told him, and took the lantern.

"Let me go first to check it—since I'm your personal squire," I said trying to keep the lantern.

"There are no ship's heads out here, and I would prefer some privacy—if you don't mind," she said and patted me on the head. "You stand sentry, and don't let anyone pass, as long as I'm talking to you, unless I yell for help. Understand?"

"Oh, I mean, yes ma'am," I said a little embarrassed. "Does that include the knights?"

"Well, I would not want them in either, but I don't think you could stop them. Just let them know that I need to be alone. That should be enough, any of the squires better not come in—including seniors, if you are able to stop them. Go relieve yourself while you're waiting."

She went inside the mouth of the cave. I told her to keep talking, I didn't want to face Caroline if I didn't bring her back. She let me know she would talk, and I should just listen, not attempt to be funny. I heard some high pitched, low yelping inside. She called out that I needed to be alert, and call for Richard—but don't leave your post. I told her we weren't close enough to be heard with the wind.

She came back a few minutes later, to my relief. "You had me kind of worried, sis. What have you got in the bag?" I had suddenly noticed a sack was moving in her hand.

"I found four wolf puppies. They might come in useful," she said.

"Now that I know that you're back, I need to ah, ah, be excuse for a moment," I asked motioning to a large tree.

"I told you to take care of that while I was inside," she said not sounding very pleased.

"Yes ma'am, but I heard the puppies and your orders to stay alert, so I waited. I wasn't attempting to disobey, just thought that was a change of previous instructions. May I be temporarily dismissed, ma'am," I asked?

"Hurry! What do you think about the puppies?"

"About what several of the other junior squires thought, when the Master of Arms said a birch tree he spotted might be useful."

"Stay out of trouble and that won't be a problem," she stated, laughing.

"Sis, I don't know if you know it, but I've been in a lot more trouble since being around you. I've got more whippings or threatened ones since we got aboard ships than the last two years combined. And yes, that includes a certain kiss that I took from a younger lady! One whipping for kissing her and one for you kissing me. My first two kisses, both got my butt busted!"

"The one ya got for me kissing ya was easier than the one I got, so stop complaining," she was still laughing. "Hurry up, let's get back with the other, before we both get in trouble or momma wolf comes back," she ordered.

That was the best idea she had come up with all morning. Then another thought came to my mind. "How did you know how bad I got disciplined that morning, I didn't tell you?"

"When I received my promotion to senior, I asked Richard. He said ya took it much better than most twelve year olds, only tears. He said he gave ya a pretty hard set. He also thought he might be giving ya a full whipping soon after, but that worked out and ya got off the hook with some extra marching."

"He shouldn't have told you that," I felt somewhat betrayed that she found out I got off easy. "Does Adam know?"

"No and neither Richard nor I will tell him, even if he asks. So don't start whining or you'll be in trouble. I'd hate to see you do a lot of extra marching at camp this evening or have to have another watch duty." She gave me a light hug and pulled me along, letting me know she was joking—I hoped.

She got back and showed the puppies to Sir Stephen, and told him my comment about them and the birch. He motioned for me to come over to them.

"You don't like puppies?" the knight asked smiling.

"Yes sir, but I was afraid . . ." I started when the knight broke in.

"Son, did you say afraid?" he questioned extremely loudly.

"I did not mean scared sir, only concerned. I don't wish the knight to question my bravery," I told him. He still appeared upset with my choice of words.

"Are you afraid of me, boy?" he asked somewhat menacingly.

"Only as it is stated in Proverbs, 'Fear of the Lord is the beginning of wisdom.' As my superior you have a great deal of power over me, sir," I said hoping that was the right answer.

"Good answer, son. I don't want to hear you say the other word again—do you hear me? It is not a word I want to hear in my presence," the knight stated.

I nodded my answer and followed it with a "Yes sir," to avoid any further problems.

"Thanks sis," I said as the knight walked off. "It's way too cold to get in trouble, please don't help me get there."

She handed me one of the puppies and told me to carry it, and keep it warm.

We walked the rest of the day and made camp for the night. One of the senior squires then asked how she planned to feed the puppies, he said something else to her too quiet for me to hear. She slapped him across the face, so I suspect it wasn't something she believed he should have said. I wanted to ask her what he said to make her so mad, but decided she would already be upset and I didn't want to be on the receiving end of her temper.

She melted some snow, put flour and grease into a pan to make gravy. The puppies lapped it up very quickly. It may have been some time since they had eaten. She then reminded me that we had not seen any tracks around the cave. So the mother may have been on a long hunt, or might not be coming back.

We got watch order set for the night in pairs. Sherry and I were on the first watch, which is the best, you're already awake. After watch we laid down for sleep. I started to lie down by her feet. Most everyone was pretty close together to block the wind, and give each other extra body heat. But I didn't think that would be a good idea with Sherry being married.

"Hey little brother, come here," she told me.

"But sis, it might not look right, and . . ."

"Shut up, and get over here. You know better than to get out of line. We don't need to discuss it, do we? Hurry up, it's cold."

I laid down beside her and we spread both of our covers over us.

_____

The next morning one of the junior squires made some comments to one of the other boys and looked at Ray and Sherry. Sherry didn't see it, but the lad did. He walked over to them, and asked what was so funny this early cold morning. The other junior squire's remarks were out of line, and Ray suggested that he should go over and apologize for his rudeness.

The other squire did not believe that would be a good idea. He had seen Sherry slap one of the seniors last night. The other squire was nearly sixteen, and a great deal larger than Ray. He suggested that it would be better if Ray forgot it.

Aaron, who had been promoted to a senior squire only the week before, but about the same age as this one came up toward the end of the discussion. Aaron quickly realized what was taking place and sided with Ray about an apology.

Aaron suggested Ray step back and let him talk to the other squire a moment. Sherry came over to Ray during this time, and asked him what was going on. Ray tried to put her off because he didn't want to tell her, he was embarrassed.

Aaron signaled for Richard to come over and get involved. By now Sherry was ordering Ray to tell her. Without saying much he informed her the other boy made a comment in poor taste.

This made Sherry more than a little upset, and she was ready to ready to hurt the other boy. The boy, James, remarked that there was only a couple of months different in their age, and since she wasn't noble she did not have the right to demand an apology or expect satisfaction for the statement. Sir Stephen and Sir Robert said that he was within his rights, but they were not pleased with his actions and any further comments would be considered disobeying orders and they would have a reason to correct his actions. Sherry was still livid, and did not see Ray go up to Sir Stephen and talk to him.

"Boy, you also insulted me with your comments, and I am noble. I require an apology for your rudeness and generally poor manners toward one the princess deemed noble enough to attend her wedding and has her direct access and friendship," Ray stated in a rather loud and clear voice. He believed he did that exceptionally well, and was glad his voice had stopped cracking—at least for the time being.

Sherry started to go to stop Ray, but Richard stopped her. "It's too late now, Ray has already stepped in it. I saw him talking to Sir Stephen first."

"I'll kick his little butt for this," she said, but she was proud of how he stood up for her.

"YOU HAVE GOT TO BE JOKING!" James exclaimed.

"No, and I'll have an apology NOW, or I'll render you useless for considerable time. I have more than martial skills to harm you with, and you should know that I posses more mental power than you. Want to play that game with me?" Ray asked.

Aaron stepped up behind Ray, put his hand on his shoulder, and suggested that the other squire quickly ask forgiveness, before he was badly hurt in a psionic struggle. He was showing that he would support my actions.

James apologized, not very convincingly, but it followed the letter of the law for such.

Sherry started toward Ray. She was mad about something, he didn't know exactly what, but he was certainly glad Richard stopped her before she got a hold of him.

"Sherry," Richard said grabbing her, "he did that for you. Don't go to him mad and force yourself to fulfill a promise that you won't really want to do when you cool down. He took a risk, for you. Don't punish him because of it."

She took a deep breath, "Tell him to get our gear together and that it would be better not to talk to me until noon break, unless I send for him. Let's switch squires for the morning."

Richard told her, "I don't think that is being fair, after what he risked. Go give him a hug and tell him you're proud of him, but that you're mad because he took such a risk, and that during lunch you can talk more about it—after you have calmed down."

She followed Richard's suggestion and by lunch was really proud of him, but put forth he not tell his mother about it. He suggested it would be better not to tell the princess either.

Aaron came up to Ray, along with Richard later that evening. "You made an enemy today. It was brave, but maybe not very smart. Could you really have taken him in psionic combat as easy as you said?"

Ray told them, "I have a little more power, but no more weapons to choose from. I'd have won, but it would not have been a pleasant sight."

Three more days passed and the group was farther than any other had gone inland. There had been no more problems for Ray or Sherry. One of the other junior squires had to have some healing after a tumble, but it wasn't too bad. A slight snow was starting to fall.

They spotted some wild apples trees growing in an area, and marked it on their map for future reference. They got to the area where they hoped to find some adequate stone for a building quarry. It appeared to be what they hoped for so they marked it and started the trek home. Some of the younger ones believed it was a long way off for building supplies, but they were told after a road was built and wagons were in use it would not be too bad. And they took a slightly different route back for additional mapping of the land.

They spent one day in their tents as a howling wind and heavy snow fall made movement nearly impossible, and chance for frostbite probable. The next day, the storm had blown over and the sun was back out, shining brightly, but it had dumped several inches of snow for the party to walk through.

On the way back, Sherry found another cave. This one was not empty and she woke a black bear from hibernating. The two left the cave area quickly, but the bear was gaining. Sherry quickly turned and put an arrow into the charging bear as Ray readied his sword. A second arrow struck the bear as it stood up and Ray started attacking. Sherry drew her sword and joined the boy in the combat. They were able to dispatch the bear, with only some minor wounds, which the healer was able to patch up and have both totally well in a couple of days.

Back in the cave Sherry pulled out a less than half-grown cub, put a rope around his neck and brought it with them also.

The party got back to town, with the information and the baby animals. One of the mages had an idea and asked for and recieved all the animals. Sherry did not know what he wanted them for, but was afraid to refuse the old man.

Sir Stephen told Ray, "Son, you did a great job, especially with the bear. I won't complain about your coming with me again. You can count on me for a supporter and I would take you as a squire. Your father would have been proud of you."

Ray thanked him, but asked him to leave out the challenge if he talked to his mother. She might not like hearing about that.

The mage, by his arcane arts, turned an animal each day into an elephant. They were still babies, but they would grow and be able to assist in the building of the city. He only came out with four elephants, as one of the wolves did not survive the *polymorph*.

Not much changed for the rest of the winter. Cold squalls came in and stopped almost all work; otherwise the city began to grow. Much of the timber continued to come from the planned fields for the spring; other trees started being taken from where the road would be to the rock quarry.

There were no more expeditions that winter, but everyone knew with the arrival of spring, much exploration would need to take place. Many of the buildings were starting to show signs of completion.

Things went reasonably well for the rest of the winter. Not much training—too much other work needed to be done. Ray saw very little of Sherry or Adam for the next couple of months. He heard that she was working with Princess Charissa a couple a times a week, training her with a sword. The princess' talent was reported to have lain in the healing arts. Ray thought that was a much better profession for a princess than wielding a sword.

Ray's mother spent more time working in town, using her healing skills that winter. The cold required more care of healing talents than Ray had realized.

Ray continued the growing spurt most of the winter and had even picked up a bit of weight to go with it. That made it a bit easier working with the older squires, which he did when the rare occasion to train occurred. He also had a noble knight request him as his squire, to work with him in all the tasks assigned. Baron William Scrope was twenty-one years old, and newly knighted, before the city was evacuated. He told Ray that Richard had suggested Ray to him. He also told Ray that he had known and worked with his older brother—Kelvin, and was about a year older than Kelvin would have been. He was one of those that helped recover the body and brought it back for burial. Lord William did not tell Ray that he had helped recover the body. Ray had met him at the funeral, and remembered the information. When Ray asked he just shook his head yes, and said that the subject was not one he wished to discuss—they had buried too many friends. They were to start working together in the spring; until then, Ray would continue his present assignments and studies.

As spring approached plans for planting started being made. Priests had asked for divine guidance on when the proper time for planting the crops would be. Through their holy spells times for crop planting were determined. The road to the quarry was a long way from being completed, but a fair start had been made. The saw mill had flattened many logs, and in areas that seem to stay muddy, they were placed as a roadway. The outer wall was starting to show signs of being useful in case of an attack. One foot-thick walls, with three feet of dirt between another foot thick wall made a nice five feet wide barricade at the top, it was about twenty feet high, and thicker at the base.

Ray was starting to worry about his mother, she seemed to be tired and almost sick a lot of times. She also appeared to be gaining weight. The weight gain seemed unusual—given their food supply.

Finally the king sent word that he decided it was time for action—plans for expeditions were made for early spring. This would include sailing one of the two large ships out from the harbor to see what was nearby, or maybe what was not so nearby. Troops were also to be sent, but of course there would be many left there to defend the city, families, and the king.

Chapter Four

Exploring the Land

"Send some men to explore the land of Canaan, which I
am giving to the Israelites." Numbers 13: 2a

Word finally came for Ray to get ready for the exploration
and mapping of the new land. He was to notify instructors and
family of his planned departure, and this raised the eyebrows
of some of his teachers. He was to have clothes, armor, and
weapons: sword and bow. All other equipment would be
waiting for him. The night before departure would be spent
in the newly constructed, (although wooden), great hall, and
they would leave before first light.

Ray hoped for a opportunity to see the princess, but
assumed she might have other duties, and would not get the
chance. This would also be his first occasion to see who his
companions for the adventure would be. He was disappointed,
because he did not know any of them, and he had hoped Luke
might be selected. The young squire had seen some of them
maybe, but did not know any of them. One of the new Mentan
senior squires, Kurt, came up to talk with him. Kurt had been
one of the squires he and Sherry had competed against in the
ship competition in front of the princess, and he had known

Megan for a long time. The senior said he would be glad to be fighting with him, instead of against—if the need arose.

Kurt was the third son of wealthy baron, who had seemed more into mechanizing than warfare. His older brothers and fathers were all lost in the last attacks on Candlewynd. Kurt was a personable individual who seem to get along with everyone. Kurt's mother had not had the spark, but had some mental powers still. He also had a younger brother and sister who were both pages.

For this task, Sir William had asked and receive magical support: a mage, a healer, and a priest. Of the spell casters only the healer was of noble birth, which suggested she would be the only spell caster with psionic skills. The warrior members of the expedition were Sir William, four senior squires, four junior squires that were all close to being seniors, and Ray. There was also an expert with traps, locks, and stealth with them. The healer, the mage, and one of the senior squires were females. Besides for the Baron, the healer, and Ray only one other was Mentan—Kurt. The rest of the members were commoners.

This would also be Ray's first chance to work with Baron William Scrope, who was to take him as his squire. This was a significant honor for a first year junior to be chosen by an important lord. Usually if a lord took a squire, it would be a senior or a junior who was close to being a senior.

The group ate dinner together, and spent some time visiting. Xell, the mage, was attired in dark blues, and seemed she seemed almost sinister to Ray, even though she was fairly young, as was the rest of the group. She had a nice smile, he thought, but it sometimes felt like it was "I know something you don't." She did not appear to want to socialize with the warriors, and stayed talking to the priest and the healer. Ray later found out she had some psionic abilities, but wasn't a true psionicist.

The priest was Mathias. He talked to everyone, and seemed to be interested in what everyone had to say. He was the oldest in the group, and he wasn't more than twenty-five. That seemed fairly old to Ray—since it was almost twice his age.

Ray didn't get a chance to talk with the healer—that was surprising since she was noble; there weren't that many in this group that were. She spent time mainly with the senior squires when she was with the warriors, but primarily she was around Xell.

A man in the King's livery came and gave Ray a message. It was from the princess. She had wanted to come and see him, but was not allowed. Some of the advisers thought it would seem inappropriate, and her grandfather was aboard ship that evening planning the ship's searches, so she couldn't appeal the advisers' ruling. She thought about disobeying and coming to the hall. She feared that would get them both another whipping, and might create problems for Ray with his new knight.

The servant was to take a reply, which Ray quickly moved off and wrote. Then the servant said, "By order of the princess, you may not discuss these communications with any member of your party—for at least a week. "That should keep you both of the hook," he smiled and gave a wink as he left.

Ray was immediately asked about the message, and he replied that a royal command prevented him from discussing the communications. That made everyone even more curious. The baron, came by and whispered, "I hope her majesty is doing well," and then walked on by, smiling.

Ray just swallowed hard and tried to smile.

Since horses were not available, the party would be walking and carrying their gear in packs. There were two large war dogs were also going with them, and they would help carry supplies. Ray was glad they were taking some tents, so if it rained they would not get as wet trying to sleep. It also would make it a little warmer for the nights—which were still very cold.

They would start off by going to the rock quarry, which was supposed to start mining next week. The partial road would make their start a bit quicker.

The morning they started was cold, and a light snow was falling. One of the junior squires commented about the lovely spring they were having. Sir William did not believe he was humorous and suggested that evening he and his senior could have the honor of the middle watch to work on their jokes, and any other discussions they needed to have.

Ray was glad he hadn't made the remark, as he had thought about it also. The baron did not seem to have a very good sense of humor, and one of those discussions usually were unpleasant at his age.

They made a good first day's march, and set up camp while it was still light enough to see what they were doing. Ray and another junior squire were sent to gatherfire wood. It would have seemed extremely difficult to start a fire with the wood wet with snow. That is when Sir William informed them that junior squires were always responsible for the fire. He sent the war dogs with the boys to serve as guards.

When the boys returned with some wood, Xell (the mage) told everyone that she had memorized some cantrips that would assist in getting the fire started. After that, the junior squires would be responsible for carrying dried wood from the fire the night before to start the next fire. Xell said since they were close to the city she had done this. From now on she would be memorizing spells that might help if there was a combat situation. A list was made of the order in which the junior squires were responsible for the kindling. Sir William informed them that failure to have the kindling would result in a serious chastisement. Further if he was upset enough at the failure, all the junior squires might suffer those consequences, which he would administer, so there would be no leniency from one's senior squire.

A meal was prepared and everyone ate and got ready for some rest. Three tents were set up. Ray thought the three females would be in one; the rest of the party in the other two. Not so; all the spell casters were to have a tent, because if they were learning spells they did not need any distractions. The trap remover or scout, was also stationed with them. The warriors were in the other two tents.

The baron made a watch rotation of three watches per night. Only the fighters had watch duty, but still they got a full night's sleep after two days of watches. Sir William decided he and Ray would have the first watch; which was fine with Ray, he was too excited to sleep anyway.

"You remind me of your father, and you look a lot like your brother, although you're smaller. That's probably because I remember your brother at seventeen, and you're a couple of years younger. In two years you might be that big," Sir William stated.

"My lord, I'm only thirteen, sir," I told him.

"You're how old? Sir Stephen and Richard said you were with them in searching for the quarry. I saw you in the ships' competition with that girl, the two of you beat two of my better squires who are seniors now. And didn't you give your partner, Sherry, away when she was married in January?" the Baron said quickly, and none too pleased. "Weren't you training with the kids who are almost senior squires? I thought I was getting a squire with whom I would work for nearly a year before he became a senior—and you're telling me you're just thirteen!"

"My Sir, even though I'm only thirteen—I've held my own against the older students. I fought a bear, on the expedition to locate a quarry. And sir, you never asked me my age," I was afraid he was going to send me back to the city. What a disgrace that would be.

"Take your helmet off and come over here. We need to *rapport* to let me get this sorted out," he ordered me.

"Sir, I've never been in *rapport* with anyone except my family. Please sir, I don't wish to do this, sir," I told him. *Rapport* is a special sharing of one's thought, you don't want just anybody inside your head.

"Ray, you're my squire—you need to trust me enough to let me do this!" Sir William was getting more and more upset.

"Sir, *rapport* is one of the few things that a knight may not require of his squire, forced *rapport* is only lawful in legal matters. And I really don't want to do this," I tried to convince him. I was afraid he would find out my dreams and other things I wanted to keep secret.

"You're thirteen, I'm not going tell everyone what is in your mind, that would not be ethical for a knight to do his squire. If I found out you'd killed someone I couldn't tell anyone." He tried to reassure me.

"Please, no sir," I was pleading now. I felt like I was a little boy trying to talk my mother out of spanking.

"Ray, do you know what discipline for general principles means?" he asked looking me seriously in the eye.

"Yes sir, that is an old and seldom used law that allows a knight to whip his squire once a month for things the squire might have done and got away with, sir," I was in trouble now—I just knew it.

"For one of your rank once a month is correct—for others it can be once a week. Would you care to start that tonight? At thirteen I believe I'm allowed thirteen strips. Would you care to assume the position across that log out there?" he asked looking and sounding sad.

"No sir, but this isn't right sir."

"Ray, I'll be easy with you on this. I'll treat you like a little brother, and you've asked a question that I wouldn't answer—you may look for that answer while we *rapport*. And I swear on my oath as knight, and I'll never force you to do this again. Would that be okay?"

"It would be better than getting my butt blistered, and I've been doing a good job of avoiding that lately, and at my age that is not easy. It seems like everyone is trying to bust us," I answered. "And you're only allowed to deliver seven cuts to one my age for general principles." I was not liking this, but I certainly did not want to get caned every month, for no reason either.

The baron and his squire began the *rapport*, Sir William had done this on multiple occasions, many times to relay military information during the war. But for the boy it was a scary ordeal, in that he was not use to sharing with anyone. He would have done so with Sherry, had she been able to, but that was about it outside the family.

The baron quickly, but gently touched his mind and found what he wanted to know about the boy. He also realized the child would be much slower to find his way about his mind, so Sir William directed the boy to where the information about his brother was, and the small friendship they had shared in training school and in combat. The baron then went back to finish getting what he wanted to know.

By the time it was finished Ray was in tears. Not because he had been hurt by his knight, but from the information that he had witnessed, and a bit from fear.

When the *rapport* was broken Sir William gave him a brotherly hug, and tried to comfort the lad. Sir William knew what the child had experienced in seeing his brother's death, and how scared he really was at the procedure they had just completed.

"You go on to bed, we'll talk about this tomorrow while we are walking," the knight told his squire.

"Sir, we're still on duty—I can't go off to bed. That is a breach of conduct that can really get a kid in big trouble," Ray answered him.

The baron let him know that it was all right, because the commanding officer gave him permission. Besides, there wasn't much time left in their watch—he *accidently* made a mistake about that.

The next morning the knight acted as if nothing had happened. Ray wasn't sure if that was good or bad. Sir William reminding him of his kindling, as if there had been no discussion of it the night before, and after first meal they started off.

Kurt came up to him when they first started off, and asked him if he noticed psionic activity last night. He thought he felt some while he was sleeping, but he might have just dreamed it. Ray just grunted and tried to ignore the question, so Kurt let it drop.

After they had walked some ways the baron sent two of the senior squires off the road and up a bit to see if they might find some game for that night's dinner. Then he signaled his squire to come to him.

"You okay, after last night?" he questioned in a concerned voice.

"Yes sir, but I'm still not pleased that you forced that on me, and don't think that the choice you gave was much of a choice, sir," I told him still, a bit upset.

"You want to report me when we get back, it is your right as a nobleman's son," he told me.

"No sir, I wouldn't do that, sir. I'm not a snitch, and I would appreciate it if you wouldn't imply that I am, sir," I told him a bit more hateful than I should have.

"Son, if I were you, I would never use that tone of voice with me again. I'll give you a little room because of what I forced on you last night, but insubordination will not be tolerated! Do you understand me?" He was upset with me now; I had gone a bit too far.

"I'm sorry sir, you're right of course, and I beg my lord's forgiveness. Please don't hold this against your squire. It won't happen again, I'm just a still a little upset about last night," I told him. I knew I went too far, and normally a kid my age would have paid a painful price for that remark.

"All right, we'll kind of start the day over. I won't give you a hard time about anything I saw that was private, but you realize I knew some of it already—such as your almost getting killed by some older squires on the way here, and kissing the princess."

I gasped when he mentioned that, I didn't think that many people knew about it, and told him.

"Ray, I was there when the prince got the news and discussed it with your father. I thought your father was going blow up. It was a good thing you weren't in camp that day."

"Now, that I've seen what I needed to know, do these other squires know how old you are?" he asked.

It seemed a strange question, "I don't think so, sir." I answered, still not sure why it was asked. "Kurt may know," I added. "He may've heard at the competition."

"Kurt," he called out. Then motioned for the senior squire to come over to us. "What do you know about my squire?"

"That his title is higher than anyone else here. His father was one of the most trusted and respected commanding officers of the king. He had a crush on a commoner, whom he defended against another squire, and the princess supposedly has a crush on him."

"What!" I almost exploded.

"Hey, many young girls have a crush on a squire—I just wouldn't kiss her again if I were you."

The baron stepped in between us, "Hold your temper squire, I'll ask the question. I don't believe this squire was attempting to besmirch anyone's reputation—especially not the princess!"

"No sir, I meant no disrespect. Little kids need to have someone to look up to. Your practice partner Sherry had a crush on your big brother. Did she tell you that?" Kurt asked. "I haven't said anything to anyone else about the princess's crush. I just overheard someone else talking about it in the great hall. That was why she wasn't allowed to come down and see us off. I've got ways of finding things out. I don't mean you any harm by it."

"Thank you Kurt, I thought you might know something useful to assist me in his training," the baron said. He was still standing between us to making sure I was not going to do something stupid.

"Oh, you mean like, he is a couple years younger than he should be to be with us, sir?" he responded innocently enough.

"Yes, that was what I meant," the baron stated, now getting upset with what seemed to be a game to Kurt.

"Sure I knew it, but I don't think anyone else does. I haven't told my junior, because I didn't think it was any of his business, or anyone else, and besides from what I've seen the little snot can pull his own weight. I figured with his title, he could use the extra training. Besides any kid his age that can back down one my age with psionic reputation alone must be okay. Also Sherry and Adam found out I was on this with you, and asked me to watch out for him."

I started to apologize to Kurt, "I'm sorry, I misjudged you, and came close to accusing you of not being a gentleman or worse."

"Sherry said if you got out of line, just to tell you I got a paper from her in my pocket that your mother gave her." Kurt paused briefly, "Not really, she just said it would get your attention. Besides I don't really need it. And you got a little close—didn't you?"

"Yes sir. How do you know all this?" I asked.

"My secret and yours is safe with me," Kurt said smiling.

The baron just turned his back on us and walked off. Glancing back over his shoulder he told me, "We'll finish this later, when you two figure out this is not a game. That way I don't lose my temper with you two. I suppose my squire is not in trouble, for his near lack of manners?"

"Good! Get out ahead and see if you can spot any tracks. Go! Go!"

"You're going to get yourself in trouble like that," I warned Kurt.

"If I was your age, I would have been in trouble. At sixteen, I can get away with a bit more. Now if you're going to pass for a fifteen-year-old, you better keep up with me." Then he took off in at a slow sprint.

I took off after him, and was having problems keeping up with him in the snow and slush. We got a quarter mile ahead of the rest and Kurt finally slowed to a normal walk.

"So, was that the two of you working on psionics last night—like I thought?" he gasped after the run.

"Why are you asking?" I panted.

"Listen, I know a lot of things because I listen well and ask the correct questions. It also helps to have *ESP*."

"You're a . . . ," I started.

"Watch it, remember I know how old you are, and I'd hate to pull rank, but if you go too far I will.

"I won't use *ESP* on you. Too easy to get caught using on people with psionics; the commoners, that's different. Let's see if we can find something to kill and eat," Kurt said.

The boys hunted ahead of the group most of the day, and had several snow rabbits to add to the meal. The group would be close to the quarry by about noon tomorrow. They were able to travel faster than the original force, with a partial road and laid out direction. Then the mapping would take place.

Kurt and Ray continued to visit, and almost forgot what was going on; until a loud call for kindling reminded Ray they were waiting on him. The baron quietly told him he thought he might have lost the kindling and was trying to find more that was dry. Ray had to get the fire started, so Kurt's squire and another cleaned the rabbits and took care of the pelts.

The fire was going, the tents were set up, and it had stopped snowing. It was beginning to look like a lovely night. The boys had not seen any predator's tracks while they were hunting out from the party, nor had any of the others. One of the other juniors suggested, in jest, that the ferocious bear that Ray and Sherry had killed that winter had scared all the others away.

Sleep was easier to come that night, except Ray and the baron had the middle watch. It was tough to get out of the warm bed roll and go out to watch. But the night passed without any problems. Ray and the baron discussed some points about psionic combat and techniques for teaming. It was an interesting discussion for the boy, who other than controlled practiced had never really used the abilities in combat.

The party got to the quarry camp by midmorning. And it was a great morning. The snow, which already stopped, was starting to melt and the sun felt great.

They checked on those who had come early to set up the camp and get things planned for those who were to work in the quarry. There were not many stone masons among those at the city, and many of the workers would be young. So they took an early lunch there and then continued on and started their mapping.

The expert in stealth; oh call him what he is—a thief, climbed a large tree as high as he could to attempt to gather information about the lay of the land from there. Standing there among the trees was like being in a light sprinkle, as the melting ice dropped water on their heads. Today was the first day it had started to feel like spring.

The next day or so the plants begin to show some signs of spring. Grasses began to make their way out of the earth. Some of the trees began to show a hint of leaves, and the ground was mush. The melting snow made for mud everywhere, and made walking a chore as the group sunk in soft places. Mud stuck to their feet and added weight to each step.

The squires continued their duty of keeping kindling for the next night's fire without mishap. The start of spring-feeling days did not stop the feelings of winter nights, as temperatures plummeted when the sun went down. The people still weren't accstomed to the dual moons, and the moons were still a source of awe and wonder.

With the change in weather, a few extra animals began to show themselves. Birds became noticeable and noisy. Small streams appeared as the thaw began to run off, and these made their way to the river, as it seemed this land was ringed by cliffs. The land was lower in the middle—at least where the party was exploring. But animals and moving water gave the night some different sounds to hear besides the wind.

After a week of walking a slow sloping rise, the party was up to a height even with the cliffs, and a small waterfall into the ocean was observed. Probably it was only sending water over this falls with the winter run-off, but it was an interesting sight. They then discovered there was a spring also. On the other side of this hill was another valley. It was a great deal steeper going down than coming up, and made for a natural fence for things on the backside. It appeared this rim went all the way to the river, so Sir William suggested that this area might be somewhat cut off from other parts of this land.

A small herd of wild goats was spotted in the distance and their locations were marked on the map. It took the party two days to get down the hill, as a path was not readily found, and repelling down the side only works down—the return trip would have been difficult. Finally the group returned to where the goats had been spotted earlier and a difficult, but workable path was located.

Ray and Kurt spent most of their time with each other, and enjoyed being kids when time permitted. The two young Mentans got along well, if with the difference in age. What the boys enjoyed most was being out of the city and doing construction work. The fresh air and a chance for adventure was exhilarating.

The baron never mentioned their *rapport* to Ray, or information that he had discovered. Ray never questioned him any more about his brother—the *rapport* had shown him everything Sir William knew.

The healer, Sarah, also begin to visit with Kurt and Ray, mainly at meals. She was a pleasant addition, boys agreed. Sarah was a couple of years older than Kurt, about eighteen, and had a great sense of humor. Ray was a bit shy around her, especially with the difference in their age; besides, it was funny to watch Kurt when she first began to eat with them. It seems Kurt thought she was extremely beautiful, Ray felt he might have had a crush on the young healer.

Sarah knew Ray's cousin, Luke, his sister Megan, and she had been on the ship with Ray. Ray didn't mention that Luke was his cousin, and neither remembered meeting the other on the ship. But she remembered the competition, on board ship, where Ray had been teamed against Kurt.

––––––––––––

"You've grown a bunch since then, haven't you?" she said looking at me closely.

"Yes ma'am," I replied, "the additional weight has helped the strength." I hoped this would imply that only a big difference in weight.

"It seems your height has changed more. Wait up, just a moment . . . you're Megan's brother, and Luke's cousin—his YOUNGER cousin! How did you get to come on this expedition?" she asked in a reprimanding tone.

"He's good," Kurt chimed in, "and don't tell anyone how old he might be."

"Does your lord know your age?" she questioned me further. I felt like I might be in trouble with her, but I didn't know why.

"Yes ma'am, he does . . . now. Would you mind changing the conversation—please?" I asked.

"Sarah, the baron knows about him, his older brother and the baron served together, before Kelric's death," Kurt interjected. "But like the kid said, let's change the conversation. The baron does not want his age made general knowledge."

"You two are finished eating," she noted. She then went over to the baron, pointed to the two boys and came back and told them, "Pick up your weapons and come with me, as escorts. We can talk more away from the group."

This did not come as a request, but as an order. Kurt continued to sit there. I quickly obeyed. She looked back at Kurt, "Well?"

"I'm a senior squire, you can't just order me around," he told her.

I could not believe what he just said. I mean, he was correct, but still.

"Excuse me sir squire, would you do me the honor of accompanying me for some privacy?" she queried in overstated manners.

"My lady, I would be honored to attend you," he stated in the same tone. Then he laughed and said, "I just liked being asked every now and again. Although your request is like a command."

Oh brother, I thought. I didn't say anything—I would have liked to but . . .

"Okay, we are out of the earshot of the others, explain," Sarah commanded.

Kurt, realizing I was in over my head, jumped in, "What'd you like to know? He was on the quarry expedition, and aided in killing a bear. He is one of the highest ranking nobles in our city; therefore, in need of additional training. He was worked well with other senior squires and knights, who recommended him to the baron."

I wasn't sure what was taking place, but I sensed Kurt was playing as a defender for me, and neither of us understood why it was needed.

"I think these questions would be answered better by *rapport*. You should not be here!" she told me to my surprise!

"Ma'am, begging your pardon, but I do not wish to enter *rapport*. It is a family matter to me and I, I don't feel comfortable with non family."

"I didn't ask you your preference, I informed you of requirements," she said extremely irritated.

"Ma'am you may not compel me to do so, it is not permitted," I reminded the healer. I was wondering why this idea of *rapport* was being so needed of late.

"Do you have the authority to discipline the child?" she asked Kurt, much to my surprise.

"Normally one doesn't discipline another's squire, on an expedition. As I understand it only the leader normally will do that." They talked almost as if I wasn't there.

"NORMALLY the junior squires aren't this junior! Now a straight answer yes or no—I will *truth read*."

"Yes, but there would need to be a good reason," Kurt told her.

Sarah turned to me, looked at me for a moment. A chill went up my spine as she looked.

"You are correct, my child," she said, seemingly to agree. Then she turned to Kurt and ordered, "Put the boy across the stump and I will have to examine him under the scourge since he refuses to enter *rapport!*"

"Sarah!" Kurt exclaimed.

"Ma'am!" I exclaimed, at the same time.

"I need more answers than I believe the boy wants to give, and I don't have time to play games. He will follow my orders, or he will regret his decision!" She was not smiling and seemed genuinely mad.

"Ma'am, begging your pardon. Ma'am it's not permitted to discipline me like that. I have the right to refuse," I tried to explain.

"Go sit on the stump, and allow Sarah and me a moment to discuss this," Kurt said. When I did not move as quickly as he desired—because of shock at was taking place, he ordered me a much firmer, "Boy, I gave you an order. If you don't comply, there will be a reason to put you over that stump!"

I went over, confused. Why were these people treating me this way? I had not done anything incorrectly, but had been in trouble just for being young. My cousin had said you could grow out of that.

Sarah and Kurt came over where I had been sent. "You're not used to this, are you? Healers practice it a great deal more, so they are not as timid about sharing thoughts as other youngsters. But I need some information, and I would prefer to know about it without your realizing everything I want to know. The baron did this the other day, didn't he?"

"Yes ma'am, and I don't understand why? He is my lord, so extra trust is expected from him, but even he can't require me to take part in *rapport*," I answered, still not comprehending why.

"What if I was in there with you? Would that make you feel safer? Ray, we've been getting along really well, and I've been kind of looking out for you, haven't I?" Kurt asked, attempting to reassure me.

"No, Kurt," she said. "I don't believe you need to be there for what I'm doing. Ray, I'm sorry, but I don't have time to continue to debate."

The next thing I knew I was on the ground and Kurt was shaking me awake. "Don't say anything right now. I'll explain tonight."

We traveled the rest of the day. Sarah spoke the Sir William shortly after he started traveling after lunch. The baron had others out hunting and I stayed close to him the rest of the day. He was not very happy about something, and that was fine. I did not want to talk much either.

Kurt came over to talk to me an hour or so before stopping for camp that evening. I was hoping he was going to tell what happened. I started what I hoped would be a good conversation, "Sir William has been somewhat sullen today. You know what has him upset?"

"It seems some youngster whom he may care about has created some problems. I believe the Baron is considering how severe he might have to be with the lad," Kurt informed me in a serious and low tone. "I don't believe at your age it is a matter of if, only how bad."

This was not what I wanted to hear.

As camp was being set up the baron and the healer came to me. They said I was to go with them, and we walked on further from where the camp was being set up.

"Our healer is not too pleased with you, lad," the baron began. "She suggested that Kurt help you remember your manners earlier today, and he declined. She has repeated her request to me. Son, do you understand what that means to you?"

"Yes sir, it means that you are going to give me a whipping, sir," I said as level as I could. I didn't believe I deserved caning, but it didn't appear my opinion was going to be asked.

The baron started again, "I have discussed this request with the senior squire and our healer. Kurt still, maintains that your station should prevent that measure of chastisement. Nor is Sarah pleased with Kurt. I would prefer not to have to administer any such punishment this time, but I am not sure if it would be appropriate to allow you, at your age, to be permitted to get away with being willfully stubborn."

"The boy may have wished his friend would have given him the punishment, given the difference in your size and Kurt's," Sarah said, with a slight smile.

The baron then took out his dagger and began stripping away the bark on a branch off a nearby tree. "Go, quickly and quietly get Kurt, and both of you come back immediately!"

"Yes sir," I said and hurried off to get Kurt. I found him and told him the baron wanted him. As we walked away from camp, "Kurt, I think I got you in trouble because you didn't bust me earlier."

"Don't talk, and whatever you do—don't make up an excuse," he told me as we walked along.

"Are you going to, ah, ah . . . Are you going to give me another whipping if I cause you to get one? I was concerned that I'd end up getting another from Kurt, besides having someone I'd gotten along with well upset with me."

"Just shut up—and no," he said to my relief.

The baron had a rather large cane ready for discipline when the two returned. Sarah was looking a bit upset when they got back. The baron pitched the rod to Kurt, and asked if he knew what that was for. Kurt looked over at Ray and said that he assumed it was to motivate the boy to do something he should not have been forced to do.

The baron asked if he was attempting to be insubordinate.

Of course Kurt, denied that statement. That would be asking to receive a beating also. Kurt asked the question Ray kept wanting to, but was afraid to. "Why is the boy in trouble for being young?"

Sir William told Ray that he'd be allowed a pardon for both he and Kurt if he would allow the four of them to go into to *rapport*.

Ray looked at Kurt, and Kurt told him to make his own decision. Ray said he didn't want to do the *rapport*, but he wasn't willing to get Kurt in trouble for taking up for him. So he would agree.

The older two members of the *rapport* gathered a great deal of information quickly, then imparted information to the boys.

Ray should not have been on this mission because some to the things they were expecting to do would have been inappropriate for him, at his age. At fifteen it could be tough to deal with, but at his age and considering his rank, very inappropriate. The lord had almost sent him back after the first night he had *rapport* with the boy, and found out how young and innocent he was. Then he considered leaving him at the quarry, but decided that could taint his reputation. He really was ready to just beat the tar out of him just because he was so mad at having been given a squire that was so young.

He and Sarah were mad at Richard, but Richard didn't know about this mission, or know what was to be taking place. There could come a point where Ray might be left behind for a while, or sent away—at least a short distance. He was impressed how quickly those orders were to be followed, or past transgressions and current ones would be paid for in full with a severe beating.

They also discussed some of their abilities that each possessed psionically. This way they would better be able to expect one another's actions. The healer also let them know that by going into *rapport* like this she would be better able to *cell adjust* them if it were needed. Then what Ray felt was the best thing happened; Kurt sent the thought out that Ray needed to be given privileges of a fifteen-year-old for the remainder of the trip. By giving him this respect and leeway that would allow, he would be able to function without some of the discipline normally forced on the younger squires. Kurt let it be known that a slight statement implying his age would prevent anyone else from questioning his age. They would just believe he was very small for his age. The four of them would be all that knew, and then only the baron would be the only one able to discipline him. And the baron agreed, as did Sarah.

Then they broke the link.

———————

"I'll even continue to put up with you two during meals—but don't start acting your age," Sarah told me.

"Kurt, thanks. That was great what you did," I told. I was so happy I was about to burst.

"It's okay, you kept me from getting caned also. Remember if you give me a hard time, I'll take you out in the woods, and just beat the snot out of you—I think that was Sherry's approach."

"I don't know about that. You're not near as cute as she is. I might not go out there with you knowing you're mad at me," I said, laughing. "You still going to explain some stuff to me tonight about what happened this afternoon?"

"I would prefer not to, but if you have to know I will. I really don't want to," he told me in all seriousness.

I wasn't sure what to make out of it. "Well, can we talk about it—at least a little? I'm really confused."

"Maybe, but there can't be any of the commoners around. Hey, and why hadn't you told me you could disappear with psionics?"

"I thought it might bother you, besides, I'm not that good with it."

"Did you ever try it with Sherry?" he asked with a mischievous chuckle.

"NO! You've got to be kidding. I can't believe you are even suggesting such an idea. She and Adam would have both killed me. Would you have tried that with your sister?" I asked somewhat surprised at Kurt's non-mannerly suggestion.

"She's not your sister, and you can't tell me you never even thought about it, as cute as she is," Kurt continued and gave me a slight push.

The younger boy blushed, and walked off, with Kurt still laughing as he went. Kurt knew he got to the boy that time—not like he was trying to hurt him—just giving the kid a difficult time.

Sarah joined the two for supper that evening, but didn't visit with them much. They were all quiet during the meal.

Sarah told Ray, in a hushed voice, that she was sorry she put him through so much that day, but she was still not pleased with his reluctancy with *rapport*.

Ray then noticed someone using their psionic powers, looked at Kurt, and told him to quit.

Sarah continued that she realized it was a bit frightening sometimes, but it was needed. Then she left and went to talk to the mage.

Ray was still mad about the exchange when she left. He challenged Kurt about using his *ESP* ability. Kurt replied he was just trying to help, because he knew Sarah was still upset about something.

Kurt's squire came over and the conversation shifted, not to one that Ray was wanting to discuss much more, but to keep the other junior squire from knowing the original conversation.

––––––––––

"I still think that Xell has prettier eyes, although Sarah is prettier in general," Kurt said as if they had been discussing the two ladies' physical appearances.

I picked up on the ruse, "Maybe but there seems something harsher behind them, a little frightening. I still think the healer is prettier overall."

"Sure, but I love those eyes—I'd like to stare into them for a while," Kurt said and made a less than gentlemanly gesture.

His squire, Thomas joined in, "That might prove to be a dangerous liaison, if your moves were rejected. You might end up a rabbit or a toad. Oh, or better yet—an elephant, still need more of 'em for building."

––––––––––

The boys laughed and joked about things boys their age would joke about, when adults or ladies weren't around. Ray didn't add much to the conversation, other than when Kurt embellished his problems with Adam, and when Sherry kissed him. Ray expanded that kiss and the one he received, in the hold of the ship, to the others' delight and Kurt embarrassing him a great deal more.

When the only female senior squire walked over and realized what they were talking about, she said they were disgusting and should be ashamed. Kurt responded it wasn't disgusting, it was discussing. She told them her reason for coming over was to find out which of these juniors squires had wood detail.

Thomas got up and went for additional wood, as the female squire went off shaking her head and mumbling.

Ray and Kurt continued to talk. The younger squire was wanting to know if Kurt found out what the point of the mission was that was so bad for him to be on. Kurt jokingly said there were people out here that had human sacrifices—virgin sacrifices, and they didn't want Ray taken by mistake. Ray didn't believe that was nearly as funny as Kurt did and said something out of character for him, that was more than just close to being rude.

Kurt's expression changed.

"How many people know how old you are?" Kurt asked angrily.

"Just the three of you from this evening, sir," I stated, concerned that I might have gone to far.

"So you understand, I know your age, but do you realize how easy it is to bust your butt. Perhaps I should demonstrate, right now—in the middle of camp?"

"My apologies sir, I lost my temper, sir," I tried to make amends. "You're one of the people I would want least to offend, as you have befriended and aided me, sir."

"Then you agree that your actions are deserving of punishment?" Kurt asked, still obviously angry. "If you were fifteen, and I reported this action to the baron, you would still receive a caning for your actions!"

"I'm sorry sir," was all I could say.

"I still believe it would be better for everyone to believe you're closer to their age. So I guess we should take a walk into the woods, far enough that your cries would not be heard in camp," he stated.

"Yes sir."

We started walking to the woods, Kurt picked up a limb from a tree to use for the rod. When we had walk a long ways from the we came to a fallen log. He pointed at the log.

"Can you think of a reason I shouldn't wear you out," he asked?

Remembering his earlier comment about making excuses, I answered negatively.

I was ashamed of my actions. "Sir, I was upset with your teasing, but I repent what I said, and hope the senior squire will not continue to hold my action against me, after administering the discipline." Then I started to lean across the log.

"Didn't I tell you to wait? I have decided that I'm going to hold off on the beating until we return. You're still going to get the whipping—just not right now. That way, there is a better chance of the others believing your age. But upon our return to the city, you and I are going to go to the stables, and I am going to tear you up."

"Yes sir, thank you for waiting sir. It would be difficult to carry out duties tomorrow after you finished with me this evening," I said relieved the caning would take place later.

"Should I not be able discipline you, on your honor, you're to go to Sherry and request that she give seven well-laid stripes," he ordered.

"Not Sherry sir, please."

"You are to explain why you're requesting the beating and in detail."

"Explain sir? Sherry would be extremely upset with me for that—sir, she's like a sister."

"Okay, you may have a second option, but I want to know which you're planning to select this evening. Your other option is requesting the beating from James, seven licks. I'm sure after your dealings with him, looking for the quarry, he'd loved to have an excuse to beat the crap out of you," Kurt said.

"I'll take it from Sherry," I told him, "Sis is going to kill me. She might lose count and give me a dozen."

"One more thing, I'm going to deliver a blow to you; one, as a reminder of the actions. You may accept this or you may attempt to defend and receive worse, Kurt told me.

"Kurt, I don't want to fight you. All that would accomplish is me really getting beat up, and both of us getting a caning for fighting from the baron. I'll stand and take the blow sir. Please don't knock out a tooth, sir. Might I close my eyes, sir, in preparation—I'm not sure if I could stand firm watching, sir?"

Kurt hit me in the jaw and knocked me flat on my back. We then walked back to camp.

"I suggest you eat with the other junior squires tonight, instead of Sarah and me. Another slip and you will pay a heavy price," he told me.

"Yes sir," I said and rubbed my jaw. "Are you going to inform the baron of my lack of manners, sir?"

"No—if I did, he would beat you badly—as you deserve. And I would prefer to have that honor when you will not need the sleep or ability to walk as much."

Sarah was sitting with Kurt when I got my roasted rabbit, bread, and thawed snow to drink. I went to sit with the other juniors. Thomas asked why I was sitting with the commoners—get the senior squire or the lady upset.

I told him I was attempting to be fair—they were both willing to be without my company for the evening.

Thomas said laughingly, "Good thing you're not one of our new twelve-year-old—you'd have been having to eat standing up." Everyone laughed but me on that.

I went to help gather some wood, to make sure it was dry for tomorrow. Thomas came up to me and took be by the head and turned my head toward the fire light. "Ray, you got smacked across the jaw? You've got the start of a bruise. You really did upset Kurt, didn't ya?"

I turned to go and walked right into the baron, who heard what was said.

"Excuse me, my lord. I didn't realize you had come up behind me, sir" I explained for walking into him.

"Are you going for wood? Yes, then when you finish come find me. We need to discuss some items," he informed me.

"Crap," I said under my breath.

"I didn't see him, Ray. I hope I didn't get you in trouble with the baron," Thomas told me.

"I think I did that for myself," I replied.

We returned from gathering wood, which did not take much time. We set it up near the fire to dry. The baron was talking to the mage when he spotted me.

"Oh, there's my squire. Get your sword and accompany me. I need a short walk after the meal to think—you shall accompany me," he yelled to me.

I moved quickly to him, as I already had my sword.

He clasped my on the back and we walked off, as if best of friends. Shortly out of camp his grip became much firmer.

"Did you take part in a fight, Ray?" the baron questioned as we walked.

Ray told him of the situation with Kurt, and that the bruise was delivered as punishment and not resulting from a fight. Then he went back to explain the entire problem, from the beginning. The lord was upset with his squire and said that the senior probably should have beaten the devil out of him for his poor manners then, not deciding to wait until they returned. The baron, however, was not waiting that long and decided to discipline the boy for his actions for the day in general. The baron handed the boy a stick to bite on, as he did not want the camp to hear his cries; this was a private beating. Should another be deserved it would be much more public.

Six stripes later the lad was allowed to stand. The baron suggested that there had better not be another day in which he caused as many problems, otherwise his discomfort would be much greater. He allowed Ray a couple of moments to compose himself before the returned to camp. He then told him to locate Sarah and return with her about one hundred yards from the camp where he would be waiting.

"The boy has been chastised for his actions today, apparently he might should have received it earlier and gotten it over with. Check his jaw, to make sure nothing is broken," Sir William said and walked off.

Sarah examined the boy with her psionic skills. "The jaw is not broken. You want to sit and talk about it?"

"Ma'am, sitting is about the last thing I want to do," he told her.

They talked, and Ray asked what was going on that she did not want him there. But she wouldn't answer that. She asked if he wanted her to heal the jaw. But it was already known that he had been struck by Kurt, so it better stay. She reminded him the other wounds were not visible, and asked whether he want those cured. Ray responded, that she knew that she wasn't supposed to cure discipline pain.

"That's right," she said as she walked off, "glad you remembered."

No one seemed to be aware of the beating that Ray received. Everyone seemed to know about the shot to the jaw. The other junior squires all reminded him it could have been worse. And Kurt never had explained what had happened earlier.

The valley already had the beginnings of grasses starting to sprout, the tender shoots making their way through the soggy earth. Birds also seemed more noticeable here. Late the first day a large pond was spotted. Water was running from it toward the river. They weren't sure if the pond was spring fed, or merely full from the winter snow that had melted very quickly.

Two of the junior squires went to make a quick check around the pond, and excitedly ran back to report tracks. But being out of breath it took a few moments to tell the type of tracks. Finally they gasped out "horse tracks, and a lot of them."

The baron's first question was then whether they were shod or not? The two boys thought just a brief moment and then said simultaneously—"non-shod!" The party moved to where the tracks had been seen and looked carefully around the pond for other tracks besides the horses'. The horse tracks were so prevalent they were unable to discern any other tracks.

At lunch Ray sat with the other junior squires again, still carefully. They were having stories about catching the horses and the fun of trying to break them. Maybe then they would not have to walk so much. Ray was trying to take part, but still didn't feel too well. The idea of trying to sit on a horse at this time was not a pleasant prospect.

Toward the end of the lunch break, Kurt motioned for him to come over. "Did you get in trouble yesterday evening, after our discussion?"

Ray was looking down, a bit afraid to meet his gaze, shook his head in the affirmative and quietly answered, "Yes sir."

"Got a nice little bruise on the jaw too," Kurt continued. "What'd the baron say, about you taking one on the chin?"

"He was displeased with my actions, and disappointed in me sir," the boy said.

Kurt sent him away and continued to talk to the healer. The boys wanted to know what Kurt had told him. Ray made up a little story about still being on Kurt's bad side and eased back down.

Thomas tried to cheer him up, but it didn't work.

The thief came back into camp and said that he had spotted the horses close to the stream, just about a mile from them. The party was excited to find out more on the horses: what type were they, their size, and the size of the herd? The thief let them know he hadn't been close enough for all that. He didn't want to scare them off.

The baron and the thief went back to check on the horses, and camp was set up where they were to allow the spell casters to memorize spells that might prove useful in catching the horses.

Sarah motioned for Ray to come over. She wanted him to finish setting things up for her, then said told him that the baron said she might need to cure him, to allow him to aid in breaking the horses. She then surprised the boy by saying that was too bad, he needed the pain to help him realize his error.

He turned on her in shock and asked what he had done to make her so upset with him. She let him know that she was not used to having children disobey her. Ray couldn't believe her. As he was walking out of the tent, the priest came to him. He told Ray that he had hurt her feelings when he refused *rapport*; that had never happened to her before. Ray tried to explain that he was not raised that way, and *rapport* was a private; family matter.

Ray attempted to talk to Kurt a bit later, but the senior squire told him that he had not been sent for. Ray went to Thomas, and asked if he would request permission for him to talk to Kurt. Thomas said that he must be in more trouble than Ray had thought. Thomas made the formal request for Ray, and Kurt told him they'd go for a walk. Ray hoped it was better than the last two he'd been on.

They talked and Kurt agreed to help Ray get over the fear of *rapport* by entering into it with him. After they tried, maybe Ray could allow the healer easier access to his thoughts. They spent some time in the exercise, and Kurt was able to ease the tension and apprehension about the mind sharing.

Ray also finally found out what had happened the day before—Kurt explained through the *rapport* that Sarah had cast *sleep* and done the *rapport* while he was out. She had actually slept both of them with the spell.

Ray also discovered that Kurt was hoping to marry the healer, since neither of them had a promise in the works, after the flight of the kingdom. Kurt was able to see how sorry the boy was for his offense, and said he would accept his apology, but he was still going to have to face the punishment for his actions—forgiveness does not absolve consequences.

They went back, a little tired from their mental ordeal, and got Sarah. She walked into one of the other tents, and Thomas was set on guard in front of it. Then Ray allowed Sarah to enter *rapport* with him. Kurt joined them after a while and made sure that Sarah understood the boy had really been afraid, not attempting to be unruly. Ray saw some other things he would want to talk to Kurt about later, and Sarah saw Kurt's idea of marriage through Ray. She let Kurt know that she was not outright opposed, but it would require some thought.

"Next time you should ask yourself—not send a boy to do a man's job," she concluded and broke the *rapport*.

Ray was embarrassed by the ending, and concerned that Kurt might be upset with him; which was not what he needed, considering what else was happening. He also wanted to be sure he was on Sarah's good side again.

———————

"Ma'am I hope I'm forgiven for having you upset with me, I don't want you mad at me. I just truly was not prepared to have others in my mind," I tried to explain.

"Were you concerned I would tell others your fantasies, or betray some trust?" she asked—still sounding offended.

"No ma'am. Sarah, my lady, if you still believe I deserve to be disciplined for my actions, not for my age, I will submit to your discipline," I stated bravely, (or maybe foolishly), and then stood at attention.

"You what?" Kurt almost yelled. Which got attention from some of the others.

"Does that mean if I tell you that you are to be caned you will accept this?" she asked in almost disbelief.

"He does not, Sarah!" Kurt interjected.

I took a deep breath and exhaled slowly, "Yes ma'am—if I must to gain your forgiveness."

"Both of you come with me," she ordered and walked out of the tent.

We walked a short distance, and Kurt and Sarah stopped and had a brief argument, that I couldn't hear. Then Kurt went and cut a limb and started to remove the bark. He walked over to me while he was peeling the bark, and let me know he was not pleased with what I had done. Basically he told me it was not too smart. He then handed her the rod and stepped back. She pointed to a good size-rock and told me to assume the position.

"Ray, this is going to be very painful, and it should be. I'll give you the first four and Kurt will give you four more, and I'm sure he will do a good job."

"Yes my lady, but isn't that a bit severe?" I said and looked at Kurt, who did not seem to be happy with this new twist of events. "Normally one my age only receives six or seven cuts from a cane."

"You'll receive eight for this, since we're pretending you are fifteen, and that is within the limits allowed," Sarah told me.

I turned and started to lean across the rock, and she stopped me.

"Boy, this is going to be on your bare butt."

"What!" "Ma'am!" Kurt and I said at the same time.

"Sarah that type discipline is not required, the child wasn't that bad. It is too embarrassing for a lady to beat the boy like that," Kurt said.

I was just stunned—I couldn't believe she would whip me that way. Not with a rod that long and large.

"I want to make sure the child is contrite," she said coldly.

I didn't even know what that meant—contrite.

I turned, then asked, before following instructions, "Might I receive extra discipline and not have to be beaten on the bare bottom—please?" She shook her head no. "Might I be permitted a stick to bite into, to keep from yelling out?" Again she shook her head no. I was terrified and embarrassed.

As I bent over the rock, I was already in tears; not sobbing out, but in tears for embarrassment.

Sarah applied the strokes extremely hard and I had begun to cry on the third lick, but then I was still sore from the beating I had received the night before. When she finished, she handed the rod to Kurt and told him to finish the disciplinary procedures.

Kurt told her that I had suffered enough, I was already bleeding from the welts I had. She said the longer he delayed the worse it would make it for me, and if he didn't give the licks hard enough then she would give five more.

I am sure it hurt worse because I was already so sore, but I wasn't sure Kurt didn't try too hard, because he was mad at Sarah, but I was the one that was not going to be able to sit for a long time, or do much of anything else that day.

When he finished, I was crying extremely hard, and was having a hard time breathing as a result. I knew I was bleeding from the beating, I could feel the blood running down my legs.

"Stand up and redress," Sarah told me.

I did what she told me, I was hurting really badly. I was also mad, because she treated me like a street urchin caught trying to steal something.

She came over and sat on the rock. "Hurts pretty badly doesn't it?" she asked calmly.

I shook my head and tried to speak, but wasn't able because of crying.

She then took me and turned me and leaned me gently against her, and gave me a small hug, the first time she had shown any spark of kindness in a long time toward me. Then I felt a strange sensation that seemed familiar, yet different. Her mind was moving in me, not in *rapport*; something else. Then it struck me as I noticed the easing of the pain—*cell adjust*, she was healing me. I could not believe what she was doing—it was against the rules. Healers weren't to heal wounds of discipline, and that was the only pain I really had.

"Sarah—ma'am, you could get in trouble for that. Sir William gave me those stripes for a reason, and . . . ," I said, before she cut me off.

"I'll deal with the baron. I'm afraid most of those stripes were because of me. You've suffered enough, and as the healer I determined your readiness required that I heal you. You're extremely brave to take what you did. Maybe not too smart, but brave. I didn't heal the bruise on the chin—the others know you got that. The other wounds can't be seen—normally. Boys, if anyone asked, I needed some privacy, which I did to test this child."

We walked back into camp joking and cutting up, with Kurt almost knocking me over with a pretty good shove, so no one knew what I had gone through.

Chapter Five

The Village

"There is a time for everything, and a season for every
activity under heaven: a time to love and a time to hate,
a time for war and a time for peace." Ecclesiastes 3: 1,8

The party worked slowly to get the horses in a favorable
spot, then the cleric cast a *speak with animals* and got
information about the herd. They had to build corrals, of
sorts. They were built and laid down among the trees close
to the river and part of it on the open land close to the river.
This all took time—over a week, since they didn't exactly have
all the right tools or materials for the building. The party then
manipulated the herd to that narrow area between the river
and some trees. The trees fences had to be set up quickly from
the laying down position. The healer and the mage were to
cast *sleep*, one night on some of the stallions, to make capture
easier. Then the mage was to cast a *web* to confine the horses
in a slightly, enclosed place, while the rest of the fence was put
into place.

While this was taking place, Ray was glad to be back in
favor with Sarah and Kurt. Sarah had treated him with more
respect than she had previously, even before she learned his

age. He was having a really good time; even with all the hard work, it had been a while since he hadn't been in trouble with someone, and he enjoyed the change.

The horses turned out to be slightly larger than a light war horse, but of course not trained for battle—nor broken to ride. So the next task was to break them—lots of fun without saddles, or other equipment they were used to riding with—right. Of course the warriors weren't used to attempting to break horses anyway. They were accustomed to that being done by someone else.

The baron had claimed the largest stallion, a beautiful roan, but said they would wait on attempting to break him. That might be a longer and more difficult task, so they starting trying to break some of the others.

Ray picked a young palomino which he thought held lots of promise, even if it was too young to ride at this time. He chose the colt's mother to ride, and set out trying to break her. Breaking horses was slow work, but the warriors enjoyed the task. The spell casters were more interested in the finished product, and they were to have their horses broken before the others were allowed to break their own.

Good natured abuse was given to the squires that were unhorsed, and all of them got the chance to sail through the air. After one of the squires, Torin, had taken many tumbles and kidding from the others he became upset. Ray who was on both sides of the teasing happened to be the one whose remark caused him to reach the boiling point, and he challenged Ray to a fight. Ray was not interested in fighting, because that normally resulted in a severe chastisement. Thinking to have a way out of this challenge without loss of honor among his fellow junior squires, he agreed to the fight only if the baron would permit it. He could not go against his lord's orders.

When the baron came out later that afternoon, the junior squires made the request to settle a matter amongst themselves, without a penalty. After all, it was requested and not done in the heat of anger.

The baron discussed it with his senior squires, without knowing which juniors were involved. The seniors did not tell him either—so he gave his approval. Kurt was not there, being off to do some hunting with his junior squire, so it wasn't known if he'd have attempted to warn the baron or not, or if that would have made a difference. If Ray was to be treated as an older squire, he would have to face some of the problems. The fight was decided that evening before dinner, after the work was finished and it was decided that no magical healing was to take place until the following morning, unless it was an emergency. Ray was not too excited about this ruling, but the other junior squires made the decision, which would hold for future fights. A senior, at least one, would be on hand to make sure things did not go too far; otherwise they would stay out of the way.

Kurt got back to camp and heard about the fight and said that it would provide some diversion, then found out from Ray that Ray was part of the entertainment.

––––––––––––

"Your going to get hurt, you little fool!" Kurt started in on me. "What ever made you agree to fight him? Torin is too much larger than you."

"It wasn't exactly my idea," I stammered. "I believe Torin thinks it's a chance to get back at a noble for some of the harsh treatment he received as a little kid before being taken for training. But suggesting he is thinking might be a stretch." I added the last bit smiling.

"Don't guess there's a chance of you getting out of this, is there? The size difference aside the difference in age is likely to show in a fist fight," Kurt told me.

"Thanks for being so encouraging."

"I suggest, if there are no rules—cheat," he told me with a grin. "Sherry won't find out."

We went out to fight and Kurt went to inform the baron that I was one of the fighters. I think I'm glad I wasn't there when he told the baron.

"When the fight's over, kick the kid in the butt for me—assuming he is not carried off," the Baron told him in disgust.

Jennifer, the female senior squire, and Torin's senior, gave the rules, "No hitting or kicking in the groins, all else is fair." Rules were a bit loose.

I asked for a clarification, "Anything is fair, but that? Biting, kick to the shins, everything?"

"Well, you can't pick up a weapon of any kind," Jennifer responded.

"Thank you ma'am, wanted to make sure of the rules. Now, Master Torin, would you care to withdraw your challenge?" I asked, with a defiant tone, as I pulled off my shirt.

I thought Kurt was going to hit his jaw on the ground when he heard what I told the larger boy. He looked at Sarah and some of the other seniors, and shook his head.

Then as Torin started for me with a bull's roar and rush I ducked under him, went into a quick trance, and became psionically *invisible* to him. [Psionic *invisibility* is different than the spell. One may only be invisible to so many people, depending on the amount of skill one has and how much skill the intended targets have. One may choose to which opponents one wish to be invisible the most.] I was visible to everyone except Torin. I caught Torin with good right to the lower right side of his back, just a couple of inches above the belt. He yelled in pain, arched his back and grabbed the spot. I followed with a vicious kick, which caught him directly in the front of the stomach. This doubled him over. I quickly hit him twice quickly to the face and delivered a blow to the stomach. When he doubled over from the blow to the stomach, I grabbed his head and slammed it down onto my knee. Then I stepped back. Except for the first punch, he could have seen and still done very little to stop the attacks. Being trained as a warrior, I knew how to make the attacks count.

Torin was still very much conscious when I stepped back. I allowed him to hear and see me, and asked where everyone could hear, "Have you had enough? Can we stop?"

"Yes," he sobbed, and remained on the ground Jennifer yelled to one of the other junior squires to get the healer, who was already there.

The others took Torin back to the camp, where Sarah could look after him. I motioned them to go on; I was fine.

Everyone left, I got back up, turned, and walked into Kurt. Kurt was livid as he began, "What in the world did you just do?"

"I won, sir?" I answered somewhat confused by his attitude and question. "Are mad that the big oaf didn't beat me senseless?"

Kurt gave me a shove with both hands, which pushed me down to the ground. "It would be better if you didn't get up," he said through clenched teeth and his hands were balled into fists.

Since I was supposed to be smart, I followed his orders, concerned that my next trip to the ground would be considerably less gentle than this had been. I rolled over and just looked at him.

"Explain to me what I just thought I saw. And it better be the truth or . . . ." he began, but was interrupted.

"The boy went *invisible* to his opponent," Bennet, the thief said.

I started to get up, and asked Bennet, "How do you come by that assumption?"

"I told you not to get up," Kurt told me. I quickly went back down. "But I too would like an answer to the lad's question."

"I felt the use of power, but wasn't certain where it came from, until I saw what transpired in the fight," the thief answered.

"You're not noble—how do you have that ability?" I asked

"I never knew my father, but my mother said he was of noble birth. I assume I inherited the ability from him. I don't have the skills and powers like you have, just some talents," the thief said as he sat down on the ground beside me. "Your skills may come in useful to us on this expedition."

"Does the baron realize that you are psionic?" I asked. "And may I get up, sir?"

"Not if you're smart! Would you excuse us, Bennet? I need to have a conversation with the boy."

"You might as well wait for his lordship to get here, you're going to have to have it again anyway. Besides he has already had one fight this evening, it wouldn't be proper for a senior to pick a fight with him now. Either that or we go find his lordship. What'd you say lad—ready to go talk to the baron?"

"If the senior will allow me to get up, sir," nodding to Kurt.

"Oh, well don't fret. Here's his lordship now," Bennet said quite happily.

"Bennet, would you excuse us, I need to talk to these squires," Sir William said as he came up. Angry again.

"Bennet is psionic," I said. "Might I rise now, sir?"

"You're psionic," the baron asked Bennet, while motioning me to get up?

"Your boy here has a right handy talent, my lord," the thief said with some glee that the nobles now realized more of his potency.

"Somebody want to explain why of the largest junior squires on this expedition is lying nearly unconscious, because my smallest squire beat the snot out of him?" The Baron looked like he was ready to explode into a ball of fire.

"Had the baron preferred his own squire to be in that situation?" the thief asked.

"Sir, I followed Kurt's instructions and cheated," I said. "There were no rules to the fight except not hitting below the belt nor picking up a weapon. Torin just never saw what hit him, sir."

A rather heated discussion followed as Lord William got all the information. Ray was glad the thief stayed for most for the discussion, as he seemed to be an unlooked-for ally. Bennet was eventually dismissed, and Ray had to face the other two. Lord William told Kurt that he was to treat Ray as if he were the age they had agreed on and, therefore would have to clear it with him before discipline was allowed. Ray was dismissed, sent back to camp, and the baron and Kurt continued to discuss things.

Ray was concerned that Kurt might have been in trouble for his statement about cheating. "I hope that wouldn't land me on his mud list," he thought to himself as he walked away.

With the order to observe the age rule, he believed Kurt was in trouble with the baron.

Sarah examined Ray when he got back to camp, and noticed the only problems were on his hands from hitting the other squire. Since they were not alone, she wanted to know more as soon as it was possible.

Ray shocked her by jumping into *rapport* and quickly giving the turn of events without anyone knowing it. He noticed a jump in brain activity with the information about the thief. She felt Ray had done well to avoid getting hurt, using his abilities. Before they ended Sarah suggested Ray not bother Kurt this evening.

Ray ate with the other junior squires, and they treated him a bit more respectfully, not they had treated him poorly earlier—just more respectfully. Before the fight they had thought he was some undersized, overly privileged nobleman's son.

Ray didn't see Kurt the next day, until late in the afternoon. That was not a big thing, as Ray had been with the horses, and Kurt hunted a lot. Lately, Ray noticed, he had been hunting with the thief.

Sarah healed Torin that morning, but apparently it had not been complete, as a large bruise was still on the side of his head where Ray's final punch had landed. Sarah told Ray that Kurt and Lord William were not happy with his use of his skills in the fight, even if she was. Kurt had almost been caned for it and apparently did lots of extra marching for demerits she let him know. "Don't give him a reason to need to remind you of manners for a few days, any excuse could be unpleasant," she warned.

Kurt and Bennet were gone for the next five days, scouting. Ray and the others continued to work on breaking the horses. Finally the squire broke enough horses to ride a bit. They couldn't really fight from horseback, because they weren't that well trained, but it was a break from walking. When Bennet and Kurt returned, a long meeting occurred with Baron Scrope, and the two of them. The next day as they traveled, it seemed to be purposeful in direction, not just for mapping. Camp was broken and the horses that weren't being ridden were led.

Ray was glad to be on horseback again, as was almost everyone else. The mage and the healer, were not too pleased. They seemed not to like horses that much, or at least the pain of getting used to riding again. The squires thought the pain was unpleasant, but it beat the ones from walking too much—Bennet was not very thrilled either.

On the second day of riding the camp was set up early. There was still at least another hour of travel, before camp was normally set up, and this was not that ideal camp site either. The baron, then really surprised them all, by ordering a cold camp—no fire or lights.

"Why the cold camp?" I asked one the senior squires.

"Ask the baron—you're his squire," was the rough reply I was given. Then he turned and walked away.

I wanted to ask Kurt—but he was still a bit upset with me. I began to suspect he got more than additional marching duty for his suggestion in the fight.

Lord William had not brought the matter up with me again except for the simple comment, "Don't ever use that on one of your comrades again!" That was it, no threats, no explanation, just "don't".

That night with the cold camp the seniors, the spell casters and Lord William were preparing for a very long meeting. The juniors were set out to make an outer defense—and to stay out of the way. From my distance on guard I saw the baron setting a *ward*, to prevent being overheard. At that point I realized this wasn't any meeting to determine watches for the week, this was going to be serious. It lasted a couple of hours.

After it was over, we were called back and were informed that a village of humans was close by and we would enter the village tomorrow, and it was expected to be a hostile.

I was so excited, I could hardly stand it—combat!

We were to leave our mounts a goodly distance from the village to prevent them from alerting the village and moving in on foot, but the baron said the rest of the information would be given in the morning.

Later that evening I asked, "Sir, why do you believe it will be hostile? Is there not a chance for treaty? And if it is, wouldn't it be an advantage to have the horses to move in faster, or at least be able to make a quick retreat . . ." I was asking questions extremely quickly, because I was so excited.

"Ray, hush! Let's go for a walk," Sir William stated tiredly.

"Am I in trouble, sir?"

"No, you're not in trouble, but my compliments' Kurt, ask him to join us," he told me.

Now I was confused.

I went to locate Kurt, whom I was concerned might still be upset with me. I located him quickly, but he was talking to Thomas. "Sir, the baron's compliments. He wishes that you join him, sir."

As we started walking to where the baron I was I timidly questioned the senior squire. "Sir, are you still upset with me?"

"Yes," was the simple, yet chilling response.

"Am I to know the extent of trouble I'm in with you, sir? Did I cause you more than marching duty, sir," I ask him?

"Are you required to return, or just tagging along?" he asked in rather stern voice.

"Required, sir," I informed him.

"Then do it quietly," Kurt told me in a less than friendly voice.

The rest of the walk to the baron was strained. I thought I might not have been in trouble with the baron, but the walk into the woods might be because I was in trouble with Kurt.

"Ray, the battle for the village is similar to battles in the Bible. We are going to capture and make servants out of some of the peoples. This is the reason your age made it difficult for you to attend this expedition. This was the main reason for this expedition, not mapping. We didn't know about the horses; they're just a bonus. At some point after the battle you will be sent back after the horses, and will remain out of the village until someone—Kurt, the spell casters, or I come for you. You are not to enter the village until then. Do you understand?" the baron asked me.

"Yes sir, I understand the order sir, but . . . ," and I was cut off in the middle of the sentence.

"Kurt will explain further, and you will accord him the respect during this that you would give me. Give us just a moment," the baron said and motioned for me to move off.

"Ray," Kurt put his hand on my shoulder, and started as the baron moved off. "This may be difficult for you, and I don't know how to make it any easier. We are not going to be taking many male prisoners. As his lordship mentioned, it will be like some of the Biblical battles where only the small children and the women were kept as prisoners."

"How young are we talking about, sir—twelve-year-old boys?"

"Young enough that they won't remember much of their life before we took them! The others and I will be involved in activities that at your age you don't need to be taking part. So you will follow orders and leave camp when instructed," Kurt instructed—leaving me no doubt as to the severity of these orders!

"Sir, I can follow orders, especially the way these have been directed. But what else are you meaning, sir?" I questioned further. I was concerned I was going to ask too many questions and get in trouble.

"Debauchery, and I don't want any more questions, do you understand—boy!" Kurt exploded. "After we have finished, you may ask more questions then, I'll talk to you then about it, but not until afterwards—a couple of days. And for God's sake, don't ask anyone else, before the attacks."

I started to ask another question, but decided it would not be healthy. But since I had already opened my mouth to start, I switched my question to another subject. "Am I still in too much trouble to eat with you and Sarah again?"

Kurt thought for a moment. "You know how much trouble you got me into with your comment about cheating?"

"No sir."

"I was reminded that even though I was a senior squire, I was still a squire, and not an adult. He did not appreciate the humor in which I gave you that suggestion, and it lost a bit for me too."

"Yes sir."

He continued, "I probably won't eat much in the morning, and will want to be by myself. Sarah might like the company; I'll put up with you following morning. But I would suggest you check with the baron before you go anywhere, since you are his squire."

"Kurt, I'm sorry I got you in trouble with the baron. I wouldn't have done it on purpose. I didn't think he would get upset. Sarah thought it was a good idea."

"Ray, I know you didn't do it on purpose. You know better. If I thought you had tried . . ." and he let the thought trail off.

They went back to camp and got ready to try to sleep. Most of them were having a difficult time, because of excitement. Everyone was on edge. The village had a population of around one hundred people. A little less than half of these were male, and approximately half that number would be adult males, and therefore combatants. So, they were looking for about twenty to twenty-five adult male warriors, and maybe ten teenagers that might assist. With the party's spell casting assistance, they should be able to capture the village—but only after a hard fight.

Ray prayed that something would make the baron change his mind, and make a treaty with the village. Killing warriors was one thing, but killing young boys that were not combatants was hard for him to take, and at that the time, to understand. Maybe when Kurt would talk to him later, it would make more sense. Even the twin moons seemed sullen tonight.

The next morning the warriors were quiet, in reflection on what was to come. The only warrior who had seen real combat was the baron. The day was quiet also, as if it knew to have the wind blow was to disturb their thoughts. Spring was starting to make a serious change, but today was gray, overcast and quiet. A slight breeze began to blow in their face as the party headed for the unsuspecting village. They noticed the fresh aroma of spring, with flowers, trees and other blooms wafting through the air. But the quietness was unusual.

Suddenly a new smell piqued their nostrils, one that did not belong to the fresh spring air—smoke! Not cook fires, but a large amount of smoke.

The baron signaled to pick up the pace, and the party began to move at a slight trot. As they moved closer to the river, and the village, the smoke smell became stronger. Also, they began to hear the sound of conflict—a battle was taking place.

As they moved to the edge of the clearing, not into it—they stayed back in the trees to see what was happening—they saw the village was the source of the fire. The small barricade fence around the village was not keeping out the attackers, and there were many dead in the village, most with arrows protruding from them. As they watched, Ray heard the cleric breathe out in a muted tone—Orcs. None of them had ever seen an Orc. These creatures lived far away from the civilized country of their home—but they weren't at that home any longer.

Orcs are a little larger than humans, and these seemed huge. Their bows had done a lot of damage, and now they were starting to advance into the village itself. Whether the Orcs were after captives or plunder was hard to tell from the party's view point. There were at least twenty of them and maybe more.

Ray's mind went back to his nightmare on board the *Silver Goose*, on the way from Saxet. These were the creatures he had seen in his dream. He had heard about Orcs, but had never seen even a drawing of one. Here was his nightmarish vision alive. These seemed larger than those of his dream, but these were not an illusionary vision. After this was over—if he survived he'd have tell Sir William of the nightmare, that seemed much more than a dream.

Baron Scrope gave some orders to the spell casters and then told the rest to get ready, they were going to attack from the back of the village; jump the fence and take the Orcs. The spell casters would get to the huts and give support from there.

Bennet came over to Ray and told him, "It will be okay to use ya skills against these foul creatures—his lordship won't mind."

Ray hoped he was correct, but was afraid to ask him, but Kurt was close enough to pose it to him, "Hell yes, and get your bow out. Use it first and as long as you can," was his response.

They charged over the open ground at the back side of the village, through the newly turned soil that was getting ready for seed. They jumped the fence and came in between the huts and attacked the Orcs before they knew what hit them.

The guard dogs were staying with the two female spell casters, to give them protection and time to cast spells.

Ray and Thomas were firing bows from the side of a hut, supposedly at Orcs on the other side of the fence, who also had bows. This was to provide cover fire as the others went into the melee. Ray's first shot, however, took an Orc in the throat as he was getting ready to cleave a young, defenseless, boy of about ten. The Orc gave a surprised expression, looked at Ray as a second arrow entered his chest, and he died. Ray shot and killed two more Orcs before his companion and he were spotted. As the Orcs closed, Ray began his psionic *invisibility* against one of the Orcs. He stepped up to that one, and to Ray's surprise was still able to see him. Luckily Thomas fired once more, hitting the ugly brute in the arm. The Orc wheeled from the arrow, and Ray caught it across the ribs. It turned back on Ray, but his blow caused the Orc to stumble, Ray ran his sword up through the huge Orc's chin, and out the back of the skull. Thomas was having a difficult time fending off the attack of his opponent. The size difference was going to tell quickly, as the Orc split the squire's shield with a crushing blow from his sword. Thomas's arm was broken from the shock, he attempted to parry the next blow, but was badly wounded in the shoulder, on the side with the broken arm. Ray then came in from the back, after dispatching his, and drove the point of his long sword through the back and out the breastplate of the Orc.

Several of the Orcian archers stopped firing as the cleric was able to stop them with his *hold person* spell. The mage and Sarah had cast *sleep*, which slept several others with a spell a piece.

Ray got Sarah's attention and she came to bandage the wounded squire. Ray got his bow and moved to cover the baron who was starting to engage an exceptionally large Orc. Ray was able to wound an Orc, and kill another attempting to go to the aid of the larger Orc. Finally, Ray drew his sword and went to assist the baron with it, as the wounded Orc moved into melee combat.

The large Orc was giving the baron all he could handle, and the arrival of a second Orc, even a wounded one, could have spell doom. Ray came in and sliced the right leg of the big Orc just as the baron took a deep gash to the chest. Ray's second attack cleaved the shield arm off at the elbow and Lord William sliced his neck and he fell, seemingly dead. The wounded Orc swung at Ray, who blocked it with his shield. The blow, however, numbed the arm and left the shield momentarily useless, as two more Orcs closed to rally to their apparent leader. A glancing blow on his helmet, from an Orcian sword sent Ray to the ground, with the ground spinning uncertainly around him.

With three Orcs facing him and the wounded Lord William, Ray was afraid his career as a warrior might be a short one. Then Kurt was standing over him flailing away with his broad sword, which seemed to have a slight glow to it, but Ray thought he could have imagined it.

The cleric closed in to assist the combat, mace in hand. He caught one of the Orcs in the head and his blow caved in the helmet as well as the Orc's head. Kurt then grabbed Ray and pulled him to his feet.

"I thought I told you to use your bow!" the thundered.

"You did, sir, but they got too close to the baron for me to shoot safely so I closed in to help. Glad you came too," Ray said.

The battle was going well, the Orcs were routed and the party followed them back to their boats and killed them—they didn't want anybody telling the tale.

They came back to the village, bloody, tired, and excited from the combat. The Orcs that had been slept were tied up for an attempt to question them later. The little boy that Ray saved with his first arrow shots came up to Ray and started trying to speak to him. Ray couldn't understand anything that was said, but the boy finally grabbed his feet and stayed there.

Lord William looked around and the saw child holding to Ray's feet. He asked his squire if he was in need of immediate medical assistance. Ray shook his head slowly, no, but it was very sore. The baron then told him to take his new friend and go get the horses, and follow previously discussed orders.

Ray started to say something, but decided against it, reached down and took the boy by the shoulder and led him out of the village to where the horses were tied. Ray was thinking, "I wonder if I saved his life twice and he doesn't know about this second time."

Ray and the boy, who called himself Jakót, got the horses, and started slowly back to the village. They stopped often on the way back, taking a couple of hours to get close to the village. Ray stopped again as the edge of the village was getting close, careful to follow his orders. The boy wanted to continue on to the village, but Ray was able to get him to stay. Ray cleaned his sword and equipment. Then he got on a horse and pulled the boy up with him. The boy was afraid; it seemed he had never been on a horse, but quickly calmed down with Ray holding him.

Finally Sarah came out and got him. She looked way too cheerful, Ray thought, for what was supposedly taking place in the village.

_____

"Did you consider what the boy's age was, when you shot the Orc that was about to kill him? That he might have been too old for the mission requirements?" Sarah asked.

"No ma'am, not at the time. I thought about it later as the battle was over and he came and threw himself at my feet. I hoped he was young enough to be spared. Is his lordship angry with me?" I asked.

"Come here and let me take a look at your head," she started, "I understand you took a blow on the helmet."

I didn't move, and asked again about Lord William being upset.

"I said come here!"

I came over, took my helmet off, and she examined and then bandaged the lump on the head. As she was doing this she started to answer my question, "No, little one, he is not upset with you, and in fact your actions helped a great deal. By the time we attacked, almost all the men were already dead, as well as many of the older boys who were trying to fight. So that part of our job was done for us; only a few teenage boys remained. I'll let the baron or Kurt explain the rest—I just came to find the two of you. Let's get back to camp," Sarah told me.

When we came in with the horses, the villagers were quite impressed. They had not attempted to tame and use the animals. I also noticed that none of the captured Orcs were still there—I assumed they had passed their usefulness.

Our wounds had been relatively light: Mathias and Sarah had been able to save everyone and the only death was the mage's guard dog. I hated to see that we lost one of the dogs, because they had done a great service for us and helped the mage survive the battle. But considering that we were outnumbered, I was grateful that none of our people were dead.

Our camp was set up in some of the larger huts and Mathias and Sarah had been tending to the wounded. Food was being prepared and most of the other guys were sitting, holding, and talking to some of the young female villagers.

The baron came up to me and checked on my wound. Kurt came up and began to talk in Sarah, who appeared somewhat upset with him.

"Sarah, I didn't do anything," was all I heard him say as they walked off to talk in private.

The baron pointed to a hut and a woman came and got both our equipment and Jakót and took them to the hut. The baron motioned for me to follow him.

"Son, you did very well today. Your bow was a great help, and your arrival to my aid saved my life. Kurt was a little upset about your inability to follow orders," he told me, and held up his hand as I wanted to protest. "I know, he told you to stay with the bow and a couple of times you took the long sword and went into the melee. Both times your decisions were good, Kurt was just worried about your getting hurt. You aren't in trouble after we talked, but it was a good thing he had a chance to calm down, after he saw you get thumped on the head."

"My lord, I'm glad I was able to serve you well, as is my duty as squire," I said, feeling quite proud of his compliment.

"And because of your action to save the child and we were able to work out a treaty with the survivors, which keeps them from feeling they were just taken as slaves, although there is not a great deal of difference," he began to explain.

"But sir, why?" I asked.

"Ray, when we escaped many of those who were away learning spell casting did not make it back—most of those were women. We have a large number of men, whose arranged marriage were no longer possible because their intended did not make it back, or missed the ships. None of the males on this trip has a matched wife any longer. The women in the village were to be wives or concubines. So after our rescue, we told them we would *allow* them to return with us for protection; in return, they would become our servants. The squires have already selected their girls, except Kurt, who has, or will shortly, ask Lady Sarah to marry him. So more of the boys were spared and will become servants, as will some of the older women.

"They are burying their dead today, and will finish tomorrow; we will finish inventorying the Orcian equipment and other items. Then we'll pack up and take them back to the city. They have some grain that is natural to the area that we can include in the grain production," the baron told me.

"So you didn't think I had an arranged marriage, and took me thinking to find me a wife? Is that why you were upset?" I asked finally seeing a larger part of the picture, and a little shocked.

"The other boys are probably wondering why you weren't involved in the selection process earlier, but with Kurt not taking a concubine, it makes it easier to think the nobles were wanting one with the psionic powers. And just in case the thought crossed your mind—no, you may not select a girl for the trip!"

I blushed and started to say something when the baron grabbed me, picked me up and spun me around, "You're a good little kid—come on, let's get something to eat. By the way it looks like you have a page, or at least a servant."

We went back to the hut where our equipment was stacked neatly, and food was being served as we came in. Jakót helped me remove my armor, which felt good to be out of after a day of combat and sweat. The woman who had gotten the equipment and brought it to the hut served the meal and she and the little boy ate with the two noblemen.

I asked the baron, carefully, and hopefully very respectfully, if the woman serving us was one he had selected. I believed, although I didn't say anything, she was a bit old for the baron, but I wasn't sure. He told me no, that he had a wife already, and that they were expecting their second child early that autumn, and looked at me like "Shut up you stupid little snot!" But he didn't say it.

The woman left and the young boy stayed, as if he believed he belonged with the Sir William and myself.

Lord William then saw my surprise, "His family was all killed today, except him. I wasn't joking earlier about you picking up a servant. Since you saved him, you are liable or responsible for him. You've grown up with servants, you know how it works."

"Yes sir, but I've never been responsible for one. I . . . ," I began to stammer trying to find the right words.

"You'll figure it out, and will do fine. Just don't treat him too harshly. You know what it is like to be disciplined. It's bad enough when you did something that you believe you deserve to be punished, but it is hard to take when you don't think you deserve it," the baron said. "Now give him a blanket and point to the bed over there, next to where you are going to sleep, and get to sleep—where I can."

"Before we go to sleep sir, I need to talk to you," I told the baron. Then I explained my nightmare on board the ship. I asked if he thought it might have been a premonition.

We talked a little more about it and he said take the information to the mages and priest—maybe they could find out more about it. Then he said sleep is what every one of us needed.

I got the blanket, pitched it to the child, pointed to the bed, and then went and got in mine. He got in the bed and I heard him whimpering, a low sob. It went on for a minute or two, and then the baron spoke.

"Squire—get your boy quiet, or both of you will have a good reason for tears!"

I went over to the young child, and reached down to hold him in my arms. He was shaking like he was cold, but it was fear. So I held him like Kelvin had held me when I had some nightmares, when I was much younger. I thought how much I missed my older brother and father. Had he been from a psionic family I could have used *rapport* to comfort his, but with him not having that ability, *rapport* was not possible—at least not for me. But I could understand his pain. I just laid beside him, to let him go to sleep, then I could go back to my bed, and sleep.

The next thing I knew the sun was coming in through the window in my eyes, and I was still holding the little boy. My arm was asleep from holding him and I noticed the rest of my body ached from the battle yesterday.

I left him in the bed, and went outside to see how things were going. I saw the baron talking to the three females of the party, over first meal.

"My Lord, may I join you?" I asked as I walked up.

The female squire looked up at me and gave a rude kind of grin and asked, "Did you have a good sleep last night?"

"He slept," the baron replied, somewhat gruffly before I could answer. "Yes, sit down. None of the nobles are selecting wives," he continued looking sternly at the senior squire.

I sat, then looked up, and blushed as I caught the implication of her question. I started to get back up and leave, until a heavy hand from the baron forced me back in my seat.

"I didn't mean offense—only he is a young male. I . . . ," she continued.

The baron broke in to stop the conversation, "That will be enough, just drop it."

I looked down at a plate of food that one of the women brought me, and then started to eat.

"Where's your young servant?" the baron asked.

"He is still asleep. I thought, since he had a pretty rough day yesterday the extra sleep would be good for him," I answered. "Sir, I was thinking. From what I remember being taught about Orcs, they don't like the sun, so why were they attacking during the daylight hours? And it didn't seem to be bothering them at all either?"

Sarah gasped, and then spoke up, "Maybe that is why our *sleep* spells were not as effective as we thought they should have been. These may be more aggressive and a higher breed than what we have always heard about standard Orcs. Wouldn't that be just lovely, a band of Orcs that render our *sleep* to half its normal effectiveness?"

"That might explain a few other things too," the baron said. "How many arrows was it taking to drop one? They were a bit larger than I thought they should have been, but I'd never fought one before. Real combat is a different experience than just studying and training, isn't it?" the baron asked his two squires.

We both nodded and gave a "Yes sir," to the baron's question.

About that time Jakót came up behind me and place his hand on my shoulder. I pointed to where the woman was serving food and motioned for him to go to her. She gave him a bowl and he came and sat on the ground beside me, as the small table was full.

"I thought maybe I just couldn't pull the bow back enough to drop them like Sherry did when she fired at things. It was taking three shots to put one down, with sheaf arrows most of the time." That also might have been why I was not able to affect the Orc with *psionic invisibility*, I thought to myself.

"How many did you kill, my young squire?" the mage asked.

"Six or seven by myself, counting the bow kills, and assisted on several others ma'am," I answered as I went through the battle quickly in my head.

"Well, my young lord, you seem to be a constant surprise: first in a fist fight with a larger squire; and then on the battle field. You are very good," the mage said in an encouraging voice.

The baron looked at me with a slightly surprised expression, then asked the mage, "Have you had a chance to check the Orcian equipment?"

"Yes sir, I knew you would want to know, so I did it the first thing this morning. The bastard sword the big Orc was wielding and a morning star were both enchanted weapons. That was the only magical enchantment I discovered," the mage replied.

"OhmyGod," I exclaimed. "My mother is going to kill me!"

"What's wrong Ray?" the baron asked anxiously.

"Mother was displeased with me for bringing home a stray dog. What's she going to say when I bring Jakót home! She is going to beat me good!" I exclaimed mournfully.

They all laughed, like it was some big joke. But this was serious, I'd have a new horse to train when we get back and wouldn't be able to sit on a saddle. Worse than that, he couldn't speak our language. This was going to get really bad. They kept laughing.

Finally Lord William spoke up, through his tears of laughter, "I'll explain it to your mother, squire. I'll keep the rod off of you for this. I wasn't laughing at your problem, but your expression and shocked look of realization."

The enchanted morning star was given to Mathias, the preist to use, since the squires all were primarily sword users, and one of the senior squires took possession of the magical bastard sword, as that was his primary weapon of choice. Other useful supplies were gathered up, especially the Orcian bows and arrows. The arrows were well made, but the bows might not be as useful, due to their length. Their other weapons were not very good, but still might come in handy if the need was great. Some copper and a small amount of silver coinage was discovered among the Orcs also.

They also packed up everything of value from the village, which wasn't much. The villagers had some small carts and the equipment and supplies were loaded in them, and they constructed another larger wagon to help carry the young and those who would not be able to keep up. Then they put the Orc bodies in one of the huts and torched the village.

The horses that were captured pulled the wagon and carts, so movement was greatly increased. The adults took turn walking and riding so the pace was reasonably quick.

Jakót was still crying every night, and Ray had given up—for the time being—of leaving him alone, mainly due to a promise the baron made about keeping the child quiet. Ray considered leaving him with the others but that made the child wail even louder and carry on. Kurt had a harsh suggestion to keep the child from continuing that behavior, but Ray was loathe to beat the boy for probably being scared. He was too close to similar motivation to want to use it on another.

They returned to the goat path, and slaughtered some goats for fresh meat and then it was decided that they would attempt to herd them back to the city. They would eat part of the garbage generated by the city and provide wool and milk. It might take a while for the herd to grow to any size, but it would be a start. And they had brought no goats with them, and very few sheep.

Herding the goats alone slowed up the process, but it gave something for some of the villagers to do, so that was an added bonus. Ray was just glad he didn't have to tend to them—he thought they stank.

The three spell casters spent a great deal of time with the villagers attempting to teach them the language of the king. It was going to take some time, but it had to be started. Too bad none were powerful enough to cast *tongues*.

The return trip was uneventful With so many noncombatants, that was a great blessing. Those learning the language was starting to make progress, and with the help of Sarah they were able to discover why Jakót was crying at night: the nightmares of seeing his family slain by the Orcs. So he didn't cry every night, and he understood that his actions were likely to get both Ray and himself disciplined. When it got too bad for him, he just moved over to sleep next to the squire for comfort.

The night before they were to reach town Kurt reminded Ray of their appointment for discipline. Ray asked if his actions during the trip might spare him from the discipline promised; he didn't think it would, he just hoped it wouldn't make it worse. Kurt suggested that they might have Sherry observe, where she would know how to discipline one his age. Kurt then suggested they stay with the original plan—which Ray agreed to after hearing Kurt's other idea.

They got back late afternoon the following day. They stored their gear in a barn, and horses, which everyone was excited about. They were almost as exited about the horses as they were with the villagers. Ray's younger brother Cord and Luke were there to meet them, they said his mother would see him when he got to the ship, they were still living there. Ray sent Jakót with them and said he had to take care of some other things and would be home as soon as possible after that. There was to be a reception with the king that evening which they were required to attend, but he would have the chance to clean up and visit for a while first.

Baron Scrope assigned Kurt and Ray the finishing-up detail in the barn, knowing of the discipline that Ray was to receive. This way, not wanting to embarrass his young squire, it could be in private. After everyone else was gone, Kurt talked to Ray and they discussed discipline for other things that Ray had been allowed to get away with. It really wasn't that much, but Ray was getting concerned that Kurt was going to add to the punishment. Kurt let him know that he felt that he did an outstanding job on the trip, and had he not promised the caning he would have considered not giving it to him, but he would not go back on his word. Ray was willing to let him do so, and Kurt told him that their honor would not allow that to be the case, as both had pledged. Kurt said just because he was wearing him out didn't mean he wasn't fond of him. Kurt reminded him, his father had on occasion disciplined him also.

After the discipline was over Kurt waited on the younger squire to regain his composer before leaving with him.

"I know you are in pain, but I still think you're a good kid. I'll see you tonight. By the way, it seems your mother is a healer—she nor your cousin, nor anyone else are to cure those stripes," Kurt reminded him.

"Yes sir, I know the rules sir," Ray told him as they part ways, to go their lodging.

Ray had continued growing on the trip. In the six weeks they were gone he had grown almost two inches, and gained close to fifteen pounds. The extra height made it appear that he had lost weight, and he looked thinner.

Ray got home and found out why his mother wasn't there to meet him. She was obviously pregnant. What Ray had mistaken for weight gain was her being with child.

Chapter Six

Celebration and Learning

"Folly is bound up in the heart of a child, but the rod of discipline will drive it far from him." Proverbs 22: 15

Ray looked in shock at his mother, hardly believing what he was seeing. It was quite apparent to her, Luke, and Megan that Ray had no idea of this when he left.

He started to speak and nothing came out. He plopped in a chair, then quickly stood again, due to his recent discipline with Kurt. He then went, hugged his mother, and started stammering, almost in tears.

She wanted to hear about the mission he was on, the horses, goats, people and what this young boy was doing here. Cord just wanted to know how much trouble he got into.

Just then Sherry and Adam knocked on the door. Megan showed them in and Sherry gave Ray a huge hug.

Ray's mother told him that Sherry had come by to check on her almost every day, and had even helped Cord with some of his page skills. Ray asked Cord how many times he got in trouble with Sherry.

"Luke would you take the two boys out? Maybe you could go down to look at the new horses or something, where I can talk to Mother? I'll fill the details in for you later," I asked my cousin.

Luke was not at all pleased, but realized I needed to have Cord and Jakót gone to talk. Cord was really mad, and I thought he was going to cause a problem.

Sherry snapped at the young page, "Cord, you are a page and expected to follow orders. I realize it's your brother, but it is a reasonable request. Now it's my order, which you must follow, as I'm a senior squire. I don't want you to cause your mother distress over this. Are you going to have to remind you of your manners?"

Cord saluted and walked out with Luke and Jakót was close behind.

"Have you had to remind him of his manners often?" I asked Sherry, with a grin.

"Just once, and if you think that is humorous—maybe you would enjoy a lesson!" she snapped back at me. "Had you acted like that at the time of his discomfort you would have been punished."

"Now children, let us act well and not have an argument the moment Ray returns," Mother said in a calming voice. "Sherry has been a great comfort to me, and assisted in caring for your brother and your younger cousin, as Megan has been given a great deal of responsibility at the infirmary."

Luke knocked and came back in, "Mother was coming and saw me with the boys, she took them—is all right if I get the story on the first telling?"

"Sure, I didn't want to exclude you. There were some things that Cord didn't need to hear or Jakót, not that he would understand much," I told him.

Ray went through the trip giving them the details, and his confusion early on about why they were upset about his age.

His mother was slightly upset, about his being forced to *rapport*, especially with Sarah. Sherry was apologizing for getting him in over his head, she didn't realize age was a consideration.

Ray continued his story. Luke was surprised that Sarah would heal him after having worn his behind out so badly. Luke also thought the fist fight was good, but neither Sherry nor Adam felt much amusement from his action. He asked them if he should have just been beaten senseless, by the older boy, who was trying to take out his frustration on the smallest kid in the camp. He reminded them he had never used his skill on them, even when he thought Adam was about to kill him.

All but Adam seemed surprised at the reason for the mission, when he got to the telling. Adam had already heard from some of the other squires about a rumor of a village, and that potential wives were going to be captured there. He hadn't said anything to Sherry, as it didn't affect them.

All five were impressed with the battle. They were surprised that he was able to accomplish all he did and only get minor bruises. Ray said all the archery practice with Sherry paid off.

Sherry told Ray it was a good thing that he got the caning from Kurt, it would have been a lot worse if she had given it to him. She also told him, he was right, she might have miscounted. Ray wasn't sure if she was joking or not.

Luke excused himself and said he'd leave, to give Ray a chance to rest up before going to dine with the king and give reports to the ministers. The others followed suit and got up to leave. He signaled for Ray to walk with him.

"You want me to heal you from the caning," Luke asked?

Sherry turned kind of pale with his question, but I answered quickly, "Are you crazy? We'd both get a terrible beating if you did that, and Kurt found out. He mentioned you by name, about not healing me."

"You're going to be sore for a while after that one, I thought it might help," Luke told me, really trying to aide me.

"Has it been that long since you got in trouble that you forgot how badly those rods hurt? The beating hurts a lot worse while you are getting it, the lasting pain is bearable, compared to the taking of it," Sherry interrupted.

"Sherry, what would happen if you disciplined a junior squire and gave similar orders and the squire disobeyed?" Adam asked her.

"Well, in Ray's case: you wouldn't be returning home after the banquet. It would be back to the barn, and someone would be sent after the healer too for his part. You'd both get a whipping probably much worse than the original one, and you'd be standing at attention for the night," she said.

"Kurt is also a nobleman, so I don't think he would give us any less than what she said. Not to mention, I think we are going back out to finish the valley. Wouldn't want to have him that mad at me to start with," I told my cousin.

Adam proposed, "Maybe we should have Luke report to Kurt with his suggestion?"

Luke was a bit scared at that prospect, "I'm not one of your squires, that you can order me to do that!"

"I guess Ray will have to report it then, and probably Lord William will get involved," Adam said with a smug grin.

"Sir, please, that won't be necessary," I asked. "He didn't heal me, I said no, it was just a test."

Adam looked at me sternly, and said, "You will inform Kurt this evening of the request. You may also inform him that you declined the invitation for curing."

I looked at Sherry for support, but none came. I wanted to plead with Adam about the order, but before I could say anything else he made it really clear there would not be any change. "You will do as ordered. If you ask another question on this matter, you and I will take a walk to a barn to make sure your manners are in excellent condition. You might have forgotten some with the trek into the wilderness, and playing like you're fifteen!"

Sometimes strict rules for behavior can be very difficult on what is thought to be inappropriateness, even if nothing happened. I was concerned that I could get in trouble for my cousin just asking to cure me!

"Yes sir," was all I could say. "May I be excused to return to my apartments?"

He waved me off, and I turned to go. I heard Sherry suggest to Luke that it might be much easier on me, if he were to inform Kurt of his mistake.

I got cleaned up and then fell asleep on my stomach. I awoke and found Jakót asleep beside me. Cord was sitting on the other bed, reading.

"Hey kid," I said to him, "how long have you been back?"

"About an hour. Mother said you'd just gone to bed when we got here, Sis went to duty, and I was surprised you were asleep already. I think you got me in trouble with Sherry," Cord told me.

"I don't think you're in trouble. Hold on a moment, let me check on Mother, I'll be right back. Then I'll tell you about the expedition—if I have time," I told him as I got up.

Beth and Caroline were there visiting her. I hugged my aunt and cousin. I checked on the time, and then ask Caroline if she would like to hear while I was telling Cord about the adventure. She said she would, so I had her get Cord quietly and return. While she was out, I told Mother I would tell them an edited version of what happened, leaving out the primary purpose of the trip.

They felt that would be fine and would enjoy hearing the tale from me. As the two came back in, Mother told Cord he was to help Jakót perform the page duties for me this evening, explaining what I would need for the formal dress affair.

"Mother what will I wear—I've grown enough that my formal clothes won't fit!" I exclaimed. "I can't go in what I wore last August; I've grown three or four inches since then." I was starting to panic.

"Beth, will you go get the seamstress? I brought some of Kelvin's clothes for such a circumstance. There in the bottom of the chest—still packed neatly. Go get them and we'll see which pants are the closest and what needs to be done. Children, I'm afraid Ray will have to tell you the story another time. Caroline, put the iron on the stove and put some more wood in so they can look nice."

I got the clothes from the bottom of the chest. There were two sets of clothes: a light-blue set of trousers and jacket, and one in gold. I so hoped the light blue would fit. Mother always told me the blue colors made me more handsome, and set off the blue in my eyes. Gold would have been Kelvin's favorite, and probably Cord's too.

Both sets of clothing were too large but the blues would be closer and easier to make fit. While the seamstress was working on the clothes, I told my brother and cousin the story of our trip, just leaving a few things out that they didn't need to hear or how much trouble I stayed in. I did tell them about getting a whipping from the baron I knew Cord would want to know I didn't do everything perfect. I know how hard is living up to an older brother that seemed to have done no wrong.

The clothes were just a bit big still, but close enough to look good still, and there was not much time to spare as I got dressed with the assistance of Cord and Jakót. He was starting to pick the language up a little and he and Cord were going to work on it that evening while I was out.

The great hall was going to have to be made of wood for a long time. Too many other projects would require stone and workers to make it a stone building. As I walked up, I spotted Kurt.

I saluted, which he returned, and said, "The squire is reporting as ordered, sir."

"I did not order you to report to me," he said, as he appeared to be looking for someone else—Sarah, I guessed.

"Yes sir, another senior ordered me to sir," I told him.

I explained what had happened with Luke, and he told me Luke had already been to see him. He also let me know how fortunate I was that I had turned down Luke's request. It would have been shameful to have bled down the back of the uniform I was wearing. Sarah had taken Luke to see Ayrus, the person in charge of the healers, and he will be disciplined tomorrow—probably by Sarah, Kurt informed me.

"Let's get off the subject of you being in trouble. That uniform looks good on you, was it your brother's? Surely none of your dress clothes are going to fit you as much as you've grown this spring, and for sure since we left?" Kurt asked.

"Yes sir," I answered glad to change the subject, as I saw Sarah walking up behind us.

Sarah startled Kurt when she began to speak, "You and I will report to the school area for the healers tomorrow at seven, and you will discipline Ray's cousin for his action. That way the discipline will occur before the students arrive, as Luke has been assisting with the instruction—he is not to be embarrassed in front of the students, but it is all right if he wants to stand all day."

"I would have thought that one of the healers would have caned him for this," Kurt said. "Normally isn't that the case? Beside I'm not enough older than he is to discipline him."

"Yes, but you are to do it since it was your discipline he was attempting to undermine. Are you taking the baby for another one also?" Sarah said nodding toward me.

"No, he acted correctly," Kurt answered. "I'll let him off this time—but it is a good thing he quickly turned down the offer.

"Are the two of you planing on getting married?" I interjected wanting to change the subject.

"Probably, and I knew you weren't in trouble. I just wanted to make you squirm a bit," Sarah said and tossed her raven black hair, that was tied long behind her, to the side.

I thought she was somewhat sadistic to be a healer, but decided that saying it would have me in additional pain, so I kept quiet about it.

"Do you have something you wish to say—child?" she asked in a taunting voice.

"Leave him alone—and let's go in," Kurt said.

Sarah then shocked me with a nice compliment, "You know kid, the difference between you and the rest of the kids your age is that you handle yourself much more maturely than they do. I give you a tough time, but for the young snot that you are, you are much better than the others, much closer to Kurt's age, than kids your age."

As we went in, I wanted to quickly excuse myself, to get away from Sarah. She seemed to take great enjoyment out of goading me, but she asked me about Mother.

"My mother is with child, I mean she's having a baby—I didn't know it when we left. How did it happen so quickly?" I questioned.

"I know you're young, but surely not that naive," she remarked, somewhat surprised at my statement.

"No, I meant, well isn't she a little old to be having a baby? If my brother had lived, he would have probably had a child," I said.

"Healers can help in becoming pregnant, using *cell adjustment*. Didn't you know that?" Sarah asked.

"I hadn't thought about it at all. Can they determine if it is a boy or a girl," I questioned?

"You come with me, time for a quick lesson. Kurt, you too," she ordered.

"Sarah, what did I do, am I in trouble for something?" I asked.

"No, just both of you come with me," she told us.

They went into a small room off the great hall and she explained that through *cell adjustment* a healer could help one to conceive a child. A healer was not able to determine the gender of a child, but could improve probability of having one. Ray's mother knew how dangerous his father's role would be, and wanted another child.

Sarah got on to Ray for not being more observant, and aware of what was going on around him. To be so smart he surely was dumb sometimes. But then, she remembered how young he was and just smiled. She enjoyed picking on him—sometimes.

Ray said he resented being called dumb, it just was a little out of the ordinary for one his mother's age to be with child.

She had never talked about it and he had been kept pretty busy since leaving home.

Sarah gave him a hug and said it was okay, she didn't mean to hurt his feelings, but she understood why Sherry thought highly of such a young squire. Ray told them he just wished his sister thought so.

They went back to the great hall, began to visit with the others there, and give information about the expedition. Many of the older members of court seemed very impressed with Ray's exploits in the battle. They also wondered why no one questioned his age before they left, since it seemed now they all knew how old he really was.

Thomas came by and asked him point-blank how old he was. He was surprised how well Ray pulled off his junior status. "Torin might like to discuss your manners with you again," Thomas suggested.

Ray thought he saw Charissa, but then decided he must have been mistaken, because when he looked where he thought she was, she wasn't there. He was hoping to see her, since the last message from her was at the send-off dinner. He continued to visit and receive many compliments for both his work on the mission and his part of saving the child which turned out to be a boon in the working out arrangement with the villagers. Several of the advisers asked him to repeat the episode where he saved the baron.

Then all of a sudden she was standing beside him in lovely golden gown, that he decided was very nice on her. The ruby tiara added contrast to the gown and her hair, which was tied in a long single braid down to the small of her back. She smiled and he again was struck dumb at seeing her. Then she grabbed his hand.

"Come on," she told me.

"Where are we going? I thought I saw you earlier and then you disappeared," I responded and followed her.

"I changed gowns, this one goes better with yours—and just come on," she said.

We went to the end of the great hall, and she told me that she wanted to kiss me. I was terrified. "We can't, we'll both get in trouble and Lord William will murder me for it. The king will have you punished too. I don't want to get you in trouble," I said in a blur of speech.

"You don't want to kiss me?" she asked as her lip started to quiver.

"Yes I want to, but we better wait for another time, please don't cry," I implored.

"Okay, but come with me to see the king," she ordered.

The king had not come into the hall, and guards were posted at the doors where she was leading. I did not think I should go, but as we approached they moved aside and opened the door. She pulled me in behind her.

King Harold was sitting at a desk looking over something—I think it was a map; when we came in. Charissa went up to him, he stood up, and picked her up and hugged her affectionately. She started to talk to him, "You were right, grandfather, he wouldn't kiss me."

I thought I was going to die, or that he would call for guards to take me to my execution. I wanted to talk, but nothing would come out. There I was a thirteen-year-old kid, and I was in the presence of my king—and I was going to be killed, and my head put on a pike.

"I see the son of one my most trusted nobleman has some intelligence to go with his youth," the king said looking at me, and putting Charissa back down on the floor. "So you don't want to kiss my granddaughter?"

"No you highness, I mean yes your highness, I wanted to, but had been told not to do so by both of our fathers in August, your highness . . . ," I stammered. Oh, I felt like a complete fool. "What did I do, God to deserve this?" I thought to myself.

"Well you may kiss her if you like, now. You have Our permission," the king told me. "But should We hear that you tell—well, you figure it out."

So I kissed her with the king looking on.

It was grand. I guess neither of us really knew what we were doing, but it was delicious.

"May Ray sit next to me at the dinner, please," she asked?

"Yes darling, but don't get him in trouble with his knight. A young squire must obey his knight, and Lord William will expect things of him," the king said as she dragged me back to the hall. At least this time it was at a reasonable pace.

"Your highness, would you grant me the privilege of escorting you back to the hall?" I asked, I thought very formally. Then I extended her my arm to escort her in a stately fashion.

"I believe the results of that kiss will be much less painful than our first kiss," she told me as we reentered the dining hall.

"It was more enjoyable also, since both of us were trying," I said with a slight grin. "Come on, I'll introduce you to my companion on the expedition. What do you know about it?"

"We can discuss that later. I would like to meet those that accompanied you, especially your knight," she said.

I took her to meet those that were already there, and I could spot. Finally I took her to meet Kurt and Sarah.

"Oh Sarah, it is good to see you made it back safely. I wondered if you'd be all right. I'd hate to have lost you," Charissa began as we walked up to the pair.

"I see you know Sarah already, this is senior squire Kurt, ah . . . ," I stammered not sure how to proceed. "Should I tell the princess that you are engaged?" I shot a quick mental message in *rapport* to Kurt, which shocked him.

"You may," was his mental message. "Aren't we being brave with this?"

"Didn't want Sarah to have you take me back to the barn," I replied.

"They recently decided on being engaged, or getting married, I'm not sure of the proper way to express it, your highness," I concluded after the brief pause on mental contact.

Sarah looked up, realizing something had taken place, but not certain what. She thought it might have been *rapport*, but knowing how much I had been afraid of it, and not the thing normally done in front of royalty—she wasn't sure.

"Sarah has been one of the teachers for healers this year. She has done an excellent job in my instructions. Oh and by the way, Ray, girls mature quicker than boys. So just because you weren't able to *rapport* at my age, doesn't mean that I don't recognize it!" Charissa reprimanded me.

"Please forgive me your highness, I did not wish to make mistake in saying something about the wedding, and have my elders upset with me. *Rapport* is not something I do lightly and there was some conflict with that on our trip," I said hoping my error in manners would not cost me serious disciplinary pain.

"We heard your question, remember We had hold of your arm," she replied, using the royal plural, looking sternly at me. "But you are forgiven this time, and pardoned also. Kurt, you are not to take action against Ray for this slight in protocol—this time."

"You're most generous and forgiving, your highness. Still, young squires sometimes have difficulty with their manners, and require reminders. Might it not be better for him to be reminded of these? Warriors don't always remember without assistance," Sarah told her.

"No, Sarah, it is Our wish that he not be punished this time, should We require his manners to be improved, We have many at Our beck and call to see to it," Charissa stated in an order.

"Might I speak with the junior squire for a moment your highness?" Kurt asked. "You and Sarah might catch up on how your training is progressing."

Kurt and I walked away a short distance, and then he verbally chastised me for my actions. "Of all the stupid things to pull. As scared of *rapport* as you act, and you do it with the princess on your arm . . . You'd better be glad that she made it an order not to discipline you or I would . . . No, I'd inform the baron and let him tear you up. I still can't believe you did that."

"Kurt, I didn't know she was already psionically aware. She is just eleven; people I know don't become aware until sometime after their twelfth birthday. I didn't want Sarah mad at me about your getting married—but I guess I messed up that idea too," I said. I was hurt at Kurt's anger at me, even though I knew I deserved it. The princess had saved my backside that time, and she knew I was in trouble.

We went back and the princess and I continued to move about the room introducing each other to those we met. As we were going along, she started talking, "You see I'm not as young as you think. You'd better be extremely nice to me, or I might change my mind about keeping you out of trouble for your rude behavior."

"Your highness, I meant no disrespect, I was just . . . ," I started when she cut me off.

"I know what you were doing, but I would refrain from doing it again. I second poor judgement like that and I won't be able to keep you from a harsh caning. And that would spoil my evening," she told me. "It wouldn't do much for yours either," she giggled.

The food was very good. Some of the mages had used their spells to add spice to the food, and some of the early spring crops were already providing fresh food. During the meal Charissa kept teasing with me, and making lovely conversation. I hope I wasn't a total boor, but I enjoyed just listening to her. I mean, considering how young she is.

After the food was served each of us on the trip were to tell part of the story. I was allowed to go early in the order, and tell my viewpoint of the battle. Then Charissa and I were to be dismissed. I would escort her with some guards, to view the horses and goats while matters that she didn't need to hear about at her age were to be discussed.

The king had arranged that with the baron earlier and he passed the information to me, that the princess was not to know of the original reason for going to the village. He also let me know that Kurt had informed him of my mistake in manners, which would be discussed in the morning. I asked if Kurt had also told him what the princess said about not being disciplined. He said he would take that into consideration, at seven in the morning, at the stables.

When I finished telling what I had to tell, the King suggested that we might leave, and they would finish talking over the details. Therefore; his granddaughter might spend some time with someone nearer her age, and not in a room of adults.

As I pulled out Charissa's chair and began to escort her from the table, Lord William stopped us. "Your highness, wasn't there another matter you were going to make known before dismissing my young squire?"

"Oh yes, thank you Lord William. Ray, son of Kelric, Marquis of Retúpmoc for actions against the Orcs at the village you are hereby given the status of senior squire, with **most** of the privileges and responsibilities of that office. There are certain limitations, which your knight, Lord William, will discuss with you on the morrow. Congratulations Ray, come back up here, and receive your new sash.

I was in shock as Charissa moved me back toward the king and gave a slight pressure on my arm to remind me to kneel, as I removed the red sash of a junior squire, and was given a new red sash with gold trim—one of a senior squire.

"Your squire is most grateful, and always at your command, your highness," I managed to say in a somewhat correct tone.

He then raised me to my feet and Charissa and I left the hall. Just before we passed the second hall she motioned for the guards to wait a moment, pulled me behind the door and gave me the most wonderful kiss I had ever received. "I've been wanting to do that, but I decided that during dinner it might not be considered good manners, and you were already in some trouble for your manners, didn't want to get you in any more," she told me. Then waved to the guards to come.

The night air was lovely and a bit chilly, so Charissa hung onto me for warmth—not that I minded. The stars were more beautiful and bright than I could ever remember, and the dual moons were extremely brilliant and lovely. We walked and talked and occasionally she gave me another kiss. Then she asked why I never attempted to start the kiss. I told her she was the princess and I didn't want to seem forward and inappropriate. She let me know that she hoped I would demonstrate some of the initiative that had served me well during the battle in the rest of the walk.

We leaned against a door frame to the barn and I kissed her a long, slow, extremely enjoyable kiss. And we hugged so hard I was afraid I might break her. She told me she wouldn't break when I released the hug—I guess she read my mind. Then one of the guards, which I had forgotten about, suggested that we should start walking back. It was a lovely slow walk holding hands, her wearing my coat due to the cold. I felt ever so much older than when the evening started.

As we got back, we kissed goodnight, and she said as I turned to leave, "Next time I'll teach you about holding a girl when you kiss."

"How do you know so much about this subject your highness?" I asked starting to feel jealous.

"I've talked to some of the serving ladies," she said, pitching my coat to me, and quickly went inside.

I think I floated back to the boat. I wanted to talk to Mother so badly, but wouldn't wake her. I was afraid she would need her rest too much. It could wait until the morning. Then I remembered I was to meet with the baron. That took a sizeable chunk of my feeling of happiness knowing what might happen with him in the morning.

The next morning, I quickly and quietly got dressed, and made my way to stables, merely leaving Mother a note as to where I had gone.

Since the baron was not there, I curried my palomino, and talked with him awhile. I put a saddle on him to allow him to get use to the feel of a saddle on his back. He was still too young for me to ride, not that I wanted to after Kurt's discipline.

"Ray, I'm glad you were not late this morning," the baron's voice bringing back to my reason for being in the stable so early.

"Yes sir," I replied and quickly moved to him.

"Kurt informed me of your lapse in manners last night, with the princess. I'm more than slightly surprised with your actions. I know what you think about *rapport*, yet you jumped into it with the princess, and unknowingly involved her," the baron did not sound pleased. "What have you to say for yourself?"

"I was attempting to avoid a lapse in manners with Sarah and Kurt—about their wedding. I wasn't sure if I could inform the princess, so I attempted to overcome my fear of *rapport*, and asked Kurt if it would be all right to tell her. And made a ah ah . . . I can't think what the term is—but I made an error in protocol."

"Yes you did, and the king heard about it also!"

I wanted to dig a hole and crawl in and pull the dirt back over the top of me. I wondered if he heard about our kissing from the guards, or maybe Charissa had told him! I wonder if I did it right?

"What have you to say for yourself?" the baron asked.

"There is nothing I can say, sir. My manners were at fault, and I will have to accept the consequences of my mistakes, sir," I responded knowing that two whippings within two days time would really have me in pain—again. I moved to lean over the saddle, expecting a severe caning.

"The princess pardoned your actions and the king asked me to honor that request this time, so my young squire, you may get up. You're pretty lucky, considering the pain you're probably already in from Kurt's discipline," the baron told me.

I couldn't believe it. I just knew he was going to wear me out good. Probably the worse beating I would have ever had. And I wasn't going to get one. This was starting to be a great day.

"Thank you sir," I managed.

"Don't thank me, son. I was ready to have blood running down your back end before I finished with you. But I guess it will be easier for you to function in class without another whipping. Oh, that reminds me. You need to report to classes while we are back—you may be a bit behind in some of studies. I'll give you a pass that says you are to report at nine, since you'll need to go back and change."

"Yes sir," I quickly responded.

"Oh and regarding your senior squire status, you may not discipline another squire on your own, unless you have the three years on them," the baron stated, giving the information the king told me to expect.

"Oh, that means I can't discipline most of the pages, because I'm not three years older than they are," I said almost laughing.

"I guess that does eliminate any squire, wouldn't it?" the baron said realizing what was meant with the age. "Well, you still could if directed by someone else who had the authority, like an instructor. And you don't have to announce it. The main thing the senior status does, is it keeps a senior from exercising their authority to bust your butt. Since a senior can't discipline another senior, it will keep some of the older bullies from trying to make a point at your expense. I understand you may have a couple who would like to beat the tar out of you."

"Yes sir—a couple at least," I responded.

"Go get ready for your classes," he told me and gave me a slight push toward the door.

"Sir, may I still have an Orcian bow for Sherry and dagger for my brother and sister? I asked after the battle, but didn't get them yet. "They would make a nice souvenir," I said.

"Sure, they are still in the cart. Good thing you asked today, this morning they will put them in a storage room at the armory," the baron told as he walked to the cart.

I grabbed a good-looking bow and a couple of mean jagged daggers and took off, back to the ship's apartment. I got there shortly before Cord was leaving for weapons class with swords. I showed Mother and Megan what I had and asked if it would be okay to give it to Cord before he left, and gave Megan her dagger.

He was so excited, maybe the most I'd ever seen him. He put it in the sheath to take to class, and then he noticed the sash I had on. His eyes got big again.

"Ray, you've got on a senior squire's sash. You get mixed up with somebody?" he asked.

Mother looked up, concern was in her eyes.

"No kid, and I didn't steal it either. The king gave it to me for the work on the mission. I think it was the baron's idea—to keep me out of trouble with the older squires. Also he said it would allow me to keep some of the younger kids in line easier," I told him and gave him a hard look.

"MOTHER," Cord almost cried, "Ray's picking on me!"

"No, he isn't, and won't," mother assured him. "Now you better run along to your class or you'll be across a saddle."

"I've got to change and go to class also. I hadn't thought about that, but the baron informed me I better get after it. May I leave a little early and take the bow to Sherry?" I asked.

"I want to hear about the senior squire sash," she told me. "Besides Sherry will have already left—she is helping with Cord's training, she told me."

"Mother, the senior status is mainly to keep the older squires from trying to find an excuse to discipline me, when I beat them in something or while I'm on duty with the baron. The baron didn't realize how young I was, and doesn't want his squire having to deal with some of the petty things."

"What about the boy?" she asked.

"He can stay and clean the apartment—whatever you need him to do. Do you think you can make him understand?" I asked.

"Probably, but you need to try to communicate that he is to stay before you leave," she told me.

Jakót was making his bed and I attempted to make him understand that he was to stay, but I was leaving. I felt like I had gotten through to him, and he was making the other beds as I left.

I took the bow to where Sherry was teaching the class. She noticed the sash before she noticed the bow, and was about ready to remind me how inappropriate that was, before I was able to convince her of the king's awarding me the status. She was really happy for me and wanted to talk that evening if we could. That was great, I told her but I had to hurry to class. I'd hate to get a caning my first day of class as a senior—wouldn't be a good example for the other squires.

I reported to a battle field cartography class. This was where we studied maps of a battle field to understand advantages in use of the land for a battle, and help in understanding the positioning of troops. I didn't recognize the instructor, nor did he know me.

"May I help you?" the instructor asked as I walked toward him.

"I have been told to report here, sir," I answered.

"You must have the wrong time, this class is mainly for first year junior squires, most of the senior squires are assisting in the teaching of pages at this time," he told me.

There was some snickering in around the map table, as the other kids recognized who I was, and some surprised expressions that I was in a senior squire's sash.

"Sir, this is class I should be with, these other students are the ones I've always been in class with. I was given senior squire status, due to my accomplishments in the recent mapping expedition—where we brought back the new horses and other things," I informed the instructor.

"Well, a sword is not appropriate in this setting, please remove it. And why are you late in arriving?" he asked me, not sounding very happy to see me.

"Might I speak with you privately—for just a moment sir?" I asked believing a small amount of extra information might help remove some problems?

"Sir, as a senior squire the king's law requires me to carry my sword. And I need your assistance with this study, as I'm already behind these other students in the study. And I really am their age—thirteen, sir," I attempted to explain.

"Well I assume it will be all right—at least for the day, but I'll check on this. And should you attempt to disrupt this class you will be disciplined like any other student in class," the instructor said with a sour look on his face.

The class went passable after that, but I felt like he was watching me for some type of poor behavior. I rarely got into trouble in class, and it had been a very long time since a classroom problem got a leather strap used on me, and then a second set from my father when I got home that evening. I might get in trouble dealing with some of the older kids, but in the classroom I was a very good student.

It was good to see my friends again, and the next study for that class was mental exercises and combat theory. It was difficult, since most of us did not have any options on our mental attacks or defenses. But the instructor knew me and congratulated me for the new status. He also used the attack on the Orcs to start the discussion, and how our mental skills could be used to assist our friends.

We went to the mess hall for lunch, and I had to tell—well, maybe got to tell them, about the combat in greater details. Some of the other squires came over to let me know they were surprised to find out my age—and let me know they would welcome me to eat with them, should I wish. Most of my friends were intimidated by the older squires, especially the seniors, and I wanted to be around them—and probably be a bit silly with them.

I got word during lunch to report to Lord William in the great hall, when I finished eating. I gulped down the last of meal and double-timed it to my knight.

He asked me how the classes went, and what the other kids thought about my being given senior status. I told him the other kids were great, but the map class wasn't going well; the instructor didn't seem to want me there.

We discussed the situation, and the baron said he would speak to him, and if it was to be a problem he would move me.

I let him know that I didn't believe I could go with another group, because they would be too far advanced for me. The baron felt the instructor might not want to deal with seniors because he didn't deal with battle field strategies as much as just map making. He might have thought I was there to challenge his teaching abilities.

I let the baron know also that the squires I was with were doing sword practice this afternoon, hoped that I might be placed with an older group for that skill lesson. I hadn't been with them since Christmas on the ships.

He then showed me the map that he had done while we were on the mission. It gave me the chance to practice reading one, and he wanted to know if I saw anything out of place or maybe thought of something left out. It looked good to me, except the village might be a little further down the river than he had it, but I wasn't sure. Xell had said the same thing, he told me.

He put some markers on the map to show me the other side of the map, to show me what still needed to be mapped. The king's staff did not believe the rest of the valley would hold any threat, but wanted to know what was there. He was preparing a follow up expedition, and most of those who went last time—were . . . occupied. So we would be getting a new group. Jennifer, the female senior squire would be going again, as would Xell, the mage. He asked who might be some of the others <u>we</u> would select.

"Sherry can't go," the baron told me before I could say anything else.

"Richard, the senior squire that worked with Sherry and I on the ship. What about Adam, Sherry's husband? How many suggestions do you want?" I asked.

"We probably need one more younger senior, it would be better if he has psionic skills—just in case," he answered.

"Aaron is one of the few that I know, and believe he would be good to work with. He was promoted after we returned from the quarry expedition ans his sixteenth birthday. I know some others, but would prefer not have them. If my lord would not mind," I hoped he would not choose some of those who had it in for me.

"I don't know Aaron, but Richard and Adam will do well. I'll see what Richard knows about Aaron. How well do you know him?" Lord William asked.

"Well enough sir. We worked on the ship together, and on the quarry expedition. He's also one of the older squires that helped Sherry with my manners one time on board ship, when she didn't want me to get a whipping, but believed I needed some rougher treatment. Aaron was tough on me, but not mean or too excessive," I informed him, "and stood by me in a little problem with James on the quarry trip. What about my cousin Luke, for the healer? He is supposed to be good, even though he is young, and he even served in the war."

"I'll consider your cousin. He is a bit younger than I would prefer, and not quite as powerful as Sarah, but there are not a lot of choices with healers. I'm trying to get Mathias to go with us again, but he does not seem interested. I may have to get someone over him to order him. Don't tell your cousin about this or the possibility of his going. That is an order! Do you understand me?" he asked.

"Yes sir," I responded. "But Luke might surprise you. He saw action in the war, before we left. He served almost a year, instead of going to train. He may have as much skill as Sarah," and he's a lot easier for me to get along with, I thought. "What about junior squires, I know many of them much better?" I volunteered.

"I'll get with the seniors first and see if they have any they want to take, and besides I would prefer fourteen and fifteen year olds, to the twelve and thirteen year olds that you would know. "We will be leaving a week from today.

"Now for training this afternoon—you want to work on jousting?" he asked with a grin?

"No sir," I said, shaking my head.

"I thought you might be a bit too tender from Kurt's discipline to want to sit on a horse. Report to the city gate—there is a group of seniors working with swords there. Work with them, and let the instructor know that you were attending me, and not dismissed until late to get to the lesson. If he has a problem, he is to see me before disciplining you. You're dismissed," Lord William told me.

"Yes sir, thank you sir," I said and hurried to the gates for the training. My first sword practice as a senior. I was excited—finally I would be training with the students, without worrying about their age causing me problems with discipline.

"Hold up," the baron yelled as I was going through the door.

I hurried back to see what the change in orders were.

"If Aaron is in the group that you are going to—send him here. If not I'll get with Richard and then send for him if needed. Don't mention to anyone that we are going or when. I guess you can tell Adam or Richard to report to me if you see them. I'll be here most of the day," he told me.

"Yes sir," I answered and left again.

I was thinking about the change in orders as I left, and was not as careful where I was walking . . . That smell would make everyone happy to see me! I hoped it would be all off before I got to the gates.

———————

Ray hurried along to the city gates, and as he was exiting the city he saw Richard, who was working with the group of junior squires that he would have been working with, had he not been allowed to work with the seniors. Ray quickly went over to them, and formally gave Richard the orders that he was to report to the baron.

Richard congratulated him and told him he heard he did a good job. Ray told him the baron wasn't too happy with his recommendation, when he found out how young he was.

Richard asked if that was what the meeting was about, and Ray told him probably not, but if it was, it wouldn't be the first time he got the senior in trouble, and then left him wondering. He wouldn't have dared to leave Richard like that as a junior squire, but he knew he could get away with it as a senior. He liked that feeling.

There weren't many senior squire groups. Ray found both Adam and Aaron in the group he'd been sent to.

Again the instructor was not pleased to have a late arrival, and was both insulting and rude.

"I don't need some newly located, undersized squire, who doesn't know his father interrupting the training that we are doing here."

Several of the boys, knowing who Ray was, gasped at the instructor's comment. The instructor was not noble, nor was he a spectacular fighter himself.

Ray turned red, and was working to control his tempter. Had this not been an instructor, Ray would have challenged him right then and there.

Aaron told Adam to grab Ray, and they both moved quickly to prevent him from reacting too rashly.

———————

"Let me go, Adam," I said turning and looking at him with fire in my eyes, "I'm noble which requires you to unhand me!"

"So am I," Aaron interrupted, "and he is under my compulsion. Are you going to act sanely?"

"Yes, now let go of me!" I demanded.

Then turning to the instructor, "I'm Ray, the son of Kelric, Marquis of Retúpmoc," I informed him through gritted teeth, "and heir to the title! If you don't get on your knees and apologize I'll report this to the king!"

"Lord Kelric's oldest son is dead, and the second is not near old enough to be a senior squire, if even a squire," the instructor said in a laughing voice.

I turned on my heels and started away.

I guess some of the other squires quickly told him who I was, so he came after me and begged my forgiveness, as I commanded.

Then he ordered me back to class. I suggested that I needed some time to cool down. He reminded me that he had followed my instructions, and now that I was assigned to his class, I would follow his or suffer the consequences of my actions, which would not involve a cool down.

I went back to the class, still extremely mad, and almost barked at Aaron and Adam, "Lord William will see the two of you—after the training session. He will be in the great hall!" I *might* have left the impression that it was for grabbing me moments earlier.

"Well, let's see what our new class member is capable of," the instructor said in a malicious tone, "James, you two will spar—so I can determine his ability level." I think he finally put things together and had an idea about me.

James was the one who had insulted Sherry, and I backed down looking for a quarry. He was much larger than I was. "Yes sir, I would be glad to aid in the evaluation of our little friend."

As I was getting ready and testing the wooden training weapons, and selecting a shield, Adam came to me, and reminded me that I had better not use psionic against him. "Too many will know something happened, and Lord William will beat you worse than James possibly could in this practice."

"Thanks for the vote of confidence," I snapped back.

"I hope I'm not too much larger than the new boy," James was saying with a slight laugh, "I'd hate to see him get injured."

"You're about a foot shorter than any of the six Orcs I recently KILLED, and probably not much dumber—so I hope you are at least a challenge," I replied and made an obscene gesture, that only he could notice.

The effects were as I suspected. He made a bull's charge, hoping both to intimidate me and crush me. I ducked under the charge and caught the older squire in the small of the back—where his armor provided very little protection. Not hard enough to knock the air out of him, but enough to really piss him off. He caught me with his shield on the way by.

He came back toward me with murder in his eyes. I heard one of the other squires yelling for him to let me have it, and another telling the instructor he might should stop it. He approached a lot more cautiously this time, as I twirled my sword around in my hand, something Lord William had shown me. This was to keep his attention on the moving sword, and less on other things I was trying to set up. As James moved closer I feinted with the sword, and caught him on the side of his head with my shield. This staggered him, so I used a quick sword slice, which was blocked by his shield, as he was going back. Another sword thrust was parried, and he was starting to regain his balance. I pressed the attack, and feinted again with the sword and again landed a solid blow with my shield, as he struck my shield arm with his sword. I then was able to swing with all my strength and got under his shield and caught him the stomach hard enough to knock the breath out of him, even with armor. Then a hard overhand stroke caught him on the top of the head—this broke my wooden sword and rendered him unconscious.

The other squires and the instructor stood there for a moment in surprise, and then ran to check on James. Adam and Aaron came over to me, to congratulate me on the exhibition.

"Just remind the instructor that it might have been him, had the two of you not grabbed me earlier in class," I stated still breathing hard. "I didn't have a wooden sword at that time, remember!"

"You wouldn't have attacked him really—would you?" Adam asked in disbelief.

"I didn't say that, I just asked you to remind him. Let him draw his own conclusions."

The instructor sent one of the other squires for a healer. Two others began to carry James in the same direction. After they came back the class discussed the combat and why James was defeated by a smaller opponent. Aaron's comment ended the discussion and started everyone else thinking.

"He got beat by a superior opponent. Ray has been in more combats than any of us, and just might be better than his size indicates."

As we were leaving, I asked why Sherry wasn't here, and Adam said she was working extra with the bow. Then he went over to the instructor, as he and Aaron preparing to go to report to Lord William. He pointed to me and said something then they walked off, the instructor became somewhat pale, as I ran to catch up with the two older squires.

"Would you inform Lord William I'll be working with my colts, should he require me for anything? Adam, what did you tell the instructor that scared him?" I asked.

"What are we your lordship's messenger service?" Adam asked somewhat sarcastically. "Yes, I'll give him the message—just like I delivered yours to the instructor!"

I went to the barn, mainly to see my colt, but also to massage my shoulder. I'd hurt it in the combat earlier, I just didn't want anyone to know. On the way over I saw Luke and went to talk to him, and I ask him to look at the shoulder. I was hoping he might use his *cell adjustment* to remedy the pain and the bruise I was going to have.

"What are you doing in that sash?" Luke almost exploded. "Are you crazy? You'll really be in trouble if someone catches you."

I forgot I hadn't seen him yet to tell him the news. "I got senior status for my part in the expedition—last night from the king. I didn't know it was going to happen and haven't had the chance to talk with you," I told him quickly. Then I mentioned a little bit more of what happened but not enough to get me in trouble, just to make him wonder.

I told him about what kind of day I had trying to get some training done. It was tough with the instructors being hostile.

He immediately reminded me how his day started with Kurt—I agreed his might have been worse, with that type of start.

"Will you heal my shoulder? I think I'm going to need full use tomorrow if I have sword practice again. I wish you could just teach me how to do *cell adjustment*, it would come in handy," I said, knowing only healers seemed able to develop that devotion.

"Sure I'll be glad to show you how, it won't make any difference, but I'll show you anyway," Luke said laughing.

"Come on in the barn and take your shirt off and let's take a look at the shoulder first."

The bruise was much worse than I thought, and Luke was impressed how I managed not to say anything to anyone about the injury. He told me it would take a moment or so to heal that deep a bruise.

"Can I watch your mind curing, using *rapport*, while you're curing me?" I asked.

"Sure, I can't do *rapport* and *cell adjust* at the same time so you'll have to bring up *rapport*. I don't know what that will show you, since you're not a healer. But that's how some of us learn the devotion," my cousin told me.

I watched through his mind as he began to send his mind through my body to the injured area. Then his mind began to mend the battered portion of my shoulder and force the blood to move along. The swelling went down. It was very interesting, I dropped the *rapport*, and tried to move my mind through him like he had done. My mind found an injured area and began to cure it—just like he had done. All of a sudden Luke yelled and jumped away.

"What in the world are you doing? You can't do that," he hollered and jumped about!

"What are you talking about? I was just thinking about what you were doing," I said, somewhat confused.

"You're going to have to report yourself to Kurt! How did you learn that?" he questioning, and still not making sense to me.

"Slow down—I don't understand what you're talking about." I was getting a bit concerned with his carrying on, and some of the others who worked in the stable area were coming to see what the commotion was about.

"You were healing me!" Luke exclaimed.

Chapter Seven

Returning to the Valley

"'The land we passed through and explored is
exceedingly good.'" Numbers 14: 7

The two young noble cousins sat in the barn. Luke was healing his younger cousin from the bruises and sore muscles from the strenuous training the younger boy had been through. Facing larger opponents, even when one is better trained, can be a painful learning experience.

"You were healing me!" he repeated. "Do you understand how rare that is for one of our kind to be able to do that, and not be a healer?"

"I don't understand. What do you mean I was healing you?" I asked in unbelief.

"You know what I offered to heal you from yesterday, and got in trouble for? You just did it for me," Luke told me still in having a difficult comprehending what had transpired.

"Oh CRAP! Kurt is going to kill me," I said in realization of what just took place. "Do you think he'll take into consideration that I didn't know I was doing it?"

"You've got senior status, he can't whip you," my cousin said coming to that understanding before I did. "But you'll have to report it still."

I asked him to come with me to tell Lord William, I wanted someone to verify this claim, and besides I didn't want him telling anyone else until I'd talked to the baron. He shook his head yes and said thanks for the relief, he just wished he'd let me finish before he pulled away. On the way over I let him know I didn't want him to tell anyone for a while.

Aaron, Adam, and Richard were all in the great hall with the baron when we arrived.

"My lord, I need to speak to you in private—please?" I implored.

"They've already informed me of your actions earlier—I'm not too pleased with you," he began in a very serious tone.

"Not that, something else, sir," I stated, waving my hand like what he was saying was of little importance. I didn't mean it that way, but that was the way it might have been perceived had he not known me.

I quickly explained what had just taken place, after the other squires had withdrawn a small distance and left my cousin and me to talk to the baron. Luke verified what I was telling him. He then told me how my waving action might have been received, which terrified me. He told us not to tell anyone, including Kurt or even my mother, of this until at he had mulled it over a while. I asked if I might have permission to tell her since she was a healer. He sent Luke away and suggested I not question his orders. Then he reminded me what would have happened to a junior squire who would have done that. He said he was glad I was not considered a junior any longer—I agreed and thanked him for his leniency.

He sent Luke and me outside while he finished with the other three, and then he would talk more to us.

Charissa came up while we were waiting and I got the chance to visit with her, and tell her again how much I enjoyed the time last evening with her. The time passed much quicker while she was there, and then Lord William dismissed the three seniors and had them send for Luke and me.

"I guess we're going to have to take him with us now," the baron started. "Richard said he is capable, and like you just needs more practical experience."

"Take me where, sir?" Luke asked.

The baron explained the plans to return to the valley to finish exploration, and that we were not to tell anyone until the day before we left, and then only our mothers. Adam was going to tell Sherry at that time, and she would move in to help care for my mother, brother and servant. The baron said I could tell Mother of my new devotion, but let her know that no one else was to discover this for a while, not even Megan.

The baron questioned Luke about some of the junior squires his age who might be going with us and then we were dismissed. He reminded both of us, (but mainly Luke) that we weren't to tell about the mission.

As we were about to leave, the baron gave us one more parting bit of information, "Since I've ordered both of you not to discuss Ray's new skill, you can't tell Kurt what you did, but more to the point you can't tell the healer who ordered the caning about it. That should save you both another beating. Since it was not a willful breaking of the rules I will consider it forgiven. But you can't finish the curing. I'm going to check with His Majesty, but I think he will allow me not to chastise either of you for this."

Then he thought a moment and asked me, "Are you going to be able to ride tomorrow?"

"It would be extremely unpleasant still," I replied.

Then looking at Luke, "Can you break a . . . never mind you have the same problem. Luke, tell Adam that he needs to start breaking a horse for you also. Dismissed."

We got back to the ship, having talked most of the way, and went our separate ways.

I told Mother about discovering the ability to *cell adjust*, and she asked me to show her. She was feeling ill again and her head was throbbing. So I did as she requested and she was able to rest. She told me that Beth had come by and taken Jakót and was showing him around town. She asked me to go meet Cord from his training classes, it would mean a lot to him, so I said I would. She drifted off to sleep and went to meet my little brother, who was in religion class, studying Genesis.

Mother was right, he was delighted that I came to walk home with him. He still was wearing the Orcian dagger that I gave him, and which Sherry had told him to leave at home after today.

A we were walking along Cord, tugged at my sleeve, looked up at me and asked, "Ray, can you spank me?"

"Cord, what did you do? Which instructor did you make mad, little brother?" I asked concerned for him.

"No, no, no, no, no, no, no. That's not what I mean. I'm not asking you to give me one, I wanted to know if have permission as a senior to do it if I make you mad," he said.

"Yes, but I would prefer not to have to," I answered trying to reassure him.

"That's not fair. You're my older brother," he complained.

"Did you know that Kelvin gave me a good spanking—once?" I asked him.

"Nohedidn't!" Cord shot back, very quickly.

"When he first came home, after becoming a senior he and I had an argument, and I told him he couldn't whip me, 'cause Father wouldn't let him. I was about ten. I was a little rude about it, and he told Father that evening after I got ready for bed."

"Father got me from bed, took us both out to the barn, and I thought we were both going to get a whipping for the argument. Father had me pull up the night shirt and handed Kelvin a sword belt, and told him to show me that he could give me a good spanking, ten licks should have my attention.

"I was in tears after the second lick, and Kelvin asked if he could stop after the fifth, Father told him he had to finish what he started. The next swat wasn't as hard, and Father told him, 'If you don't make the licks count, I'll finish the spanking and then you'll have to have one for not following orders.'"

"After he finished, Father went back inside and Kelvin picked me up and hugged me. I was really hurting and mad at him for spanking me. Then I noticed he was in tears too, and he told me that I better not ever make him have to spank me again.

"So, I don't want to have to give you one, but I will if needed. And next time I tell you something you better not yell back at me in disagreement, as you did just a moment ago," I concluded.

The rest of the week went much better and things got into a nice routine for the boys as the final plans for the renewed mapping expedition got readied. They had two days of construction detail, and another of scouting. Scouting with others his age was a relaxing time. Ray got the chance to be with those his own age and act like them. They all loved it because with a senior around they could get away with a bit more.

Ray enjoyed seeing Sherry some, and was glad she was going to help at home while he was gone, even if she didn't know it yet. The King also agreed with Lord William that Ray's new skill could be kept quiet for the time, and did not require the baron to discipline them for the accidental healing.

Lord William convinced Mathias to go again, but Ray thought it may have been more coercion than convincing. Only two junior squires were to go with them this time. Jennifer asked for a female junior, Cindy, a fiery red head that she felt showed promise, and Adam suggested a slight built junior who had been working with Sherry, and was outstanding with a bow. Jelu, whose mother was a noble woman married to a commoner, appeared to have a slight amount of elven blood. He had some psionic ability, but was not going to have the strength of a true psionicist. Rumor had it that he could use his psionics to assist his bow skills. Bennet would also accompany them again.

The party left by horseback, before anyone realized they were going. Ray missed not having Kurt, having become accustomed to having him around during the last trip.

Luke decided the female junior squire was pretty, and Cindy did not seem to mind his attention. This didn't look like a good idea to Ray.

The party quickly made it to the quarry, taking some fresh supplies to the people working there. This was part of their cover. They were taking supplies to the rock quarry. They would be a long way into the valley before people realized they had not returned in a timely manner.

Back over and down the goat trail, back to the burnt village, and from there the mapping would begin again. As the party got to the bottom of the other side, a spring thunder shower soaked them in a very quick manner. They continued moving along, but it was tough slogging through the mud.

During this trip, with other young psionics along, the baron had the squires work on their psionic skills. He also set up the map and worked with Ray, as his instructor had been displeased with his skills or in the progress in them while he was there.

When they arrived back at where the village had been they discovered some fresh Orcian tracks. Well, they might not have been Orcs, but that was the guess. With the rain of several days ago the baron felt it must have been very recent. They seem to have come from the river, as the tracks lead back and forth from there.

The baron decided to follow the river upstream, to the top side of the valley, and then they were to go back to the coast, following the mountain range there. They discovered lots of good timber for construction and the land seemed fertile for growing, and at least for now it was getting plenty of water. It was raining nearly every day. The run-off made little mini-rivers in the valley heading to the river. As the party cut over to the coast, the weather remained miserable. Cool temperatures and rain made for a lousy time, and tempers were on edge. Fortunately even with frayed nerves the kids were able to focus enough not to have any fights. The threat from the baron dealing with fights probably helped keep them from occurring.

Bennet kept leaving, to scout—trying to make sure the Orcs were not setting up a surprise. A of couple times he requested that Ray go with him. They found nothing but they kept feeling like they were being watched.

Finally the weather broke. A couple of days of dry weather, and much warmer weather, made for a great change. The party took the day to rest, and to hang up wet items to dry. Jelu and

Adam brought a small deer back into camp for some fresh meat. This added to the improving spirits that the dry weather had generated.

Bennet got Ray up several hours before daylight and told him they were off again. He was to dress quietly and get ready to go on foot. After dressing Ray lets him know that the idea of sloshing through the mud on foot didn't seem like a very good idea. Ray tried to convince him that they should go on horseback. Bennet reminded him of who the adult was here, and who was in charge. Then he asked Ray if they need to wake the baron to prove the point. Ray knew better than to continue his complaints and said he was just tired, but ready. Jelu was going with them this time.

The boys would have preferred several hours more of sleep, but yesterday's rest helped a great deal.

"I feel like my eyes would like to stay shut and it is hard to keep them open," Jelu yawned as they moved out of the camp.

"Be quiet, or I might be inclined to show a way to get you wide awake very quickly," Bennet snapped. He may not have wanted to be out this early either, but he definitely didn't want to hear any more complaints from the youngsters.

We traveled a couple hours, then it was daylight. We ate a sparse first meal and continued on. That morning, which was bright and clear, and we were glad for that. About nine, Bennet came back down from looking over a ridge. There was a gully on the other side and an Orc camp was there.

"We are going to move up slowly and very quietly. I couldn't see how many were there. You two stay below the crest—just keep your eyes on me and be ready to move down for a quick retreat," Bennet told us. "The camp may be almost deserted, so stay alert for them coming up behind us."

He moved back up and we trailed. Jelu signaled to me and then unwrapped his bow and strung it. I followed his example. Bennet slid back to us and said there were only five or six Orcs in camp.

"Looks like they are drying stuff like we did yesterday. The camp looks like a pretty good size war party, but everyone else is gone. You children want to play with your bows and those pointy things," he said pointing at the arrows, "at two to one odds? That means they might get to us with one each, and they are a lot bigger than we are. I can take one from surprise, but it could be tough, especially for you, Jelu."

"I believe between the two of us we can drop at least four of the six with bows that will make them think its two of them, against the two of us, and you can help out. Remember, I'm much better with a bow than a sword," Jelu said.

I asked Bennet to describe where they were and what they had out, then suggested to Jelu that he take the guard with a bow and I'd shoot the one with a sword who was closest to us.

We moved where we could stand up and fire from behind small trees and then raised up and fired at the same time. Just before we fired all three of brought up our psionic skills, and made the others jump a bit. Jelu was really good. I thought I was decent but he was able to fire quicker than I could. He shot the Orc with a bow as I sank an arrow up to the feathers on the one with a sword. To our surprise neither dropped. We quickly fired again and both of the Orcs dropped on the second shot. Jelu was already loosening his third shot while I was attempting to find another target. It was going to get easy to find targets—they were charging right at us. I fired twice, hitting both shots, and had not killed my second one,

Jelu fired his fourth shot just after I fired my third, but it took his fifth to drop his second target, and then turned to finish off my second target with his sixth shot. He had managed to fire and hit six times during the time I had fired four—and I thought I was good.

So we had been able to kill four of the Orcs, but we thought at least one more between us would have been dead. We moved back a little down the ridge to give Bennet a better chance to take one from the back. Jelu and I were a little spread out to make it harder for an Orc to get from one of us to the other. Jelu realized I would go *invisible* to the one attacking me, and didn't want to be double teamed.

Bennet was able to kill the one he hit from the back, and I disappeared on the one charging at me, and was able to quickly dispatch him. Bennet was moving to help Jelu when I yelled at him to look out, another was charging at his back. He turned to in time to parry the Orc's thrust. I closed to help Jelu, hoping Bennet could take care of himself, because I was pretty sure Jelu couldn't in a melee against the huge Orc.

Jelu was bleeding badly from a gash to the chest and another on his left arm, when I arrived and caught the unsuspecting Orc between the shoulder blades with my sword, but he didn't drop. I thought I caught him pretty well, but his armor must have deflected more of the blow than I realized.

The Orc turned to face me, and couldn't find me—thank God; as Jelu collapsed. I ran my sword up to the hilt in the Orc's stomach and had to jump away as he nearly fell on me. A second Orc had shown up and was attacking Bennet, who was now in need of help. I looked at Jelu, who was bleeding badly.

"I can hold the wound a bit, hurry and help Bennet," he called as he saw me waver.

I quickly ran to Bennet and saw a third Orc starting to close on us. Bennet was bleeding from a couple of small cuts on his chest, and gash over his right eye. I yelled to him as I ran which one I was going hit and he tried to move to help set up the attack. I caught the Orc leaning over to try to take out Bennet's leg, and cleaved through his neck, severing his head. Bennet would have to deal with the wounded one, while I took on the fresh attacker. With only one to deal with Bennet was able to go *invisible* to him and kill him in a reasonable time. But he was badly injured.

The last (I hoped) Orc, was carrying a massive two-handed war axe, and was almost a foot and quarter taller than my 5' 6" frame. He let out a howl, and swung shortly after I had attempted to be unseen by him. The problem was with the muddy ground, my feet sloshed and he seemed to be able to keep a general idea where I was, and I didn't realize it.

I caught him in the ribs below his left arm with a decent slash, but it didn't seem to make much of a difference. Another slice on his right arm, and a slight wound to the head, but the Orc kept on fighting.

He broke my shield, and possibly my arm, with a blow that might have cut me in half had my shield not caught it. It still sent me to the ground several feet from him. He howled and came back at me, watching to see my footsteps. I thought, if I had realized this sooner, I could have moved away and hit him with some arrows. Then he might have killed Bennet or Jelu.

I let him go by me, then made a hard swing and caught him in the back of the leg. He went down and I pounced on him before he could regain his balance, and was able to finish him off with a thrust to the back of the neck.

I went to Bennet who was lying unconscious and bound up his wounds, and then went to check on Jelu. I knew I could *cell adjust*, but very limited amounts, and I didn't know who would need it the most. I was in need of medical attention also. Jelu had passed out from loss of blood and was still bleeding. I bandaged him, and checked him; he was not breathing. I had to heal him; and hoped that Bennet was going to be okay without the cure. I had expended almost all of my ability on the junior squire when he finally came around. I told him I'd be back and went to check on Bennet. He was worse than I had originally thought. I made sure all his wounds were wrapped and expended the last of my *cell adjust* on the thief. It apparently was enough, as he coughed and moved.

"Go get my backpack, I've got something in there," he told me.

I went down the ravine and dragged the backpack to him with my good arm. He dug around inside it, and pulled out a small box. Inside the box was a carefully wrapped vial. He drained the contents and his wounds started to close.

"I wish I had some more of that, looks like you could use some too. How is Jelu?" he asked.

I just stood there and stared. He had a healing potion, and I was wishing he had some more, too.

"Ray, how is Jelu?" he asked again. "I was nearly dead. I had to drink the potion. Did you just heal me a little or did I imagine it?"

"Jelu is pretty bad off, and my arm is broken. And yes I healed you, but that is it for my skills today," I answered.

"Probably a good thing you did, I don't think I'd made if you hadn't. You're more of a surprise all the time. Let me see the arm."

He looked out and said, "Yep, it's broken. Let me set it, and maybe you can heal yourself later, if we don't get back to camp."

Then he yanked my arm, and I passed out.

When I came to, Jelu was sitting there looking at me, and smiling. He still looked pretty bad but his eyes were open and alert. Bennet was coming back down the ravine again with a bag.

"I found a few goodies they left behind. I don't think we want any of their food, but a drink of this wine might relieve the pain in your arm. And we really need to move," he said.

"Sir, where did you learn to count?" I asked, grinning. "I hope you do a better job next time."

"Don't go getting too big for your britches, I might count them licks that way for a caning of a young squire if his manners don't improve," Bennet replied, but he was laughing also.

Jelu and I were moving very slowly with our wounds. I suggest that Bennet go ahead and try to find the party to bring them to us. Bennet said he couldn't really leave us, a possum could take us in the condition we were in. Unfortunately he was correct. It was after dark before we made it to camp, and I was starting to run a high fever with my broken arm.

I came to the next afternoon, and was still laid out nicely in our tent. Cindy hollered when she saw that I was awake. Luke and Mathias came in to check on me.

"Seems you went off and had too much fun," the cleric told me.

"I must have missed it, when was that?" I asked.

"You boys got into a bit of action, and I understand there may be a lot more. How are you feeling? Want to get up and get something to eat?" the priest asked me.

"Yes, and something to drink—I feel like a bunch of dust devils had a dance in my mouth," I answered.

———————

They stayed in camp and rested the following day. The baron did send out some scouts to try to avoid the Orcs getting a counterattack. Even after being cured all three were pretty well spent. Bennet gave an estimate of the size of the Orcian camp, and Ray reminded the baron of the thief's math skills, in jest, from the original encounter with them.

Bennet had also given the baron a map that he had found in one of the Orcian tents. The baron believed that it would be better for the expedition to avoid the raiding party if possible; there were more than they might be able to handle.

Bennet handed both of the boys twenty silver pieces and a gold piece—he said it was their share of what was in the tents.

Jennifer wanted Ray to talk to his cousin about Cindy. They were spending a lot of time together, and Jennifer thought Cindy was promised. Jennifer thought perhaps Luke also had marriage arranged. Ray talked to him and Luke suggested that he mind his own business, and that he didn't need any assistance like that from someone two years his junior. Luke let Ray know he didn't appreciate the interference with his love life.

Cindy was not much better when Jennifer approached her. Cindy was promised, although her fiancé would be killed later that summer. Finally Jennifer discussed her concern with the baron, who spoke to both of the teenagers and told them to cool down. Any inappropriate action would be extremely painful for each of them, and might cause a lot of problems for their families when they returned to the city.

Bennet informed the baron that he thought there may have been some human footprints with the Orcs. He hadn't said anything to anyone else, as the children might not think clearly with that information.

The next day they started moving again, with Bennet out in front scouting. They continued following the hills to the coast and back and forth to map out the rest of the valley. They discovered a small pride of lions, with young cubs at the foot of the mountains. Bennet was excited about this as the cat hearts were important in some type of alchemy production. Ray and the other squires weren't privy to the information he was telling the baron but Xell believed the animals might prove useful.

The party stayed upwind of the big cats, and kept the horses well away of them. They caught a lone male first and it went down in a hale of arrows from Jelu, Ray and Adam. The four females were going to be more difficult, as they were together looking out for their cubs.

Finally the party was able to catch them after a kill. Again archery made the task easier, but the job was finished off with sword work, as Richard and the baron finished the last lioness. Four very young cubs were taken, and some young adults were allowed to get away.

The squires seemed to enjoy playing with the cubs.

Much of the rest of the mapping trip was extremely uneventful, but it was getting hot. The party was nearing the pass back out of the valley when Ray discovered what appeared to be a wild peach orchard. If it wasn't wild, someone had been here earlier and abandoned the area. These peaches they were enjoying were ripening in early summer and quite tasty; some other peaches had already ripened and fallen off. The spot was marked on the map. Ray decided this would not be a bad place to live, and would like to build a castle in the area where he could watch the waterfall into the sea and get to the peaches. He wondered why they hadn't spotted them on the original journey in the valley.

Bennet returned from scouting the evening before they would getting to the pass. His news was not good, nor was it what they wanted to hear.

———————

"The Orcs are set up at the top of the pass, apparently waiting for us," Bennet told the baron while I was lying there in the tent.

The baron looked at me, and said "I guess it is too late to send him out now. You aren't to repeat any of this," Lord William told me.

"I didn't see the kid there," Bennet said apologizing to the baron. "But I probably wouldn't have thought much about it if I had. He has been with me on the scouting and he handles himself well."

"Ray, you are dismissed, I want to hear the entire report, and have to think about it before everyone else knows. Don't say anything still," Lord William told me.

I wanted to protest, but I didn't think this was the time to . . . annoy him.

I left and went to talk to Adam and Aaron. I was really glad Aaron came; I enjoyed his company more than any other of squires. And he treated my like I was his age. Adam still thought of me as a little kid, almost a baby brother-in-law. Adam also still wanted to give me orders, and (I guess) look out for me.

Finally the baron called for me, and then he sent me to get the Mathias and Xell. I was wondering why Luke wasn't called in with the other spell casters. I was allowed to stay for this planning session and even asked how I thought we might set up with the bows.

My suggestion made sense and the adults decided to act on it. Jelu and I were to go around and climb up to the ridge and flank the Orcs. Then as the rest of the party attacked their position, we would be able to fire at them from the flank. I told them two of us would be able to sneak up on them, and set up. Mathias put a wet blanket on the plan.

"What happens when the Orcs go after our two young archers? They won't be able to defend themselves if they attack in strength and we won't be able to get to them," the priest contended.

"Well squire, what do you say to that?" the baron queried.

"We don't have to stand and fight them toe-to-toe, sir. We could shoot and move, and if too many came at once, we'd run for it," I answered sounding much more confident than I felt.

"Xell, can you make Jelu *invisible* to get up and into position?" the baron asked.

"Yes, it will last a day or until he attacks. I could cast it tonight, and he and Ray could move out. I'd then sleep and relearn spells, and we could be ready by tomorrow afternoon—around three. Can you two be there by then?" Xell turned to me and asked.

"I don't know how long it will take us, and this weather will make climbing and moving more difficult. And we'd have a tough time finding a place to climb in the dark," I answered.

"Let's move camp, further away from the pass, and think on it some more tonight," the baron ordered.

We broke camp and moved further from the pass, hoping to keep enough distance from the Orcs where we wouldn't be attacked. It was decided that if the night passed without our being attacked that Jelu and I would leave in the daylight, around noon. That we would have enough time to find a way up the ridge and could be on the flank by the next day. Aaron believed that it was too dangerous for two kids our age, but couldn't come up with a better idea, and a straight frontal attack against superior odds would be suicide.

That night almost everyone was on alert, except Jelu and me. Jelu and I slept to be ready to make our move and the rest were going to try to rest up during the day. Then we would all attack the next following day, around ten. Hopefully Jelu and I could get set up while he was *invisible* from Xell's spell, and I would use my psionic skills to hide—the problem was that I couldn't hide from many opponents—apparently only one of the War Orcs!

I found the place that we had climbed earlier in the spring, but with the recent summer rains, and a slight mist falling today, it would be tough, especially when I couldn't see Jelu.

We spent most of the day getting to the top, and then ate and rested. Jelu said he would watch first and let me get a bit of sleep, then he'd catch a quick nap before we moved on. A half an hour nap isn't much, but sometimes it can give you enough of a lift to keep going. We went on another hour and half before it got too dark to see, and by then we were as close as we wanted to get to the Orcs for the night. We took turns on watch and sleeping.

Early the next morning we ate another cold meal and began moving into our final position. We saw two scouts or guards moving toward us. I told Jelu to stay *invisible*, and I would try to take them both using my psionic skills.

"We're too close to their camp and it's still an hour before the attack," Jelu whispered to me, "It is too dangerous to risk it."

"We can't have them behind us when we start, that would ruin our retreat," I countered. "I've got to take them out."

"Then I'll have to help, and we will both just have to move carefully afterwards to set up," Jelu told me. "Let's both shoot the one in the brown cloak and try to kill him quicklly, then switch to the one in green."

"Alright, on my count of three," I said. "One, two, three!"

We both stood up and let our longbows twang, and two sheaf arrows sped toward the unsuspecting Orcs. Jelu was already preparing to fire a second shot before the first two arrows hit the Orc. Both our second shots hit their mark also, and they were both dead before they realized they weren't alone. We went to check the bodies, and to make sure they were dead. Jelu reminded me to check for papers or anything else that might prove useful. I didn't like digging through the dead's pockets, but he was correct.

We finished that ghoulish business, and then slowly crept along to get positions to aid in the attack. This would be much harder than our last attacks on Orcs. They would know the party was coming. When we parted to set up, both of us were shaking.

Ten o'clock came and so did the rest of our comrades. They came up the pass firing bows as they found Orcian targets. The problem was that there were only six warriors down there, and three spell casters. Xell and Mathias could cast combat spells, Luke didn't have anything but three curing spells, and those would all be needed.

I expected Mathias to cast his *hold person* spell, like the last time, and for Xell to cast a *sleep*, but that would still leave a lot of Orcs. If each of their spells affected three Orcs, we would still be outnumbered two to one.

The Orcs were ready and answered with their own bows. Jelu and I were firing into their flanks, and that made them pretty easy shots. Our fighters continued to fire and close, then all of a sudden the Orcs dropped their bows and charged.

Charging down hill gives the attacker a great advantage; you have momentum with you and you are swinging down on our opponents.

Jennifer was already down when the charge started. Her leather armor was not able to stop the arrows that the Orcs were firing. Richard and Adam were also wounded. Lord William was the only one in the battle with chain armor, everyone else from both sides were in leather. As the War Orcs closed, Mathias's *hold* was cast on the front members of the charge. Two of the Orcs stopped and those behind them tripped over their immobile companions. Xell *sleep* got three in the back but the others were quickly among our friends.

Jelu and I continued to fire as long as we could, and did a great job in damaging Orcs, but there were still thirteen Orcian warriors attacking the five fighters we had, and the thief. The fighters coming up had scored a number of hits on Orcs with their bows—killing two and wounding several others. Jelu and I had killed three others and finished off the one who was wounded, but we couldn't keep firing from here. I moved down to help in the melee, and Jelu moved to have open shots down the ridge.

Lord William was attacked by three of the creatures and it looked like they were trying to grapple him and take him down. Richard was holding his own with two Orcs, both armed with broad swords. Aaron and Adam were both in bad shape as they were not a match for two opponents each. Cindy went down quickly, and may not even have gotten a swing in, Bennet had taken one as they charged her and Mathias had gone to her aid, but there were still two large Orc warriors there.

Xell cast another *sleep* spell, but only two of the three Orcs on Lord William fell asleep. Luke was attempting to position himself to cure Adam, when I arrived and took one of Aaron's from the back. Jelu released his deadly bow where the Orcs were attempting to kill the priest.

Then Lord William dropped the last Orc that was attacking him. Free from his attackers, he moved over to help Adam who was closest to him.

Jelu dropped one of the Orcs, then he, the thief, and the cleric together took down the third. Lord William sliced the head off one of Adam's Orcs and the cure kept Adam from going down, but he wasn't making much progress against the Orc. Aaron and I dropped his last one and tried to move over and help Richard, who was starting to waver from multiple wounds.

Jelu finally closed, no longer able to fire safely into the combat and so he closed to protect the priest as he checked on Cindy. The baron and Adam finished off the one that was there and also started to move to Richard. Aaron and I had arrived and interposed for Richard, whom Luke was about to cure. I had forgotten to target my opponent with the psionic *invisibility* and almost got my head taken off. Luckily I was much shorter than the Orc and could duck. Aaron and I finished off the Orcs, which were already wounded from dealing with Richard. The priest was getting Cindy revived by the time I got there, and Luke had gone over to see if he could help Jennifer.

The entire battle had only taken about fifteen minutes. But they had been very bloody. Jennifer was dead, she had been hit multiple time with arrows. It seemed that many of the Orcs just happened to shoot her. There was nothing we could do for her. We would roll her body in some canvas or whatever the Orc tents were made from. But that would be later. Now we had to make sure the Orcs were dead; tie up the *held* and *sleeping* ones. We cleaned up our wounds and Jelu and I went to check their camp as Bennet went to get our horses. When we got to the camp there was an eight-year-old or so human girl tied to a stake, in one of the tents. We tried to communicate, but weren't able to, no matter how slowly we talked.

She appeared quite scared of us. I tried getting down on my knees, so I would be closer to her height, but she screamed bloody murder. That brought Richard and Lord William dashing into the camp and to the tent. They saw my expression and the yelling little girl, looked at each other and begin to laugh.

I, frankly, didn't see the humor, and told them so.

Richard asked, "Do you often have that effect on the young girls?" Then they both starting laughing, even more.

"Squire, take off your helm and wipe the blood from your face—you're probably scaring her to death. We all look pretty gruesome," Lord William said between laughs. "Then untie her from the stake, leaving her tied, and take her to Xell to look after."

Jelu agreed it was not that funny, as he wasn't use to having little kids scream in terror at the sight of him either. I quickly follow the lord's command, and Jelu continued to search for things that would help us. Bennet returned with the horses and aided in searching the bodies. I returned and helped Jelu.

Aaron came in the tent we were searching and nealy scared us to death, as neither of us heard him come in. He thought he was extremely funny, and suggested that had we both been juniors, and were paying so little attention to things after a battle, that we might have been in trouble with the lord, or a senior. But since a senior was on duty, he would not report it this time. Jelu knew he was older than I was, and wasn't sure if the senior squire was attempting to be funny again or was serious—I figured it was both.

"His lordship's compliments to his squire," Aaron started in a more formal tone, "he said I was to report to you. He said you might be able to assist me with this wound, but I'm not sure what he expects you to do?"

"I'll try, if you won't let the baron know how unaware you caught us immediately after a battle. Jelu is a junior squire, and you know how old I am, and you were correct, we could get in a lot of trouble," I said moving to look at a gash in his leg and side.

"Hey kid, I told you I wouldn't report it. And yes, I remember you're thirteen, I'm not going to try to get you in trouble with his lordship. I thought we were good enough friends that you wouldn't have to ask," Aaron responded, sounding hurt.

"How old did he say you were?" Jelu asked incredulously.

"My apologies, I thought we were that close too, until you said what you did. It kinda scared me a little, due to my age. We have enough injuries without have a birch inflict any more. I'm sorry I sounded in doubt, sir," I answered not wanting Aaron upset with me.

"Excuse me, how old did he say you were?" Jelu asked again.

"He's thirteen, and deserves his senior rating for his combat skills," Aaron told him, as I was starting the healing trance.

"I knew he got a rating advance, but I had no idea he was that young. I thought maybe a bit younger than me, and still a bit small too. But thirteen!" Jelu exclaimed.

Then Aaron realized what I was doing. When I came out of the trance he looked down and said, "Son of . . . where did you learn that?!"

"Did you just *cell adjust* him?" Jelu asked, his eyes wide in amazement.

"I just found out I could do it while you and Adam were talking to the baron, when he told you about the mission. That was what Luke and I came in to report," I told them. "It is kind of hush—hush."

"Is that what you did for me, when we attack the Orcian camp with Bennet," Jelu asked?

"Yes, you weren't conscious, and may have stopped breathing. I don't attempt this if I can avoid it—kind of an emergency. So neither of you are to discuss this, Jelu consider this a direct order, from a senior. Aaron, I can't order you, but you know if I'm giving Jelu one it is important," I told him.

"Jelu, take off. Let me talk to our surprising baby senior squire," Aaron said.

Jelu left, and Aaron asked, "Does Adam know?".

"No sir, only Lord William, Luke, and Bennet may know, 'cause I cured him also after the battle. Not much, but I did cure," I told him. "The baron ordered me not to tell, or I would have told you. The only person I told was my mother, not even Sherry."

"Or the princess," came the baron's voice through the tent flap, with Jelu?

"No sir," I responded, "you told me no one, save my mother."

"You two aren't to discuss this devotion MY squire has," the baron ordered.

"Ray already gave me the order, sir," Jelu stated.

"Now I've given it, and it applies to you also, Aaron. I don't wish to loose him to the healers. And you know that *cell adjustment* is normally only able to be learned by healers of our race. Occasionally one with wild talents discover this, but not very often," the baron concluded.

"Sir," Aaron began, "wouldn't it be advisable to have the party members aware of this—in case there is a need. Especially the priest, maybe Ray could tell him in confession, then he couldn't say anything to anyone?"

"Should I need a sixteen-year old's opinion on matters of policy, I shall ask you, or possibly just cane the response I require from you," the baron responded extremely harshly. "Will the latter be necessary squire?"

"No sir, begging the baron's pardon, I . . . I . . . ah, I apologize sir," Aaron finally got out.

He motioned the other two boys out, and then sat down on a camp chair, and looked at me. He motioned for me to sit also, and then continued to set there. I was wondering if I was in trouble for something. Maybe he knew Jelu and I weren't alert while searching the tent?

"Are you injured, sir?" I finally asked.

"Nothing serious, and the others definitely are need of curing more than I am," he replied. "What about you kid, you okay?"

"My ankle is sore, I kinda turned it going down the hill after the Orcs," I told him. "But nothing like the others needing attention."

"Do you want to remain my squire?" he asked me.

I was almost in shock by his question. It caught me totally off guard. "YES SIR! What have I done that would have the baron wish to dismiss me?" I asked, trying not let the tears swell up in my eyes as my voice crack.

"I will not be as active the rest of the summer or in fall, and have considered allowing you to be the squire of another that will be in the field. You haven't done anything to make me **want** to dismiss you," he told me.

"Then I'll stay with you, but if you loan me out or send me out for an expedition it would still be fine, sir," I said overly relieved I wasn't in trouble or inadequate.

We moved our camp to the top of the ridge and rested the rest of the day, planned to get a lazy start the following day. The baron got out the map out we had taken from the Orcs and allowed me to attempt to match up their map with ours. Their map was very crude, and not very useful as far as cartography goes, but it did indicate where their village was, and a few other tidbits of information. I had practiced a great deal with our valley map, and another old map that the baron had brought from Saxet.

The summer sun felt great that next morning as they started back to the city. The little girl seemed scared of all of them, but she seemed to relax when she was allowed to play with the lion cubs. Xell was about the only one she didn't scream in terror around, and that may have been because she was female, and not in armor.

Luke tried to examine her, but she was pitching such a fit that he was going to stop. The baron asked Luke how he would treat a young student with that attitude? Then deal with her similarly. Luke tried to convince Xell to take that responsibly, but she declined and reminded Luke that he was given that task—not her.

Luke disciplined her and she settled down and he was able to examine her and did not discover anything wrong with her except some scars on her backside from bad beatings. Then he cured her pain from the discipline, and gave her a big hug. After that she calmed down, and clung to Luke like he was her protector, but she still was given to Xell to take care of, much to Luke's relief.

The party returned and was surprised how much the city was beginning to take shape. The stone from the quarry was starting to show in the construction of the city wall.

The villagers were starting to get a slightly more adjusted to the city, and their ways. Some of the mages got the idea across that they would have to worship God, not their pagan worship they were used to, or the priest would have them executed. The priests were concerned that some of the older women might be a snare to new husbands, and try to get them to worship in their pagan rituals. This is one of the reasons they did not want them to survive the expedition's capture of their village. The children were punished if they reverted back to their old religions, but the priests were willing to give them a chance—a painful chance, but a chance. The older ones might be burned as a heretic. Ray had not heard of anyone being burned like that, and prayed they would see the light of the Lord and convert in a quick manner. Not only for their souls, but their physical lives as well. The clerics set up catechism classes for the villagers to help them learn about the Trinity, and religious rituals of the faith.

Ray discovered on his arrival that he had a baby sister, Anne, and that Sherry was to be the godmother, which didn't displease him. He also noticed that Sherry was carrying a bit of extra weight, and suddenly realized why she was not allow to go on the mission. He also realized how loud little babies could be.

Kurt and Sarah were married that summer while Ray was out finishing the valley, which was the reason they did not return with the baron on the second expedition.

The extra horses that were brought and the *polymorphed* wolves to elephants were being trained and starting to do a bit of work. The elephants, in spite of their young age, helped a lot. Things were looking good, and the crops for the first year seemed to be doing great. Grain silos were being constructed in preparation for an expected bumper crop. The ship that had gone off to explore had not returned, and they were beginning to expect it.

Ray began training with the other squires and enjoyed being around some of the squires his own age, being able to relax, do more normal things a thirteen-year-old would do, and be a bit silly at times. He did things with Jelu and Aaron often, and sometime Kurt would join them, but except for combat skills he worked mainly with this age group, and got to enjoy a little bit of being a kid still. He discovered he wasn't the only young squire who got disciplined this spring. Most of the squires it seemed had the same problems, especially with the new seniors, but it was always that way with the new squires. New rules and expectations, little patience from their superiors, made for a rough couple of years for the new junior squires. But the more they learned of what was expected and how to follow the rules, the easier that part of their life would come. Ray had it easier than most of the mates his age. His senior status prevented some beatings that would have occurred during his training.

The senior squire status created other problems for him. Having to discipline a junior squire at an instructor's, or some other's request was difficult, especially when the reason was nearly invented. He was required to carry out those orders, several times, and it was painful not only to the other young squire but to Ray.

He went on patrols with other squires, to keep a lookout around the city, but nothing interesting went on them. Still, it was a chance to be out of the city, and off work details. He even had the opportunity to lead some of them, even with other senior squires.

The church was being built of wood, and was much smaller than the one in Candlewynd. It was difficult for many to think of any building as the church except the grand structure that had been in their capital city. But this was to be a temporary structure until time permitted the construction of a true cathedral. The wooden structure which was presently the church would have other useful purposes in training and living quarters for the clerics, and storing manuscripts and other writings.

With a building erected, even if uncompleted, Sunday's Masses seemed more normal to the citizens. It was a chance to visit and see those one didn't have time to see sometime in the busy week. Ray had seen the princess several times, and got the chance to talk to her once, before being invited to sit with her, King Harold, and other young nobles one Sunday.

Ray spoke to the king about the land he thought he wanted to build his castle on—eventually. The peaches and the waterfall were his idea of a place to live.

The baron spoke to the King about Ray's ability to heal, and thought he was too valuable as a warrior to switch to a new profession. The healers agreed that it was unusual for a warrior to have *cell adjustment*, but agreed that his talents were in war, not spell casting.

On the subject of his skills Lord William spoke to the king, "That squire may be the most powerful sixteen-year-old we'll ever have seen when he inherits his father's title."

"We agree," the king said thoughtfully, "and possibly inherit more than that."

Ray spent a part of each of his summer evenings with his young colt when he was in the city. Many times he allowed Cord and/or Jakót to come with him. One night as he was returning home, a little later than normal, accompanied by Jakót, Ray was grabbed. A large sack was placed over Jakót's entire body. That was all he could see, it was a rare moonless night in the land of twin moons.

Then, Ray was being pummeled by an attacker as two others held him. He was unable to throw off his attackers, and they beat the young teenager unconscious. Then they continued to inflict pain on the motionless body.

Chapter Eight

Pain and Tough Love
....

> "Trust in the Lord with all your heart and lean not on your
> own understanding; in all your ways acknowledge him,
> and he will make your path straight." Proverbs 3: 5-6

Ray regained consciousness, with Sherry holding him in the street. Jakót had gotten out of the sack and went to get Sherry, and said "Ray—hurt." When they found him, she sent Jakót to get Luke and Adam went to locate Sarah and Lord William, in that order. Megan was out on a patrol, so she couldn't send for his sister.

Luke arrived first, and asked what happened. Jakót tried to tell them what he knew but still had a language barrier to overcome. Luke tried to help stop the bleeding, as he explained to Sherry, "I don't have any spells or psionic healing left today. I was assisting with the seniors jousting, and that was pretty rough."

"Do we want to take him to the ship?" Sherry asked.

"No, let's wait for Sarah to get here. We don't want to cause any additional injury by trying to move him in this shape," Luke told her. Then Luke noticed that Sherry looking pale. "Are you all right? You're getting pale."

Luke wanted her to lie down, but she sat there holding the young squire, and stroking his hair.

Sarah and Kurt arrived shortly thereafter, and both gave an explicative oath. Sarah cast a healing spell of some sort. Ray opened his eyes, but still looked pretty bad.

"Why didn't you do something, besides sit and watch? You've got enough skill to figure he needed a cure," Sarah said in demeaning manner.

"I don't have any left today, I was at the jousting area today," Luke replied defensively.

Ray tried to ask what happened, and was wondering what he was doing on the ground and why everybody else was in his room, but he was having a difficult time talking. Then the baron showed up, and Ray tried to stand up, but Sherry had a firm grip of him and wouldn't let him.

Luke went over to Adam and said he needed to get Sherry home, and to take Jakót. "Have her go to bed and stay there, the excitement is causing her some problems." He then went to Sarah and spoke with her and she went to Sherry and examined her before letting her leave. Then Sarah changed Luke's order, and told Adam to take her straight to the infirmary. Luke, you need to take Jakót home and stay with Ray's mother. She doesn't need to come to check on him tonight.

Luke wanted to know where she was taking Ray, so in the morning they could come see him. "Tell her I wouldn't tell you, but he will be well cared for," Sarah told him and then dismissed the younger healer.

"Are we taking him home with us?" Kurt asked.

"Of course, we can't let the baby lay in the street," she said as Lord William picked up his young squire.

"Sarah, you have your young students there. Isn't that going to create a problem," Kurt asked?

"No, some of them can already *cells adjust* a little, they can use their powers on a real victim. He'll love the extra attention," she said as they walked along back to the apartment.

Kurt and the baron carried Ray back, and Sarah went on ahead to make some preparations. She opened the door for the men to bring the boy in, and the baron noticed the three young children, each around eleven, there near the pallet made for his injured squire. These children were training to be healers, and Charissa was one of the young healers. There were also another girl and a boy there for the training exercise.

Lord William did not believe this was a good idea. The king would not want his granddaughter there, even with all the other people—appearances.

"This is what they need to see, to learn to heal better. Broken bones are not as simple as a cut or a bruise. The *cell adjustment* works better—making certain they heal correctly," Sarah said.

The baron had her come out where they could discuss something without the younger healers hearing. Sarah left orders that no one was to touch the squire until she was back. Sarah, then informed, Lord William that this was her decision to make, not his on healing. She would make sure things were handled properly, and if her young healers did not follow correct procedures and orders they would face serious discipline. They knew better than to think they would get away with anything.

The baron left, still not pleased with Sarah's decision, and decided he better let the king know what was happening.

Sarah then returned to the room. Ray had been laid on a pallet with Kurt sitting next to him, and three very wide-eyed young healers knelt across the room looking on.

"This is a chance for us to learn about healing from one who is actually injured. He has been healed, a little, but we need to discover what else is wrong with him. I want you all to think for a moment what we need to look for, and questions that we might need to ask."

"Charissa, come here for a moment, I need to talk to you before we all get started," Sarah said, and stepped back outside the room.

"Yes ma'am," Charissa said as she also stepped out into the cooling summer night.

"I know you like Ray, and that you have kissed him before. Even a few times more than you had permission. You got in trouble with His Highness, after the party, when you kissed him several times. You may not kiss him here! That is an order, do you understand me?" Sarah asked.

"Yes ma'am, but he . . . ," Charissa started.

"You will follow my orders, or you will receive a good spanking. I don't think you want that. Nor would you want me to give you one with Ray in the next room. What if you got him in trouble and he is already injured? Make sure there is no kissing, and let him know it is not allowed," Sarah said in a very commanding and threatening voice.

They went back and Sarah had them all to go into *rapport*, while she went into a *cell adjust* trance, to see all the injuries. Even after she had cured the young squire, there were several broken ribs, a crack in his jaw, and multiple bruises—some very bad.

Sarah communicated to the young healers that the broken ribs were the most serious problems. Had he not already received the medical attention, he might have died. With all the young healers' limited abilities they repaired one of the broken ribs, making it as good as new, with Sarah's assistance. The rest would have to wait until the next day, when they could use more psionic skills, and Sarah would have to relearn her spells.

Kurt said he would watch him for the night, and Thad, the young boy said he was willing to assist him.

Sarah said that was good, but Thad would need his rest to regain his psionic skills. If he awoke during the night, however, he could check on the patient. The ladies would retire to the next room, and were not to return until the morning.

The night passed without incident, and without Thad waking up to check on Ray or being needed. Kurt kept a careful watch.

Sherry, on the other hand, did not have a good night. The sight of her young friend being hurt so badly had a terrible effect on her. She spent the night in the infirmary, and would be in there for several days. Morning sickness was bad enough—now this really had her upset and worried, and made matters worse.

Ray was still in pain the next morning when Sarah and her young charges went back to examine him. The chest wrap helped, but he had at least one more broken rib, and all the other injuries from the severe beating he had gotten. The three children and Sarah rechecked the injuries and then began healing some of those most painful. The children weren't mature enough to cast healing spells, and their psionic healing ability was very minimal, but every little bit helps—especially when one is in pain. So, Sarah directed their efforts, and then sent them to get ready for their training for the day. She would still have to memorize spells before she would be able to help Ray much more.

Sarah sent Kurt to Lady Martha to let her know where Ray was, and to assist her in coming over. Lady Martha would be able to add to the healing process, if she had been able to learn spells, but even better, she would be able to *cell adjust*.

Ray was moved home that evening; Luke and his mother would be able to finish the healing process. Sarah allowed his mother to cure the jaw, so eating would not be so difficult, and then as time permitted they would attend to his other ribs, and the general bruises and scrapes. Megan returned home the next day and also was able to assist in the process.

Ray discovered when he got home that Jakót had been punched a few times also. Nothing very serious, just enough to have the child in pain for a while—bully actions.

After a couple more days of resting and healing, Ray returned to duty, not in the best of moods. He was sharp to the junior squires his age, and with a senior squire's rank, intimidating. With the senior squires with who he was accustomed to working, his attitude was not any better, and wasn't well tolerated. Finally it was decided that Kurt, Aaron, and Adam would assist him in getting his head back on straight. They determined to meet him in the barn, while he was working with his horse.

Cord and Jakót were both there, so Adam went over to them and sent them to Sherry, who knew what was going on. Others had also discussed it with Lord William, in case things progressed along an even more unpleasant path than the painful one that was planed. The baron would have gone with them to allow his squire to know his view of the meeting, but left it with the young senior squires instead.

———————

"We need to have a talk with you, kid," Kurt said, as I was brushing and talking to the palomino.

"Talk away," I responded, probably somewhat surly, and never turned toward them.

"It would be in your best interest, to act a bit more civil—with those who are older and **larger** than you," Aaron stated in a manner that made me a little more concerned.

I didn't want to give the impression of fear to them, but I decided that I better at least listen closer. Then I noticed that everyone else had left the stable.

"Consider yourself a junior squire again, and act your age," Adam said, "I'm here on Sherry's behalf. She said to 'Pay attention, little brother!'"

Now I was worried.

"Your attitude has been wrong for the last, well, since you got beat up. We believe that they may have knocked something wrong with you, and we are getting ready to get you back in the correct mind set," Kurt began. "You have been acting a bit big for your britches with the other seniors, and kind of throwing your weight around with the junior squires. It is getting ready to change!"

"Yes sir, the squire apologizes, and will immediately change his behavior, sir," I stated, hoping to get my older friends to back off a bit.

Adam walked off, as the two noble born seniors continued the verbal battering. "Ray—that's not going to be enough," Kurt told me. "You are going to have to pay for your past actions. You have several seniors and more than a few junior squires that would like to kick your butt."

"Sir, might the squire be excused due to the circumstances, sir?" I asked.

"No, Ray, you've gone too far," Aaron told me.

Then I noticed Adam walking back with a large, birch rod. "No, you can't whip me, I have a senior rating!" I complained.

Adam walked up testing the limb, "Remember what I told you about be a junior again? You're getting ready to get a whale of a beating, kid!"

"You're going to get five from each of us," Kurt said.

"Even if I was still a junior you could normally give me only seven. Come on—no," I pleaded. "Aaron, please?"

"Too late kid, if you don't take it from us, the odds are you're going to get the tar beat out of you again, multiple times, by some seniors," Kurt said.

"Just tell them I've been out of line because of the beating I got, and I'll behave—honest," I told them.

"Ray, quit whining like an eight-year-old and let's get this over with," Adam said. "You sound like some of those kids Cord's age."

"I'm taking a whipping from you three? As a senior I don't have to!" I told them getting a little belligerent, and taking off my shirt.

Kurt looked down at me, and said, "Don't act like a fool, you can't take any one of us, without psionics, and with three of us you know better than to try to use them."

"Are the three of you going to gang up on me, three on one? Or you going to at least give me a chance?" I asked hope some show of bravery might help.

"Ray," Kurt told me, "you are going to get a caning. The only option is, are we going to have to beat you up first, or are you just going to take the caning?"

The discussion did not improve any for Ray, and Kurt said that he was the oldest and largest of the three seniors, and he would fight him, if Ray really wanted to get beat up again. But he wasn't going to waste any more time with a thirteen-year-old, and punched him hard in the stomach. Ray went down, stayed down as Kurt instructed at the time, then submitted to their discipline.

When they had finished, they told him it was not really their idea, and that they didn't like having to do that to him. But without them punishing him, he would have gotten it worse from several others. They would let those others know that he had paid for his actions and that his behavior had better improve, or the next time they might not be able to help him.

Ray wasn't so sure they had helped.

Richard came in as the others were leaving, and asked if he survived. At the time Ray wasn't really sure, he just knew that he hurt.

"Baron Scrope wishes to see you, when you are finished with your companions," Richard told me.

"Right now?" I asked, still in tears.

"I'd wash my face, if I were you, and report immediately. Unless of course you'd like some more of what you just got?" Richard told me in a sarcastic manner.

"No sir, I wouldn't care to experience any more from a birch this evening, sir," I said realizing I could still be in for more trouble. "Where is his lordship?"

I washed my face, went back to retrieve my shirt, which I almost forgot, and reported to Lord William's and his wife's apartment.

I knocked and Lord William answered the door, and asked me in. "I'll offer you a seat, but I don't think you're wanting to sit right now."

"No sir, I'll stand, with your permission. Did your lordship believe I was or my older mentors made me aware of the problem, before I had to be disciplined, sir?"

"I wasn't aware of it, until they talked to me. They hadn't noticed how bad it was, because you didn't act that way with them—you knew better than to challenge them too much," the baron told me.

"Sir Stephen is going on a scouting party, and asked my permission to take you along on the expedition. He is taking three juniors, including Jelu, and he will allow you to select another to go that is your age. He believed you would select Timothy. Aaron and Luke are also supposed to go. So you should be pretty comfortable as far they go."

"Yes sir, I'd love to go sir, with your permission, of course," I blurted out, interrupting the baron.

"James is also going, and will be taking Torin with him," the baron concluded.

That took some of the wind out of my sails, "Does that have anything to do with the beating I just got, sir?"

"Yes, some," he answered.

"I've never been in trouble with Aaron before . . . ," I started.

"Ray, it wasn't their idea. It was Sir Stephen's. Now, you have my permission to go if you want to, but you do not have to," he told me, putting his hand on my shoulder. "But you've already paid for the ticket!"

"I'll say, that was the severest beating I've ever had. The one from Sarah and Kurt might have hurt worse, because I was already sore, but fifteen licks. I'll go."

"I think Sir Stephen suggested a two dozen—eight from each of them, and they took up for you, especially Aaron," the baron told me. "Go by his barracks on your way home. Dismissed."

"Sir, begging your pardon, but with recent events, I'm not sure I want to discuss things with him right now, sir," I offered, hoping to not have to talk to Aaron considering the pain he had put me through.

"Would you like to walk back to the barn with me, squire, or would you prefer to follow orders?" came back the baron's response.

"Yes, I'll be reporting immediately to the senior squire, sir," I said and quickly left.

I went quickly to the barracks to find Aaron, still upset with him for his part. I probably shouldn't have been, since he saved me about nine additional cuts from a cane, but my backside still was hurting.

I knocked on the barrack's door, and one of the older senior squires answered, "What do you want, little boy?"

I considered answering him as an equal, then decided that since I had a senior's sash on I'd try a smart mouth approach. "As a marquis, a bit more respect to start with." It worked.

"Excuse me my lord, I didn't see the sash," he responded, stepping back and showing me in.

"It's all right, I was a bit sharp too. I need to see Aaron," I said not wanting to push it too hard and get into any additional trouble.

Aaron saw me, stood up, and motioned for me to come over to him. The scowl on his face may have been because he heard the interchange between the other senior and myself.

"Reporting as ordered, sir," I said as I came up to him.

"Did you just forget your manners—again?" Aaron asked in a quiet, level, but ominous tone.

"No sir, I may have been a bit sharp, but I'm due some respect also," I answered.

"As a junior, what would your action cost you? And come to attention," Aaron ordered.

"As a junior I wouldn't have been able to given the answer I gave, sir, and my tone might have cost me some disciplinary action," I answered.

"Hand me the sash," he said, holding out his hand and sitting back down. "Now go and ask the senior if he wishes to discipline you for your actions."

"Aaron, please, I'm senior, this isn't right," I pleaded with him, without success.

I went over to the senior and asked if he might step over and allow me to discuss something with him, and with Aaron. He looked at me and questioned the absence of the sash. When I got back to Aaron, I explained the situation, and asked for his forgiveness.

He asked Aaron if he had anything to add, then instructed me to get a rod leaning up against the far wall, and wait for him at the table in the middle of the room, before Aaron could answer. I went for the birch, as he and Aaron talked. I handed him the rod, and to my surprise he handed me my sash.

"Neither of us treated the other with the proper respect I didn't see the gold trim on your sash. Had you not had the sash, you would've been more respectful. I got caned more than a few times too, at your age, and since Aaron said he wouldn't mind if I let you off this time, and hoped I wouldn't cane you, I'll accept an hour of marching in full armor at Aaron's convenience. Is that fair enough or would you prefer a quicker punishment?" he added.

"No sir, thank you for your leniency," I answered greatly relieved. "Should you need my assistance in a manner, I'll try to return this favor, sir."

"When I become a knight, I might need some assistance—I'll call, but will not hold you to a promise. Aaron wants you outside, and try to keep quiet the rest of the evening," he answered. "Put the cane back before reporting."

I followed his instructions and found Aaron outside. I walked up to him and he caught me with a right punch that knocked me to the ground. This was the second time I had been struck by my "friends" this evening.

"Should I get up, or stay down?" asked rubbing my jaw.

"Oh, get up. I won't hit you again," Aaron answered. "That was for not learning the lesson the first time. I tried to get you out of the caning, but Sir Stephen was adamant about your getting busted."

"What about inside? That senior could have blistered me good, again. How did that fit in with your helping me . . ." I asked and then added the "sir? How long have I lost my senior privileges?"

"You may have those back in the morning. And you better be glad that Kurt and Adam agreed to give you the caning. Sir Stephen had some others in mind for the honor. What orders were you given after we caned you, besides to report to Lord William?" Aaron asked.

"None sir, that I can remember." I wasn't sure where this was going.

"Are you still sore from the discipline?" he asked.

I started to really mouth off at that question. Three older squires take turns wearing me out, and he asked that question? "Yes sir," I responded simply and truthfully.

"Then why don't you do something about it?" he asked grinning.

"I don't understand, sir," I said, somewhat confused. "What can I do about it? I don't think taking a swing at you is going to help the pain."

"Use your mind—literally," he said grinning and rubbing the top of my head.

"Oh, but . . . ," I started.

"You aren't a healer, and didn't receive orders not to use your skill. Of course, Sir Stephen doesn't know about it," Aaron told me. "Do I need to beat you again to get you motivated?"

"No sir," I said with the realization he meant for me to use *cell adjustment* on my welts.

"Go ahead while I'm here with you. If anybody notices the activity they will believe that we are practicing *rapport*," Aaron told me.

"Hey, sir, are we going to have any mage support on this expedition? Or is Luke the only spell caster?" I asked before I left.

"There is still some discussion about bringing a young novice spell caster, but it hasn't been decided yet. It may have been one that your cousin is newly contracted in a marriage arrangement," Aaron told me in an uncertain manner.

I hadn't heard of this yet, so I decided I'd better check with Luke, when I got the chance. He had been pretty busy lately. With his training, and helping to train the younger kids, we hadn't seen much of each other since we returned.

I marched the penalty duty the next day, after my classes. I also apologized to the seniors with whom I had been working with for my poor attitude, hoping they would forgive me because of the beating I received that night. I didn't mention the beating I received last night, but several knew that it had occurred. I also asked those my age to not to hold my disposition against me since it had been poor after being beaten up.

I met up with Jelu that afternoon. I told him I was tired of training. I wanted to learn more from action. Jelu asked about the learning from the actions of the seniors the previous night. I told him I didn't think it was very funny, and asked how he knew. He agreed, and hoped that neither of us got one on the expedition. He said he said he heard Torin and James discussing it, and said they wished they could've assisted.

Timothy was thrilled to be allowed to go, he was the only other junior our age who was being allowed to go on any more than scouting parties close by the city.

King Harold was to officially christen the new city Candlewynd, in honor of their former land, that week, but it was decided to delay the christening until the fall banquet for promoting pages to junior squires. This would give extra reason to celebrate, and since many would be mourning the passing of loved ones at that time it was decided to postpone the ceremony. Since the new squires would not be leaving for training, it could make another reason for a grand party. This would give the troop about five weeks from when they would leave to return for the christening.

The walls were coming along well, especially with the addition of the stone quarry. Other buildings were starting to take shape, and streets had been laid out. Spell casters can greatly add to the building process, even without *wall of stone*, just by the power of their spells. The city was a long way from being complete, but as the long days of summer stretched on, the city has growing well. Not only had physical aspects of the city but the living ones as well. Many new babies, besides Ray sister, Anne, were being born: most by women whose husbands did not make the trip by ship to the new land. Many of the senior squire age girls, who had been married after the arrival, were expecting children soon. Sherry and Adam believed their child would be born soon after the promotion celebration.

The fishing vessels had been having great success fishing around the new land. They had discovered some reefs near the new harbor, where the fishing was exceptional. The fresh fish and the new crops that were coming in were working wonders on the morale of the city, as well as the health. The few healers the city had were able to spend most of their time assisting with training, taking care of expectant mothers and newborns, rather than on illnesses. Megan felt as she might as well be a midwife. She had hardly had time to do anything, and with Luke or Sarah gone a great deal in the spring, she had to take up the slack.

Plans were being made to expand some of the fields next year, and to prepare others. This was to allow the part of the land to lay fallow every seventh year.

No news came from the other ship which had gone off exploring early in the spring, but there really wasn't a time table for its return, as far as most knew. But still they were hoping for some information. One of the larger fishing vessels had journeyed around the coast some, to see what was in the immediate area, after the party had returned with the villagers. They had gotten a general idea where the Orcs were from that trip. Another trip was planned about the time Sir Stephen was to set out with his group. The ship would sail out a few days to see if anything like islands were nearby.

The exploration that Ray and the others were going on was toward the Orcs. There had been some sighting of them by scouting parties. Not ever very close, but the signs still had some people upset. People were concerned about the possibility of the Orcs raiding the crops, or fire the fields.

So a party was going to be sent to check on them, and they would be allowed to take some of the newly trained war horses for this. Quicker travel, and retreat if needed, was much better than walking. And should they have to fight, a calvary charge with a lance can be very effective in dealing with foot soldiers. Granted, it would be a small charge, but it would also allow the party to swing down on the Orcs, instead of the other way of around.

The party started off, and was greeted by a much needed summer shower that morning. The town, and especially those working the crops, were hoping for a nice slow rain all day long. It would cool things down and settle the dust, however, it would make building in the city more difficult and slow that down.

The party consisted of: Sir Stephen, a knight; Aaron, James and Ray senior squires; Jelu, Torin, and Timothy junior squires; and Luke, the lone spell caster of the party. They also were bringing along three war dogs. All but Luke were in armor: Sir Stephen in chain mail, the squires in studded leather. Each warrior was mounted on a war horse, and the juniors were responsible for a pack horse each, which were those found in the valley. Supplies were on the pack animals, as was leather barding for the seven war horses. One did not normally travel with barding on one's horse, it tired the animal too much. The barding was put on before a battle, provided one had enough time.

Ray missed not have Bennet and Xell with them on this expedition. It seemed odd that they weren't along. Ray and his friends would have really like to have had Xell's magic support, but maybe it would not be needed. And needed or not—it wouldn't be available.

The first night out, after it had rained most of the day, Xell's cantrip to dry the wood could have come in nicely.

"You three junior squires go gather some wood for a fire. As close as we still are to the city, I'd prefer not to have a cold camp the first night out," Sir Stephen instructed.

"It's going to be tough to start it when it rained all day," Timothy said to me as he dismounted to go look for the branches.

Torin retorted to Timothy, "They can dry some of the branches off by using them across your backside!"

Timothy looked at me, with some fear in his eyes. I told Torin, "Oh, that's what they brought you for. I was wondering about that." Then I to motioned Timothy to get going. Torin didn't seem to think my response was near as humorous as his.

When the three returned they each had an arm load of soaked wood, for the fire. We'd never be able to start a fire with that stuff. Then Aaron walked up and handed Timothy a big double handful of straw.

"I grabbed it before we left, decided it might come in handy the first night. Now each of you will take turns making sure there are some dry wood for each night's campfire. Lay some out to dry by the fire each night and put it in your saddlebags," Aaron told the three junior squires. He passed his order along to Sir Stephen who gave the rotation order, making sure all three juniors knew they would be responsible for following Aaron's order.

———————————

The three tents were set up, and watches set for the night. Sir Stephen suggested to Luke that he share a tent with him. Then the seniors could share one and the juniors could share the other. Luke said that he would be honored to share the tent with the expedition leader, but suggested that instead of the tents split up along those lines, it might be better to divide more on age, which would have normally been done.

Luke suggested that Ray and Torin switch tents. Ray and James had not been on good terms for some time, and he was much closer to the other squires in age and friendship. The knight accepted Luke's suggestion, and Ray was thankful to his cousin for the idea. He believed it would be easier on Timothy, if he was there instead of Torin.

Aaron told Ray he was not too thrilled about the sleeping arrangement, but then told him that he was just giving him a hard time about it, he would be able to deal with those other two.

After the rain, the next morning broke warm, and got hotter very quickly. They decided to send out two advance scouts and rotate them. The others would go without armor, until the scouts came back with word that it was needed. Even without the armor, the troop was sweating a great deal, and had to often walk the horses to keep them from tiring too much, should they be needed for a fight. They all agreed this new world was much warmer in the summer than where they live on Saxet.

Ray quickly volunteered himself and Timothy for the first scout party, but Aaron suggested that the two youngest together might not be the best combination. He suggested that Ray take Jelu, and that he would work with the youngest junior squire.

Sir Stephen agreed, so Ray and Jelu started off in advance.

"Why'd you volunteer to go first?" Jelu asked as the boys rode away.

"It is going to get hotter, before it gets cooler—so I wanted to get out of the armor in the warmer parts of the day. Assuming we don't have a fight," I answered rather smugly.

"Don't get too proud of yourself, I think that may have had something to do with the conversation between you and some other senior squires," Jelu reminded me, in good humor. "Don't want to deal with Aaron again, do you?"

I asked him, "Have you been disciplined by Aaron?"

"Once, I argued with an instructor about the use of a bow. Even though I was correct, my manners were considered inappropriate. The . . . ah, instructor, had Aaron remind me of my station as a junior squire. Aaron isn't quite a full year older than I am, and we always get along great, but I thought he was trying to kill me. Apparently he believes his duty to discipline a younger friend is serious, and is more stern with us than a kid he has no interest in," Jelu told me.

"That explains why he was so hard with me. He almost cost me another one that evening."

"Jelu, I have a question to ask you, and I don't want to be rude. So if you believe the question is inappropriate, I apologize. I have heard you have some elven blood, is that true?" I asked hoping it was not offensive.

"Well, it is not something I talk about much, but I'll answer you, if you swear on your honor not to discuss it with others," Jelu responded.

"I promise not to betray your trust, as you have kept mine about my healing ability," I answered.

"If I remember correctly, I got a direct order from a knight, of noble birth to keep that information secret—Lord William! But thanks."

"Yes, several generations ago, an elven grandmother was captured by some humans, that were less than honorable. She had a child from the ordeal. When she was rescued by some other humans, they stayed with them and her son grew up as a human. It seems the elven skill with a bow was passed on to me through the generations. If I remember my math correctly, I'm either one sixteenth or one thirty-second part elven, I think it is the later. My psionic skills, I inherited from my mother's side of the family. I also have inherited the elven listening skill too, which helps when seniors are looking for an excuse to give a younger student a beating," he finished.

"Can you speak the tongue of the elder," I asked?

He shook his head yes.

As we traveled, we noticed the land seemed good out here, too. The others felt that at some time the city would be able to start crops out here too—assuming the Orcian threat was dealt with. Some of the people in the city had suggested a treaty with these creatures. I for one, didn't think that was a real possibility—given what I knew of Orcs.

If nothing else, some people should return, and cut this high grass for winter feed for the animals. I thought this would make fine hay, even if it was a little farther out from the city than was normally worked. A troop could be sent to guard the workers. I suggested this to Sir Stephen, who looked at me with surprise, and said he would include my idea in the report.

We moved most of a week without any sight of hostile creatures. We did see some deer-like animals, with longs straight horns, that went straight up. It seemed strange that the herd size was so small with the abundant grass, and we hadn't seen any predators. This suggested some predators were about, we just hadn't seen them. Aaron had come up with the same conclusion, and told us keep extra alert, remembering the big cats we had seen this spring.

Jelu had started working on a smaller bow, when I asked why he had a second smaller bow. He answered, "The long bow works great when I'm standing on the ground, but on horseback it is too large. I need a bow that I can fire while riding. I won't have near the range, but if we are trying to get away, it could slow down pursuit or reduce the odds if we are trapped, before we make a stand. Besides, I've spent so much time with a bow, I don't really know how to use the lance, I'm afraid I'd get it stuck in the ground, and it would send me sailing in the air." He laughed as he moved his hand through the air, showing his flight.

Timothy, Jelu, Aaron, and I enjoyed each other's company a great deal, and were having a wonderful time. With Aaron and I both being seniors, James nor Torin were giving Timothy too difficult a time. Jelu worked with Timothy in fencing practice to help him improve his skills, while Aaron and I worked a lot together. Aaron and I also worked together in close quarter fighting, while Jelu and Timothy used long sticks to approximate spear's thrust. This was done after the travel day was over, and then we would collapse in the tents for a brief rest, and prepare for night duty, or whatever duties that were assigned.

I told Aaron that I wished Kurt was with us, and it seemed strange for Lord William not to be here. I was careful not to seem disrespectful to Sir Stephen if I were overheard.

One day we day we spotted a group of mountains in the distance. That evening Sir Stephen came out to practice with us. He had some wooden swords for us to use, which were no more than a stick about the weight of a sword. He kicked Aaron pretty quickly, then disposed of me, then defeated Aaron and me both at the same time.

"Sir, permission to try something, sir? It may not work because you are more powerful than other opponents I have encountered, but could we try again," I asked. Then I told Aaron I was going to attempt to become *Invisible* to the knight.

"Are you skilled enough to hide from him—he's not an Orc?" Aaron questioned.

"I don't know—that is what I want to find out, which is why I asked first," I answered.

We made another attempt, and as I suspected I was not strong enough psionically to overcome him with my *Invisibility*. He asked me to explain what psionic skill I had tried on him, that apparently didn't work.

"I attempted to become *Invisible* to you sir," I answered. "It works well on the Orcs, and allows my smaller size to survive."

"I don't think it will help a lot on horseback, but one never knows," Sir Stephen responded. "And yes, I knew about your skill, so I'm glad you sought permission first; otherwise I might have felt insulted." Then he walked off.

"Good thing you asked, or you might have gotten both of us in trouble," Aaron said looking at me. "And that might have meant an unpleasant conversation between us afterwards."

"You can't take the sash back again, can you?" I asked.

"No, but I believe I'm still big enough to beat the snot out of you, should I choose to do so," he answered. "Just like my older brother did to me a couple of times. Yours ever kick your butt?"

"No, but he wore me out once. He never punched me in anger, but pushed me down once or twice when I wanted to swing at him," I told him. "I'd prefer not have to fight you."

"Me either," he told me.

They moved closer to the mountains and noticed more Orc tracks the closer they got to the mountains. Small rivers and streams crossed the land; they been gone nine days when they spotted the mountains. The mountains were not very large, "over-sized hills" might have been more accurate.

Near one of the streams a large canine paw print was discovered. It was larger than the war dogs that were with the party, and a bit deeper.

"What do you make of it sir?" Timothy asked Sir Stephen about the paw print.

"I'm not sure, but it's bigger than a poodle," Sir Stephen said as he laughed and rubbed the young squire's head. "I think it's some kind of a huge wolf—I'm guessing around 300 pounds."

James spoke up, "Sir, would a dire wolf fit what you're discussing? I remember that some Orcs use to use them as guard animals. But since we never met any Orcs on Saxet. I thought they might have just been made up. That is, until Lord William's expeditions encountered them this spring and early summer."

Then everyone looked at Aaron and me. "We didn't see any with them on the one I was on," Aaron answered the unasked question.

"It is a lot bigger than prints of the wolves that Sherry found on the search for the quarry. The puppies were timber wolves. Don't you agree James?" I asked to get him back in the conversation, and to appear to yield to his age.

"Agreed," was James's one word answer.

"We'd better keep a sharper lookout from now on. Looks like we'd better stay in armor all day, and you might better sleep with the leather chest protectors close by. Guard duty will be in full armor. Any questions," Sir Stephen finished.

We had none, those orders were clear, and we would have all come to the same conclusions on our own.

"Luke and Ray with me, if you please," Sir Stephen called out as everyone began to get their armor out of packs, and put it on.

We went to him, and I told Timothy to get my armor out while I was with the knight.

"Luke, are you capable of casting *sleep*?" Sir Stephen asked.

"Yes sir—one, and that would be in place of my more powerful healing spell," Luke responded, somewhat confused sounding.

"Relearn it then. Dropping one or two of those big wolves might be worth more than the cure. If they don't attack, we won't need as much curing—I hope."

"Ray, I don't think you are going to be able to go *Invisible* to those big wolves. You might be able to, but don't bet your life on it," he told me.

"Do you want to stop now and let me relearn the spell, while everyone is getting in armor? It will take more than a quarter of an hour to relearn that spell," Luke informed the knight.

"Yes, we'll get in armor, and have an early lunch. I'll tell everyone to leave you alone while you are studying," Sir Stephen answered.

Everyone got into their armor, Jelu and I said we'd take the horses to get some water, while lunch was being set up—stale bread and cheese. This gave the horses an early rest, and we decided not to armor the horses at this time.

After eating James and Torin went ahead to scout and we got ready to move through the still high grass of this land. An hour later they came back at a fast trot.

"We saw Orcs with human slaves," James told us.

Chapter Nine

Beasts in the Fields and Mines
••

"... He has sent me to bind up the brokenhearted, to
proclaim freedom for the captives and release from
darkness for the prisoners ..." Isaiah 61: 1

With the troop on a full alert, James and Torin came back
from advance scouting at a full gallop. James was signaling to
others as they rode up to make sure they knew they were coming
hard, with what appeared to be important information

James began when the two had reined up. "We almost
came out of this high grass, when we spotted a grain field, of
barley. There are humans working in the fields—I think slave
labor. There are four or five Orcian guards in leather armor
with swords, whips, and in leather armor. There are also five
huge wolves—we believe them to be dire wolves. That was all
we saw. We didn't want to get too close, it is possible there are
more."

"How many humans did you see?" Sir Stephen asked.
"Were any of them armed?"

Torin looked at James and answered, "Sir, we didn't
count the humans. They weren't armed, and may have been
hobbled."

"Well boys, are you ready to earn your King's bounty that you have been receiving, and his training?" Sir Stephen asked. "James and Torin, give us a rough map of how things are, so we can put a plan together."

It was decided that Jelu and Ray would step out to the cover of the grass and start firing arrows—at the wolves. Sir Stephen said they would be able to track the party better than the Orcs would, so they needed to die first. The rest of the party was to stay hidden in the high grass, and would come out as the fell creatures got close. Hopefully the Orcs would run after the two young archers also, so the five remaining warriors could catch them in a lance charge, and would be able to slay them.

Luke was to attempt to *sleep* the wolves as they converged on the archers on the ground. Whatever was left Jelu and Ray would have to deal with.

I was thinking I would have preferred to have been fighting from horseback as they got that close; besides, that big horse's hooves could help in that type of combat.

"Sir, would it be okay if some of you helped with the dire wolves before charging the Orcs? On the ground it would be a bit hard if more than one wolf got to us?" I asked.

"You afraid of a little puppy? Besides, you'll have the three war dogs to help you. If looks like more help than that will be needed I'll have Aaron stay and help," Sir Stephen agreed.

We stepped out of the high grass, stuck the arrow tips in the ground so we could fire quicker, and both shot the wolf closest to us, (that was doing a perimeter search, I guess). He was about thirty yards from us, facing away, when we let fly our arrows. Both missiles hit the large carnivore. It yelped in pain, then turned and snarled and started toward us. Both of our second arrows also found their marks, and the beast dropped dead—one down, four to go. Three of them were completely across the field, the last was on our right, so it became the target of arrows. We both began to fire arrows at the wolf.

By now the Orcs and the remaining wolves had seen us, and as expected started to charge. My God, those big wolves could run fast. The closest, the one on our right, was going to get to us faster than we expected. Jelu's first arrow hit the wolf in the flank, mine was a glancing shot and slid harmlessly off its hide. Both of our second arrows hit, and I yelled that I would get my sword out, but Jelu told me just to keep shooting. He fired and hit, but it was not a very effective shot. I fired my third shot as the creature was leaping with its maul open wide to devour us. My shot went into his open mouth and into his throat and it died in mid-leap, landing on me. Jelu switched to a new target as I climbed out from under the dead beast. As I got out from under the wolf, I decided it would be a good time to bring up *Invisibility*. It might not work, but it certainly wouldn't if I didn't try. While I was doing that Jelu fired twice more, as the three remaining wolves bore down on us. Jelu fired once more and then the *sleep* was cast, as the Orcs were starting to get close to our position also. Only one of the wolves went to sleep, it was an uninjured one, but only one slept from a healer's spell?

The horses then bolted out of the grasses. Aaron lanced the other uninjured wolf and I moved up to interpose between Jelu and the one he'd been firing at.

Aaron's lance broke off in the wolf he attacked, knocking the creature down, but not killing it. While it was down the horse, reared and plunged down on the creature with its steel shod hooves. Aaron was pulling his sword, throwing away the broken part of the lance that he had been holding.

The wolf I stepped up to didn't seem to care about my attempt to be *Invisible*. It leaped up at me, which I caught on my shield. The animal's weight nearly knocked me to the ground, despite being deflected by the shield. I hit the wolf with my sword and put a large gash across its rib. Jelu's next shot sunk the arrow up to the feathers, and still the creature wouldn't die.

By now the mounted part of the group had reached the Orcs with their lances. Sir Stephen skewered the one he attacked; the lance went all the way through and lifted the Orc off the ground. Sir Stephen dropped the lance, started to pull his sword, and his charger hit and trampled the Orc in the field of barley.

James and Torin both hit their Orcs with their lances, but neither were killing blows. Their horses knocked the Orcs over, and as they turn to come back at the Orcs, they pulled swords. Swinging down on the stunned Orcs they were able to dispatch both of theirs in short order, as both charges struck with their hooves also.

Timothy was having a more difficult time. His lance attack missed as the Orc was able to parry the charge with his sword. Timothy lost the lance and it fell to the ground. Timothy swung the horse around, and drew his sword to continue the attack. While he was turning the Orc picked up his dropped lance, using it for a large pole arm. The Orc caught Timothy with it, as he returned and unseated the young squire.

The wolf I had to deal with had got under my shield and was clamping down on my right leg. It was a good thing I had leather leggings on, or it might have bitten my leg off. I brought my sword down, hard across the skull, and another arrow shot from Jelu dropped the creature.

Sir Stephen had the last unoccupied Orc. He charged and swung his sword down, splitting the Orc's shield. The Orc swung up at him and sliced his armor, but the armor held, and he was uninjured from the blow, except for a slight bruise.

Aaron charged to assist Timothy who was wobbly from being unhorsed. The Orc charged him as he struggled to regain his feet. Fortunately the trained war horse protected him as he was starting to rise, and reared and plungeded, keeping the Orc away. The Orc attacked the horse, and put a nasty gash across its front right thigh.

Jelu, seeing the threat, shot the Orc that was attacking Timothy's horse. The Orc hit the horse in the chest, and then turned to see where the arrows were coming from. Aaron rode in and decapitated him, with a strong sweeping motion at a full gallop.

Sir Stephen was still attacking the last remaining Orc. The Orc somehow managed to grab the knight and yank him off his horse. As both fell, Sir Stephen was able to roll free and spring back on his feet.

The Orc gave out a great cry and charged, swinging his sword with both hands. Sir Stephen caught the sword on the edge of the shield, which split a quarter of the way up. Sir Stephen countered with a swing that caught the Orc across the stomach, for a deep gash. The Orc swung again, and again Sir Stephen deflected it with the shield. This time the shield buckled and Sir Stephen pitched it to the ground.

The rest of the troops were finished with their foes, and we moved in to assist the knight—it wasn't needed. Sir Stephen caught the Orc with his sword in the breast for a slight slice. The enraged foe made a mighty swing, hoping to catch the knight and crush him with the swing. Sir Stephen ducked under the attack and plunged his sword up to the hilt through the back of the Orc, severing the spinal column.

At this time I was lying on the ground, with a serious gash on my leg where the giant wolf had attempted to have me for lunch. Timothy was still dazed, but not really injured. His horse was another matter. She was badly wounded, and those trained horses would be hard to replace.

Sir Stephen had Luke bandage my leg, and prepare to cure me.

I suggested, "Sir, I'm not that bad. But if Luke doesn't heal the horse we might lose her, and we can't afford to do that sir."

"I believe one of my squires is more valuable than even a well-trained war horse, so let the healer do his work," Sir Stephen said.

"But sir, he can finish curing me tomorrow, or *cell adjust* me after the horse is cared for. So if we need to leave, we have all our mounts."

Then I whispered to Luke, "Don't tell him I can *cell adjust*, just let him know that my plan is workable."

Luke followed my lead, and the knight agreed. Aaron came and Jelu came over to me, and asked what I was doing. "If Sir William didn't inform him of my second skill, we can't," I told them. "He can think Luke is curing me while I do it myself."

"Be careful, or you'll get a heck of a beating," Aaron warned me. "But you are sworn to Lord William."

Luke cast both his remaining curative spells on the horse, then checked on Timothy to make sure he was not injured from his fall. He had to psionically cure him a little, just to get rid of the cobwebs in the young squire's head.

Sir Stephen took James and Torin with him to try to communicate with the slave laborers, leaving Aaron in charge of getting things ready to leave. Aaron was getting ready to slit the throat of the *slept* dire wolf when Timothy yelled for Aaron to stop.

"I can communicate with it—we might get some information. Let's tie it up until Sir Stephen gets back to decide what questions we need to try to get answered," Timothy said.

"You can communicate with animals?" Jelu asked.

"Well so far, just mammals, but we might get some get some good information," the junior answered.

"All right Jelu, you and Timothy get it tied up, and then check your arrows, to see if any are retrievable. Luke, you go and tend to your cousin," Aaron commanded.

Jelu looked from Luke to me, and then followed Aaron's orders. I cured myself, and got most of the wound taken care of. The bandage made it feel better, but without additional curing the bruises from the bite would be with me for a long time. Even with the curing, I still had a pretty good limp.

Sir Stephen and the squires came back with twelve humans the Orcs had enslaved. There were eight males and four females, all were relatively young—under twenty-five—and in fairly poor condition (due to harsh treatment). Aaron went out to meet them, and to inform Sir Stephen of Timothy's idea for information.

Sir Stephen and Timothy discussed things for a couple of minutes to plan strategies for questioning the wolf. Timothy reminded the knight that his devotion was not as powerful as the clerical spell, *speaks with animals*. The creature was not forced to cooperate, but it sure helped when training creatures.

Luke examined the humans and treated some of their injuries, but got them some food to eat, before examining them. Luke also had Torin cut the ropes off their ankles, where they had been tied together to prevent running.

Now animals are not smart in the same sense as humans, so getting information from them is not as simple as questioning a human, even a child. Timothy had never attempted *animal telepathy* with a hostile animal—and the wolf was definitely hostile. He eventually discovered wolves counted by number of paws, a full set of paws being four. There were five other sets of wolf guards like this one: twenty-five more of these creatures. One set guarded the workers in a mine that produced metal for weapons, another was a scout patrol, two other groups were in fields, and the last one was off duty. The way it worked, they would get a day off in each rotations set—work five days and have one day to rest. The wolf had no concept of the number of Orcs in the city, too many for it to count. But Timothy did find out, the city was above ground and these Orcs did not mind the sun.

Then right before he had planned on finishing his question, a couple of things frightened him. First he discovered that at least one of the Orcs in the city could cast spells—a witch doctor. The second (and Timothy believed worse) the Orcs had a pack of Worgs to ride. The wolf didn't know how many; he stayed away from the horse-sized wolves. These creatures were supposed to feed on other creatures that got too close, and were many times fed slaves—alive.

Timothy was tired from his questioning of the dire wolf, and the battle. He relayed the information to Sir Stephen, which was much more than they had been able to get from the humans. The language they spoke was similar, but not the same as those taken from the village. This surprised the party, but it was possible that their language was adapted to Orcs, or maybe there were other villages that spoke different languages nearby.

Finally, Aaron drew the field and the hills further back in the dirt and remembered the word for map that the villagers used. One of the older men realized what was being asked and drew in the city and fields of the city.

While they were drawing the map in the dirt, Sir Stephen sent Torin and Ray to check the guard post to see if any equipment was there that might be used. He sent Timothy to lie down, and to try to sleep to regain some energy after his trial of battle and what was required to communicate with the wolf. He was visibly exhausted by his ordeal.

Sir Stephen now had a dilemma: what to do with the grain field. James suggested that they take all they could get and fire the field. This would add to the city's growing food supply, and make a more difficult winter for the Orcs.

Luke suggested that would invite retaliation from the Orcs on the city's grain fields. He suggested that they only take what the Orcian pioneers could carry off with them in some sacks, and leave the rest—including the wagon and its contents.

Sir Stephen said he would make the final decision, but that he would like to hear each of the squires' opinions, as if they were advising the king. Torin and Ray returned during these discussions.

Jelu believed that doing the most harm to the Orcs was a good idea, but agreed with Luke about not inviting that type of retaliation. Aaron believed that Luke's logic was sound—even if he wasn't a warrior. Aaron believed you made war on armies, not the land. Torin, of course, agreed with James.

Ray said that in general he would like to see them do as much harm to the Orcs as possible, but since Candlewynd was not ready to go to an all-out war and siege the city, he would agree with Luke, that burning the crops would set a dangerous and possibly costly precedent. Further he believed that they should withdraw, back to the city—as they were out of spells and curing.

Sir Stephen was not pleased with Ray's extra unsought advice. "I didn't ask for your last statement, squire. I'm aware of spell ability, or the lack of it that is left, but I'm loath to leave humans in Orcian hands. Since you brought the subject up, unsolicited, what do the rest of you think?"

Ray was embarrassed by the manner the knight responded to his opinion, when he believed it was warranted.

Luke was adamantly opposed to any attack with spell support: no cures, or *sleep*, especially with some injuries already incurred. Timothy's horse was still hurt and Ray's leg needed more healing. A score of peasants wasn't worth the risk.

Torin, surprisingly spoke up next, without waiting to say what James already had said. "I want to kill some more Orcs. The more we kill today, in small parties, the less we will have to deal with when it comes to all out war—and it will!"

Ray was shocked when Jelu agreed with Torin.

James's opinion was somewhat caustic to the young senior squire. "I believe that the two cousins are being overly cautious. Our battle plan was good that time, just a slight change to improve it is needed."

Aaron looked at Ray and just before he spoke Ray knew that we would also side with the attack. "I'm not sure over cautious is a good term. I believe they have a good point. It will be dangerous to continue the attack, but I believe it is what we must do. In good conscience, I cannot see leaving the humans as slaves."

Sir Stephen then informed the expedition of his decision. "We will leave the field. Let's try to communicate with the prisoners to take as much as they can each carry and have them travel toward Candlewynd. We will make at least one more attack, and meet them at one of two locations, tonight or by tomorrow night. Luke, since you have no spells, go with them, having them lead the pack horses, and help them find the sites for camps."

Luke was shocked at his orders. "Sir, I still can bandage and treat the wounds from combat. I believe I could still be an asset to the team, and would prefer to stay, sir."

"Come with me," Sir Stephen stated, very angrily.

Aaron began trying to get the former prisoners to understand what Sir Stephen wanted them to do. He got a sack and motioned for them to fill them, and then pointed to a place on the map. With a great deal of gesturing and pointing, he believed he got the point across.

Luke and Sir Stephen returned to the rest, neither looking very pleased. Ray asked his cousin what happened. Luke said he was staying, but he might have an unpleasant night—Sir Stephen hadn't yet decided how unpleasant it was going to be.

The former slaves started off, with the pack animals, and the party started to the next field they wanted to liberate. It was decided that Aaron would fire his bow also, at least to start and then would mount and attack on horse. The lancers would attack dire wolves first and assult the Orcs. They would also set their war dogs into combat this time, and Luke would be responsible for that.

Ray quietly asked if maybe he and Timothy might should switch. Timothy could fire a bow and Ray would attack with a lance. He also apologized for speaking out of turn earlier.

Sir Stephen wasn't in the mood for apologies or changing his plan.

Ray was limping badly, and James suggested to Aaron that they should say something to the knight about him being on the ground, and unable to move well. Aaron agreed.

"I don't like the little snot, but . . . ," James started.

"Yea, I know. But you'd like to be the one to kick his butt, not an Orc," Aaron said with a grin. "Let's see Sir Stephen."

James began, "Sir, Ray's leg is pretty bad off, even after a little curing. He is going to have a difficult time fighting from the ground like that. We were thinking maybe it would be better to have the little snot on a horse, because of that."

"The healer didn't say he wasn't fit to fight—why should you two?" the knight responded.

"With all respects, sir, I don't think we gave him much of a chance, when we discussed attacking, sir," Aaron suggested.

James was sent to get Luke, while Sir Stephen and Aaron continued the topic. "It seems a bit more dangerous than it should be," Aaron said.

"Do you believe, I think this is some game we are playing out here," Sir Stephen asked—starting to get mad?

"No, sir! But that's a young marquis you're gambling with—and he has an injured leg. He suggested something different, without complaining about the leg where he could get on a horse."

"You're getting extremely close to being insubordinate, squire," Sir Stephen said very cooly, as James returned with Luke.

"How bad is your cousin's leg?" Sir Stephen asked, as his younger companions returned.

"It is pretty bad. Had he not been in the leather armor, it would have probably been broken, and I can't tell for sure, because I've exhausted my *cell adjust* for the day, the leg might have a slight crack in it," Luke answered.

"So . . . ?" the knight questioned.

"He should be off it until he gets it healed. If we had more troops, he would not be cleared for battle," Luke informed him somewhat coldly—even a bit dangerous at his age.

Sir Stephen changed his battle plans and switched Ray and Timothy. Timothy was to fire his bow, with Aaron and Jelu. Aaron and Timothy would step back into the grasses and remount and fight from horseback, while Jelu would continue to fire his bow. If time didn't permit, Aaron would stay on the ground and fight, and he would tell Timothy when to cease firing and mount. Luke and Timothy would also switch horses, to keep the injured mount out of the combat.

The party got into position. The three boys stepped out of the high grass and started their deadly rain of arrows on the surprised canines. Two attacks, and two complete surprises—they were indeed fortunate. It was predetermined that if a wolf was very close they would all fire at it; if not, Aaron and Timothy would take the closest and Jelu would start on the next threat, assuming it was not too far off.

The closest wolf was about fifty yards away when the boys fired, the next one was about another forty from that, so Jelu decided to shoot the wolf at ninety yards. Aaron's shot caught the huge lupus behind the right front shoulder, and Timothy hit with a grazing blow toward the back of the ribs. And to everyone's surprise Jelu—missed. Well, he hit the creature, but it just caromed harmlessly off its side.

The first let out a tremendous howl of pain, and limped toward his assailants. The second, an uninjured one, also howled but she took a moment to find his attackers before it charging the boys with a great burst of speed. But the moment of indecision allowed more time for extra shots to be fired.

Jelu's second shot at his target was true. He caught the animal in the right shoulder, just after she had begun its charge, which sent it tumbling forward.

Aaron's and Timothy's second shots were close behind Jelu's and both hit the wolf square in the chest. It still didn't drop, and it would be close if the boys would be able to fire again before the wolf attacked. Aaron told Timothy to get mounted, but the boy was pulling another arrow to fire instead. Just before either could fire again, Jelu's bow twanged, and dropped the wolf four yards in front of Aaron. With their original target down, both squires fired on Jelu's original target, which was limping on three legs after the previous shot by Jelu. Aaron's shot hit the right back hip and Timothy missed, since he fired too quickly on the switch of targets. Aaron again ordered Timothy to go get mounted. Timothy started to argue when Aaron yelled, "NOW!"

By now the rest of the wolves and the Orcs were closing on the boys, and Timothy reluctantly went to get on his horse. Jelu and Aaron both fired again on the wounded wolf and killed it, then Jelu also started to get on his horse when Sir Stephen and the others charged out of the grass. Sir Stephen told him to start firing on Orcs, one of whom had pulled a bow and was preparing to return fire.

James, Torin, and Ray each charged one of the remaining wolves, keeping them from getting to the archers. Jelu and Aaron both concentrated on the Orc that was getting prepared to shoot at them. Timothy started to charge in the direction James and Torin had gone, thinking he might finish off one that was only injured, hoping Ray could take his own. Sir Stephen then spurred his mount and took off after an Orc that was attempting to flee for help or sound an alarm.

James and Torin both caught their wolves dead on with their charge and then trampled them with their chargers, just how it was described in class: neither wolf moved after the horses had trampled them. Timothy then moved to take an Orc that was trying to get to James before he was going to get his sword free, as it was somehow tangled in the sheath. The young junior caught the Orc just before he was going to split James with a huge, two-handed axe. It wasn't a clean kill, but it did knock the creature to the ground, allowed James to get his weapon clear and finish it off, and Timothy's lance didn't break.

Ray wasn't as fortunate with his lupus. He missed and the wolf almost knocked him from the saddle when it bit him on his right arm. Luckily the wolf didn't stay locked on and Ray was able to charge on through and come back around for another attack. The second charge was much better, catching the big wolf in the chest and breaking off the lance in it. The horse veered over and trampled the wolf on the way by. Ray pulled his sword and wheeled about, but the creature was dead.

Jelu and Aaron made short work out of the Orcian archer. Jelu quickly hit him twice and Aaron added another shot before he ever finished stringing the bow and notching its first arrow. The pair then turned to hit an Orc that had flanked the party and come up close before being spotted. Aaron fired, then dropped the bow and picked up his sword and shield which were right beside him. Jelu added an arrow before the creature arrived, catching the female Orc in her left shoulder, as she closed with another two-handed axe. The huge female Orc was howling in pain, or making some curse, as Aaron collided with her. Aaron's shield swept her axe to the side and sent a slicing long sword across her right ribs.

Torin had found a new target and bore down on an Orc with his long sword. The Orc waited for him with his own weapon. It seemed that all of the Orcs were wielding the great axes. Torin was wishing he still had his lance; that axe was a huge weapon and it was likely to make contact before he could reach the Orc with his shorter weapon. Just before the moment of contact an arrow by Jelu struck the Orc, just below the armpit, causing it to flinch and allow Torin to cleave its skull with the charge by.

Sir Stephen caught the fleeing Orc in the middle of the back with his lance, lifting the creature off the ground, then trampled it with the charger. With his lance intact, he wheeled to make sure the job was completed. To his relief the field was theirs and all hostiles were apparently dead.

They started to get the humans together and speak with them, again this was extremely difficult with the language barrier. This group was a younger, mixed group, almost all children between ten and fourteen. Most of them looked pretty ill-used.

Luke bandaged Ray's arm and then started to care for their injuries. James and Timothy checked all the orcian and dire wolf bodies to be certain they were dead, and gathered their weapons.

Torin showed the young prisoners the map, but it didn't seem to mean anything to them. They attempted to communicate with some of the language of the people from the village, but they didn't seem to understand it either. Mostly they just sat down and cried.

Aaron was having a heated discussion with Timothy, and Timothy looked scared.

Sir Stephen was getting impatient. "We've got to move, if we're going to rescue the other group."

"Sir, these kids aren't going to be able to make it to the rendezvous without assistance," Torin told the knight. "They are too young and scared."

"All right, Luke, you'll have to take these back. No argument, just get them packed and moving. That is an order," Sir Stephen told him.

Then turning to me, he said with a grin, "Would you try to avoid getting injured the next time? Your cousin won't be there to wipe your—ah, tears and look after you."

Then Torin asked, "Sir, what about those patrols of wolves? They meet one of them and it could get really ugly. Some of those patrols might be making it back this way this late in the day, if they caught us in the attack—we could be in real trouble."

"Luke, have the children dump the grain out of one of the wagon, and harness your horse to it. Some of those kids aren't going to be able to go very fast, put them in the cart. When you get back to the meeting place, have them fix a big meal to help with their strength and hope that we will be back soon too," Sir Stephen said.

I went to help Luke harness the horse to the cart. It could hold six of the smallest children and they would be able to make quicker time. Luke wouldn't even have a guard dog if they got attacked. We had a quick prayer that he'd get to the meeting place safely, and that he would survive the meeting when Sir Stephen returned.

Luke and the kids moved toward the meeting place, and we started to the last field. I was tired, and I knew everyone else was too. I thought Sir Stephen was pushing us too hard, and after a hard fight we would have to still get back to the meeting place that night. We couldn't stay this close to the Orcian city.

This time the field was not surrounded by high grass. There was a lot of open space between any cover and the field. That meant a knight, six squires, and three guard dogs against five dire wolves and five Orcs. I didn't like the odds, especially with us and our mounts so tired.

We walked most of the way to the last field, and it was within an hour of dark when we got there. The prisoners were already starting to load the carts for the return trip to the Orcian city.

We moved out into the open and made it almost to the field before we were spotted. A wolf howled and then they all howled. Everyone but Sir Stephen and me dismounted and prepared to fire bows. We held the horses. The guard dogs, we had left back a ways, and were going to call them up when we wanted them to charge. Each of the five squires would fire a flight arrow first at the charging wolves, then fire a second shot with a heavier sheath arrow, preferably at the two lead wolves. If there was time, a third volley would be fired before mounting up.

Moments after spotting us, the howling wolves sprang toward us, with the Orcs close behind. At extremely long range only Jelu's arrow hit and did damage; others glanced off the animals' flanks. Sir Stephen whistled for our dogs, who came bounding up to our assistance. The second volley of arrows was much more effective as Jelu's and two other arrows hit the animal, dropping it dead. The other two squires hit and injured another wolf.

Aaron and Jelu fired once more as the other three squires mounted their horses. We were going to be in for a much tougher battle this time, too many opponents were going to reach us. Aaron and Jelu both struck the wounded wolf in the chest with arrows.

Sir Stephen and I charged wolves. James, Torin, and Timothy did not have time to get a charge in on a wolf, only to get horsed and ready for combat. James took the remaining wolf, allowing the two junior squires to charge Orcs, who thankfully were armed with long swords, instead of those great axes.

Two of the dogs jumped the wolf attacking James, and Aaron swung up in the saddle to prepare to meet the Orcs.

Sir Stephen lanced his wolf through the mouth and down its throat, breaking the lance and killing the wolf. I still would have preferred to have used a sword. Not enough practice with a lance, but I suspected I would get plenty of practice when we got home, if we survived this battle. I made a decent hit with the lance, and knocked the creature over. The horse took me past the creature and I continued my charge to attack an Orc that was closing. I hoped Jelu would see the wounded wolf and finish it off with arrows. As I glanced back, I saw Jelu had mounted, and pulled his lance to attack the injured wolf.

A big Orc rolled under my lance attack, came up and almost knocked me from the horse when he hit my shield—luckily it was the shield instead of me that he hit. I wheeled and came back around in time to see Jelu and the last guard dog attacking the wolf I had injured. The second pass at the Orc, I made a good clean hit, knocking him to the ground, and breaking the lance off in his shoulder. I pulled my sword and closed again, but to my surprise he ducked under again and pulled me off the horse.

I rolled under the horse, to free myself from the Orc. The horse protected me while I got back on my feet. I went into a quick trance and brought up *Invisibility*. The Orc was busy with my horse and I took him from the flank across the neck with the long sword. I then remounted and got ready for whatever else needed to be done. Then I saw five more wolves bearing down on us—the patrol!

Jelu heard my yell and dismounted and started to fire at the five fresh wolves. We had all been a little slow from fatigue, and had not quite finished the Orcs when the new onslaught hit us from our left side.

Jelu had managed two good shots before the dire wolves were among us. Sir Stephen closed with his sword on one of the brutes, while Torin was finishing off the Orc that he had been attacking. James and the two dogs had finished the wolf with which they were dealing, and one of the dogs was badly mauled from the encounter.

With our lances all broken, it would be a battle with swords against the large wolves. Timothy charged up to help Torin. who had been knocked off his horse by a leaping wolf. Aaron was having a difficult time with a jet-black wolf that seemed to be larger than the others. I closed and intercepted the wolf that Jelu had shot to allow him to keep firing. With those two deep arrow wounds in the wolf I was able to dispatch it reasonably swiftly.

Jelu was able to get off a shot into Aaron's wolf, distracting it long enough for Aaron and his mount to finish it off. Torin had gotten back on his feet with Timothy's assistance and between the two had finished off their wolf.

James was the last to complete the killing of the wolves. The second guard dog had died in the struggle, but we were lucky it was only the dogs. Had the wolves arrived two minutes earlier, it would have been us lying in the darkening field.

I hurt all over from the strain of the battles that day, and my wounds were throbbing as I dismounted and led my tired horse back to where Jelu was standing. Then I moved to Torin. "Let me see the arm. I'll try to clean it up a little until Luke can look at it," I told him.

"Thank," he said. Then looking up at Timothy, "Thanks kid, you saved my butt. If you hadn't showed up, I would have been dog food."

Sir Stephen and James had gone to round up the slaves, had them dumping out the grain from the cart and pulling it toward the rest of us. One of the women came over and looked at the bandage on Torin's arm, then nodded in approval. She went around and looked at each of our wounds, cleaned, and dressed them.

They harnessed Jelu's horse to the cart. The war horse seemed upset that it was being harnessed. It was the freshest of the horses, so it would have to pull. The human prisoners were a lot older than the last group. I couldn't guess their ages—just adults.

We were all leading our tired horses, when Aaron came up to me and told me to get in the cart. "You have to stay off that leg, or it will be harder to heal."

"I can't ride like that, Jelu's horse doesn't need the extra strain," I answered, as he walked off ahead.

I dropped back and saw Timothy was dragging along also, just from exhaustion. "You did a good job today. A couple of saves, and kills. Not bad for a junior squire," I told him.

"You think so?" he said somewhat discouraged.

"Yeah, you did good!" I answered.

"Would you talk to Aaron for me? He's going to wear me out," he answered.

"Why?" I asked.

"I didn't follow orders and mount up when he told me to."

"I doubt I can help you on that, he's going to bust your butt for it," I told him. "Maybe I can convince him to wait 'til we get back, or at least until we've healed up from the battles. It would be hard to fight when you can't sit on a horse."

Sir Stephen dropped back and told me, "Get in the wagon and off that leg. You don't need to walk on it, and it's at least three hours back to the camp. Get some sleep, and you'll be able to handle watch."

The next thing I knew we were at the camp. A late meal was quickly prepared for the prisoners we had rescued and our forces. Luke redressed the bandages, and put some salves on the wounds.

Timothy and I had the first watch, and then Sir Stephen and James were going to finish off the night. We planned to get a late start in the morning, to allow Luke to learn his spells. Thankfully the night was uneventful, and the summer morning broke with what promised to be a bright and hot day.

Slowly the camp started to move, food prepared, and Luke began to check the wounds to see who needed his help the most. Because of my multiple wounds, it was determined that I was in need of his most powerful curing spell. Torin and the lone remaining dog received his the other two. Luke used his *cell adjust* on some of the injured former prisoners.

Luke told me, "Save your *cell adjust*, in case of an emergency. I know your leg is still in need, but I don't want us to be totally without any healing if someone goes down."

With our horses exhausted from yesterday's battles, we all walked the entire day. I got the chance to talk to Aaron about Timothy's trouble.

"Since he is your junior squire for the mission, you need to discipline him," Aaron told me.

"I can't," I replied.

"Why not? He is your junior squire, and he needs to be punished," Aaron responded.

"For the same reason you can't discipline Jelu. There's not enough difference in our age," I reminded him.

"What, he's only thirteen . . . Oh, you can't discipline any of the junior squires, can you?" he asked.

"I can't even discipline a bunch of the pages without orders from someone older, but don't mention that, please. Sir William's orders," I informed him.

"Well, I can give you the authority, but I don't think that is what is needed here," he told me, thinking.

"Why don't you wait until we get back and then cane him? That way if we need to fight, he can fight from horseback," I suggested.

"Let's go talk to Sir Stephen and see what he thinks we should do," Aaron countered.

Sir Stephen wasn't at all pleased about this. He suggested that perhaps I should be caned for not having taught the junior squire to follow orders, and then I would do a good job of disciplining Timothy. He said he would think about it, and let me know that evening. I gave my suggestion about postponing the discipline until after we returned, and he said he'd keep that in mind also.

That day was uneventful, and Jelu and I moved back behind the party to see if we were being pursued. It made for an intense day, but we saw no sign of Orcs. That evening we made it back to camp and were in need of food and a good sleep.

Shortly after dark, Sir Stephen led Timothy and Luke into the woods. It was a fairly long time before they came back, with the younger boys moving very sorely. Apparently Sir Stephen decided the discipline would take place immediately and not wait any longer. Luke said that both of them were beaten pretty severely.

That night Sir Stephen called all the squires together for a meeting. He wanted to remind us that there was a strict "hands off" policy in regard to these new humans we had rescued. That was met with something less than enthusiasm from the older squires, some of whom the younger girls were giving attention.

Sir Stephen said, "Most of you have a contract marriage in place. So your obligations should prevent an affair, and since Luke did not have a *cure disease*, it would be better not to contract some Orcian disease."

I was a bit shocked with the order but apparently, from what Luke told me, James and Aaron had been getting lots of attention from some of the females we had rescued. It didn't seem to bother them.

Sir Stephen asked them if they would require a walk with him to understand his orders clearer. Having seen Timothy and Luke returning from a "walk" they understood that their status as a senior wouldn't keep them from discipline if they didn't obey.

After a couple of days of walking slowly, medical assistance, and large meals the newly rescued captives were capable of picking up the pace. The slow movement also allowed the horses to rest some too, but they were still not ready for another prolonged battle. The pack animals were able to pull the wagons and allow the war horses a rest from that chore.

Sir Stephen was still sending riders to check the back trail every day, but after a couple of days he began sending out advance scouts to make sure the Orcs had not circled ahead to cut them off from the city. But still there had been no sign of pursuit.

The troop made it back to the city in ten days, without incident, and with that many noncombatants. The boys did a good job of both keeping them moving and of staying out of trouble themselves, which is not always easy for young boys.

Ray was looking forward to seeing his family and working the young palomino. He was also looking forward to seeing Charissa again, although he couldn't figure out why seemed so special to him. After all, she was so much younger than he was; she was only eleven and he was thirteen.

The Fall Festival and christening of the city would be soon, within a week. Preparations were being made for it as the group came proudly to the city, after the city gates were closed for the night. It took some effort and calling of the guards and checking before the gates were opened and the party was allowed in.

Sir Stephen, Luke, and the three senior squires, (which included Ray) were called immediately to the king for a report. The three junior squires were to assist the humans in finding a place to sleep for the night. It was decided they were to stay in one of the barns until other arrangements could be made and their conditions carefully examined. The three junior squires were required to stay with them, as guards and to help in the transition in the morning. This was not exactly what the three wanted to hear. They had been looking forward to an enjoyable bath, and their own beds. Unfortunately for them, it would have to wait at least one more evening.

The knight and his other four boys went to the great hall for debriefing and reports. They were divided up among the king's advisers and asked about certain aspects of their journey, the land, plants, animals, and of course the hostile creatures they encountered. One of the advisers was assigned hear each person's take of the three battles. Another, what they had learned from the prisoners they had freed, even with the limited language skills, etc. In all it was a lengthy process, and much more intense than any other questioning through which the boys had been.

Food was brought to them and the questioning continued while they were eating, answering questions between bites of cheese, pork and bread. The group was questioned about information for mages to know, about the creatures, the damage potential of the opponents for the healers . . . many of whom had to answer "I don't know, sir or ma'am."

After the long interview process, they were finally dismissed and allowed to go home. As it was getting late, Ray wondered if those in the great hall had sent word to their families that they had returned. By now it was so late everyone should be asleep.

As Ray and Aaron were walking out of the meetings, a very sleepy-headed page approached them—it was Cord.

"What are you doing here, and up so late?" I asked my brother.

"Sirs, Lord William's compliments," he began. "You are both to attend him at six, in the morning. You are to meet him at the Knight's Hall for first meal, and you are to be in dress attire."

"Very good page. Are you to report back that the message was received, or are your duties completed with the delivery of the message?" Aaron asked.

"No sir, I must also inform the healer, sir. Then I will have completed the assignment," Cord responded.

"I'll stay and wait with you," I told him as I grabbed him and gave him a good hug. "I'm glad to see you're doing well, and getting an important task for a page."

Aaron excused himself, and went back to the barracks to get some rest, in what was left of the night.

We sat back down, and Cord told me that Lord William sent for him, so that mother and Aunt Beth would know that we had arrived back safely. He also let our mothers know that it would be a late night and early morning for us.

Cord also told me that Jakót had wanted to come and wait with him, but he was in trouble, and mother wouldn't let him come. It was then that I noticed that my little brother had a slight black eye.

"Is that what he is in trouble for?" I asked Cord, pointing to the eye.

"Yeah," he replied looking down at the floor.

"Is that the correct response you're suppose to give a senior, as a page?" I returned, in quite a stern voice.

"No sir. I thought I was just talking to my big brother, and wouldn't need to be so formal, sir."

"You're still on duty, and what if someone else overhead the statement? You'd have been in for it. Now, let's try it again. Is that what he is in trouble for?" I repeated the question.

"Yes sir, we had a fight, sir," he answered, still looking at the floor.

"And what happened after that?" I asked.

"Mother wore both of us out, real good, and the only reason I got to come was because Sir William had sent orders, and he didn't know I was confined to the ship," he said very rapidly. "Had he come, himself, Mother probably would have told him we were grounded and asked if another might have the assignment."

"Well kid, it could have been worse—I could have been home, and given you the whipping, and I'm stronger than Mother," I said, teasing with my brother.

Luke came out and Cord gave him the formal message from Lord William. We then all walked home together on the warm summer night to get the four or five hours of sleep that we could before having to be up early in the morning.

"It looks like the baron could have met us for lunch instead of first meal. As tired as I am, I would have liked to have slept that late," Luke said.

I agreed. After a trip like that with the pressure and worry of getting back, I really would have liked a long sleep.

When we got back to the ship, everyone was asleep, except those on watch duty. I left orders to wake me up at five, so that I might have time to prepare for my early appointment with Lord William.

I wondered what tomorrow would have in store.

Chapter Ten

The Gold Squad

....

"Praise be to the Lord my Rock who trains my hand for
war, and my fingers for battle." Psalms 144: 1

I felt like I just had laid down, stretched, rolled over and
closed my eyes when the cabin boy shook my shoulder and
woke me up.

"It's five, my lord. You left instructions to have you woken
at this time," the young boy said nervously. I guessed he
was hoping this wasn't some hoax fir which he would be in
trouble.

"Thanks," I mumbled as I rolled over.

I went over to the washbasin, poured some water from the
pitcher, washed my face, and was trying to convince my eyes
to stay open. It was still too dark outside to see anything, so I
had to light the lamp. I tried to stay quiet, so I wouldn't wake
the two younger boys that were still sleeping—quite soundly.
I thought about "accidently" waking them up since I had to
be up, but decided against it. They would need their sleep,
and Cord had been up late last night delivering messages for
Sir William.

I dressed in the light blue trousers and jacket. I met with Luke on deck, who came up moments after I did.

"I'd still rather be asleep," he said, letting out a huge yawn.

"Well, you could have ignored the orders. I somehow suspect the extra sleep wouldn't have been worth the discipline you'd have gotten for disobeying an order from a knight at our age," I told him laughingly.

"What is this 'our age' stuff? I'm two years older than you, still," he replied, in what seemed an upset tone.

"What're you mad at me for? I just meant we still get busted if we don't follow orders," I said.

"Never mind," he said, shaking his head. "Let's just go."

I wasn't sure what I had done to upset my cousin, maybe it was just the early hour, and lack of sleep. The wind was still, and the bay was barely moving, just enough to gently rock one to sleep. The two moons over head gave off decent light, and it still seemed strange seeing both of them in the night sky.

The unpleasant smell off the bay was worse than usual—rotting sea weed and dead fish, and with no breeze to stir it up, in this heat I was ready to get moving. Hopefully the breeze would pick up soon; if not, it would get unpleasant here.

Luke and I arrived first. Neither Aaron nor the baron were there, nor anyone else I knew very well. Some young squires and pages were setting up for first meal, and the aroma of freshly baked bread smelled lovely.

Shortly afterwards another younger, slightly built, apparently junior squire aged boy came in and sat down. He was dressed formally, and Luke and I wondered why he was here. Neither of us recognized him, and I knew all the younger squires, and Luke knew all the healers and most of the spell casters. We guessed he was an older junior squire. Then Aaron arrived, and the three of us went and got some hot tea.

We sat and talked, and Aaron asked one of the pages, "Has Baron Scrope arrived and is he waiting in another area?"

"No sir," replied the freckled-face page, "there is no other area ready for first meal, sir."

Some knights and other squires came in and begin to be seated and to get fresh bread, hot grain cereal, butter, and cheese. Kurt and Jelu then walked in, and seeing the three of us they came over. They were also dressed in formal attire.

"Any idea what we are here for?" Kurt asked still trying to rub the sleep from his head.

I wanted to reply that it was because the baron ordered us here, but decided against smarting off this early in the morning. So I grinned and shook my head no.

"You start to say something, and decided to remember your manners kid?" Aaron said looking at me with a grin.

"My last conversation with the two of you together wasn't a lot of fun. I didn't want Kurt to volunteer to repeat it," I answered with a slight chuckle.

Kurt's look made me glad I hadn't smarted off, as Jelu leaned over and asked, very quietly what I was going to say. I decided that if I told him later it would be safer. Even if Kurt didn't have authority to bust me, he could still pound my head into the ground.

Just then Sir William arrived with what appeared to be two senior squire aged boys. Both were in formal clothes too. He motioned to us and to the other boy that had come in early and we all went to the back of the hall, into a meeting room. He also summoned a page. He gave the page some orders, then took us into the room with a large table, with four chairs on each side and one at the head. He had us sit, and took his place at the head of the table.

"Good morning, gentlemen," the baron stated as he looked us over.

Eight voices returned his greeting.

"Our first meal will be served shortly, and then I will let you know the reason for this early morning meeting. Aaron, how long before your arranged marriage is to take place?"

"Sir?" Aaron questioned.

"How long before you are supposed to be married? I know that your intended is or is getting close to the marrying age," the baron said.

"About a month, sir. I haven't had a lot of time to think about it. We are suppose to meet the day after the christening and Fall Festival to work on the plans, sir," Aaron answered.

"Good," Sir William said.

We discussed rather mundane things: how our families where, who had family here. The food soon arrived and we began to eat.

The first meal was good, but we really were more interested in knowing what we were doing there—so early.

After we finished first meal, Sir William began to tell us what we were there for. "We are putting an elite group together—a small raider unit. You eight will work behind the scene as an independent unit. Most of you were expecting to serve in the army, and possibly command large units of the army. What we have in mind is quite different. Each of you are young, and talented in your field. The fact that you are too young to have responsibilities with the regular armies gives us a chance to develop your talents—more as individuals for a unit than with the army."

We all just sat there—trying to make sense out of what the baron had just told us. Not really sure what it would mean to us. I looked around and the other boys looked as bewildered as I did.

"You eight will be the center of this elite unit. You will have additional people working with you or leading at different times. The idea came as some of our scouting parties this summer performed things not entirely expected of them. You will train together and work closely with each other. You are to know each other extremely well, and know what to expect of one another. His Royal Majesty and I have put together an excellent group of youngster in you. Your training will be somewhat secretive, and it will be assumed that you're preparing for other things as some of you have been doing this summer already."

"Luke and Jelu will be promoted, so that you'll have senior ranking with the others, with some minor limitations. That will make your training somewhat less disruptive, as Ray will attest. For informational purposes you will simply be known as the Gold Squad. Which of course is misnomer as your group is not even a full unit."

For combat purposes the army had been traditionally divided into parts. The smallest part of the army was a "unit." A unit normally consisted of between twenty and twenty-five troops. The next up the chain was a squad, which would consist of two or three units. Then came a "Company," which would have multiple squads which would number between 200 and 250 troops, followed by a regiment with approximately 1000 troops. If multiple regiments were involved, it was a brigade, or just "the army." Neither Candlewynd nor its neighbors on Saxet could rarely field an army of more than a single regiment at a time. There were some empires that could field multiple brigades, just none that was in that part of their world. Normally each squad would have spell casting support attached to it that might be sent with individual units. Ray's father, Kelric the Marquis of Retúpmoc, had commanded the brigade.

The boys asked many questions in a short amount of time. They asked about other people with whom they worked who might be able to work with their squad. It would be an all male unit, it was decided that females would be too much of a distraction for the boys, especially close friends such as Sherry or Sarah.

The boys found out that each of them had psionics, so together they would have formidable psionic power at their disposal. The group had a great combination of talent also. Besides for the four squires, Ray's cousin, the healer Luke, there was the mage Markél; Andrew, a cleric, and Tarrin—who was a thief. They found out from Bennet that the boy was Bennet's distant cousin or something like that. As did Luke, the spell casters had a very limited amount of spells they were able to cast, but in a small group like this, they would be able to train quickly, and be able to learn more and more powerful spells as they progressed.

Some rather surprised looks were directed at Ray when Sir William informed the group that he was also able to use *cell adjust*. They were told this ability was a closely guarded secret, but they would need to know what each of their associate's skills were. Even a leader wasn't to be told of their skills unless that person had been cleared. Nor were the boys to tell their wives about the squad or what its members could do.

The boys had some individual things to work on, and some group things to learn, such as special hand signals to communicate quickly and quietly when time demanded it. Other normal school work was also crowded into their day, especially for Ray. Being the junior member of the squad by at least two years, he still had a great deal to learn in the academic classroom. The other boys had all finished formal schooling—at least traditional education, which usually finished by the end of their fourteenth summer. Their training now was in their professional area: arcane knowledge, sword use, tactics, etc.

To absorb what was required Ray spent less time in training with his weapons and more in mathematics, cartography, and other much needed subjects. All of the squad members spent time with the more recently freed captives to learn Orcish.

The Fall Festival and christening day finally arrived. It had been decided that from now on promotions to page, from page to junior squire, and from junior squire to senior squire would officially take place at the Fall Festival. Those that would have been promoted next month would have to wait an entire year for the promotion day. In the past only those going from a page to squire had to wait, now all the others would be required also. Only those going from senior squire to adult would take place in between the Fall Festival, and that one would cease to be a senior squire on the nineteenth birthday, if not promoted earlier. The purpose was to make this a bigger celebration, but it made a number of the young upset at the prospect of having to wait longer for promotions.

Those children who had been promoted during the summer were formally recognized again in the ceremonies. Ray was one of those who was given formal recognition who having already been promoted. Jelu and Luke both were given their early promotions.

There were some that were close to the correct age, but weren't quite old enough that also received early promotions: Torin as a senior, and Richard was now considered an adult, and was knight, due to the change in age requirements, and his skills.

It was a grand party, the first real celebration in the new land. Cord had been assigned duty as a page at the party, and was feeling quite proud that he had been selected. The food was good, and plentiful, but much less remarkable than in years past. The herds were still trying to establish themselves here, so the meats were in small servings, and mostly wild game.

The members of the Gold Squad visited with one another. They all met Sarah, and Andrea—Andrew's wife; which were the only wives of the group at this time. Aaron's fiancee, Deborah, was there, with him and was given a great deal of attention by the other boys. She was quite beautiful, already fourteen, and was nearing fifteen. She was blonde, slightly darker blonde hair than Aaron's, but she was lovely in her light green gown. More than one of the boys found himself staring. Although she was of nobility, she didn't have the "spark" to train as a true adventurer, but she could learn and cast a single per spell a day. She worked as scribe and assisted in record keeping. Her intelligence and charm, made her very good at that and Aaron was in love with her.

Luke's intended was in attendance with him, Ginger. She was a relatively thin girl of thirteen, slightly younger than Ray, with light brown hair that was tied in a long, single braid worn over her left shoulder. She was attractive for her age, but nothing like Aaron's fiancee. Ginger was training as a mage.

Charissa was also there, and she allowed Ray to escort her around much of the evening, after the formal greetings were over. Charissa enjoyed several dances with the young squire and with others as well. Ray danced with others, his younger cousin, and even danced once with his older sister, at his mother's request.

Two days after the christening the ship came back. It had been spotted from afar by the keep at the entrance to the harbor, so the word spread through town quite rapidly. Much of the city had tried to come to the harbor to see what word the vessel brought. The Gold Squad was training on hand signals when they heard the news of the ship. Like everyone else, they wanted to go. Lord William was working with them at the time, and said they could find out later; they would have to continue their training. It was probably just as well that he didn't see some of the hand signals that boys used regarding his decision.

Later that day the squires and Tarrin were to work on firing the smaller bows from horseback. At first they would just fire mounted, then they began to ride at a full gallop, attempting to hit targets as they rode past. This seemed to be a lesson in futility, but Sir William agreed with Jelu that this might be a useful tactic at times.

The lessons were extremely important today, as Aaron's wedding was in three days, and he was to be given time off to assist in the final plans. Since several of the team were also members of the wedding party, there would be some disruptions. Kurt was the best man, with Jelu, Luke, and Ray as groomsmen. So today was their last day of real work with the entire team.

That evening as they were getting ready to leave, one of the new junior squires appeared, gave Sir William and the rest of them a summons to the great hall—at once.

The nine arrived and were shown to the meeting room. There was a map of the island they occupied. The entire outlined loomed before them for the first time. There were two other markings on the map, similar to the one at the site of the Orcian city—an "O." Ray and the others got a sick feeling in their stomachs that there might be these additional cities of Orcs on the island.

Ray then noticed where Jelu's gaze had locked. Sitting in the corner of the room was young, robin-red haired, half-elven woman. Her golden eyes seemed to have Jelu in a trance—he was unable to look away. She spoke in a wonderful singsong voice and in the language of the elder. The boys thought she was completely enchanting.

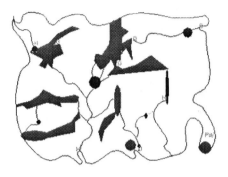

Jelu shook his head after she spoke and replied to her, also in the elven tongue. Jelu didn't have the same enchanting singsong type voice quality, but the language was still lovely to hear. The two spoke, for a while then Jelu began to translate what she was telling them.

"She has asked all but my companions and the king to leave. She will then speak to us, of things we need to know," Jelu stated, as if he loathed to return to the human tongue. It had been a long time since—well, five years, when he was a young page, since he had spoken in the tongue of the eldar. "She is called Eldalië, meaning elf-folk."

The half-elf told the group of many things, many of which they would have preferred not to know. Having looked at the map they had already guessed there were three Orcian cities on the island. Other news was there were several islands which were inhabited by Bugbears. These islands were nearby, and thankfully these giant goblins had no desire for shipping.

The Orcs were another matter; as were those labeled "G" for giants.

There were also two other outpost of humans still on the island. They had not been wiped out as they provided sport for the Orcs, and made for good slave labor. Slaves did not last long once they were captured. Candlewynd was drawn in on the south side of the island, with its harbor and river.

The Gold Squad learned that she was a scribe on an Orcian vessel, and that she had been in the Orcian ports. The vessel she was on sunk in a storm, and she had been rescued by the flagship this summer as it sailed around. She did not know a lot about the waters, as she was normally kept below deck. She did know a bit of the trade in the area, however.

The humans were kept from the coast and Orcs patrolled the rivers and coastal area to prevent their escape. The human village in the eastern part of the island provided a lot of lumber for the Orcian ships, with a canal built to send material across to the city. This was the larger city and there are some Orcian guards stationed in the city. The city is much more likely to survive as it provided material for the Orcs. The northern city was another matter: that was the one that was maintained for sport. There was another village, but I heard that they had planned to assimilate it this spring. That village was the one the party had rescued this spring.

Unfortunately, she had no nautical charts to help find other human lands. It seemed they were in a part of this world that was control by fell creatures, of their legends, having never seen any until this spring. With the other information given, the whole process took almost three hours.

The group left with the exception of the Jelu and Sir William. Jelu stayed as a translator, and then he left with Eldalië, to show her around the city.

"I heard you really hacked off Markél," Luke said to me. "I understand it was pretty amusing."

"I didn't think it was too funny. He doesn't care for younger kids," I responded.

"I understand he threatened to bust you good—for you running your mouth again. I thought Aaron, Adam, and Kurt had taught you better than that," Luke said laughing.

"He started it, and was really giving me a harsh time. He said that he only could think of one use for twelve and thirteen year boys! You don't want to hear his idea of usefulness. I told him he couldn't cane me. He didn't have the authority! After some other unpleasantries, he wanted to know if I wanted him to show me that he could do it? I decided not to challenge a mage," I told my still laughing cousin.

"It's a good thing. One of the juniors tried his bluff, and it wasn't a bluff. Markél cast *sleep*, tied the junior across a saddle and blistered his bare butt with a large hickory. He didn't go through one of the other seniors or a knight, just tore the poor kid up, then left him tied to the saddle until someone else found and untied him. Markél got disciplined for it, but none of the other juniors have challenged him since. You might give him a little more respect, at least until he gets used to you, and realize you're not a typical little snot," Luke concluded.

Just then Aaron and Kurt came up behind us and grabbed us, scaring the daylights out of us. They seemed to think it was extremely funny.

"What the . . . was that for?" Luke yelled.

"Oh come on, it was pretty funny," Sarah said laughing. "You should have seen the startled look you and the baby gave."

"Evening, Sarah," I said. Having Sarah around always worried me. "To what do we owe this honor?"

"Luke, you are to report with me tomorrow at eight for some training with Ayrus. He wants to see if he can show us some things. He also said we are to bring our spell books!"

Ayrus was the highest ranking Healer at Candlewynd. Usually a summons from him at Luke's age meant he was in trouble. The fact that he and Sarah were both going sounded like he was being given a boon, at least that is how I took it.

"Also, we have a meeting tonight after dinner, around eight. We are meeting in same the conference room we were in this afternoon," Kurt told us.

"I'm going to check on your mother, Anne, and Sherry during that time, and visit with your sister—you know, girl stuff—to plot against you" Sarah told me. "So you won't have to worry about the little boys either."

"Thank you, Sarah," I answered her. "What are we meeting for and with whom?"

Aaron gave me a look of disapproval, and said, "Just be there!" Then turning to Sarah and Kurt, "You two stay out of trouble for the next couple of hours. I'm going with these lads."

After Kurt and Sarah left, I looked over at Aaron, "I guess from your expression that I asked the wrong question?"

"You know better to ask question like that in front of Sarah or anyone else," Aaron said turning on me.

"I'm sorry, I forgot," I said, wishing almost immediately I'd said something different.

"Maybe the baron needs to help you with your memory! Or would you prefer to discuss it with Kurt or me?" Aaron said still very angry.

"That won't be needed. Come on, Aaron, I'll be more careful," I said. I really didn't need Aaron mad at me.

"All right. Hey, what did you do to Markél, to upset him with you?"

"He hasn't had enough birthdays," Luke said, starting to laugh again.

The boys got home, cleaned up and had a great dinner. Ray noticed Cord was acting like he didn't feel well. More like something was upsetting him.

After dinner Ray asked his mother if he might take a nap before the meeting. He could sleep for almost an hour, and the meeting might run late.

His mother said that was probably a good idea, she would have one of the boys wake him in time to go.

After the nap, Ray got up and washed his face. Still feeling a bit groggy, he got ready to meet his cousin for the walk over. Cord still looked like he was troubled, so Ray checked on him before leaving. Cord wanted to talk, but wasn't sure how to start. Ray said that when he got back the two of them could talk and he'd try to help him. Then Luke knocked on the door and the two older boys were off.

"What do you think this about and who called it?" I asked.

"I don't know, but you better be more careful about that question in the future. I don't think Aaron was joking," Luke responded.

We walked the rest of the way in silence, and arrived at the Great Hall just after dark, but then dark is a relative term there—the twin moons usually gave off some decent light.

The days had started to get shorter, but it was still hot. The guards admitted us without any questions, I guess they were used to us by now. It still seemed strange to me, going into the Great Hall, and it was only wood.

As we were walking to the conference room, Charissa ran up to meet us.

"What are you doing here, this late?" she asked as she tossed her hair behind her, and smiled.

Ray thought "Lovely."

"He wishes he was here to just see you, but he has a late meeting that he'd better not be late for," Luke interjected, but smiled and walked on.

"Your cousin seems a bit curt with his greetings," she said with a frown.

"He's just trying to keep me out of trouble. A couple of the older squires have wanted to remind me that I'm still thirteen, and if I'm late—it could be quite unpleasant. Luke knows how I can lose track of time with such a pretty girl around," I answered, thinking I was paying her a nice compliment.

"Oh, you've had this problem with other girls? I shan't keep you then," she said and turned on her heels.

"My princess, that's not what I meant. Only you make me lose track of time," I said, trying to figure out how or why she acted that way.

"In that case—I still don't want you late. Good night, my knight," she said and gave a mischievous smile and left.

I felt a hand on the nape of my neck, and turned to see Aaron. He was nudging me gently to the room.

"I'm going," I told him.

"I knew it, was just making sure you did. Kurt is a little put out with you. He wants to talk when everyone is finished," Aaron told me.

"Crap!"

"Better watch your mouth in here, little boy," Markél said, with a less than friendly grin.

Andrew rose when we all gathered in the room, and let us know he was the one who had called the meeting.

"As the oldest member of this group, I'm taking charge of the meeting, and since none of us are very old, I don't presume to mean that as an official position, but just at this time. First on my list, I want to reprimand Markél for causing disharmony among us. I realize his attitude toward working with younger students, but he needs to get over it, so that we can succeed."

I wanted to stand up and applaud, but figured Aaron and Kurt might do more than want to verbally reprimand me for that.

"If your inability or unwillingness to work the three boys that have been given an advance status above their years due to their skills, then I will recommend to Sir William that you be replaced," Andrew continued.

"Wait a bloody minute!" Markél thundered.

"SIT and let me finish," Andrew stated and slammed both hands down on the table. "You younger boys need to remember that you aren't our ages, especially Markél's and mine, and attempt to act a bit more mature. Now let that sink in," he said and looked directly at me.

"If I have been out of line, I apologize," I said. "However, I will not be talked down to—without reason."

Kurt and Aaron both shot a look at me, that let me know I'd better be quiet. They might not have the authority to discipline me, but with an extra three years of growth they were fully capable of getting my attention, and they had informed me that they would treat me like their little brother. Which meant if they thought I was out of line they might feel obligated to remind me of it—unofficially, of course.

"The second and hopefully the most important thing to consider what I believe will be our first mission," Andrew stated this and sat back let us absorb it. "I believe we will be called on to rescue or at least scout out the human city to the north. It's the one that the Orcs are much harsher on. It is smaller and we might be able to get the inhabitants down the river to the north, and to one of our ships."

"There are still close to fifty men in the town and total population of close to two hundred and twenty-five people, according to the half-elf!" Markél exclaimed.

"Her name is Eldalië!" Jelu interjected.

"That's true, but I still expect it to be what we are sent on first. There are a couple reasons for this. First, with three Orcian cities, we may need help holding out. Second, we can absorb that many people without endangering the city. Now, the way I see it, we may not move the people, but we may have to scout the city and the route out."

Andrew again allowed what he was saying to sink in.

Kurt asked, "What kind of numbers are we talking about on the Orcian patrols?"

"I don't know, yet. Jelu, pump Eldalië for information about the patrols and information about the city," Andrew ordered.

"Remember, the priest said only to pump her for the information," Markél said laughing as he said it.

Jelu jumped up and I believed he was going to attack the mage had Kurt and Aaron not stopped him.

Jelu was fifteen, Markél was eighteen. Even though Jelu was a warrior, the difference in age would have made a difference in a fist fight. I thought Andrew was going to come undone when the mage made that remark.

Andrew regained control, "I want each of you to think of plans how we might take an expedition to scout and/or rescue the city."

"Markél, your actions will be reported. Let's go—we'll meet tomorrow evening to discuss plans, unless of course we are called for earlier."

"What about the wedding plans?" Luke asked. "Some are obligated there."

"We'll meet at seven, here. That way everything else should be finished. If Aaron is preoccupied and unable to come up with ideas—he's forgiven, in advance," Andrew answered.

Everyone got up to leave, but I waited to talk to the older squires, as I had been told to do. I wasn't looking forward to this, but decided I better. I figured Aaron would be there as a referee.

Aaron was talking to Jelu, who was still pretty upset I just sat there. Kurt came over and said, "Let's take a walk."

"Am I in trouble, Kurt?" I asked him.

"Some, but we don't want it to get worse," he answered.

"Is Aaron in on this?"

"No, just us," he said as we left the Great Hall. "I want you to be careful about the questions you ask with others around. If it continues, I'll ask Sir William to discipline you, or allow me to."

"Yes sir, Aaron warned me this afternoon, when you left with Sarah. I'll work hard not to let it happen again," I said, feeling a bit relieved.

"Also," he started again, "you need to act a bit more respectful to the older members of the squad. You've hacked off the older spell casters. Hey kid, I'm really trying to keep you out of trouble. I know sometimes it's tough, and I want you to know Aaron and I are on your side."

"When I smart mouth them, it is because of their actions toward me," I complained. "Markél makes a stupid remark about me and I respond. If he took a swing no one would be surprised if I swung back, but you act like that I should stand there and let him talk all he wants. If I were a junior squire, I wouldn't have to put up with him, and he wouldn't be around to verbally abuse me."

"Ray," Kurt interrupted, "Aaron and I don't want to have to bust you again—so stop. Do you understand me?"

"Yes sir," I answered, not really pleased about being dressed down that way.

"Good. Let's go home and think about the plans Andrew is wanting."

I got home, and was ready for bed. I had almost forgot about Cord needing to talk to me. When I sawing him lying in his bed, I started to let it wait until the morning. I softly called his name, as I sat on by bed and started undressing.

He got up quickly and began to assist me in disrobing. "I didn't mean you were on duty as a page. I just wanted to see if you were awake, and still wanting to talk." I told him.

"I'm in trouble with the mathematics instructor, and I need you to escort me to class early in the morning. He asked if I had an older brother that was a senior squire or a knight, and when I answered that you were a senior, he told me that you need to come with me early tomorrow. He's going to have you discipline me," Cord told me, and then began to cry.

"Cord, I don't want to have to do that," I told him.

"If you can't then I'll have to get Adam. Big brother, Adam is a lot bigger, I would prefer to get it from you than have Adam to spank me."

We laid down on my bed and talked for a long time. Then Cord fell asleep still holding on to me for comfort. He was really worried about being in trouble. Not that it was the first time to be in trouble—he was all little boy, but that I was going to have to administer the discipline.

We got up the next morning and got ready for our discussion with his teacher when Timothy knocked on our apartments.

"Sir William's compliments, sir. You are to attend him as quickly as possible, after first meal," Timothy informed me.

"My compliments to his lordship," I began, "I have an early meeting schedule this morning with an instructor. I will be with him as quickly as I may when I've finished with the instructor."

Timothy shook his head and asked, "Are you sure you want me to tell Lord William that he'll have to wait on you?"

When Timothy left, Mother asked who was there so early, and I told her about needing to be two places at once. I didn't think about Cord not having let her know he was in trouble. She gave Cord a stern look, but said nothing at that time. Later they would have longer discussion about his behavior.

When he got to the appointment, I remembered the instructor. I was concerned that it might be more difficult for Cord, with the instructor knowing me also.

"Cord, is this your brother? Are you truly a senior squire?" he asked me, before Cord could answer.

"Yes sir."

"Have you ever disciplined your brother before?" he asked.

"No sir, I never had to perform that duty," I answered. I didn't like the way this was starting.

After a bit more discussion the three of us went into the stable. The instructor stood at the door, and Cord and I went to a saw horse, and I disciplined him with a leather strap. I was glad I didn't have to use a rod on him—at his age that would have really been improper. Ten licks with a leather strap are bad enough for little kid, I thought I was going to cry also, for having to spank him.

The mathematics instructor left, and I told Cord how bad I felt about having to spank him. He was still pretty upset too, not to mention hurting. I held him for a while then told him I had to get to my other meeting, before I got a busting too.

I hurried on to Sir Williams, the others were already there. They were looking over the map again when I knocked and was motioned to wait at the door. The baron came out to discuss the reason for my tardiness.

"Next time I send for you, you will attend me, and have the other person wait—unless it is his royal majesty. Do you understand me, squire?! Because if you have to been shown the error of your ways, the discipline you received from your three senior friends will seem gentle," the baron told me, in a less than pleasant voice.

"Yes sir, I understand. Might I send the squire or page that is sent for me to inform the other my reason for not showing up, sir," I asked?

The baron turned back on me, with anger flaming up in his eyes. "I mustn't forget how old you really are. It seems your advanced rating doesn't keep you from asking questions with the impertinence of a thirteen-year-old," he said as he took me by the arm and led me quickly out of the grand hall!

On the way out, I attempted to explain that I was trying to ask a real question, not wanting to have others waiting on me, but the baron was not interested in listening. My being late, combined with the question that I asked, plus the dealing with the older spell casters had the baron ready to kill me. The baron gave me the worst disciplining I had ever received, and suggested that we might continue this discussion again that evening if my behavior was very near-perfect the rest of the day.

The rest of the day was spent working through possible plans that Andrew had suggested they create.

That was the first time in a long time that I had been treat so harshly or as such a young junior. The baron kept me that evening after everyone else left and then merely said, "Let's go."

As we started walking back to the barn, I was—was scared that the baron was going to give me another caning.

Then I sat up straight in the bed—cold sweat running down my body—it had been a dream. It was the first time I had any kind of really bad nightmare since Kelvin's death. But it made going back to sleep tough. I was glad I hadn't awakened Cord. If he had asked about the nightmare, it would have been tough to tell him about it. But the dream seemed so real.

I knew one thing: if the baron sent for me in the morning, I wasn't going to tell him to wait.

The next morning arrived too early, since I hadn't slept well the night before. I got dressed quickly and went in to break my evening fast on cheese and bread. Cord came in later, and was worried what the day would bring for him—he had a pretty good guess it wasn't going to start well. I wondered if he had told Mother about being in trouble for behavior?

Just moments after we finished eating a knock at the door startled me, and made the cold sweats start again. I went there and found a junior squire, but it wasn't Timothy.

"Sir William's compliments, sir. You are to attend him as quickly as possible, after first meal," the junior squire informed me.

"Thank you. Do you have other messages to deliver for his lordship," I asked?

"No sir, you're the last sir."

The squire was one of those that had been with me on the ship from Saxet, and was a year and a half to two years older than I was. He didn't seem to enjoy his errand this morning.

"Very well, then I have a task for you. You're to escort the page to a meeting that I was scheduled to attend, and give my compliments to the instructor. Inform the instructor that I was called to attend my knight, and will be there as quickly as I may," I told the squire.

The squire was upset at this assignment, and protested my orders. I finally reminded him that I was a senior squire, and informed him that I would let the baron know of his unwillingness to follow orders. That got his attention he knew I was younger than him, but had forgotten the baron in his smug attitude.

I told him to wait for Cord on deck, and hurried off to meet Lord William. He had just arrived at the Grand Hall and was setting up the room for our meeting. He was quite surprised to see me so early, and without Luke.

I then explained my other meeting, and asked if my handling of the matter was appropriate. Then, before he answered the first question, I asked, "if it wasn't how should I act in the future?

"Your actions are correct, as your first obligation is to me," the baron said.

I told him about the dream; well, most of it. I said it upset me, and had me scared. I also gave him the problem with the junior squire's unwillingness to assist in the matter.

"Go take care of the other meeting, and you won't even be very late. Have the junior report back to me. I have some other errands for him, before he attends his first class or assignment for today—which I believe is working on the wall," Sir William told me.

I hurried off to the other meeting and was only about ten minutes late. I gave the squire his instructions, and then gave my attention to the instructor, whom I didn't really know.

Enough of the dream was true to annoy me, but much wasn't true either.

Cord was really in trouble. He had talked back to the instructor, under his breath, and was heard. There was another page there, Bradley, who was also in trouble.

The instructor didn't believe at first that I was a senior squire. I told him that I wasn't really old enough, but had been given the rank with some others this summer early, for the work we had done.

I was instructed to discipline both boys. I requested that he give me guidelines on the how severe the discipline was to be, since he had chosen not to discipline the boys himself.

"Your families' rank makes it inconvenient to discipline, when one is a commoner. So, to avoid the problem of striking a nobleman of their rank, I called on you, or would have gotten another senior squire."

"At their age, I assume a leather strap is to be used on the boys," I asked?

"They may have their choice, seven with a rod or a dozen with a leather strap," he answered.

"They will choose the leather, sir," and motioned the boys toward the barn. "Sir, might I asked for a bit more leniency, and only administer ten licks, as they are under the age of ten. I didn't want to ask in from of the pages, but at only nine years old . . . ," I started as the boys left for the barn.

"Are you telling me how to discipline children?" he asked indigently.

"Oh, no sir, I just haven't been required to exercise this authority, and wanted to make sure I wasn't being too severe at their age, sir," I stated quickly. I didn't want him to inform the baron that my behavior was disrespectful.

"Oh—very well. You know, you might be right. I'll stop you after the tenth stripe, saying, 'that will be enough,' and then you may discipline the other child, who is also noble. That will sufficiently remind them of their manners," he decided once he realized I wasn't trying to argue about the discipline.

After that unpleasant task was over, I returned to the Grand Hall. I hoped that the rest of the day would go better than my dream.

They began setting up plans for the rescue of the village, just as Andrew had predicted. Ray was extra careful to be respectful of the two older spell casters, and was surprised to see Kurt show up not too long after he had returned. Ray had thought Kurt and Aaron would be working on the wedding plans.

Kurt told him he was there early, but had to deal with an unmannerly junior squire, which made Ray swallow hard. Kurt asked if Ray was on next on the list, but Andrew told him the boy had been very respectful and asked some good questions on the plans.

Jelu had gotten as much information as he could from Eldalië. She reminding Jelu that she had never been to the human town, but it was information that she overheard the Orcs talking about.

Kurt went to work on the wedding plans, with no battle plan close to workable, but Lord William knew that Aaron would be needing his help. Besides, sometimes, you think of a solution to a problem when you are not working on the problem.

Ray suggested some approaches that the others had considered. Being younger, he looked at problems differently; some of his suggestions were immature, as his age would suggest. But around lunch, one of his ideas in a thinking session proved to be a good one.

"Andrew, if the Orcs are watching the river to the coast, and out to sea—why don't we walk them the thirty miles around the mountain, and go down stream the other way? I understand that getting a boat to move them that far would be a problem. But—wouldn't we have the same problem getting boats to take them down river to the ocean?" I asked before putting a large slice of cheese in my mouth.

Andrew, Luke, and even Markél looked up with a sense of surprise: that might be the plan. Markél stated, "We could send a ship around, off coast, as a diversion, while we are going the other way. The Orcs would be checking the river to the coast, and we would be moving around the mountains. I believe the little snot has a workable idea."

"Thanks," I said feeling much better than I had the rest of the day.

Markél had been somewhat subdued in his actions that morning, and I thought he might have gotten in a great deal of trouble because of his actions with Jelu yesterday. If he had been in trouble with the Baron, I was being extra careful about my behavior. I had asked Luke to warn me if I said something that might start me down a dangerous path, or if someone said something to me that might get me started.

We started looking at my original plan, to see how to make it work. When the baron returned that afternoon, Andrew allowed me to describe what we had come up with. Most of the plan, (well, everything else), except the original idea had come from the others, but Andrew still gave me the credit for the plan. I quickly gave credit to the others for fleshing out the rest of our details.

The baron liked what we had done, and sent me after some of the advisers to help with the additional and finalizing the plans—back to junior squire duty, but I didn't mind.

We were given the rest of the day off, and I wasn't required to attend any training classes. Usually if we were working, when we finished the baron sent me to cartography, mathematics, or some other training that I needed, but today I was given two hours off to relax.

I went to the stables for the first hour, and worked with my horse. He was getting to look really good, and he was nearly old enough to start riding. I went by and spent most of the last hour visiting with Sherry. Her baby was due any time now, and I hoped to see it before I left on the mission.

We had a great visit, and I hadn't been around Jakót for a while. He was helping here with Sherry and spent the night many times. I couldn't tell her about the mission or anything connected with the Gold Squad, but I did tell her about my dream.

"Sounds like God was taking care of you, little brother," she said.

A messenger from Charissa came to check on Sherry while I was there. Sherry told me she had come by to visit once, and had inquired on her several times. Sherry had worked with the princess a couple of times with swords, while I'd been out that summer.

Adam came in soon afterwards. He'd spent most of the day working on calvary charges and maneuvers. He was hot and tired, so I left and Jakót came with me.

It was nice to be home early. Aunt Martha was just getting ready to leave as Jakót and I walked in. I took Anne from her and held her for a while, and Jakót went into the bedroom to work on studies with Cord.

Mother had found out from Cord the particulars about the morning. She asked when I was planning on disciplining him again that evening. Coustomly we were given a second disciplining for poor behavior in school. Being rude was normally going to have us in trouble when we got home also. Not being able to complete a task satisfactory and being disciplined for that would not get us in trouble at home. Doing something you knew was wrong—that was different and not acceptable. Apparently Jakót had also been in trouble lately. So what I thought was going to be a nice enjoyable evening became very unpleasant, and much more so for the two younger boys.

———————

Planning for the mission was taken over by the royal advisers, and the squad got the chance to catch up on scholastic training and preparations for Aaron's wedding. Ray even went on a day patrol duty, with mostly junior squires. He enjoyed being with kids his age, and having the chance to act a little crazy. The senior squire supervising the group had told them they would have some leeway, and a late afternoon swim in the river was a great deal of fun. The young teens took their armor off and dove in the river water with their clothes on—as was proper, since this was a mixed group. The other juniors enjoyed getting to dunk each other and especially Ray—since he was a senior. Timothy got him a couple of times by sneaking up behind him and jumping on top of his head. By the time they got back there were eight very tired young squires, and one sixteen year old senior squire, who had done a great job of both working with them and allowing them to have some fun.

The wedding was lovely, and the boys had a bachelor party for Aaron. It was not the type that might be had today, but these were different times. Not to mention, much younger were couples being married than in our society.

Then it was back to normal training while final strategies were being planned by the royal advisers. Ray and Jelu spent several days working on the wall construction. Even aided by magic, the wall was taking a long time to build. Other work was being done on the inside of the wall as the city construction was going quickly.

Ray was finally getting cartography down. Understanding maps was not an easy task for him, and some of the other kids seemed to think it was so easy. His hard work was beginning to pay off, but it might have been because he was using what was taught in the planning of the rescue mission. October had come and still they had not left on the rescue.

The beginning of October also brought Sherry's and Adam's first born into the world. It was a fine baby boy, and Ray thought, thankfully he looked more like Sherry than Adam. The boy was named Michael, after both of their fathers. As much as Cord and Jakót had been around Sherry, they almost felt like they had a little brother.

Ray had begun attending the early mass each Sunday. Andrew many times had responsibilities in those services, and he thought it would be good to be supportive of his new companion. Things had been quiet, and he had even managed to stay out of trouble in class and with the baron.

Sarah had asked him to assist in a training exercise with the healers and clergy. She told him that some of the children had requested that he help, since they had gotten to work on him when he was . . . injured. He agreed when she said that a young female was particularly interested in his participation. He had enjoyed all the attention, and since he was the only senior squire that was taking part, the younger children were impressed that he would help out.

While he was wrapped up like a mummy, Kurt suggested that it was a good time for the would-be doctors attempt to discover if their patient was ticklish. He suggested this only to the girls, as he believed Ray might have attempt pay-backs for any of the younger boys taking part. He would have to endure it from the girls. Sarah didn't find it nearly so amusing, but since Kurt had instigated it, she couldn't be too mad at the girls.

The second week of October the squad learned the plans were ready for implementation. The original plan was changed to include one of the ships sailing around the coast and drawing attention to itself. While the people where going overland to the other side of the mountain and down river, the ship would be trying to lead the Orcs to believe that the humans would be going down stream. When the town was evacuated, the squad was going to fire the town, and try to give the impression that the ship might have raided the town and looted and burned it.

A snag had developed in the plan. Eldalië informed them of a small fort at the mouth of the river. It was garrisoned by about twenty to thirty Orcs, but it was usually lax about being alert. She had left it off her original map, only trying to identify settlements. The fort would have to be neutralized before the plan could work.

Chapter Eleven

Problems with Neighbors

"For he has rescued us from the dominion of darkness
and brought us into the kingdom of the Son he loves,"
Colossians 1: 13

"That Orcian fort is going to be a problem. We'll have to neutralize it before the ship could be believed about going up stream," Andrew said in disgust, as the boys had all been staring at the modified map.

Sir William came in the room and they stood to attention. Xell and Richard were with him, which caught them by surprise. Of course it was Sir Richard now, as he had been given the title at the christening.

"This will be the team for the rescue of the town. It was decided that additional help would be needed when we found out about the garrison," Lord William began. "We had planned a smaller group, but decided a couple more participants would be helpful. I've chosen Sir Richard to lead the expedition. Sir Richard and Xell, if you would get with the chamberlain—I think he has our list of supplies. Verify the list and bring it back. I'll bring the rest of your group up-to-date."

Sir Richard and Xell left, and the baron held his hands up for silence, knowing there were a lot of questions we wanted to ask.

"Sir Richard knows that there have been plans going on, and that he was brought in late. He does not know of the squad, but that you had been pulled together, and that I'm not leading the mission. He shouldn't ask any questions about the change in leadership—he believes I was originally going, but with the fort, more spell support will be needed. Some of you have worked with him before, so he was selected," the baron informed us.

"Sir, why don't you lead us? Wouldn't that have made it simpler?" Aaron asked the question that I wanted too, but was afraid to ask.

"Other things played a part in this decision; besides, Xell will add a great deal of support with a couple of *sleep* spells and a *web* or something else. And I have other responsibilities. But thanks for asking," Sir William said.

Xell and Sir Richard returned with the supply list, and another map. This one had a route laid out on it, up the river to the city. Then down the river to the fort, with little "x's" marking camping spots along the way—I assumed.

"I'm sorry if this is going to change all the plans, at the last moment, especially with the leadership. All the details have been gone over with Lord William, and changes approved by him and the council. I'm looking forward to working with several of you again, and some for the first time," Sir Richard began.

Details of the plans were explained to the group. The short version was that they were to travel—by horseback to the town, once they arrived they would notify Candlewynd by use of a ***mind link medallion***. The medallion allowed for telepathic communication over a long distance, similar to our cell phones, but using psionic power to send the messages.

A day or so after the squad left another group would travel to the base of the mountain where the river began, and start making rafts. The squad would inform the city of the evacuation, and have them prepare to leave. While the city makes preparations for leaving the squad would travel to the coast and attempt to destroy the fort at the mouth of the river.

As the party prepared to go neutralize the fort, one of the ships would leave, to draw attention to itself, and make the Orcs believe the ship was the primary attack. Hopefully by the time the ship reached the fort, the squad would have taken care of it and be returning to the city to start the evacuation of the city, around the mountain and down river. Once the city was evacuated and reached the raft, the city was to be set on fire, in an attempt to look like it was sacked and looted.

By the time the squad returned they would be saddle weary and worn out from the hard travels. At least there were not supposed to be Orcian villages or towns along their route—patrols were another matter. The days before the squad left a war party of Orcs that had been previously spotted by another unit, which were wiped out by a cavalry unit and infantry, but this was only accomplished after the small unit had been attacked and suffered heavy casualties.

It appeared the Orcs were planning on some pay backs for damage done by the raids lead by Sir Stephen earlier. Fortunately for the city they had been spotted, and units of twenty-five lancers and twenty-five infantries made short work of the 20 Orcs. The infantrymen were carrying bows and started firing on the Orcs as the light cavalry hit them on their left flank. The infantry put up their bows and moved in to mop up. The entire battle lasted less than half an hour. Most of the small portion of the city's army that had taken the field that day were senior squires. Some men-at-arms and a very few older junior squires took part in the infantry.

The horse situation had improved a little with the horses that were brought back that spring. They helped with the plowing and other work where their strength was needed, and most of the war-horse mares that had been brought had nice foals late in the summer.

The young adventurers started off in the predawn light of the two moons. Ray was excited about being out again. Having Xell as the lead mage made him feel better about the expedition. Although they weren't close, he believed she respected his skills, especially knowing his age. That didn't mean she wouldn't get onto him, or make some wild threat about his actions in jest, to let him know if he was getting out of line. She never had really tried to pull rank as the other older spell casters had done; she just convinced him in her own way. Whatever the reason, he would take more abuse from her than any other spell caster with whom the boys had worked, without getting unduly upset. Maybe the work that Ray and Jelu did on the hill with Orcs helped, maybe Sir Richard had something to do with it.

In an attempt to avoid Orcian patrols, the group went back over the range and into the valley again. Then they would move to the northeast and cross the river, and the move to then next river, and keeping it on their right, move up stream to the mountain source. After that it was around the mountain to the village. If only it was that easy.

Things went well initially. The trip back into the valley went smoothly, no sight of Orcs or any other hostile creatures. Once they crossed the river and started to move northeast to the next river, problems started to occur. There were some large cats that had the horses spooked. Although the cats were never spotted, their roars were heard across the rivers and horses did not like a large carnivore so near. This made night duty much more difficult. One was not only on alert for a raid, but to keep the horses calm. As they got close to the mountain, they came upon some giant footprints. The map showed that giants were in the area—but the squad did not want to wander up close to them.

When they got to the base of the mountains, before they made their northwestern swing around the mountain to the city, Andrew communicated to the city, with the *mind link medallion*, about the giant footprints. They rested for a day where the water began to flow out of the mountain for the small river. They knew the next several days would prove very difficult and strenuous.

Communication informed them that the troop that was to build rafts left the morning after they had—on schedule. Also a new twist had been added that might assist them, but was not directly related. A large contingency would move toward the Orcian city to the east. It was just a military exercise, but it might keep the Orcs preoccupied. A unit of twenty-five medium cavalries would go, composed of older seniors and adult warriors, two units of twenty-five infantries, (all were senior squires); and a unit of long bowmen, mostly female senior squires. Having a force of that size might get their attention. While they are out working on drills some men were going to cut the grass (as Ray had suggested) for hay. They make a strong guard and maybe it would draw attention away from the Gold Squad.

The Squad got to the edge of the town. It had a wooden wall around it. The wall appeared old and in need of repair. Since it was nearly dark the gates were closed, presumably for the night. The guard tower, at the gate, was manned by a single figure, in leather armor. The squad discussed whether to attempt to gain entrance this close to nightfall, or wait until morning. Youngsters their age were liable to bring more attention than desired this late in the evening. Sir Richard decided that Xell should make Tarrin *invisible*, and he could get over the wall and look around that night. They wished they had arrived an hour or so earlier to have a chance to look around town that night, but they didn't.

"I could also climb the wall and just wander around the town. I would probably be able to blend in with other kids, and nobody would think anything about a kid on the street," I suggested.

Some of the others felt like this was a good plan, and Tarrin would be there, unseen, for support.

Sir Richard overruled the idea, saying, "There might be a curfew in effect, or something else that might create a problem that he could escape. Tarrin was safer with the *invisibility*, and we could move around quieter—alone."

"Sir, if trouble happens, I could go *invisible* also, and . . . ," I started.

"Squire, this is not open to debate! I remembered that you have that skill, but it only works on so many targets. Any further discussion on your part will have painful consequences. Do you understand me—boy!" Sir Richard exploded.

"Yes sir," I responded, not needing any demonstration of the threat. Later that night I decided I'd apologize, for seeming to argue his decision—but right now wasn't the time.

The rest of the party moved away from the town about two miles to make camp, and Tarrin, with the help of Kurt and Aaron, climbed quietly over the wall to survey the town.

Resting that night in the camp was difficult. Jelu, Luke, and Ray talked for a while. They discussed girls with whom they had worked with for a long time. Telling the others who they thought was cute, and well, they talked like young boys do when discussing girls' physical attributes. Ray got a little embarrassed when Jelu brought up his sister.

"Ray, your sister is cute, and she has a great sense of humor," Jelu said.

"She is a pain in the butt," I responded. "She gives me grief, and if I respond she tells Mother. Lately she has decided to just let her fianƒe deal with me. She is planning to become engaged to an older senior squire whose marriage contract, like hers, fell through. Megan, because her intended didn't make it back from the front, and his because the young girl was killed in one of the raids on the city. I guess I should be glad he is not a knight—then he really could take me to task. It's not official yet There are some complications with it that I don't understand yet."

"What can he do to you?" Jelu asked. "You're a senior, he can't cane you. So what's the big deal?"

Luke interjected, "He is almost eighteen, in under a year and half he'll be an adult, and then he can bust him. In the meantime he is still seventeen to Ray's thirteen years. He can give Ray the choice of getting caned or getting beaten to a pulp."

Jelu laughed.

"It's not funny. I shouldn't have to take caning because of my sister, and fighting him is out of the question—he's bigger than Sir Richard," I said.

"Well, try telling him that as Sir William's squire you're not allowed to fight like that," Jelu said, trying to help.

Luke then added more information than I felt was needed. "She also has suggested that Kurt and Aaron deal with him. That's got him worried, because those two have known his sister for a long time, and Sarah will help motivate Kurt to kick his butt."

Kurt and Aaron walked up just as Luke was telling Jelu about Megan's other plan.

"Oh, that reminds me, I was supposed to help remind you of some manners. It seems you have not been treating your sister very well," Kurt said. "Something about your attitude is incorrect."

"Ah, come on guys. I should be able to at least argue with my sister," I complained.

"Her point was if she were male, she would be a senior, and you wouldn't be. So you should have to give her the respect you would your older brother," Aaron joined in.

"She is not Kelvin—and there is a difference! I don't have much of a problem with either of you, and if I was a junior then I would have to behave differently. But since I'm a senior, and that's all she'd be if she were a warrior, she still shouldn't be able to have me disciplined," I said, feeling my temper starting to rise.

"Cool off kid, we aren't going to give you a beating out here, but when we get back we might use Sherry's method of changing your attitude," Aaron said rubbing my head. "Besides, if you were too out of line your mother would say or do something."

"All right—get quiet and get some sleep. First watch stand to duty," Sir Richard ordered.

———————

The next morning, before the first light, the camp was struck, first meal eaten, and the squad was heading back to the town and the rendevous with Tarrin. Xell was watching the younger squires like she expected them to say or do something. The boys weren't sure what she wanted, but she just kept an eye on them.

Tarrin had a sense of humor, not a good one, but a sense of humor, nonetheless. He sneaked up on the party, got behind Jelu, and yelled in his ear, and poked him in the ribs.

Jelu jumped and yelled as if he had sat on something hot. Ray and Luke both laughed until their sides hurt. Jelu's comments were not exactly poetic, but did express his displeasure toward the young thief. Richard said he felt it was inappropriate, but seemed to be having a difficult time not laughing himself.

They finally got back under control and Tarrin gave his information. The town was very subdued, much more than Candelwynd had been before they had evacuated. The town closed up at dark and no one was on the street. Even the tavern was closed.

That morning the farmers went out to tend crops, and others went out to check lines across the river for fish. Still everyone seemed subdued, even the children seemed extremely quiet.

Sir Richard decided to try to make contact with a farmer out from the city, to see if additional information could be learned. They moved out from the city, until they came to a farm and Richard was going to remove his armor, go up, and try to communicate with the peasant. As Sir Richard was getting ready Kurt asked for another plan to be considered.

"Sir why not let Ray and me go up to talk to him. You're a lot larger than either of us, and might be intimidating. Ray and I would be less threatening—just a couple of youngsters, and you could be ready, in your chain armor, if assistance were needed," Kurt suggested.

Sir Richard paused a moment and reflected on the suggestion.

"Ray is not going to draw attention, and no one is going to realize how dangerous the little snot can be with a sword, especially when it is strapped to his back—out of sight," Aaron added.

Sir Richard finally agreed, so we got ready.

"Does this means you're not still upset with me for my sister?" I asked.

"No, but I wasn't really upset with you anyway. Just thought a small reminder might be needed. I'll get Aaron and Adam when we get back again," he said alluding to the discipline they gave me previously.

"That's not funny, Kurt," I told him, and about that time my shirt was being pulled over my head.

"Think we should just pound on him a little now," Aaron's voice came from behind me. "With his shirt over his head, he'd have a hard time fighting back."

"Naw, we don't have time now. Just help him strap the sword on."

"I sometimes think your senses of humor leave a lot to be desired," I told them, somewhat put off by their actions!

"Aaron, if his manners don't improve, and we don't start getting a bit more respect—we may have to remind him of his lack of age. I think you told us about your older brother having to remind you of this when you were younger. SO we might have to assist our brother in his education," Kurt said.

"Ok, let's get this done, before I get in real trouble. All right—sirs" I decided I didn't want my older friends mad at me. Especially when either one could beat the snot out of me, and we had worked with each other enough be close. But they had also taken up for me in the past, and they were becoming like older brothers.

Kurt and I moved out to talk to the farmer. Each of us had a small dagger that could be seen and our swords were strapped to our backs. Tarrin had noticed most men carried a dagger. We also had put on some extra clothes. Kurt put on one of Sir Richard's shirts, I used one of Kurt's, and we rolled in the dirt and smeared mud and leaves on them, as if they had been worn a long time.

Kurt was to do the talking, I was to crouch and attempt to look smaller, like a frightened child. The farmer looked up as we approached, and Kurt pulled me behind him like he was shielding me.

He asked where we were from, and we told him from a small village that the Orcs had destroyed in the spring.

We were having a small problem with the language, but Kurt was doing fairly well—I thought.

Kurt asked, "Can we find safety in your city?"

"City not safe, for us. Even worse for strangers. Orcs all upset. Hunting all—now, very bad," he told us.

"Can't the city guards help?" Kurt asked.

"City guards," he said and spit, "owned by Orcs. Thane owned too. All city scared. Monthly hunt coming soon."

About that time four large Orcs came out of the woods to our north. They spotted the three of us in the field, shouted, and began running toward us.

The old farmer appeared to have frozen in fright. Kurt grabbed his arm and pulled him toward our troops. The old man began to run reasonably well. As we neared the edge of the trees, it was apparent to the Orcs that they would catch up before we could hide in the trees. As we continued to run, Xell becomes visible in front of us and Aaron and Sir Richard bolted from the trees on their horses. Xell had cast a *sleep* spell, and although two of the Orcs had been affected, the other two got the point of lances from the warriors.

I thought the farmer was going to have a heart attack.

When Sir Richard returned, Kurt and I had moved to tie up the sleeping Orcs. The man fell at his feet. We questioned him carefully, and discovered that the Thane was the Orc's man, and would have to be eliminated before a rescue could be effected. Several of the guards were loyal to the Orcs, others were not, but were just trying to survive. We got a list of those he thought were loyal to the Orcs, mainly older guards who had been in their service for a long time. The town's name was now called Tabok.

The sleeping Orcs were awakened, questioned, and dispatched, while Kurt and I put on armor.

Xell went to sleep, where she could relearn spells. The farmer drew the city for the rest of us. It was decided that evening we would move into the town, in armor, and denounce the Thane as a traitor to humanity. He would be slain as would any guard that came to his aid. After that we would announce to the town that they were moving and display the body of the Thane in the public square.

Xell got up, and she and the other spell caster memorized the spells desired for the taking of the town. We armored ourselves and our horses, and moved to enter the town.

A young guardsman challenged us at the city gate. The farmer announced us as friends that had come to see the Thane, with a message. The guard allowed us to pass, and the old farmer said that the boy would be a good man—if given the chance. We continued to ride through town, and were gathering into a nice parade by the time we got to the city hall of records and the Thane.

Sir Richard remained on his horse as Aaron, Jelu, and I stepped down and held our previously strung bows at the ready.

"I am Sir Richard of Candlewynd. As a knight and vassal to King Harold of Candlewynd, I pronounce you a traitor to humanity, and sentence you to death!" Sir Richard yelled.

At his pronouncement of death, Aaron, Jelu, and I all fired our sheath arrows into his chest. He was dead before he hit the ground.

Sir Richard continued, "You are now under the protection of his majesty King Harold. Kneel before our authority or perish."

Several of the guards rushed toward the Thane or us. A guard rushing Sir Richard was greeted by an arrow from Jelu's bow, and dropped as the arrow penetrated his skull between his eyes. Aaron and I fired at the two guards going to the Thane. Everyone else in the city square was on his knees. It took both of us two shots to kill the guards, but our orders were to shoot to kill those that attempted to aid the Thane. Aaron's target may have been trying to surrender as the second arrow caught him in his throat, thus silencing whatever he had to say.

I looked at the dead bodies of the humans I had just killed or assisted in killing. I got sick, and I threw up all over myself. It was the first time I had ever killed a human. I thought I was going to pass out. Kurt grabbed me as I started to fall, and he and Luke took me inside the city hall.

"What's wrong?" Kurt asked, as he helped me get my helm off.

"I—I never killed a human before. Orcs are different, it didn't bother me to kill them, they're like animals. But these were humans—I . . . ," I stammered as I started throwing up again.

"Luke, look after him, I'll let Sir Richard know," Kurt said. Then patted me on the head and started to leave. "Don't worry about it, kid, it was my first time also—I feel a bit ill too."

The guards were all brought to the square and a trial was quickly held for those that had been in the Orc's service for an extended period. Six of the guards were declared guilty by the populace, two of those pleaded their innocence. Sir Richard had Xell used the ability to *detect lie*, and found them sincere in their innocence, and granted them their lives The other four were hung.

Sir Richard informed the city that they 1should pack up all they could and get ready to leave in the morning. He wanted to check on me, but had Xell do it.

"I understand that killing another human is tough," Xell started, "but that's okay. If it wasn't hard for you at your age, we'd worry about you. You performed your duty well, then it hit you."

"Xell, what's Sir Richard going to think of me? That I'm too young and can't handle it?" I was almost sobbing from the shame I felt.

Xell came over gave me a small hug, and said, "Ray, it is okay. He's not mad at you or upset, and neither am I. You did well today. Just rest a bit and you'll be fine."

The other boys came by to encourage me. Andrew said he was proud that I could still feel that way about taking another human's life. That just meant I had a good strong soul in me.

That evening, using the **mind link medallion**, Sir Richard informed Candlewynd of our success. One of the mages would use his science of *telepathy*, to inform the party building rafts to send someone to lead the people back to the location they were to leave from down river. We were informed that the rafts would not be ready as quickly as the citizens of Tabok would be.

Word was spread through the city that a man would arrive in the morning to lead them, and they would leave the following evening, under the cover of darkness, to begin their journey. They would take all their money and easily carried items with them, but half would be given to the king for his service in the rescue. The city's treasury was forfeit to the king. In the new city they would be assisted in establishing a place to farm or ply their trade. We also wanted to take all the grain they could carry, to help with the food supply.

We set up in the city hall. Sir Richard was pleased with our efforts, and told us all that we did well.

Andrew discovered a boarded up church in town that had not been used since any of the inhabitants could remember. He got Aaron and me to help him remove the boards, and open the doors.

It was in a sad state of disrepair. The altar had been desecrated, by slaying a human on it, probably the priest, who's body was still on the altar. We cleared it out and Andrew discovered a secret compartment in the altar. Inside the compartment was a lever which released the altar and allowed it to swing out, revealing a secret chamber.

Andrew held a brief service for those in the town who wanted to come. The dilapidated structure was fairly filled with people wanting to know about God. Then we swung out the altar.

We went down the stairs and in the chamber discovered a silver crucifix and candlesticks. Inside a closet was an ephod, which must have had some strong magic, because even with age it was still in splendid but condition. Andrew reverently removed the ephod, and behind it was a suit of chain mail, mace and a shield. On the floor of the closet was a sack of gold, with almost 100 gold coins, and a locked box. We carefully took our newly found treasures back to Sir Richard.

We were pretty excited. Sir Richard suggested that since we found the item on our own, that Andrew keep the ephod and the mace. The chain mail looked close to Aaron's size, so he might make use of it, and I should use the shield. The money would be divided amongst us all.

He sent for Tarrin, who came in and had a fit at the danger we ignored by not sending for him earlier. "That place could have had some nasty traps, and you might all three been lying dead on the floor. Now granted, it is less likely in a priest's room, but still you need to be more careful!"

Sir Richard agreed, and also reprimanded us belatedly. Then he ask Tarrin, "Would you please use your skills to check the box, and attempt to open it?"

"Yes sir," he replied and began to carefully examine the box. After several minutes had passed, he exclaimed, "The lock is trapped. It's a good thing you didn't try to force the lock!"

Sir Richard asked, "Can you disarm the trap?"

"I believe so, but if not some curing may be needed in quick order," Tarrin replied. "Everyone back up—just in case."

I thought he was being a bit melodramatic, but I stepped back, as everyone else did. We watched him work with his tools, then he breathed a sigh of relief, and proclaimed success in disarming the trap. Now for the simpler task of unlocking the chest. That task seemed much quicker, and the box was opened. Inside were some scrolls, and six beautiful fire opals.

"Andrew, examine the scrolls. Tarrin, what do you think those gemstones are worth—assuming they aren't magical?" Sir Richard asked.

Xell said, "I'll relearn *detect magic*, to discover that information—then get ready for sleep to relearn spells."

Xell cast her spell, and told us, "The mace, chain, ephod, and shield are all magical, along with the scrolls. Since they were found in a priest's chamber I suggest that Andrew examine them—he may be able make use of them."

Now we were really excited. A magical shield was a great prize to me. The chain mail was really fine workmanship and magical. These would splendidly aid us in our endeavors.

That evening Aaron and Kurt continued to give me a good-natured hard time. I pleaded with Jelu for assistance, but he sat back and laughed as they took turns wrestling me. It wasn't very fair, but they were careful not to hurt me—too much. Then they both jumped Jelu. I yelled that I would come to his aid, but was too battered to assist. By the time the two older squires had finished with us our ears were sore from head locks, and the tops of our heads from being scrubbed. We had a great time.

Then Kurt and I paired up against Jelu and Aaron. It was still unfair, I was too much smaller than Jelu to make up the difference between Aaron and Kurt. But it was still grand, getting to be just boys.

Sir Richard came in after a long time and told us to settle down and get some rest, we would be needing it. Besides, as loud as we were, he and Xell weren't able to rest.

When Sir Richard left, Jelu asked how much rest he was trying to get? Kurt popped him across the head, and said, "That remark was inappropriate."

Jelu looked a little stunned by the reaction of Kurt, but Kurt nor Aaron appeared to joking.

Jelu responded with a "Yes sir."

We went to sleep pretty quickly after that. But I asked Kurt, "Weren't you a little sharp with Jelu?"

"Do you think he would like to explain that remark to Sir Richard, or Xell?" Then he suggested that I might should get some sleep before I got myself into trouble.

Early that morning the guide arrived. He helped organize things and then suggested that everyone try to sleep for the rest of the day after a late lunch.

We were ready to pull out early the next morning to go down to the fort overlooking the river.

It had been suggested that the party could take boats down river, but with the river slow, as it normally was this time of the year, it would not save much time, and the return trip without horses would take longer. Then some of the younger guards suggested that they could aid in the rowing the boats, and that terrain along the way would be difficult by foot. They would also know where to put the boats in close to shore, to stay out of sight of the fort. They had spotted these while taking supplies and . . . prisoners to the fort. With their assistance rowing on the return trip, it would be quicker. Sir Richard weighed the information, and after learning of the difficult terrain decided to take the boats. He also did not realize at first that these boats had small sails on them which could increase the speed, especially early in the morning coming back up stream, with the wind coming in off the ocean. They would be able to leave that morning, get close to the fort, and get a couple of hours sleep before attacking the fort, and be ready to start their return trip. At least that was the plan.

Then there were other suggested changes in the plan. The town would wait for their return before leaving, that way they could provide an armed escort for the populace. Sir Richard wasn't too pleased with this idea. But the senior squire, sent to guide the people to the rafts, reminded him that the horses would be safe in the city when we returned.

Sir Richard was adamant about their leaving. Use the horses to help move the people quicker, but have them gone. We can travel quicker without the very young or the old. You have the people evacuated.

Sir Richard told the squire, "We will return, fire the town, and meet you at the debarkation point on the river. As slow as you will be with the town, we may get there before you have had half the populace on the rafts. That is assuming that they are not still under construction!"

His order was final, so the town would be leaving just a little before the party attacked the fort.

The trip down river was much quicker than it was thought to have been. The current and then afternoon breeze moved them quickly along. By mid-afternoon the boats were beached and a makeshift camp was set up—to wait for the attack. Xell cast *invisibility* on Tarrin, then *sleep* on herself where she could get her rest and relearn spells.

The boys took it easy slept and rested, along with the guards who had come with them. Close to midnight they would get back in the boats, get to the base of the hill, and move up to the fort. Normally the landing wasn't guarded but the boats were going to stop before getting that close—just in case.

"You nervous?" I asked Aaron, who was in the boat, next to me.

"With this new magical chain mail—yes," he replied and patted me on the shoulder. "Never taken on a fort before. I sure hope Tarrin can slip in and open it up for us."

"I still think I should have gone to help—just in case," I told him.

"You better not let Sir Richard hear you make that argument again, or you're really going to catch a good one when this is finished," he said sternly to me. "And it would be better if I didn't hear of it again either!"

"Yes sir."

We waited at the bottom of the hill as Tarrin quietly went up the slope to the barred gate.

Xell came up to me, and tapped me on the shoulder. I didn't hear her come up, and I really jumped.

"I want a word with you young man," she in an ominous tone.

We moved off a bit from the others, as I answered "Yes, ma'am."

"Are you trying to get in trouble?" she asked peering at me intently.

"I don't understand, ma'am. What am I supposed to have done that was improper?"

She put her hands on my shoulders and looked me in the eye, and said, "Where did you sleep last night? I heard you slept in the village!"

I stood there for a moment, then the realization of what she was asking sunk in. "No ma'am, I was in the city hall—with Aaron, Kurt, and the others—honest!"

"Boy, if you're lying—you're in double trouble," she told me in a rather cold voice.

"Xell, I don't think I've ever lied to you, even unintentionally. I don't make a habit of that. My father told me, as a little child, that the spanking for lying would be worse than the one that I was lying about. Which meant I would get an extra one. I listened," being both a bit scared at her anger, and the thought that she thought I would tell an untruth.

"All right, I believe you. You've never lied to me or anyone else in authority that I know of. Like you said, getting caned twice isn't much fun. Don't worry about it—get back and let's get ready to kill some Orcs," Xell told me.

I went back and asked Aaron about what she said. He just laughed, and said the mage was probably out in the town, since everyone else was accounted for.

Waiting seemed to be forever. I walked over to Markél, and let him know about Xell's questioning of me. He just chuckled, and said "Thanks kid, but I'm not the one she'd be worrying about. But thanks still."

I guess being eighteen allows extra confidence, or you can just get away with more.

Tarrin came back after unlocking the gate. "There're two guards on opposite sides of the gate. Each has an alarm. I'm going to need your help to take them both out," he told me.

"Go tell Sir Richard," I answered. "And next time, warn us you're back before scaring the wits out of us."

"What! Get your little butt up and let's go," Tarrin responded, sounding more than a little miffed.

"I'm ready, but you're going to have to tell Sir Richard—I can't," I told him.

Before Tarrin could say anything else Kurt interrupted, "If he says anything, Sir Richard is going to raise blisters on his butt, so you really do have to go to Sir Richard."

"I guess it's a good thing you can't see me right now. The sign language might have you upset. Go over to him and I'll inform him," he said, sounding rather pleased with his comments.

"Sir Richard, I'm going to need the little snot to assist me in taking out the guards. There're two guards on opposite sides of the gate, in the towers. He is better with a sword and I need the help, sir," Tarrin told him.

"You didn't ask him for this—did you?" Sir Richard asked me.

His tone concerned me as I answered, "No sir."

"All right, you boys get it done," Sir Richard told us.

We started back up the hill, and Tarrin gave me information about the guards. They were across the gate from each other with an alarm bell. I wasn't sure why he couldn't have handled both of the guards, and asked him.

"I didn't want to lose the *invisibility*, it might come in handy in the rest of the battle," he answered.

"Yeah, but you can go invisible with psionics," I said.

"It's not the same, and you know it," Tarrin said. "Just make sure we take care of business. We can hug the wall, and only one guard has a chance to see you. You can become invisible to him and then move up the stairs to his station. You should be able to get a clean kill and we can prop the guard up to make it look like he is still there, only asleep. Then we move to the other."

"All right, but you could have handled all of this yourself."
I told him.

"Yes, but I would have lost the spell, and I knew you wanted to take part, so I was trying to help you get the chance."

I had wanted to take part, but not exactly this way. We moved up the stairs as Tarrin had said, and were able to dispatch the first guard and then the other. We then went back for the others, and all moved back up to the fort, with Tarrin still invisible. There were approximately twenty guards still here. We needed to move quickly and quietly. The barracks were arranged with ten soldiers in each, and then there was an officer's quarters.

We started to just set the buildings on fire and then let them come out into a hail of arrows. Then we remembered the guards that came with us saying something about prisoners being brought here. If we just fired one of the buildings and the other had *sleep* spells cast into it we could be more careful about firing arrows at the beings coming out of the burning building.

Sir Richard had us put kindling and straw around one of the barracks. The back door was barred and barricaded so there would be only one exit. We found some pitch used to shoot flaming missiles at ships and put it around the building also; that would make it blaze up very quickly.

Sir Richard had Tarrin and me sit up near the officer's quarter. "Do you think the two of you can handle the officer, since he shouldn't be armored? Tarrin, you should be able to get a good back stab, and Ray you should be able to go *invisible* to him. If not, sing out for help, if you need it. When we fire the building, Jelu, Aaron, Kurt, and will fire bows as they leave, Ray you're to help until the officer comes out—probably with the other barrack. Luke, Markél, and Xell will cast *sleep* into the other barracks. Andrew, you be ready to assist there if any are left. I'll move to your assistance if needed. That building should burn quickly, so get ready."

It was really a good plan. The building caught fire very quickly. By the time someone on the inside yelled it was a blazing inferno. Their screams woke up the other barracks, and they came streaming out of their barracks. The *sleeps* were cast, and all but three of the Orcs from that barrack were slept. As the first Orc that didn't get slept was tripping over his fallen comrades, I hit him with a pair of sheath arrows, and Aaron caught him with a third. Andrew stepped up to an Orc with just a dagger in his hand, as Aaron and I dropped the remaining Orc. I didn't see much of anything after that as the garrison's commander came bellowing out of his room, except the glow of Kurt's broad sword as he pulled it for combat.

I selected him to be *invisible* to, and then fired arrows at him. The first he deflected with his sword, and started moving toward me—a little unsteady, but toward me. I fired again, this time hitting him in the shoulder. He howled in pain, and began moving more quickly toward me. I moved and he adjusted to the movement—this wasn't good. I fired once more then dropped my bow and pulled sword and shield. I certainly hoped Tarrin made good his backstab, otherwise I was going to be in real trouble. My last shot was a good one, and gave the Orc a severe chest wound, but he kept coming. His sword crashed down as I blocked with the shield, but it made a shudder run up the length of my body.

Just after that Tarrin caught him in the back with a strong thrust, as he parried my sword slash. He wheeled on Tarrin, and took a step back so that neither of us were directly behind him. He caught Tarrin with an overhand slash, cutting through the thief's leather armor and blood began to seep through it. I tried to pick up the speed and ferocity of my attack to aid Tarrin, but this Orc was good. He obviously was more powerful than other War Orcs we had encountered, as neither Tarrin nor I were able to be *invisible* to him. That kind of fouled up our plans—we hadn't counted on him having that much skill. Somebody forgot to tell the Orcs that our scouting reports didn't describe them as having that much power.

I got a couple of little cuts on him, but nothing seemed too serious. Tarrin was taking the brunt of his attacks; I guess he was mad at the young thief for the back attack. He caught Tarrin with a glancing blow on the helmet, and the thief buckled at the knees and went down. I tried to yell for help but couldn't, as I was breathing too hard. As he hit Tarrin in the head, I got another shot into his ribs. Now he was starting to feel the effects of our attacks, but I was also his only target.

I was hoping the magic of the shield was REALLY good!

He got past the shield, sliced my armor at the stomach, and gave me a slight cut, but as he got past my shield with his sword, I delivered a great shield thrust and caught him on the jaw. This stunned, him for a moment. During the moment he was stunned I pressed the attack and was able to catch the leader with a quick slash and then a very forceful jab, piercing his heart, and killing him.

I looked quickly at what was going on around me, as I headed to Tarrin. No Orcian threat near, so I pulled off Tarrin's helmet to check him. He was breathing, but not very strong breaths. Since no one else was near, I *cell adjusted* a little to see if he would regain consciousness.

It worked. He blinked, then looked up at me, and asked if the Orc was dead.

"Yeah, but you picked a fine time to take a nap," I told him.

"Did you just cure me?" he asked.

"Yeah—a little. I better not do much more. I'll find Luke and send him over or Andrew over to you," I told him then moved off to see if my help was needed elsewhere.

The rest of the battle was over also. Several of us were wounded, but only very slightly. I got Andrew to go to Tarrin and assist him. The battle hadn't lasted more than about ten minutes.

We looted the fort, killed the sleeping Orcs, and then set the rest of the fort on fire. Some of the items we took were papers, that would require translating. We thought there might be useful information in them. We also found a dead prisoner. We burned her body in the funeral pyre with the Orcs. Then we went back to our boats and started back up river.

We traveled about two hours then Richard called a halt. We were exhausted from the battle. I was aching and my stomach was hurting from the wound. When we stopped Andrew asked, "Do you have any healing left?"

"Yes sir," I answered.

"Then cure your wound, while I bring up *rapport*. If Xell asks, I'll be getting the information about the battle with the commander, and helping you get over the fear of *rapport*," Andrew told me.

So I cured myself with *cell adjustment*, and everybody went on the alert when they felt the power being used. And just like Andrew said, Xell asked. The rest of the Gold Squad assumed that I was using *cell adjustment*, but Andrew did have the story of the battle as a cover.

Sir Richard let everyone sleep for a couple of hours, then it was back on the river. The morning breeze had not come up yet, so they were having to work hard paddling against the current. At daylight they stopped again for first meal and rest. Also they figured they could wait and relax, waiting a while for the morning breeze.

At the first hint of a breeze they were back in the boats. The wind wasn't strong enough to even move the sail. They continued to row for another hour, then a real gust hit the sails, and made the boats lurch. A nice steady breeze filled the sails, and the boats picked up speed.

The trip up river was uneventful, and with the wind they made good time. They got back to town, ate, and slept. Watches were set, but the spell casters were going to get a full eight hours, so they could relearn spells. As everyone woke from sleep, they started putting brush around buildings to start the fire. Hay, straw, and anything that would burn easy, (including the boats), were piled up around the building, especially the city hall. Some tar and oil was found and smeared on the city walls, especially the gate area. Then the Sir Richard gave the order to pull out and set the city ablaze.

The night sky lit up with the glow from the city. The party moved out to meet at the rendevous. They were reasonably well rested, and the urgency of getting back to the safety of Candlewynd spurred them on. Xell contacted Candlewynd as the party was ready to depart, to let them know of their progress.

Trudging along at night was not a lot of fun, but it was safer. The nights were starting to get a bit cooler, and tonight it was nearly cold. An early cold blast from the north dropped the temperatures, and a slight overcast kept the twin moons from shedding much light. With the cold, it was better to be moving. When they stopped for a rest, a cold camp was not too exciting.

After traveling all night, they got to the rendevous by midmorning, just shortly after the town's people had arrived.

There were still not enough rafts made, so the rest of the morning everyone pitched in and started working to finish. When they finished, it was kind of late in the day to start down river, but a sunset was still a couple of hours further away. It would also be a good test, then things might be changed for the morrow, when they would be on the river all day. The trip down river to Candlewynd would take twenty to thirty hours on the river. That did not include getting out into the river, coming to land for camp, or rest/food stops.

Sir Richard was not in charge of this part of the expedition, Baron Bellun was. The baron got everyone onto the rafts and the little armada began to float down the river. With the river low and slow as it was this time of the year, it was a peaceful float. As it started getting close to dark they began to look for a good place to either beach or to anchor the rafts for the night. They found a place just before sun set. It was several hours after dark before everyone was off the rafts. This looked like it could be a nightmare, keeping everything organized.

Sir Richard and Xell met with leaders of the evacuation. Then word was spread through the camp that they would need to prepare food for the next day's meals, as they would remain on the river all night. The moons were sufficiently bright to see well enough to travel, and there was too large a chance for mishaps when getting to land, and when trying to get back out into the river's currents.

Sir Richard decided that our group would just move on horseback; that would allow for more space on the cramped rafts. By taking the party and their mounts off, there would be much more space for the Tabok's people. Ray thought it might just be because Sir Richard didn't want to take orders from the evacuation force's leader.

The rafts were in the river before dawn, and would be at Candlewynd at least a day before the party would arrive. But they all preferred to be on horse than on the river. There was no rush to return, so the party took a slow pace with frequent breaks. They enjoyed the colors of the leaves that were turning in the late autumn weather. They made sure their horses were well rested and took three and half days to make the journey that could have been made in a day and half, had it been needed.

They worked on their cartography skills on the return trip and assisted Ray with some of the studies that had plagued him that year. They visited and in general relaxed.

———————

"Andrew, I was thinking . . ." I began, and was interrupted.

"That is dangerous for a little snot like you," Aaron said proud of his smart remark.

"Why don't you go sit on your sword? Anyway, it looks like if we had our own training area, we wouldn't have to be as careful with our training," I continued.

"What'd ya mean?," Andrew asked, as moved over closer to hear me, while we were walking our horses.

"Well, I remember Father having and training troops on our estates when I was real little—before I was even a page," I added before Aaron could make another retort.

"That's an interesting observation. But I think you've got a point. When we get back you and I will talk about it more, when we don't have to be careful. Or we might just give the idea to Sir William, and let him ponder it," Andrew said.

"Well, if we did something like that it would take an estate like the boy had before we came here, to have study material for us, and everything else needed. But I agree that it sounds like a good idea," Markél said. We hadn't noticed that he had dropped back to where we were. "Better be a bit more careful with your conversations, and I hate to admit that the little snot has a good idea, but he does."

They got back and were debriefed by the royal advisers. Sir William then sent word that he would meet with the Gold Squad in the morning for their evaluation. It would not be until ten in the morning, so he would have time to talk to Sir Richard and Xell about the boys. They were all allowed to sleep in, except Ray, who had to go to a special math tutoring to help him keep up with the others his age. The older boys gave him a tough time about this—they also reminded him how lucky he was that they had assisted him during the trip with his studies. But they all had the afternoon off to relax and take care of their gear.

Chapter Twelve

Too Little to be Big

"Give everyone what you owe him: If you owe taxes, pay taxes; if revenue, then revenue; if respect, then respect; if honor, then honor." Romans 13: 7

It was late in the afternoon, the day they returned. Ray was relaxing and brushing his horse; both he and the horse seemed to miss that time while he was gone. His palomino was maturing nicely, and was going to make a lovely stallion. This breed was too small for a heavy war horse, but they would work well for the light cavalry, or scouting. Those extra new horses would at least be able to help in the fields, and there had been some talk of cross breeding with the larger horses, to improve their size for draft labor. All that was far removed in the future, and Ray was enjoying some time off without having to worry about Orcian warriors, or older squires trying to show him how much younger he was than they. His mind was on the peace of brushing and talking to his colt, when one of the healers, just a little older than he came in the barn.

"Are you Ray?" she asked as she walked up to him. "You've grown so much since I was around you the last time, before . . . we left."

"It's Darla, isn't it? I haven't seen you in almost a year. How did we miss at the party," I asked?

She shook her head yes to the query about her name. Her shortly cut auburn hair was just to the top of the shoulders, and her green eyes had a mischievous look in them.

"I've been on duty a great deal, helping with the wounded and sick. I didn't even get to go to the christening—on duty then too. I hear you've been pretty busy yourself. Out saving the sons and daughters of Adam."

I gave her a puzzled look, and asked, "Sons and daughters of Adam—what does that mean?"

"Those people you helped rescued, that's what they said the Orcs call them, most of the time," Darla told me. "Why don't you put that brush down, come and sit, and visit with me? I want to hear about you tripup river. I've heard a few rumors, but I want to know from someone first hand."

She took my hand and led me over to the stairs. "Hayloft is comfortable for sitting and talking; besides there's too much of a cool draft down here."

I began to tell her about the journey. She asked questions about the land, the trees, and other questions. Her interest was encouraging. I was careful that I didn't tell her anything I wasn't supposed to, about the team, but just about going on the trip. She just looked intently into my eyes as I told her about the it.

Then all of a sudden, she grabbed my cheeks in her hands and kissed me. I never really kissed anyone except Charissa. Well, I guess Sherry kissing me didn't really count. She did that just to show me the difference in a little kiss and a KISS.

It was different, this wasn't some preteen, this was a fourteen-year-old girl that was kissing me, and it was . . . well—different. It was also fun.

She kissed me a several times, and then she bit me on the ear. That hurt. I was sort of shocked by that. But she kissed me again, and then pushed my head to kiss her on the neck. We kissed several more minutes then Luke came in the barn looking for me.

"Ray! Are you in here," he yelled?

"Don't let him know I'm here," Darla whispered. "Tell him you were getting hay for the horse."

"Luke, up here—I am pitching down some hay for the horse." Then I reached down and grabbed an armload and threw it down to the floor below.

"Come on, your mom wants you to come and eat. Sherry and Adam are coming over also. Hurry up," he told me. "What happened to your hair? You trip in the hayloft?"

"How come you came to get me instead of sending one of the little kids?" I asked as we were starting to leave.

He looked at me, looked back up in the hayloft, and shook his head, without answering my question.

I went with my cousin, but I would have preferred to have stayed in the loft. Sherry was back on duty some, there were many new babies, and many of them had mothers that were trained professionals—not just warriors, but mages, healers, and some priestesses. A nursery was set up to allow the mothers to continue with training. Some of the ladies, like my mother, helped in the care. They had new children and were no longer training, some of the healers in training also assisted in the care of the newborns.

Adam was picking up some size. They had duty on the wall construction, a lot this summer, and he was while gaining a lot of muscle mass, he also had gotten a little taller. Carole, as always, was glad to see Sherry. Megan was on duty at the hospital, which made the evening more pleasant for me. Megan had been giving me a great deal of grief before we left, and her actions were about to get me in trouble for my reactions toward her.

After dinner Sherry and I talked, up on deck, about the problem Megan and I were having getting along. Sherry suggested that Megan was having a hard time accepting her little brother having a rating equal to hers, especially at my age. So I should just try to understand and not speak unseemly toward her, or I would be the one with blisters on my backside. I really enjoyed talking with Sherry, I had missed that. When we went back in, Luke and Adam were discussing the differences between battle techniques in large armies compared to the small forces we had all worked with this last summer. Adam was being slated for infantry work, and had been spent most of his training of late in close order drills.

The next morning Luke and I reported to Sir William at ten. We arrived early, and hoped I might see Charissa there. Luke saw me looking and reminded me that younger students would already by in one of their training classes, without mentioning the princess by name.

Sir William arrived a short time later, and the rest of the team also filtered in. Sir William notified them of the pleasure he had to inform them that they had been commended by the king for their work. He also collected the magic items that we had discovered and let us know they would be returned soon. They were to be properly *identified* by some of the more advanced mages.

The boys were then given assignments for training. They would be working with some of the other squires and knights for a while, to remove suspicion of always working together.

Jelu was spending a lot of time with Eldalië—every chance he had. Ray and Luke decided he was in love, and left him alone with it. Kurt and Aaron attempted to keep Ray out of trouble with the older squires. His maturity level showed the difference in age when dealing with things outside combat. Kurt finally had enough, and showed him that he was enough larger than Ray to bend him over his knee and bust his britches. He didn't actually do it, but let Ray know that it was a possibility if he got out of line too much.

Ray was still having trouble with Megan—he believed his sister was attempting to torment him. And after one very loud argument his behavior was called into question by their mother.

"If I were a warrior, you wouldn't have the senior rating, and would have to follow orders from me as a junior squire," Megan told him.

"If I were a junior, you wouldn't have the problem with me being your equal, that seems to be bothering you," Ray responded. "You also wouldn't be treating me the way you've been treating me."

The argument heated up and he said something very inappropriate, just as Mother walked in.

He was dead. His mother was going to kill him or worse, send him to Sir William for punishment, since Ray was his official squire.

He was sent to his room while Lady Martha and Megan had a discussion. He was truly sorry for what he said to his sister, and would probably be a great deal more remorseful when the punishment was over.

His mother and Megan came into the room, and Ray stood as they entered. Both were still extremely mad.

"Your sister is going to discipline you for your actions," Lady Martha began. "Don't you say a word," she told him as Ray started to complain. "You know better than to act that way. Even if she isn't a warrior, you still should give her the respect she deserves by the difference in age over you, and her birth rank. She has the limitations on the severity which she can administer the punishment. If you don't submit to her authority in this matter, young man, you will regret it!"

Ray decided that Megan was not near as compassionate as his older brother had been when he disciplined him. She made every stroke count, not to mention the embarrassment of having your sister wear your bare butt out with a hickory rod. She gave him seven very hard strokes. Since he was thirteen, that was the maximum she was allowed to give.

The next day Ray didn't report to classes, and Luke told instructors he was not well. He complained to Mother that Megan had been tormenting him and started the argument yesterday. Lady Martha asked if another trip to the barn would be required.

For the rest of the week Ray couldn't seem to do anything right. Kurt and Andrew were both upset with him, for various things. Kurt was trying to give him some extra tutoring in math, and Ray got mad about something with him. Kurt lost his tempter and picked Ray up, and like a little child put him over his knee and gave him a good spanking with a leather strap. Then Kurt picked Ray up and put him in the corner, and held him.

The spanking was more embarrassing than anything else. Kurt was like an older brother in helping him, it hurt, but it really hurt his feelings that Kurt would treat him like that.

"Listen, you little snot, you better remember how old you are, and start being a bit more respectful of those who are older than you. In combat you're great, but in the city you need to be more respectful," Kurt told him, breathing hard after the exertion.

"I can't believe you just whipped me like that!" Ray told him. "You don't have permission to do that."

"Would you have preferred a fight? We could do that—I believe I'd have hurt you if we'd fought," Kurt told him

"No—sir."

"I'll report myself to Lord William, because you're right, I don't have permission to spank you like a six-year-old, which is about how you've been acting," Kurt told him.

"No, don't tell him. I'd rather Sir William, nor anyone else know about it," Ray told him, somewhat embarrassed, and rubbing his sore behind.

True to his word Kurt explained what happened to Baron Scrope. Ray was called in and the baron was upset with both boys. He let them off with penalty marching. After talking things over with the older members of the Gold Squad, the baron decided Ray needed to be reined in a little. He was having a hard time fitting in with other seniors because of his age. In combat and on missions he could handle it—but in normal day to day things Ray was still barely in his second year, still a thirteen-year-old squire.

He called in Ray, Kurt, and Aaron and told them his decision. Aaron and Kurt would have permission to discipline Ray for infractions for which a junior would normally be disciplined, in behavior toward his elders, but only with a leather strap—not with a proper caning. The two older squires could only do it if Ray truly deserved it, and no one else was to know about it. He would not get a beating as badly as others his age, as a senior would use a rod on them; so his senior rank aided him, but he was going to have to mature.

Kurt and Aaron would remain his mentors and help him adapt to his rank beyond his years, but they would hold him more accountable—without having to get a hickory or birch every time. If he were in big trouble, the baron would make sure he knew his manners.

Kurt or Aaron would just give a light touch on the shoulder when the boy was getting out of line. His problem was at home where his sister seemed to delight in making him miserable.

———————

"Mother, may I move into the junior squire barracks?" I asked Mother one evening in late October. Eldalië had told us the calendar that used in this world by humans, had thirteen months, with twenty-eight days in each month, but I couldn't remember it yet. Rumor had it that we would be switching to it at the next Fall Festival.

"What? Why? What brought this on?" she asked.

"Megan is giving me too much trouble. I'm having to treat her as a superior, or get in punished. I'd rather not have to have that pressure," I explained.

"You know she was disciplined a couple of days ago for starting it with you. You two need to get over this and get along," she said in a sad voice.

"Mother, she gave me the caning, and has made it difficult with some of the other senior squires that deal with me. It's not fair," I complained.

"Do you think you should have disciplined your older sister? Or do you believe I didn't do a good enough job of disciplining her?" mother asked.

"No ma'am, I didn't mean that. I just believe we might get along better if I wasn't around as much—for a little while. Maybe a month to six weeks," I suggested.

"Son, you're not a junior squire, I don't think you would be in their barracks, and I don't want you in the senior's barrack. You are too young to be with those boys, especially without Kurt, Aaron, or Adam around to look after you. And I won't allow that," she told me.

"May I have your permission to ask Sir William about the junior barracks?" I persisted. "Even if I was in the senior barracks, there aren't that many in the younger senior barracks anymore. Most are married."

"You may ask—but you may not move into a senior barrack," she told me with finality.

"Did you know Megan's planned engagement was canceled? That might have something to do with her poor attitude of late," Mother told me.

"What happened that it was called off?"

"With the nobility depleted as it is, they didn't want to dilute the psionic power of the nobles anymore, and he was not psionic," Mother told me. "They are still upset with the marriage of Xell and Sir Richard, and she wasn't even nobility."

"Wouldn't it be more difficult for them anyway if he wasn't psionic? He wouldn't understand some things that sharing in *rapport* does," I asked, still surprised at the news.

"I think they made a wise decision, but your sister is still upset. Remember, you can't be assigned to a senior barracks," she reminded me.

I asked Sir William that morning about moving into the junior's barrack, when I saw him before going to Bible class. He said he would consider the request.

I talked to Timothy before class started, and told him of my request.

"That would be great. I'd love to have you around. Also, that might keep some of the seniors from being so hard on some of us. If one them gets in trouble they come in looking for an excuse to cane one of us or beat up on us," Timothy said.

"Have you had this problem? Why hasn't someone complained to a knight?" I asked.

"Then we'd really be in for a hard time from them—no one has a death wish to get beat up by several of the older boys at once. Even some of the girls have been pretty tough on us. You know, a lot rougher than Sherry was on you when you got her in trouble."

That evening the baron told me we'd try the junior squire's barrack experiment for month, but he believed I should just work out the problems with Megan. I informed him it was difficult to work things out when she wasn't interested.

It was fun being around the boys close to my age. I'm sure that didn't have the effect on maturity that Kurt had in mind, but it was fun. It also stopped some of the bullying tactics from some of the younger seniors. With my senior rating it kept some of the sixteen-year olds from terrorizing the younger squires.

It also allowed me to see Darla more often.

———————

The Gold Squad was still training with different groups. The baron had us training with some of the older seniors. This wasn't too bad for Kurt and Aaron, but it was a bit of a problem for Jelu, unless it was using a bow, and it was really tough on Ray. Some of the older boys took great pleasure in bouncing him around during sword practice. He could hold his own for a while, then the difference in size and strength would begin to show. The worst was when it was group exercise—he just didn't have the size to do what they wanted done. Ray's inability to match their size had him in trouble with the instructor, who suggested a trip to the barn might aid his memory in the tactics. Luckily, one of the older seniors reminded him that Ray was where he was suppose to be, he just wasn't big enough to hold the spot.

That remark got some laughs, and it kept the boy from a beating, but not from extra work as punishment for not being able to do what was required. Ray fared better in lance practice and especially when he was allowed to use one of his family's stallions. War Champion was the prize stallion of the city, and was from his estate. The ability of that horse made up for much of Ray's lack of skill with the lance—not to mention the respect it brought from the students and instructor alike for who he really was.

One afternoon, Ray was with a group of young adults, with the new age breaks, but before the change in age rating they would have still been senior squires. They had been doing individual fencing drills, and he had held his own well enough. None of these men were of noble birth, and were in the city when it was evacuated, recovering from injuries. They would again be formally placed in the army—and this group was going to be mainly infantry. They still trained for cavalry, but would be infantry in the army, as they were adults. They would be shortly formed into a unit for combat, with a nobleman in charge of the squad. They were really just waiting for a sergeant to be properly trained to take over the unit from squire rating. Then after a while they would be the leaders of the younger squires that would be a well-trained army.

One of these young men made what Ray believed to be some disparaging remarks about Jelu and Eldalië. Ray challenged him for his statement, and demanded a retraction. The one making the remark was nearly twenty, the largest in the group, and suggested Ray withdraw his challenge before he got hurt.

Ray maintained his challenge, and a dual was to be fought, fortunately for Ray, using the wooden practice swords with which they had been training with. Some of the others suggested that he just use the sword and give Ray a good caning with it.

"Laddie, don' ya' think you're a bit small to be challengin' me?" Deveron asked.

"Well, you're only about four inches smaller than the Orcs I have taken on this summer, so I hope you'll be a good challenge," I said with false confidence. He was a better warrior than most of the Orcs I faced, just not as large.

I stayed with him well, and almost got a shield thrust to work, except he had seen me use it before. He blocked it with his shield, and just grinned and said, "That's a nice try, laddie."

Deveron eventually caught me with a leg sweep and pinned me to the ground, forcing me to yield. He then extended his hand and gave me a hand up, and told me, "Ya' did a good job there snotty. Ya' handled yerself moch better than I thought ya' could, even after I'd seen you train with us."

That evening I got a summons from Kurt—I wasn't sure what it was about. I hadn't been in trouble with him but once since I moved into the barracks, and I hoped I wasn't in for another session with the leather strap, but at least the baron hadn't taken me to task for any problems of late.

Kurt was furious about my challenge of the older student that day, when I met him at his home. "I'll be back shortly," he called to Sarah, as we started to walk.

"Why are you mad about that," I asked? "Jelu is a friend, and I was taking up for his honor, just as I did for Sherry this summer!"

"I thought your manners had been discussed about dealing with older squires, and Deveron is an adult. I guess you are in need of a reminder," he told me.

"Come on, Kurt. I wasn't out of line on the challenge. I was within my rights, and I didn't do it disrespectfully toward Deveron. I don't deserve to get busted."

"Little brother, you better just be glad I'm not allowed to use a rod on you. If you were a true junior squire, the beating would be worse than the one you got from Aaron, Adam and me. And I would have given it to you in the barracks in front of the other junior squires."

When we got to the barn, he was still pretty mad. I asked if we could wait until he wasn't quite so mad to give me the whipping. I knew he couldn't give me one too bad, but I still didn't want him that mad at me.

He wasn't waiting and it really hurt, then he made me mad. After getting disciplined for something for which I didn't believe I deserved, I was ordered to report to Deveron and apologize for my manners. I complained about the order, and Kurt wanted to know if we needed to repeat what had just happened. I decided that I would follow instructions, but I didn't like it.

I reported to the older senior barracks, and asked for Deveron. One of the seniors I had worked that day showed me into the barracks. Deveron was going over the duty roster for the next day, which had them doing construction work on the wall.

"Hey Deveron, that wee snot is here to see ya," the senior who answered the door called out. "Maybe he wants to try to take ya on again."

Deveron stood up and asked, "Wha der' ya' need young sir?"

"I've come to apologize for manners this afternoon, sir," I stated in front of the entire barracks. I'm sure I was red-faced from anger and embarrassment for having to do this.

"What? Come with me," he then said.

He led me out of the room, where I wasn't having to talk in front of everyone, then asked why I had apologized.

"I was informed that my manners were inappropriate, sir. I ask your forgiveness," I said again.

"There's nothing to forgive, yer actions were totally reasonable. I didn't realize I was talkin' about a friend of yers. Who ordered ya to apologize?" he asked, as he stroked his small red beard.

"Kurt, he's—my mentor, kinda like a big brother. He was pretty upset with my actions toward one that much my senior in years."

"Were ya disciplined for yer actions?" he asked, beginning to sound a little upset!

"Yes sir, I've already been disciplined. Please sir, will you accept my apology?" I asked, thinking he was still upset with me.

"So Kurt can discipline ya, or least did soo? If you'd get Kurt and ask him to meet wuth us at the stable, again," he ordered.

Now I was upset and getting worried. I was afraid Deveron was going to say that I wasn't disciplined severely enough. Deveron was huge red headed squire, soon to be an adult, and

I had heard people with red hair had a hot temper. I got Kurt, who was not too pleased about being interrupted about this. I went into the barn as the two older squires talked. I figured I was getting ready to have to take another whipping. Kurt came in, and was extremely upset.

Deveron had told him he was out of line for whipping me—with which I agreed. Kurt told me he would report it to Lord William in the morning.

"Wait—what?" I asked. "You're going to report it. But you've already disciplined me, why are you reporting it?"

"Because, it seems, I disciplined you without proper cause," he answered—waiting for what he told me to sink in. I must have seemed extremely dense, but I wasn't expecting this.

"Kurt, if you do this, you'll get in trouble. I don't want you upset with me for getting you in trouble," I said. I didn't need to be on Kurt's bad side if he got a caning because of me. "How about the next time you believe I need reminding of my manners, you don't whip me instead?"

"I can't. I have to report it, you know better than that," he told me, still upset.

"Kurt don't report it. I'd rather you not."

"Listen, little brother, if I disciplined you unjustly it's supposed to be reported, and I'll have to accept the consequences. It's not your fault, you told me you didn't feel like you deserved to get a whipping for your actions. I'm not going to be happy if Sir William takes a hickory to me, but I won't hold it against you."

"Sure."

The look I got from Kurt at the remark was not very kind.

Sir William was going to show Kurt the errors of his way in handling of me yesterday. I suggested that the next time

I was out of line, they just let the previous day's discipline count for that. But, as Kurt had said yesterday, that was not acceptable. I then ask for the Baron not to discipline Kurt. I would prefer to forgive him, and not have him mad at me for getting caned.

The baron decided since my plea was sincere he would not use the hickory on Kurt, and merely use a leather strap, like he had used on me. I hoped that kept Kurt from being too upset with me. Having him mad could be unpleasant, especially when we fenced each other.

I then found out I could appeal the discipline from him, just like a junior could from any senior, but if I deserved the discipline I might have to take it with a rod instead of a leather strap.

I was able to spend some time with Charissa that evening. I was invited to bring materials and study with her. I would also be able to ask questions of the tutors, if I needed any assistance.

I confess that I was a bit distracted with Charissa there, but I did get some much needed help with math—algebra and I were having a difficult time. Oh, I guess I should mention I was not the only student there with the princess, but the other three students were not even squire age.

I got back after lights out in the barracks, and Timothy gave a message. "You're to report to the older senior barracks when you return. Deveron wants to see you; it was a request, not an order. He came by, and gave it himself—didn't even send a page."

"Thanks, I guess I can still go—it won't be lights out for them. Thanks, Timothy," I said and put back on my cloak, and went back into what felt like a winter night, with the wind blow hard from the north.

I arrived at the barracks shortly afterwards. It was cold enough to motivate one to hurry. When I knocked, I was informed that as a senior I was not required to knock, but could come in unannounced.

Deveron met me as I walked toward him, not knowing what he wanted me for. Just as I got to him he kneeled. "Sir, I din't recognize ya' the other day. Sir, I served briefly with ya' father, and da here now swear total allegiance to ya' as your man, save the king direct ma actions elsewhere!"

I was in shock. I didn't really know what to say.

"Deveron, I'm not old enough to have the title, and so I don't believe I'm allowed to accept your offer," I answered quietly. "But I do appreciate it, and if I'm allowed to," then a more formal voice, "I do readily accept you into my service, as my man."

"May I talk to you about this?" I then asked him.

"Sure, we can go ofer ta the corner—it's along way from the fire, but it will be a wee bit quieter, and better than bein' outside," Deveron answered.

We talked about twenty minutes before it was "lights out" and he said he would inform the baron of our discussion. That way if there was a problem, I wouldn't have to face the wrath of Sir William.

The next afternoon, I received a summons from the baron to meet him at the castle at five. I arrived and was glad to see the rest of the Gold Squad was there also. He informed us that an expedition was going out to cut some additional grass for the winter. A younger group of adults were leading and providing guard duty, and since we had been training with them, Jelu and I had been invited. The baron had volunteered the rest of us for magic and other support.

Deveron was in charge of escort. He asked Sir William if Jelu and I might accompany the escort party, then he informed him of his pledge last night. He told Deveron that Kurt and Aaron were my mentors and asked if they might attend also, and that he would arrange other support if Deveron didn't mind. Mage and clerical support was unusual for this, but the baron had told him they had asked for a chance to get out of the city. So instead of a short unit of twenty there would be a total of twenty-eight. We weren't expecting any trouble, but it was a good excuse to get out and ride, and not have construction duty. Another group was going to cut additional wood for a winter supply. With the extra people we had brought back to the city, it might be needed.

Deveron was in charge of the mission, and the baron informed him that he was responsible for things, including keeping a young nobleman in line. Ray was present when the baron said it and did not have to ask for an explanation. Aaron and Kurt were going to spend a lot of time drilling with lances for the unit. Jelu, Ray, and Tarrin would be doing scout duty, and Ray would work with the lancers some—Jelu would stay with bows. Ray decided to take his family's big charger War Champion.

Two huge wagons were being filled quickly with the grass, and with the weather was getting cold, everyone was working harder, just to stay warm. Drills were going well, Aaron and Kurt had no problems blending in with the new adults in lance and horsemanship, and with all the extra experience in combat over the last year they were surprisingly more than a match for them with swords.

Ray and Jelu spent more time working with the bows from horseback, as did Tarrin. Although it cut into Ray's work with the lance, Kurt thought it was a good idea.

After three days of cutting and crushing down grass they were ready to return to Candlewynd, when Tarrin returned and informed them that about a squad of Orcs (close to fifty), Orcs was moving toward them. It appeared they would have the opportunity to put their training into practice.

Tarrin went back to scout as the workers hitched up the wagons and hurriedly started back to town. Tarrin was to get behind the Orcs to make sure it was not just a large advance scout for an army coming to the city. Deveron, Kurt and others looked over the map for a good location for a battle, one that would allow the horses to be most effective. The unit moved out to take advantage of the position—assuming the Orcs continued their original movement. They sat up a cold camp and awaited their young thief to return with information. It was a long night, and most of the boys did not sleep well.

Tarrin returned early the next morning, gave his report to Deveron and then went for food and rest—he'd have about three hours to sleep before it would be time to prepare for the upcoming battle.

Now since most of these adults were on the ship because they had been sent home to recover from wounds, it was not their first encounter of battle, but it was their first against Orcs. The plan was to allow the Orcs to move across a large open area that came up to an area of light woods. The cavalry would wait in the shadows of the woods, and then charge into the Orcs. Jelu would add missile fire as they started their charge. Spell casters would move to the flank of where the attack was to begin, to assist combat once the cavalry had started its charge. If things went as planned almost half the Orcs would be dead before the horse charge was finished. Then pitting mounted troops against infantry would be a relatively simple matter; or so they hoped. Kurt suggested that Ray and Tarrin could fire bows also: one, that would give more damage from bows, and two Ray could ride in and pick targets, seeing who might need help, and Tarrin would not be riding in on a lance for any reason. Ray did not like this change, believing that Kurt was doubting his ability with a lance, but Deveron reminding him it wasn't his duty at this time to argue tactics with his elders.

"I don't like it, Kurt, you might have asked what I thought. You make it look like I can't hold my own in a fight," I told him after Deveron had left.

"That's not the intent. I wanted the extra arrows, and that horse of yours is good enough to help you set up targets in close quarters. If one of the men goes down, when you come up just a little later, you can go to his assistance until he can get back on his horse or you can pull him to safety. You've proved enough times already that you can pull your weight in a fight. You don't have to prove that to me," Kurt said. "Now quit disputing the orders before you get in trouble, and then not feel like riding!"

We set up and got ready. I felt better after Kurt's explanation. Jelu, Tarrin, and I had our bows ready, waiting for the order to stand up, and fire from the waist-high grasses. At extremely long range we fired flight arrows, with unknown results. We continue to fire over the heads of the lancers until they were close enough to be in danger of a misfire. Then we mounted up Tarrin and Jelu were switching to the smaller bows Jelu had crafted, and I drew my long sword for close quarter work. I was much more comfortable with the sword than the lance anyway.

Deveron's battle plan worked fantastically. The Orcs were scattered and confused by the time the cavalry had ridden through them. Spell casters had cast *sleep* on their flank, while

Jelu and Tarrin cut down those attempting to go forward to the woods, and the cavalry wheeled and charged again, most were using drawn swords as lances were expended in the initial charge. I came in and helped and discovered just how good War Champion was—so did a several Orcs, but they would never be able to testify to it. After the second charge there was only mop up work to prevent survivors from escaping. To our knowledge the Orcs had yet to have a survivor tell of our cavalry charge. We had quite a few causalities, but they were mild—no deaths. We had defeated a war party twice our size and had a good haul of treasure to show for it, especially in weapons.

The young soldiers stripped and burned the dead. They piled their plunder on their horses and hurriedly caught up to the wagons with the winter grass. Much of the plunder was then placed on the wagons to ease the work of their war steeds, who had played a major part in the day's victory.

That evening the horses were checked again, and allowed to graze on the grass while the young warriors gave them a good brushing. Luke tended to four-footed patients as well as his two legged ones.

When they arrived back in the city, Deveron gave the report to the Royal Advisers and King Harold—Aaron had assisted him in preparing the report. Everything seemed to have gone well.

That afternoon Ray received a summons to the castle. When he arrived, Sir William met him, and he appeared to be very upset. Ray had not asked about taking the big stallion with him on the expedition, and it seemed a great number of people were upset about this.

"By what authority did you take such a valuable horse on an expedition like that?" one of the noblemen asked. "Did your knight give you leave?"

"Sir the horse belongs to my family. Why would I need to ask permission to use what is mine?" I responded, somewhat surprised.

"That stallion is helping the country to raise new war horses. Had it been lost, we would have lost the most valuable sire in horses. One that could not have been replaced," the noble responded.

"Child, your actions are clearly out of line, even if the horse belongs to your family. A junior *aged* squire is not allowed to take a valuable horse like War Champion on a training exercise, without permission. He and the four mares from your family stables are on loan to Us to assist in restarting Our royal herd. It has therefore been decided that you are to be severely disciplined for your action," King Harold said from his throne.

The Master of Arms then came forward with what seemed like an entire tree. Ray was ordered to assume the position across a table, and the king ordered the Master of Arms to give a full score of stripes with the birch rod.

The boy asked if that wasn't extremely severe, since he was only thirteen?

"It seems to Us that you're a senior when it is convenient, and *only* thirteen at other times—such as when you are in trouble. The Master of Arms may continue, and may give two dozen stripes—since you are a senior squire," the king said.

The boy was then leaned across the table, and given the caning ordered by the king, with the king and all the advisers there to witness. Most of those in attendance believed the lad had been pampered too much and was richly deserving of the beating he received. Because of the senior rating they perceived he had not been beaten enough this year, and this would allow for a flaw in this young character. Besides, it was written that a good beating would drive folly from a child.

After the two dozen stripes had been delivered, the boy was allowed a few moments to sob, before being told to stand—if he was able.

"That should help the little snot remember his age, and encourage respect of his elders," one of those present stated, in a quite unsympathetic tone.

The Master of Arms assisted Ray to stand, who was having difficulties in getting the legs to support him after the beating.

"Has the boy learned his manners?" King Harold questioned him.

Ray nodded, still not able to speak through his sobs.

"Come up here, child," the king ordered. "The rest of you are to leave Us. We would speak to Our young squire, in private."

The king motioned for me to come up to the throne, and the Master of Arms assisted me, as the others left. I was standing, although a bit uncertainly next to the king while the blood was running down my legs. The room finally emptied. The king then stood and put his arm around me to steady me, and asked, "Do you understand why your punishment was so brutal?"

"Not really, my King," I answered through the tears that were still streaming down my face.

"Because many of those men fear you."

"But sire, I'm just a child still—thirteen. Why would they fear me?" I asked.

"Because they see much in you, and are concerned that We might not control you. You remember the Bible teaches, 'Of whom much is given, much will be required.' They want you to be willing to follow orders, as you should, and as you are accustomed to doing from your youth. That is why many times discipline is harsh on Our young squires. Now, We understand that you have the skill to heal psionically with *cell adjustment*, if that true?"

"Yes, my king," I answered.

"Then We wish you to demonstrate this skill," King Harold told me.

"Sire, who am I to heal?"

"Child, you have wounds enough from the beating to show a great deal of healing. You may heal yourself, as much as you are able—those on the council that demanded your beating are not aware of that skill."

I got into the healing trance and began to send my mind to the area of pain, quickly curing the welts, cuts, and bruises the rod had left. That made me feel a great deal relieved. The memory of the beating was still with me, but the pain that would have lasted at least a week long was gone.

The king then gave me a slight hug around the shoulders and suggested that I try to maintain a bit more respect for the nobles of the council, and not show off my senior rank at my junior age. He struck his scepter on the throne, and one of the attendance returned. The king asked for Baron Scrope to return and meet with the two of us.

When Sir William entered the king had him lay out a map with plans for a castle and grounds. "Here are Our plans for your new estates, where you requested it this spring. We believe that having the estates built will enable you and the other members of the Gold Squad to train without interference. As Our marquis, your estates should be one of the first to be built."

The king and Lord William discussed their plans with me and the royal advisers before Baron Scrope and I left. We were to plan a survey expedition quite soon to have things ready to commence construction in the spring. I just listened in shock.

Sir William was still upset with his squire for taking War Champion without permission, and the treatment he received from some of the nobles at court for not having better control of his young squire. Since Ray had been allowed to heal himself from the previous beating, the baron was none too gentle about returning seven of the welts to his young squire in the presence of the rest of the Gold Squad. Then he gave Aaron and Kurt five good stripes for not having kept him closer in line.

After Sir William had finished disciplining his young warriors, he explained what was going to happen in the spring with the new castle. Besides giving the squad a more reclusive place to train, it would provide a protected new area from which new lands might be cultivated.

Over the next week the squad trained with some different groups. Ray normally trained with either Aaron or Kurt, but rarely were both with him, and they were all considered first year seniors, even though Ray was only a second year squire.

Not long after returning from their last battle with the Orcs, and finding out about the new castle, Ray realized he had learned a new psionic devotion—*expansion*. This allowed the boy to enlarge his body, and the larger he became the stronger it made him. Because of his skill with psionics he was able to grow about three feet in height with this skill. His other abilities also had improved. The others in the squad also had learned new skills. Even Luke had learned a new skill, and a more complicated spell. This was even more unusual for a healer, as advancement in learning new spells for them was both more difficult and longer than for other professions.

It was starting to get much colder. Ray and the others were wondering if they would make the survey expedition before winter set in too hard. Training was going well, but Ray still had a problem with some believing he wasn't good enough to deserve his senior rating. Ray's patience was wearing thin and Aaron and Kurt had to keep a constant watch on him to keep him from getting into big trouble, without having to discipline Ray themselves.

Ray asked for the warrior members of the squad to meet him in the barn after dinner one cold, mid-November evening. He was brushing the palomino when they finally all arrived.

———————

"On board ship, about a year ago, I decided to increase my intensity in training, and those in charge were forced to move me to work with the older squires on the ship. All our skill levels have increased due to our training and our combat experiences during the past year. I was given a senior rank early; Jelu and Luke were given their rank a bit early—although richly deserved. I want us all to attempt to raise the level of intensity again—I mean really push one another. I want anyone your age to hate to fence with any of us because we are so mean in combat," I told them.

I let them think about what I said for a moment, then continued. "Jelu, I wish you would work on the great sword as a melee weapon. I know your main weapon of choice is the bow, but in melee it might be good if your weapon was different than the others. At least consider the ideal. Kurt uses a broad sword and Aaron and I both work exclusively with long swords, so a different weapon might be good. I believe Deveron would be willing to work a little extra with it, as it is his weapon of choice."

"The word is idea, not ideal," Aaron told me correcting my grammar. "But I think it is a good one. And I believe that stepping up our intensity is also warranted, but you realize it will cause some resentment."

"I really don't give a . . . care," I said catching myself before saying something that would have gotten me at least a reprimanding!

They agreed to my plan, and they next day Aaron and I were scheduled to with a mixed group of first, second, and third year senior squires. The instructor had never seen combat, and was not very skillful either. I was paired with a first year senior, and was not pleased, as I didn't consider him much of a challenge—he thought the same of me before we started.

The wooden swords that we trained with kept injuries down, but had the size and weight of real swords. I quickly took care of my opponent, who had not benefitted from the encounters with the Orcs that I had this last year. Then I encouraged Aaron who was matched up against James—it didn't take Aaron much longer to best him.

The instructor in charge of the exercise that morning didn't believe my skills were that good, and that I had just been lucky to defeat my elder squire so quickly. I told him that with the exception of Aaron and Kurt, there wasn't a first year senior that I couldn't defeat. His opinion of me was not very high, and stated that a good caning might improve my attitude.

I suggested a trial by combat to prove my point to him. A thirteen year old challenging an instructor was unheard of. He had been noble born, but didn't have what it takes to be a good warrior. He gave me a last time to repent of my impudence; seven good stripes would be much easier than the dozen I would get if I went through with the challenge.

"Sir, are you ready?" I asked.

He nodded and told me that this was going to be brief.

"You're right," I told him, then used *expansion*. "Aaron, better send for a healer."

Growing to more than eight feet in height shook him and everyone else in the area. I quickly pressed the advantage of surprise, and knocked the instructor off his feet with a shield butt, allowed him the chance to regain his footing, but not his composure. I feigned with the shield and hard over hand attack ended the combat, with the instructor on the ground unconscious. After that I challenge all of the squires to work harder because we were in a poor situation with Orcs—War Orcs inhabiting three cities on the island.

"If you aren't going to work harder—don't waste my time and effort in fencing. From now on anyone who fences with me had better be ready to go to war in the competition—because it's going to be that way from me!"

I then challenged James and Torin, and made quick work of both of them at once; not because I was better than they were combined, but because of the novelty of my size. After that I went back to normal size and asked one of the oldest squires there, a third year senior if he would do me the honor of fencing with me.

Eric was the best third year senior I had seen. We fought for close to three minutes before he was able to get inside my guard and defeat me. I then selected another very good third year senior for Aaron to compete with, and matched the others with people close to what I thought were their skill levels.

While everyone was fencing, Luke came out to look after the instructor, and I visited with Eric.

"Why did you challenge me, and stay small for the fight?" he asked.

"Sir, I respect your skills, I had none for the instructor. Also, you have normally treated the juniors fairly, and treated me with respect for my senior rank, without regard for my age."

"How young are you?"

"I'll be fourteen—just before Christ's Mass," I answered.

"You're really good for a such a little snot. Why do you defer to Kurt and Aaron? They're not that much better than you, if they are at all, and they are only first year seniors," Eric asked, as he sat back watching one of the other contest? "Hold your shield higher, Bruce!"

"They're my mentors. Sir Williams felt like that they could help me keep out of trouble, with the difference in age between me and those with whom I work, in weapon training."

About that time Bruce was hit across the top of the helm by his partner. "I told you to keep your shield up," Eric scolded. Then he told me, "You realize you're going to get the devil beat out of you for what you pulled today?"

"Not by him," I said pointing to the instructor who was being helped to the infirmary. "If they want us to improve, then they better have people who can teach us something.

But I suspect I might have problems sitting tonight, once Sir William gets to me."

"Oh, by the way, don't try going *invisible* to me, it won't work and I'll probably get upset with you for it," Eric told me.

"I wouldn't do that with you—unless it was really serious; like life and death. I respect you and your skills."

I ran the rest of the training that day, and Eric backed me up. No one was really sure they wanted to test my skills with *expansion*, to challenge the orders. Things went very smoothly—until just before the end of the session. Sir William and another knight showed up. The other knight was blustery and demanding to know by what right I took control of the class, and was giving all the orders.

"By right of conquest," I answered looking very carefully at Sir William. "The instructor was inept, and didn't know what he was doing. I believed he was wasting our time—so I took over, sir."

"You will be thoroughly caned for this!" he nearly shouted.

Eric then interrupted, "Sir, the boy was correct. He had no business instructing senior squires. Our time is too valuable to be squandered by his ineptness."

"The lad will be properly punished for his action, Sir Tomas. I'll see to it this evening. He will regret his lack of manners in dismissing his elder, but not for his ability to do so," Sir William stated. "This class is dismissed. Aaron, you and Ray will attend me!"

We explained the meeting that we had held, the previous day, and the decision to try to intensify our training. Sir William was none too gentle with me, showing some intensity with a birch. I only got five stripes that time, but Sir William made them count. Aaron received a reminder that he was also to help me maintain a correct attitude in dealing with my elders, but only three stripes. He then informed us that I would probably be called before the council for my actions, but it might take a week to do it.

After a couple of days of moving very slowly Sir William had all the Gold Squad meet in one of the barns, for a discussion.

Sir William asked, "Ray, can you stop any of your older companions from physically taking you down and giving you a whipping?"

"I don't know sir, maybe Luke, Tarrin, maybe Jelu—they aren't that much larger than I am?"

"We are getting ready to find out," he told us. "We'll start with Kurt."

He then had every one of my older comrades physically take me down and give me five swats with a leather strap. The priest and the mage were old enough that their size was too much for me to stop. A brief curing in between bouts kept me from being too exhausted to take on the next person. Finally the difference in size, with the three smaller and younger members of the squad, was not enough to take me down for a whipping. The three of them asked not to have to try, and I could actually beat Luke. Tarrin was close; Jelu just beat the snot out of me.

"Now the point of this is, that most of the senior squires can do the same thing to you, if you don't have a sword in your hand. So start being more respectful—because you have already seen what can happen if you get jumped in the night, this summer. Luke, cure your cousin up."

Chapter Thirteen

A New City

> "Unless the Lord builds the house, its builder labors in
> vain." Psalms 127: 1

The next day the Gold Squad got their plans for going on
the survey of the land where the new estate would be. Sherry
was going, which made Ray extremely happy, as was Timothy.
Sherry was taking a first year junior squire with her, Joanna,
and Markél was taking Tanya, a young squire that would be
his wife at the end of the year, when she turned fourteen. She
was officially assigned to Jelu as his squire. A couple of other
young, first year junior squires were also going with them, as
Kurt and Aaron's squires—Peter and Davy. The manager of
Ray's family estate, Jerome, was also going to see about the
land, as well as some surveyors, an engineer, and six villagers
to turn over the soil to make planting easier next year. With
Tanya and Timothy, Ray was getting to be around some others
his own age, even if not his rank.

Ray didn't take War Champion this time, and as they left
he got a little bit of kidding from Kurt about it.

"What—where is the big stallion? No War Champion
this time? Good thing—if you'd been on him you'd be off

him—he'd have been back in the stables and you'd been having to walk for painful reasons," Kurt told Ray, with a laugh. "I don't want to take another busting for you bringing that big horse."

Conversations were light on the trip as they started out. It had also been raining for the last two days, making the horses have to slog through the mud.

That night as they made camp and set up tents, Kurt told the junior squires to get wood and start a fire.

"Sir, how are we to start a fire with everything as wet as it is?" Timothy asked.

"That is your problem. But I know five junior squires better figure it out before long, or they will all deeply regret it," Kurt told them—and meant it.

The youngsters scrambled to find some drier wood, twigs, or something that might get a fire started. The three younger kids were almost in tears when they realized they were not going to be able to start a fire. Timothy and Tanya just resigned themselves to what was coming.

Then Ray motioned to Timothy to come to him while Kurt was getting a limb from a tree and starting to strip it down. Ray reached in his saddle and pulled out some dry straw that he picked up before they had left.

———————

"This should be enough to get a fire started, in the pit instead of on your backsides. Hurry up before Kurt gets that rod finished," I told Timothy.

Timothy quickly set some very small twigs over the straw, and started the straw on fire. Then he carefully added other wood, a little at a time to allow the fire to dry the wood as it burned. Larger pieces were set close to the fire as it began to burn nicely to dry out for later use.

"I'm glad one of you little snots was smart enough to bring something to get the fire going. Ray, set up a rotation for who is responsible for dry wood each night—you know how it works," Kurt told me.

"Thanks sir," Davy and Peter told me. "How did you think to do that?"

"I've been out on wet days before. I figured you wouldn't want Kurt to dry a couple of limbs out from the heat of your backsides. Timothy, Tanya, you two should have known better. Timothy, I know you've been out and done this before. It would have served you right to get busted. Don't make me have to cover for you two again," I told them in a scolding voice.

"Would Kurt have really whipped us, if you hadn't had the straw?" Tanya asked.

"Juniors are responsible for the fire—I think he might have. Why don't you ask him? But then again he might show you," I told her.

The younger kids got a nice supply of wood for the night and dinner was prepared. After a full day of riding we were all tired and ready for an early night. The watches were set and the fire rotations were established. Just before we turned in Peter came up to me.

"Sir, Kurt's compliments, he wishes a word with you."

Formal summonses were not usually good. But I put my boots back on and went to see what Kurt wanted.

"You saved five kids a beating this evening. Did you know that?" Kurt asked.

"I suspected you might have really whipped them—those first years were scared to death. Besides it's kind of cold to have to get blistered," I responded.

"I'm glad you saved them. I was ordered to test that way. I couldn't warn them or anyone else. Glad you stepped in, we've got too far to travel to have the five of them having to walk this early."

"Is it all right if I ask Jelu and Aaron for other suggestions for them that I might not have thought of?"

"You figure it out, I can't answer. Be the way let, them think I was upset with you for keeping them from the caning. It will help keep them on their toes if they know any screwup will get them whipped," he told me.

"Why do you want them to think you're so hard?," I asked.

"Because I'm in charge, I have orders, and I have to be—so you better stay out of trouble too, or you'll be having to walk," Kurt told me and showed me some orders—some of which were still sealed.

I went back to the tent, took my gear out of the tent I was sharing with Kurt, Aaron, and Jelu, and moved into the tent with the three younger boys. Then I went back and asked if they had any suggestions to keep the junior squires out of trouble.

"Make sure they keep their bows covered and dry. What's going on? Where are you going," Jelu asked?

In a voice loud enough to be heard in the other tents I answered, "Kurt is upset with me for having the straw and keeping the juniors from getting a canning. If I stay here, I'll say something to him and I'll get busted. Since he is in charge, he reminded me that he could use a cane on me!"

Kurt came in as I was walking out, I grinned at him. He shook his head, and said in a very quiet voice, "Nice, little brother."

Timothy set up and ask, "What's going on, Ray?"

"Oh shut up and go to sleep, unless you want some extra duties!" I told him and got in my bed roll.

Things went well for the rest of the trip to the site. We dropped off extra supplies for the quarry workers and checked on them. Luke took care of some injuries they had, and gave them a good checking over. I stayed with the younger squires, who were much closer to my age, although Kurt suggested that my behavior did not improve around the younger kids—I still enjoyed being with them.

The survey went well. The engineer made some sketches of where different things might go. They cleared ground around the peach trees and decided that it had been a well cared for orchard at one time. With the rain the other workers were not able to turn over the ground—it was just too wet. Other things were done: digging around the peach trees was extremely difficult with the wet ground, but it was still done. Two rather large honey bee hives were located. Plans for their care were set up also. Jerome was pleased with the orchard and said with the honey bees' hives were large enough to split them in the spring and make at least four colonies.

Areas for clearing trees for additional farm land were marked on a map, as well as planned crops for the coming spring. Ray still thought the small spring that bubbled up and ran off the cliff into the ocean was a lovely sight. The engineer said that a water reservoir would be set up to hold a large amount of that runoff, and that the rest might be directed to do more good for a village planned below, or a moat around the outer wall.

Things went well—the junior squires stayed out of trouble, for the most part. The mischief they did cause was minor and was handled by extra guard duty and marching. About three days before they were to leave some of the older squires had a very big argument. Ray didn't hear what it was about but Sherry and Markél seemed to be extremely upset with Kurt and Aaron. The younger squires didn't think much about it—as long as they weren't the ones with whom the seniors were upset, then it could get painful. They just stayed out of their way.

Ray was talking with Peter and Timothy, just kid stuff. They were discussing what their dreams were, what they were hoping for when they were adults or at least senior squires.

I told them, "For me it hasn't been that different than for you. I'm young enough no one thinks of me as a senior. I've missed a few canings, of which I'm extremely thankful, but I've had it rough in other ways. Maybe by the time I'm fifteen I'll get more of the respect a senior is suppose to get from the others. Even Kurt and Aaron don't treat me like a senior most of the time. They don't let the others abuse me—but it's like, well, they're the only ones that get to pick on me."

"I wish I had those two as my big brothers," Peter said. "Some of the other seniors are always looking for an excuse to use a hickory on the first year squires. And some of those guys swing real hard, come to think of it so do the senior girls."

"It doesn't improve much as a second year junior," Timothy chimed in. "I think about the third year they start to ease up a bit."

"What are you little snots plotting?" Sherry said as she came up and set down with us.

"We weren't plotting anything ma'am—honest!" Peter exclaimed.

"Hey sis. We were discussing how hard it is being a first year junior. They believe I was pretty lucky to have you, then Kurt and Aaron looking after me early on. Then I got the senior rating," I said to Sherry.

"Well, you probably shouldn't have gotten the promotion so young. Maybe when you are out on a patrol or mission or something, but in town you should have lost the senior rating, and had to deal with being a junior squire," Sherry told me.

"Come on Sherry, Ray deserved the rank. He can take almost all the first year seniors, and most of the second year seniors, even without psionics," Timothy said, trying to come to my defense.

"Oh, and what makes you such an expert on training? One needs to know how to follow orders and understand the chain of command before one leads. Ray will lead one day, but will he have the proper understanding since he missed out on so much by not stay a junior squire even a full year?" Sherry queried.

"Sherry, you don't think I deserved the ranking?" I asked, shocked by her statement.

"No, you should have had to deal with the first year seniors, as a junior—just like everyone else did. How do you think you would have fared with Torin and James as a junior this year? How much time would you have had to spend in the barn across a saddle? You think Megan was hard on you this year, what would it have been like with the seniors able to discipline you for your smart mouth?" Sherry exploded on me with an anger I wasn't suspecting.

"Sherry, you're being too hard on Ray. He's proved himself in battle many times this year," Timothy stated somewhat defiantly.

"Oh I guess you're taking up for him, because of the help he was in the barracks, keeping some of the seniors from being too hard on you poor little boys. So Birdy gets a body guard to keep the mean ole seniors from hurting him and making him work harder. Poor little Birdy can't make it on his own—so his good friend helps him survive," Sherry said. Sherry knew how much he hated that name.

"Don't call me Birdy—you, you, cow!" Timothy screamed, almost in tears.

"That, my junior, will cost you. Report to the central tent for discipline," she told him.

"Sherry, that's not right—Peter, you're dismissed," I turned realizing the stunned twelve-year-old was still sitting there. He got up and left very quickly.

"Sherry, you know he hates that name. You baited him to get him in trouble."

She and I argued about it for a while, and I knew she wasn't going to change her mind, and that he was out of line also. Then she really surprised me, and made me extremely angry. Since he was officially my squire she told me that I would have to administer the discipline, seven strokes with a hickory. We continued our "discussion" until she reminded me that she was still older than I was and it was an order and that I had no choice but to comply. Besides, if I didn't discipline him, then she would have Kurt do it, and that he was enough larger than me to make it much more painful.

She then escorted me to Kurt, who told me, "You should have followed orders that she gave you. Now you're going to have to give the boy ten hard stripes, or I'll give him a full dozen—if you argue this with me, it will get worse for him."

———————

Ray was really upset with the two older seniors. He believed they were being unreasonable. He followed orders and disciplined his good friend in a public beating there in the tent. It was bad enough to have to get a beating that bad, but in front of everyone made it so much worse.

When Ray had finished, Kurt came up and told him he had not swung hard enough, and his actions in not following orders given by one of his seniors were inexcusable, and that it was now his turn to get the beating. Kurt then blistered his backside harder than Kurt had ever whipped him before. By the next evening every one of the juniors had received a caning.

Another day later they would be leaving. It would be an uncomfortable ride for the younger squires, with the welts and bruises still very sore. Ray saw Kurt away from the camp and went to confront him about his actions—without anyone else present.

———————

"We need to talk about the last two days—sir," I told him taking off my sword belt, and helmet. I was getting ready to have fight I could not win, but was mad enough to try.

"Stop right there, *little* boy. I don't want to hurt you, but if you throw a punch, not only will I beat the snot out of you, you'll have to lead your horse all day tomorrow," he told me and stepped back.

"I can't believe what you just did the last two days. You and the others made up excuses to whip every one of us. Now take off your sword and helm!" I hollered at him.

"I had orders, Ray. We were ordered to bust every one of you, fourteen and under, I didn't have a choice. Sherry picked the argument with Timothy, knowing what would happen, and figured you'd get yourself in trouble taking up for him. You weren't that far out of line, but it was a semblance of a reason to whip you. Don't make this mistake and force me to give you another one. Little brother, I didn't want to do it, but I have to follow orders. And listen to me very closely. If you tell the other kids—you'll all get another one, and it will be worse."

"Is that what the argument was about the other night? Is that why Sherry and Markél were mad at you and Aaron?" I asked.

"Yes. Markél wasn't too upset about you boys getting a beating. He figures you boys need them every so often to you in line, but he was upset about his wife-to-be getting one also," Kurt answered.

I started picking up my stuff. "Tell Markél, I said thanks for the support!"

"Ray, don't ever challenge me again—it will hurt real bad. Do you understand me?" he asked.

"Yes sir, but I was so mad. I had to do something about it. I didn't want to lose my temper and bust one of the little guys. Splitting their lip open wasn't going to help, and I'm still not old enough to discipline them on my own authority. Besides, you were who I was mad at."

"What good would picking a fight with me do? Don't you remember an exercise in the barn, where we took turns wearing out your backside with a leather strap? If you'd thrown a punch, I would have beat the snot out of you and then you'd have gotten another beating. Don't be stupid—you little snot," he told me.

Then grabbed me by the shoulders and gave me a hug. "Your adopted sister would probably like to know you're not as mad at her as you have been the last two days, if you can tell her without the juniors around."

The trip back was uneventful, but wet and cold. Ray spent some time each evening, just as they had while they at the camp, working with three twelve-year-olds on the long sword. Aaron worked with the other two junior squires, and things went well. Fires were made and watches went off without a problem.

Kurt helped tutor math for Ray, Timothy, and Tanya. Timothy didn't need the extra help, but worked with the others to keep them from getting too far behind. The semester would be ending and grades were important. Aaron worked with the twelve year olds in math.

Markél worked with all of them on cartography, while Andrew assisted with religion. Religion was used not only to teach the children God's word, but was also a way to teach them to read, and get writing exercise in writing down scripture.

The two younger boys said they could have done without the school work each evening. Aaron asked what happened when they returned and couldn't do their lessons. After that thought went through their brains they decided maybe it was a good idea to study.

Arriving back in the city, Kurt and Aaron gave their report to the royal court, while Ray reported to Sir William. Sir William was at the court, but found his squire waiting for him on his return to his office in the castle. Ray was still upset about the beatings ordered for general principles, and wanted to know if the Baron had ordered them or even knew of them.

Sir William was unaware of the order, and would call Kurt in on the morrow to question him. He suggested that Ray get a good night's rest. His academic group started with math in the morning at eight, and he had better have done a good job of studying on the trip or his instructor might attempt to motivate his learning through his behind. He and Timothy were to be there at seven to go over things they were to have covered while they were on the survey trip.

Ray and Timothy were both exhausted from the return trip and eagerly looking forward to a good night's sleep. They had dinner with Luke's and Ray's family before returning to the barracks. They told Lady Martha and Lady Beth of what the area looked like and what was to be built as well as they could remember, and drew it up on a slate. It was a wonderful evening, and Megan was extremely charming—something Ray was not accustomed to of late. Luke seemed a bit upset, but Ray never had the chance to ask him what was wrong.

Sleep was peaceful that evening, and a light snow was beginning to fall. It wouldn't stick on the ground, but it looked lovely coming down in the twin moons' light.

The next day math class was as Ray expected—hard. While Ray had several questions about assignments they had been given before they left, Timothy was well ahead of his larger friend. Ray was still getting caught up when the rest of the class arrived. The math instructor was ancient, but worked well explaining things to his classes. They worked his fractions with military sizes to allow for practical applications of the studies; such as what fraction of the army of a certain size might be used for escort duty if a particular number were sent. Another might be how many miles would need to be covered to move an army a certain number of miles in so many days. Every level of math being taught was used to further the boys in the military duties or in things of economic importance, such as grain calculations.

Religion class was next. They were finishing a month long study on the Gospel of John. It was interesting and young students were expected to remember certain verses, most of which Ray, Tanya, and Timothy had missed, but Andrew had assisted them with the study, and so they were more than equal to the task in this class. The rest of the morning would be the same: get to class, hope they were at least close to where they were supposed to be, and not be required to do too much tutoring after dinner.

The next week went well, November was getting to the end, and another of the Gold Squad's member was to be married in a month. Having the mage married might improve his attitude, Ray hoped.

Ray asked the priest in charge of his biblical studies if there were books of law for Candlewynd. It seemed a strange question from a boy not quite fourteen, but he answered in the affirmative.

———————————

"Sir, I was thinking—I wondered how our laws were like the ones that God gave Moses in the desert. I know the Pharisees added a great deal to the body of law, and much of our laws are based on these—I wanted to see them to help me understand things better. As a noble, I'll need to know a little about the laws to be just," Ray informed the shocked priest.

"Well, you couldn't take them to the barracks to study, but I believe I could arrange a room for you to study them. Would that help you in your quest for knowledge and justice?" the priest asked.

"Oh very well indeed sir, there will be three or four of us studying together. I may need assistance in understanding some things and I have some older boys that will be assisting me—they may just not know it yet," I concluded, gave a slight nod and left.

I knew I could get Luke to help me with this, and I thought some of the others would help. But I needed to know something about inheritance and when a squire could have control of the estates and title. I didn't want to do the work this spring and summer and someone find some point of law and move into the area the Gold Squad was building for their base of operations.

November closed cold and a good snow began that night, as I told my concern to the other members of the Gold Squad and Baron Scrope. He believed it was unneeded, but thought it would be a good exercise for us in studies.

I thought Aaron was going to beat the snot out of me when we left. He had other plans in the evenings, which didn't include putting up with us, or at least me.

He pinned me against the corner of the building, and gave me a good fright, then told me he was just giving me a hard time. "But the next time you sign us up for extra duties—ask first. Some of us would like to spend time at home."

Sir William came out, just as Aaron released me, and called us back in. He checked to see if I was in trouble with my older friend for something. I informed him of the Aaron's jest, and said that I thought I was in trouble, at first.

"There is an arranged marriage for you! It is still several years off, as both of you are presently too young, but you are pledged," Sir William told me.

I sat down in shock, without being asked to sit. Finally I found my voice, "To whom?"

"Congratulations," Aaron said.

"It still a secrete. Just know that it exists, and act accordingly. Your mother signed the contract this week. Don't ask any questions about it at the time, just realize it is a younger girl than you. Ray, you're dismissed. Aaron I need another word with you."

I numbly left the hall, and went back toward the barracks. I was supposed to meet Darla that evening. I got my horse brush and went to the stables and started to brush the palomino, which I had named Gold Leaf.

Darla came in and we held hands, talked, and she allowed me to kiss her—well, really she kissed me. I told her about the contract. She didn't seem to care much.

"At least you'll know how to kiss your new bride. The way you tell it she could be a six-year-old, and you'll be older than Markél before you get married," Darla said laughing.

I decided I better go talk to Mother about this. I wasn't ready to get married, but I didn't think I wanted to be in my twenties as a warrior getting married either.

As I walked up to the ship, Megan was just coming in also. She reached up and pulled a piece of straw out of my hair, gave me wink, and tousled my hair in a mischievous manner. She didn't say anything, just grinned; like you're in trouble if I tell.

"Mother, Sir William has informed me that I have a marriage contract—who is the girl?" I asked.

"It is to remain secret for a while until you are both of age, or at least one of you," she told me. "Your manner was not very subtle when asking the question."

"Ma'am, I didn't know how to ask the question any other way. Shouldn't I be allowed to know?" I asked.

"We're keeping it a secret for the time, in case there is a problem that occurs, like in Megan's case. But likely, because you have been in harm's way a great deal at a young age—and appear to be continuing in it. Her family doesn't want her to be a widow, as Megan was, before she's a bride," she told me. "Now let's not talk about it any more for a while. Are you staying the night on ship, or are going back to the barracks?"

"I have to go back, Timothy is helping me with some math," I answered and got my cloak, ready to leave.

"Congratulations, little brother. I'll walk with you a ways," Megan told me.

As we got back on deck, Luke was heading off to the infirmary, for a night duty. Megan asked him to go on ahead. She needed to talk to me, and he agreed. "You want to explain the straw in your hair this evening?" she asked—still smiling.

"Not really, sis. Are you going to tell?"

"No, but I think I know who you were with, and with a marriage contract it better stop, or you will be in trouble. Just giving you a warning," she told me and gave me a slight kiss on the forehead, and turned to go back to the ship.

The snow was starting to fall harder, as I caught back up with Luke. I decided I'd better tell him about the contract, otherwise he would be hurt. He discussed it until we parted ways to our destinations.

Timothy was a little put off that I was late to study. He had been working on other studies while he was waiting, but some of the seniors had come in for an inspection, while I was late. These inspections were usually much easier if I was present. When I wasn't present more made up faults were found, and some of the junior squires were disciplined. Sometimes minor infractions were given marching duties, but usually much quicker and more painful punishment were given, as the older squires were attempting to bully the younger boys. Timothy had been one of the unfortunate junior squires to have to report to the center table and then was ordered over it and caned that evening. James and Torin seemed to delight in making up reasons to discipline some of my friends.

After that we didn't get any math studying accomplished or any other studies.

The next day was class was a surprise. Our normal instructor was missing and Eric was there in this place, and to make matters worse—I was late.

"The squire begs your pardon for being late, I was attending my knight," I stated with formality. I wasn't sure how he would accept my reason, without a pass from Sir William he was in his rights to discipline me, and at the very least assign lots of extra marching duty.

"Report up here to me," Eric told me. "Just because you're a senior squire, do you think that allows you to be late? Perhaps we need to make sure that a young boy knows his proper place and age in the classroom," he said to me quietly, but in an ominous voice.

"No sir, the squire realizes his short comings, and requests the instructor understanding for his tardiness," I answered.

"You show up late again, and friend or no, you'll find yourself across the table receiving **ten** hard stripes. Do you understand me, boy?" he said between clenched teeth.

"Yes sir!"

I quickly returned to my seat, relieved that I was still able to make use of it. Class did not improve from there. He began a review of things we were supposed to know to prepare for the end of the term tests. Everyone was still in shock at having a new teacher this time of the year, especially one that young.

"All right, I'm not pleased with your efforts. They're many of you ladies and gentlemen that I don't believe are giving me a good effort. I have a set of questions that I will call each of you in order and ask a question. If you are unable to work out the question, you will come up to the front and receive three stripes from the cane. And tomorrow we had better have much exemplary participation."

He began to ask the questions, and the first couple of students were able to answer, then one of the young male mages went blank on what was supposed to be done on a problem. Just as Eric had promised the lad was given three hard licks with the cane. Several other students answered questions, or least were able to give a good enough account of themselves to avoid the hickory. Timothy was very capable and received some praise for the quickness and correctness of this answer. Other students were not as fortunate, including Ray and Tanya.

At the end of class Eric had Ray stay. Ray was concerned that he was in for more trouble. Eric wasn't upset with him, just trying to make sure he knew what was expected of him in class, and to remind him not to be late again.

Ray then asked him if he might come to the barracks and give some extra tutoring that evening, after dinner. Eric agreed and Ray was to pass the word that he would be there at seven for those who needed extra help. Ray was scheduled to work with the books on law that evening, but he would have to leave early for the tutoring session.

Aaron and Markél gave him a hard time about setting up this study of the law and then leaving early. When he explained what had happened in class that day they agreed it would be okay—since he wasn't going to meet some girl. Ray reminded the mage that Tanya would be able to benefit from the extra assistance.

Eric had made arrangements for a female to tutor the girls in their barracks, while he was tutoring the boys. It was decided that would prevent problems with the girls in the boys' barracks. Females were sometimes in the barracks, but usually not for that length of time. Females gave inspections and would discipline, just as the male senior squires, either gender that was lacking in their duties or skills.

During the tutoring, several senior squires came in for another inspection. Kurt was one of the inspectors this time, although he was not in charge.

―――――――――

"Everyone will stand at attention for inspection!" the lead senior ordered.

Junior squires jumped to their assigned locations.

"Sir, we are having a tutoring session, this evening, and this barrack was inspected last evening," I informed the senior in charge.

"Boy, what are you doing wearing a weapon? Report to the center table for discipline," he ordered me.

"Sir, I'm a senior and required to carry the weapon," I responded.

"Then place it in the weapons locker for the inspection, and stand to for the inspection."

"Sir, you're interrupting my tutoring session. Come back another time for the inspection," Eric ordered.

"I'm sorry sir, we have orders from Sir Stephen," Kurt stated, stepping between Eric and the other senior squire. He then moved over to me and quietly said, "You'd better get that sword put away, as you were told, before you get into trouble."

I put the sword in the locker, as ordered, but I wasn't happy about it. The inspection was over quickly with no one getting in trouble, partly because Eric walked with one of the seniors and Kurt with the other; therefore, they weren't able to invent infractions.

Then we got back to our studies.

The next day in class everyone was more confident with their answers after the extra studying. It might have also been because we weren't surprised about Eric's being there.

After the work detail that evening I went to the stable to brush Gold Leaf, and to see Darla. I knew with the marriage contract it wasn't the smartest thing to do, but it was fun getting kissed. The problem was Kurt and Aaron came in after Darla. That was a little awkward. They sent her off, and suggested that I stay for a conversation.

"You know you've got a contract. You want to explain what you were doing?" Kurt asked.

What I really wanted to ask was if, after being married, he needed a thirteen-year-old to explain kissing. But doing that would have gotten me busted for certain, and they didn't appear to be in a joking mood.

"I don't know who the contract is with, or when. So I was just enjoying Darla's company. Are you going to tell," I asked?

"No, but we should probably bust you," Aaron answered.

I then wasn't smart enough to leave well enough alone. "You never wanted to kiss a girl before you were married?"

Kurt backhanded me, and knocked me to the ground. "How would you like to have us use a rod on you again? It won't be the first, maybe you need a good reminder."

"No sir, I'm sorry. Don't bust me," I begged.

"All right, but if it happens again . . . ," Aaron started stepping between Kurt and I.

Kurt was not quite as forgiving of my smart mouth comment and decided a short conversation with a leather strap would aid my manners. Aaron convinced him that five ought to be enough, and then they escorted me back to the church where we had been going over the law books. I was lucky that my smart mouth hadn't gotten me ten from Kurt, and I pressed my luck on the way over to the church.

"You know you shouldn't have hit me in the mouth, like you did."

"That was why you only got five swats, little brother," he replied with a grin. Then he pushed me into Aaron, who pushed back. After bouncing me between them for a bit they both grabbed me and took me down in the snow and we wrestled around long enough to get really cold.

When we got to the church Andrew looked up at us and shook his head, "I see you children have been playing in the snow."

I looked at the laws they had found, and it was what I had hoped for. Kurt thought it was a dangerous plan, but he and Aaron both would back me up on it. Andrew was going to ask a legal expert about it to make sure before we, or I, proceeded. Just to make sure.

Two days later in sword practice the opportunity presented itself to attempt. A rather boring and seemingly bored individual was in charge of us. I was working with Kurt and Aaron, with Eric's mostly third year seniors squires group. We had done some close order drills, which I loathed, being smaller than everyone else. Deveron came over to watch, and I requested that the instructor allow some multiple group work. I suggested that it would assist our being able to depend on comrades in arms, if we were on patrols like we had been last spring. I suggested that the three of us who were not second year seniors might go back to back and defend against a larger group of the third year seniors.

"What gives you the right to make request like that at your age, boy? Just who do you think you are?" he asked.

"I am the Marquis of Retúpmoc," I replied, using the title for the first time as my own.

"WHAT! You're not old enough to claim that title, boy. That boast will get you disciplined severely," he mistakenly told me.

At my pronouncement of the title Deveron slid off his horse and came over to me. Just as the instructor finished his threat Deveron kneeled and presented his two handed, great sword to me, "Your Grace I again pledge ma allegiance ta ya above all others, save the King!"

I hadn't seen Deveron come up, and was surprised by his actions, although they had already been promised. Kurt and Aaron, as if on cue from a play, knelt and gave a similar oath, but they had known this was coming sometime soon, they just didn't know for sure when.

"Now sir, if you plan to discipline me, it will have to be through might of arms," I answered.

This person wasn't a fool, nor was he a genius, but he knew he was going to have take me in order to discipline me. He knew he couldn't, especially with Deveron, Kurt, and Aaron standing there. As he was contemplating what to do, I asked if any of those present wish to dispute my claim. There were no takers.

The four of us left and went to the castle, stopping to put on proper armor, not practice attire. While we were changing, I sent a page for Baron Scrope, and asked him to join us at the throne room. I hadn't told him my plan. I also sent word to Sherry and asked her to meet me there. When she arrived I told her what was going on, and told her I would be honored to have her stand with me also, but would understand if she chose not to. Other than Andrew the other members of the Gold Squad were not there. We did not need to draw attention to ourselves more so than we had already done. Sir William was not too pleased that we had not informed him of this in advance, and stated that we would talk more later. That didn't sound good—but it was too late to stop what was started.

The king was meeting with many of his advisers. When we arrived, I asked to be announced, and had the guard on duty announce me as, "Marquis of Retúpmoc wishes an audience with His Royal Majesty!"

When we walked in with my coat of arms blazoned on my magical shield, Kurt, Aaron, Deveron, and Sherry with me, there were quite a few raised eyebrows. Andrew followed us and then moved to the side. His role was to verify the answer if a question on the law came up, and he had the books with him.

"Your Majesty and members of the royal court. I present myself as a vassal of the King Harold of Candlewynd, in accordance with our law upon laying claim to the title of Marquis of Retúpmoc. I hereby swear my allegiance and sword to you, my king."

"Your Majesty, this boy is too young to lay claim to the title, he is but fourteen," Robert, Earl of Athlon stated.

Several other voices rose in opposition to my claim.

"My lords, Your Majesty, the law states, that the heir to a title may claim it when becoming a senior squire. As you yourself gave me this rank, sire, I lay claim to, what by law is mine," I stated.

The Earl of Athlon again protested. The earl was of warrior class, but not really a warrior. He was very good at organization, and determining the logistics for an army, but never took the field himself. He was a widower, in his mid to upper twenties with four children, not that I knew that at the time. "Sire, this boy does not have the right to the title."

With this remark a gauntlet hit the floor and slid across in front of the him. "I stand ready to defend my right of title by trial of combat," I stated looking directly at the earl.

No one moved. It became extremely quiet. The earl became a bit pale, as he was not armed for combat, and I appeared not only armed but extremely willing to back up my challenge.

"Squire, pick up your gauntlet!" came a booming voice from Baron Scrope.

I looked back to see anger in my superior's eyes. Although I could lay claim to the title I was still bound to him as a squire, and required to follow orders. I held his gaze a moment, then he nodded toward the gauntlet.

As I moved to retrieve the leather glove I heard the king say, "Give Us time to review the information. We will meet back in the morning at eight, day after the morrow, if none can show just cause why the lad shouldn't be received as Our marquis then he will be approved. In the mean time We suggested that We adjourn and allow for cooler heads. Young squire, if you and yours will attend Me after the others have left, We would have a word with you."

The others filed out of the throne room, while the baron, and my four warrior companions stayed with me

"All right child, now that the others have gone, would you care to explain your actions here today?" King Harold demanded.

I tried to explain about the problems some of the nobles had been given me with a senior rating, and looking for excuses to use a rod on me. I also justify the idea of the land, and a rumor that one of the other nobles had planned to take it because there was no one able to hold the title. It would also give a measure of protection for some of my friends who were being bullied and abused, just because they were my friends.

The king suggested next time I give him a bit more warning, as he didn't care for surprises like this. "Our granddaughter may think it is wonderful staging and great for some of the plays she was read, but future surprises by a young squire like this will have the Master of Arms deal with the boy or girl. You may go. Sir William, a word with you before leaving."

"Yes sire. Ray, Kurt, Aaron, I will see you in my office. Wait for me there," Sir William said as we turned to leave.

After we got outside, Kurt said to Deveron and Sherry, "I suggest you two find somewhere away from here to be by the time he comes out. Boys, I think we are in trouble."

Trouble was an understatement. He believed we had intentionally mislead him while looking up the laws. We had set out to do this, but when we found the information it just presented a different plan to us than we had originally thought. It was a good thing the meeting wasn't going to be for nearly forty hours, because the next day we were all too sore to move much. He was really upset with the entire squad and showed it with the strength of his right arm. The mage and priest protested that they weren't children and shouldn't be disciplined in that manner. Sir William said if you act like a child, then you deserved to be treated like one. Sherry and Deveron weren't in trouble, because they hadn't been involved in the "plot," but Baron Scrope was mad for the next couple of days. He wasn't the only one that was *warm*.

The council meeting was full that morning. There were several who objected, but none with legal grounds, and Sir William was standing beside the lad in full armor, appearing to be his champion should someone challenge his right by trial of combat. Deveron had passed the word, and many of the young adults with him had let it be known that they would support Ray if a show of force occurred. None did.

With his hereditary title assured, Ray was more confident that things were going to go right with the new castle. Also, the boys' training took a sharp increase in effort. The new title didn't keep Kurt and Aaron from keeping him in check, a light touch on the shoulder to remind him to respect his elders, otherwise the reminder would be less pleasant. Plans for the spring were being made, and possible new squires that would go there for training during the spring. Although they would not be squires until the Fall Festival, they would be treated and trained as squires that spring and summer at the new castle site.

Markél informed them that Gerron, the most powerful mage, was researching a spell that would greatly aid in building the castle, and would assist them early this spring, before returning to the city to help in its continuing construction. But it would jump start the process at the new site. He didn't try to explain the spell, only that *Fabricate* would greatly speed things up. Between that and summoning an earth elemental, a lot of work would take days instead of months. However building a castle would not be the only worry.

People of the Story

"Like arrows in the hands a warrior are sons born in one's youth, Blessed is the man whose quiver is full of them."
Proverbs 126 4-5ᵃ

Aaron starts as a junior squire on board ship with Sherry and Ray. Accompanies party on quarry expedition. As a senior squire accompanies expedition to complete mapping adjacent valley. A noble born with psionic skills. Becomes one of Ray's closer older friends, and mentors.

Adam starts the trip as a fifteen year old junior. Will become a senior squire when they made landfall, and marry Sherry. Problem for Ray on ship. Both try to get along with the other for Sherry. Looks out of the younger squire.

Andrew noble born cleric assigned to the Gold Squad, recently married to a young priestess—shortly after land in the new world.

Anne Ray's newborn baby sister. Born after the arrival in the new land. She is Sherry's godchild.

Bennet the expert stealth person—thief. Psionic skills, but not a psionicist. Unknown father was of noble birth. Does a good job with his skills, and helps the younger squires to survive.

Beth Luke's mother, Ray's aunt, and Martha's sister in law. Also a healer, although has not practiced the skills since marriage and children.

Charissa, Princess granddaughter of the king, who has a crush on Ray, and he has a crush on her, but he won't admit it, because she is a two of years younger than he is. She is training to be a healer.

Cindy a non-noble junior squire who goes on the second expedition into the valley. Is nearly killed in the attack on the ridge

Cord Ray's eight to nine year old brother. Still too young to know where his skills will lead him. Cares for his brother, but doesn't think it is fair that Ray is older and can tell him what to do.

Deveron older, non-noble senior who will swear allegiance to Ray. Will be his sergeant for a group of older seniors who made the trip, due to injuries sustained from a battle before the city had to be evacuated. One of Ray's body guards.

Eric older senior squire who will be Ray's math instructor and tutor. Will work with Ray using psionic skills of combat. To be his Captain when new castle gets built.

Jakót young boy about ten, who was rescued by Ray in the village when the Orcs attacked it. Due to his village's custom he became Ray's servant. Will help around Ray's family's apartment, and assist Lady Martha and Sherry.

James squire of noble birth who strongly dislikes Ray. Insulted when Sherry and Ray backed him down from fear of psionic combat. Gets the chance to "evaluate" Ray when Ray joins a senior group for training. Suspected of being one of those who jumped Ray at night and beat him senseless.

James, Father priest who teaches class on Proverbs and one of the leading priest, in the city. Expert on the city law also.

Jelu son of a noble woman and a commoner father. Rumored to have small amount of elven ancestry. Expert with the longbow, and has psionic skills that assist him in this endeavor. Accompanies party on second trip into the valley. Will become part of the Gold Squad.

Jennifer female senior squire who accompanies Lord William and company on both trips into the adjacent valley. Is killed by Orcian arrows as the party takes the ridge on the way home from second expedition.

Kelric, Marquis of Retúpmoc. One of the leading, most trusted nobles in the war effort. Is lost as the country is overrun. Ray's father.

Kelvin oldest, and deceased son of Kelric, Marquis of Retúpmoc. Died two years earlier in the war. Fair haired child who never got the chance to grow up.

King Harold, the hereditary ruler of the country and leads the people in the exodus that ends up being to a new world.

Kurt begins the exodus as a junior squire, but is one of those promoted when land is reached. One of the squires Sherry and Ray defeated in dual competition. Becomes a good friend of Ray, and somewhat of a mentor—protector, but helps to keep the Ray in line. Marries the healer Sarah.

Lions, Lieutenant an officer on the ship that took Ray and others unknowingly to the new world. Assisted in training the warriors on the ship.

Luke Ray's older cousin who is a healer, and like Ray, is extremely talented for his age. Had actually served briefly in the war effort before the exodus.

Markél noble born mage assigned to the Gold Squad, plans to marry a young warrior just after the first of the year after being assigned to the Gold Squad. Does not care to be around younger males—especially squires.

Martha (Marchioness) Ray's mother. Has healing skills, but had not practiced them since the birth of her children. May have to knock off the rust in the new world.

Mathias priest who occupancies both parties into the adjacent valley. Would prefer to serve in the city and work for the population's souls, instead of adventuring, but is an important part of Lord William's team.

Megan Ray's sister older by three years. Torments him, and he believes resents his rank above his years. A Healer, whose fiancee died in Saxton before they were to be wed.

Mentans The nobles of Candlewynd, and other countries of Saxet. They are a race of humans with psionics (mental magical) powers which help them hold their power.

Ray The second, but oldest living son of Kelric, Marquis of Retúpmoc. Barely teenage protagonist. Gifted in warrior skills and psionic skills. Self conscious, and as many young teens feels like everyone is out to get him, even when well accepted by peers, older teens, and adults.

Richard a non-noble born, older, senior squire who worked with Ray and other junior squires on board ship. Had seen duty in the war, before returning due to wounds. Accompanies second mapping expedition, and others. Will eventually fall in love with the mage Xell, and marry her.

Sarah beautiful noble born healer, who accompanies the party on the initial exploration of the adjacent valley. Very capable in spell and psionic support. Seems to enjoy tormenting Ray, even though she appears to care about him. Ray mistakenly believes she is somewhat sadistic. Marries Kurt, after the first trip into the valley.

Sherry starts the trip as a fifteen year old junior squire, and became Ray's partner on board ship. Promoted to senior squire when they made landfall. Marries Adam. Special friend of Ray and family, Ray considers her as a sister, and a good friend in spite of her commoner status.

Stephen, Sir knight of noble birth, but without a title, a younger son of the Count of Windborne. Works with Ray onboard ship and may make use of the squire in expedition about the city. Thinks highly of the Ray, but wants to make sure he learns how to act as well as fight. In charge of expedition to find a quarry. Feels like Ray needs to be controlled better—may have ulterior motives.

Tarrin noble born thief-scout, distant cousin of Bennet. Gold Squad member.

Thomas non-noble junior squire accompanied Lord William and others for first trip into valley. Worked hard, was wounded in the battle at the village while firing bows with the Ray.

Timothy—Birdy a noble, junior squire and friend of Ray, who has a birthmark above his left eye that looks like a bird. Doesn't like the nickname. Has the psionic ability that allows him to communicate with animals.

Torin older junior squire who challenges Ray to a fight while they are breaking horses. Ray uses his psionic skills to defeat him in the fight, although Torin is unaware of this. He is suspected of being one of those who jumped Ray at night, and beat him senseless.

William Scrope, **Baron** knight of noble birth, has Ray assigned to him on mapping expedition, unaware of the squire's youth. Thinks the squire is worth having and willing to let him go for additional training if Ray wants it. Was a friend of Ray's older brother Kelvin.

Xell a female mage of non noble birth, although she has limited psionic skills, but not a psionicist. Seems sinister to Ray, but proves a valuable ally in both expeditions to the adjacent valley, and elsewhere. Dark blue colored clothing makes for a dark perception, not confirmed by actions. Eventually will convince Richard, (even though he is not psionic), that he wants to marry her, and make him think it is his idea. Causes some problems by marrying a non-psionic.